I0823978

EASTER EGG MURDER

Books by Leslie Meier

Lucy Stone Mysteries
MISTLETOE MURDER
TIPPY TOE MURDER
TRICK OR TREAT MURDER
BACK TO SCHOOL MURDER
VALENTINE MURDER
CHRISTMAS COOKIE MURDER
TURKEY DAY MURDER
WEDDING DAY MURDER
BIRTHDAY PARTY MURDER
FATHER'S DAY MURDER
STAR SPANGLED MURDER
NEW YEAR'S EVE MURDER
BAKE SALE MURDER
CANDY CANE MURDER
ST. PATRICK'S DAY MURDER
MOTHER'S DAY MURDER
WICKED WITCH MURDER
GINGERBREAD COOKIE MURDER
ENGLISH TEA MURDER
CHOCOLATE COVERED MURDER
EASTER BUNNY MURDER
CHRISTMAS CAROL MURDER
FRENCH PASTRY MURDER
CANDY CORN MURDER
BRITISH MANOR MURDER
EGGNOG MURDER
TURKEY TROT MURDER
SILVER ANNIVERSARY MURDER
YULE LOG MURDER
HAUNTED HOUSE MURDER
INVITATION ONLY MURDER
CHRISTMAS SWEETS
CHRISTMAS CARD MURDER
IRISH PARADE MURDER
HALLOWEEN PARTY MURDER
EASTER BONNET MURDER
IRISH COFFEE MURDER
MOTHER OF THE BRIDE MURDER
EASTER BASKET MURDER
PATCHWORK QUILT MURDER
BRIDAL SHOWER MURDER
HALLOWEEN NIGHT MURDER

Carol & Poopsie Mysteries
A MATTER OF PEDIGREE

Books by Lee Hollis

Hayley Powell Mysteries
DEATH OF A KITCHEN DIVA
DEATH OF A COUNTRY FRIED REDNECK
DEATH OF A COUPON CLIPPER
DEATH OF A CHOCOHOLIC
DEATH OF A CHRISTMAS CATERER
DEATH OF A CUPCAKE QUEEN
DEATH OF A BACON HEIRESS
DEATH OF A PUMPKIN CARVER

DEATH OF A LOBSTER LOVER
DEATH OF A COOKBOOK AUTHOR
DEATH OF A WEDDING CAKE BAKER
DEATH OF A BLUEBERRY TART
DEATH OF A WICKED WITCH
DEATH OF AN ITALIAN CHEF
DEATH OF AN ICE CREAM SCOOPER
DEATH OF A CLAM DIGGER
DEATH OF A GINGERBREAD MAN
DEATH OF A TOM TURKEY

Collections
EGGNOG MURDER
(with Leslie Meier and Barbara Ross)
YULE LOG MURDER
(with Leslie Meier and Barbara Ross)
HAUNTED HOUSE MURDER
(with Leslie Meier and Barbara Ross)
CHRISTMAS CARD MURDER
(with Leslie Meier and Peggy Ehrhart)
HALLOWEEN PARTY MURDER
(with Leslie Meier and Barbara Ross)
IRISH COFFEE MURDER
(with Leslie Meier and Barbara Ross)
CHRISTMAS MITTENS MURDER
(with Lynn Cahoon and Maddie Day)
EASTER BASKET MURDER
(with Leslie Meier and Barbara Ross)
HALLOWEEN NIGHT MURDER
(with Leslie Meier and Liz Ireland)

Poppy Harmon Mysteries
POPPY HARMON INVESTIGATES
POPPY HARMON AND THE HUNG JURY
POPPY HARMON AND THE PILLOW TALK KILLER
POPPY HARMON AND THE BACKSTABBING BACHELOR
POPPY HARMON AND THE SHOOTING STAR

Maya & Sandra Mysteries
MURDER AT THE PTA
MURDER AT THE BAKE SALE
MURDER ON THE CLASS TRIP
MURDER AT THE SPELLING BEE
MURDER AT THE HIGH SCHOOL REUNION

Jarrod Jarvis Father-Daughter Mysteries
MY FATHER ALWAYS FINDS CORPSES

Books by Peggy Ehrhart

Knit and Nibble Mysteries

MURDER, SHE KNIT
DIED IN THE WOOL
KNIT ONE, DIE TWO
SILENT KNIT, DEADLY KNIT
A FATAL YARN
KNIT OF THE LIVING DEAD
KNITTY GRITTY MURDER
DEATH OF A KNIT WIT
IRISH KNIT MURDER
KNITMARE ON BEECH STREET
A DARK AND STORMY KNIT
LAST WOOL AND TESTAMENT

Collections

CHRISTMAS CARD MURDER
(with Leslie Meier and Lee Hollis)
CHRISTMAS SCARF MURDER
(with Carlene O'Connor and Maddie Day)
IRISH MILKSHAKE MURDER
(with Carlene O'Connor and Liz Ireland)
IRISH SODA BREAD MURDER
(with Carlene O'Connor and Liz Ireland)

Published by Kensington Publishing Corp.

EASTER EGG MURDER

Leslie Meier
Lee Hollis
Peggy Ehrhart

KENSINGTON PUBLISHING CORP.
kensingtonbooks.com

KENSINGTON BOOKS are published by

Kensington Publishing Corp.
900 Third Avenue
New York, NY 10018

Library of Congress Control Number: On file

ISBN: 978-1-4967-4945-1
First Kensington Hardcover Edition: March 2026

ISBN-13: 978-1-4967-4947-5 (ebook)

10 9 8 7 6 5 4 3 2 1

Printed in the United States of America

The authorized representative in the EU for product safety and compliance is eucomply OU, Parnu mnt 139b-14, Apt 123
Tallinn, Berlin 11317, hello@eucompliancepartner.com

Contents

EASTER EGG MURDER

Leslie Meier

Chapter One

"We're way too early, Bill," said Lucy Stone, speaking to her husband. The couple were standing in line at the Air France counter in Boston's Logan Airport, and there was nobody else there. "The flight's not until six forty-five tonight and it's only two now."

"It's better to be on the early side, Lucy," said Bill, repeating one of his late father's favorite bits of advice. "We've got to get through security, and that can take forever."

Lucy glanced down the long hallway to the TSA checkpoint, where she was surprised to see that only a handful of people were waiting in line. Even the dogs who sniffed for drugs or explosives were snoozing at their handlers' feet. "I don't think that's going to be a problem."

"All it takes is one idiot who's packing a gun in their carry-on and everything stops."

"Try to look on the bright side, Bill," urged Lucy, with a smile. "This is going to be fun.

We're going to Paris to see Elizabeth." Lucy shook her head in amazement. "I never thought I'd see the day. She's actually pregnant and we're going to have another grandchild."

"That's all very well and good," said Bill, "but I think

Elizabeth and Chris ought to be married before they start a family." He stepped forward to the counter and turned to Lucy. "Passports?"

"Oh, right," said Lucy, producing the passports from the purse pocket where she'd tucked them.

"Ah, Mr. and Mrs. Stone," cooed the agent, an attractive young Black woman with the slightest French accent. "You've been upgraded to first class."

"Is that going to cost extra?" asked Bill suspiciously.

"No, no. We have a special relationship with Devonshire hotels and are pleased to provide this service to favored guests."

"Our daughter works there, in Paris," said Lucy, beaming at the agent. "We're going to visit her because she's expecting a baby."

Lucy could hear a sort of low growling noise coming from Bill that indicated she was oversharing. She knew he considered all personal details to be top secret, only to be divulged under the most extreme circumstances.

"Well, congratulations," said the agent, beaming. "Now if you'll just put your bag on the scale . . ."

After completing the weigh-in, the agent handed them their boarding passes. "After you pass through security, turn right and go straight to the elevator marked Lounges, and it will take you up to our First Class lounge."

"We don't—" began Bill, but Lucy cut him off.

"Thank you," she said.

"Have a pleasant journey," added the agent, as they headed for the security checkpoint.

They were whisked through the security checkpoint with record speed and had seated themselves on a bench while Bill laced up his shoes. "I don't like this, it's not like we deserve special treatment. If you ask me, they shouldn't even have first class. Everybody should be treated the same."

"Are you crazy?" asked Lucy, who was eager to experience the First Class lounge. "Elizabeth did this for us, it's a gift. You shouldn't look a gift horse in the mouth."

"Maybe it's a Trojan gift horse," grumbled Bill. "Honestly, Lucy, I don't know why you're okay with this."

"About first class? What's to be upset about?"

"Elizabeth is only fixing this first-class stuff for us because she knows how I feel about the fact that she and Chris Kennedy are not married and aren't thinking about getting married, either. They're doing that French thing, some solidarity pact. PBS or something."

"It's a *Pacte Civil de Solidarite*, PCS, and it's just like being married but without the church and all the bells and whistles. Face it, Bill. Elizabeth's not getting any younger, the clock is ticking and this is probably her last chance to have a baby. I'm pretty sure she'd feel ridiculous in a white gown with her baby bump showing." She stood up. "Now, c'mon, let's go check out that lounge. I bet there's beer for you and chardonnay for me."

"At a price," grumbled Bill, as they headed for the elevator.

The elevator doors opened opposite the Air France lounge, where a receptionist checked their boarding passes and welcomed them, advising them that they would be informed when it was time to board and would use a special exit that would take them directly to the gate.

"Membership has its privileges," whispered Lucy, giving Bill a nudge as they proceeded into the lounge. There they found a posh sort of cafeteria, where a variety of tempting foods and snacks were available, as well as a self-serve bar featuring drinks. A handful of people were already occupying the varied seating options, which included tables and chairs for eating or working, as well as sofas and recliners for relaxing. Quiet music was playing.

"So this is how the other ten percent live," said Lucy with an approving nod.

"There are no prices anywhere," said Bill. "Is this stuff all free?"

"I think the ticket fee covers it. C'mon. Let's grab some seats and see what's on offer, okay?"

"Okay."

Once seated with a Sam Adams beer beneath a large-screen TV displaying a Red Sox game, Bill finally relaxed. Sort of. "You know, Lucy, Elizabeth has to become a French citizen in order to qualify for the civil pact."

"That's what she said." Lucy was happily sipping a delicious chardonnay and nibbling on an assortment of cheeses and crackers.

"Doesn't that bother you? She won't be American anymore?"

Lucy shrugged. "She's been living in France for years, Bill. She only comes home to Maine every couple of years, and then she's gone practically before she's arrived. I think she's really found her home in France." She spread some brie on a cracker. "Maybe she can have dual citizenship. I don't know how that works."

"Why can't Chris switch his? Why does it have to be Elizabeth?"

"Because Chris's security business requires him to keep his American citizenship. His customers are American businesses and high-net-worth individuals, it's all very complicated and he travels a lot and needs his American passport or something. I don't quite understand the complexities of visas and things, but Elizabeth was quite certain this is the way it has to be." People were drifting into the lounge, and Lucy was curious about the other first-class passengers and was observing them while attempting to be discreet. "Bill," she whispered. "Look."

Bill was already looking at the gorgeous, tall blonde who was sauntering across the room in thigh-high boots with stiletto heels. Her skirt was short, her hair was long, and she was well aware that every eye was upon her. "Wow," he whispered, agog as she plopped herself down in an easy chair, crossed her legs, and began staring at her phone.

"We're not in Tinker's Cove anymore," said Lucy, referring to the Maine seaside town where she was a reporter for the local weekly paper and Bill was a highly regarded restoration carpenter. It was mud season when they left wearing their duck boots, and they knew the snow would still be melting when they returned, so those duck boots were in the parked car, ready for them. Elizabeth had absolutely forbidden them to wear duck boots in Paris, ordering them instead to wear conservatively styled walking shoes. "No sneakers, either!" she'd warned.

"Look at that couple," said Bill. "Looks like they've brought the whole family."

Lucy had already noticed the middle-aged couple with two grown children and wondered how much first-class tickets for four people cost. Probably quite a lot, but the mom and dad didn't seem at all concerned. Neither did the kids—especially the boy, who looked to be college age and was loudly asking a server why they didn't have any Dr. Pepper. There was every other soda, for goodness sake, but this kid had to have Dr. Pepper. Talk about entitled!

The family soon settled in at a table with a banquette, making themselves comfortable. Laptops were opened, phones were produced, all sorts of belongings were spread around them. Shoes were even taken off. The waiter delivered a Dr. Pepper—Lucy figured they must have sent out for it—and the kid was now wiggling around in his seat, apparently responding to the music from his earbuds. The daughter, older than the boy and dressed in a business suit, was sipping tea and studying her laptop. The mom, a heavily made-up bleached blonde, not fat but definitely curvy, was flipping through a magazine, and the dad was snoozing. Actually snoring.

Getting a jab in the ribs from Bill, Lucy realized she'd been staring. She took a sip of wine and opened her book, but she wasn't really all that interested in the *Thursday Murder Club*. The human drama taking place around her was definitely first class.

Chapter Two

Monsieur . . . Carole Capobianco was having doubts about the wisdom of this trip to France en famille. It was hard enough keeping Frank under control, just look at him now, snoring away. And Frank-O, who had artistic sensibilities, had to go and make a fuss about getting a Dr. Pepper. So embarrassing. Only Connie was remotely civilized, but as a junior member of the Dunne and Willoughby law firm, she was practically a slave working sixty- or seventy-hour weeks. Look at her now, pecking away on her computer, preparing some brief. Carole sighed. What was a brief, anyway? And why did they seem to take so long?

Carole sighed, glancing around the lounge, her attention caught by that dowdy couple sitting opposite. Obviously from some teeny hick town in New Hampshire or Maine, maybe Vermont, but they didn't look quite whole-grain enough for Vermont. He had a backwoodsman's beard and she, poor thing, had a terrible haircut. To their credit, she decided, they were wearing nice shoes. But what were they doing in the first-class lounge? Maybe they were old money, thrifty Yankees who wore their L.L.Bean and Brooks Brothers clothes until they disintegrated?

Carole's thoughts turned to the reason for this trip, a

call from her mother, Polly, who had recently relocated from Paris to Provence, where she'd bought a *mas*, or French farmhouse. "Come for Easter," she'd said. "Plenty of room for the whole family, and I want you all to meet my fiancé, Benoit." This was the first Carole had heard of Benoit, and she had to admit she was curious. What man would be brave enough to take on Polly?

Despite her curiosity about the fiancé, she'd actually been reluctant to make the trip. For one thing, she hated leaving her temperamental dog, Poopsie. Poopsie was a highly strung Brittany spaniel and Carole wasn't confident that her in-laws, Mom and Big Frank, could successfully manage her. She and Poopsie were a team and Carole already missed her lively canine companion, but she was used to making compromises. That was the name of the game when you were in the sandwich generation, squeezed between the demands of a mother like Polly, the in-laws, the kids, and—who could forget—a husband like Frank.

It hadn't been easy to convince Frank and the kids to agree to the trip, she remembered, thinking that she could have used Madeleine Albright to help with the lengthy negotiations. Frank didn't need to work anymore—he'd made a boatload of money with his Bye-Bye Toilet, a highly efficient low-flow toilet that dominated the market—but he wasn't about to give up running the family plumbing business, Capobianco and Sons, in Providence, Rhode Island. She suspected the reason wasn't so much that he loved plumbing but that it gave him an excuse to avoid things he didn't want to do. Top on that long list was spending time with Polly, and coming in a close second was anything to do with Frank-O. "Thinks he's something special, an artist," Frank would say with a dismissive eye roll. "That's why we have to call him Frank-O instead of just plain Frankie."

And, oddly enough, Frank-O hadn't been enthused about

the trip to France, which everybody knew was chock full of art. "Absolutely lousy with the stuff," as Frank said, after touring the Louvre on a previous visit. Frank-O, who was a student at the Rhode Island School of Design, better known as RISD, claimed he was way too busy to go, as he was currently working on a piece of art that would be, in his words, "revolutionary, cataclysmic, and genuinely radical." Frank had been somewhat doubtful, telling him that somebody already thought of taping a banana to a wall with duct tape, and Frank-O had been sulking ever since.

She glanced at her son, catching his eye and giving him a smile. He was impossible, but she was Italian and he was her bambino, so she absolutely loved him to bits. She made weekly deliveries of food to his squalid apartment, she kept him in socks and underwear, she'd even arranged for a weekly laundry service. And, most important, she tried to be a buffer between Frank-O and his father, although that was often mission impossible. She could only hope the two would get through this trip together without tearing each other apart.

Then there was Connie, bless her heart. Working, working, always working. It was unnatural, she feared, the way the girl was so focused on her job that she didn't even seem to think about finding a husband. She didn't date, which was a shame because Connie was absolutely gorgeous. She had a terrific figure that she hid under those horrible suits; Carole often gave her lovely, lacy lingerie as a way of reminding her that she was not a legal automaton but a young woman, but she had no idea whether Connie actually wore the stuff. And that hair, naturally lustrous and wavy, she didn't have to do a thing to it except run a comb through it in the morning and it did its job, announcing to the world that despite her best efforts to the contrary, Connie was a beauty.

Carole's attention was drawn by the hick woman, who was standing up and looking around, as if in search of something. "The ladies room is back there," she said, smiling and pointing her in the right direction.

"Am I that obvious?" asked the woman, laughing. "Thanks."

Definitely newbies, thought Carole, studying the bearded husband, who was watching the ball game on the overhead TV. Maybe they were airline employees of some sort, maybe travel agents, something like that. People who occasionally got upgraded to first class as a reward for a job well done. Or maybe they won a contest. That was probably it, a round-trip vacation in Paris, all expenses paid. Lucky them.

The woman came back just as boarding was announced, and the couple quickly gathered up their things, as if the plane might leave without them if they didn't hurry. That was one of the nice things about first class, you didn't have to hurry or jostle with the crowd of people eager to board. You could take your time, make sure you hadn't forgotten anything, make sure your husband and your children had all their belongings as you proceeded down the exclusive escalator and continued past the red ropes to the boarding agent, who always greeted you by name and wished you a *bon voyage*.

The one disadvantage was that once you entered the gate, there were all those economy passengers, staring at you and giving you the evil eye. Well, too bad for them, thought Carole. Instead of being envious of first-class passengers and their preferential treatment, well they could have preferential treatment, too. All they had to do was cough up the price of a first-class ticket!

Chapter Three

It has to be karma, thought Lucy, who had hoped she would be seated as far from the unruly family as possible, when she noticed the dyed blonde taking the seat directly across the aisle from her. Oh, well, it wasn't as if she was crammed next to the woman in the dreaded five middle seats in economy, fighting for space on the armrest. Feeling a pang of guilt, she reminded herself she should be grateful for this roomy first-class seat, which was a sort of mini-cabin just for her. There were little cubbies galore, a nicely sized TV screen, all sorts of switches for lights and whatever. Not to mention a big, plump pillow and a luxurious blanket for sleeping, which would actually be possible because the chair converted into a bed, which allowed one to lie flat. And now, the flight attendant was offering her a flute of champagne. This is indeed living large, she thought, wishing she could catch Bill's eye, but that was impossible, as he was sitting directly in front of her behind the privacy screen. Grateful, she told herself, time to be grateful.

She accepted the champagne and took a sip, cold and delicious. She leaned back in her seat and let out a big sigh, preparing to relax.

"Are you a nervous flyer?" It was the bleached-blond woman, sounding concerned.

Lucy met her gaze, noticing her sympathetic expression. "Oh, not really. I don't fly very often, so I guess I'm not used to it. The whole idea seems fantastic, crossing the Atlantic Ocean at thirty thousand feet in an aluminum can."

The woman laughed. "When you put it that way, it does seem pretty weird. I'm Carole Capobianco, by the way. From Providence, Rhode Island."

"I'm Lucy Stone, from Tinker's Cove, Maine."

Economy passengers had begun filing down the aisle, struggling with their carry-on bags, but that didn't deter Carole, who stuck her arm across the aisle, blocking a woman carrying a baby, to shake Lucy's hand.

"Lovely to meet you, Lucy. Is this your first trip to Paris?"

Lucy gave a quick squeeze and withdrew her hand, smiling apologetically at the woman. "Oh, no. My daughter lives there and we're visiting her. She's expecting a baby, her first, so I'm really looking forward to seeing her."

"First grandchild?" Carole had drained her champagne and seemed about to signal the flight attendant for a refill, but realized it was impossible because of the boarding passengers and gave a resigned shrug.

"No. I have a grandson, Patrick, who's eleven. He lives in Alaska, though, so I don't see him as often as I'd like. How about you?"

"None yet. In fact," continued Carole, peering between two passengers who were waiting for the queue to move, "we're visiting my mom, who lives in Provence and wants us to meet her fiancé."

"Wow," said Lucy. "Grandma's getting married." She thought for a minute. "Not her first marriage?"

The line was beginning to move. "No, this will be her third."

"Busy lady."

"You have no idea."

Conversation paused while the boarding continued, and Lucy opened her book. She felt as if she were on display, and she wasn't comfortable being seen as someone she wasn't, which was a woman who could afford to fly first class. I'm just like you, she wanted to tell the economy passengers, I just happened to get upgraded. I thought I'd be in seat 33E, which is where I belong. That was impossible, of course, so she did the next best thing, which was to bury her nose in a book and ignore the passing stream of less fortunate fellow passengers. Fortunate or unfortunate, she realized, they were in one way all equal. If the plane crashed, it wouldn't matter if you were in first class or economy, they were all doomed.

It seemed to take forever, but eventually everyone was seated, the flight attendants did their safety presentation, and they were told to fasten their seat belts and prepare for take-off.

"I'd kill for another glass of champagne," commented Carole, who was twirling her empty flute.

"I'm sure they'll come around again once we're in the air and the seat belt lights go off."

"Crazy, isn't it? We can get to France in a matter of hours, which people simply couldn't do for years and years, they had to take a boat that took days or weeks, even months, but somehow six hours in the air seems to take forever."

Lucy was beginning to like Carole, who seemed to be very down-to-earth underneath the eyeliner and foundation and lip gloss and designer clothes and expensive hair-do. "I've never been to Provence," she said. "Do you go often?"

"First time," said Carole. "Mom lived in Paris until this fall, when she bought the place in Provence. It's a *mas*, or French farmhouse."

"That sounds lovely," said Lucy, thinking she'd prefer Provence to Paris, which she wasn't all that crazy about. It was gray and grimy and crowded with tourists from all over, huge tour groups from China, rugged Swedes in hiking shoes, Germans speaking that guttural language.

"Well, you know how it is with family." Carole paused. "They bring their issues, wherever they go. Provence, Providence, Paris, you're dealing with the same personalities."

Lucy nodded in agreement. "Yeah, my husband and I aren't entirely happy that Elizabeth, that's our daughter, isn't marrying the baby's father. They're doing a French thing called a PCS or *Pacte Civil de Solidarite*, which seems to be a complicated way of avoiding doing the proper thing."

"It's a bit funny, isn't it? Your daughter and my mother are both engaged," said Carole, laughing. "May and December."

That struck Lucy as funny, too, and wouldn't you know it? The flight attendant was coming down the aisle with more champagne! Carole held out her glass for a refill when her husband slid open the panel dividing their seats and tapped her on the shoulder. "Do you mind? I wanna get some shut-eye."

Catching Lucy's eye, Carole rolled her eyes and made a gesture zipping her lips. Settling back in her seat, she pulled out her phone and started scrolling through her photos while sipping her champagne. Lucy opened her book and began reading but was interrupted by a tap on the shoulder.

"Look at this photo," whispered Carole, holding out her phone. "Isn't this the cutest thing you've ever seen?"

Lucy took the phone and studied the photo, which pictured a cute white dog with orange spots, giving a doggy smile. "Really cute," said Lucy. "What's the dog's name?"

"Shady Brook's Madame Pompadour, but we call her Poopsie."

"I bet you already miss her," said Lucy, passing the phone back to her.

Carole nodded, staring at the photo, and Lucy returned to her book. It wasn't all that interesting, however, and she began wondering when they'd serve dinner, and what it would be.

As it happened, there was a choice: filet mignon or shrimp piccata, and Lucy was amused to notice that Carole's husband had both! After the dinner service, the plane quieted down, the lights were dimmed, and for the first time ever, Lucy fell asleep watching the in-flight movie. She woke when the lights were turned on and they were informed they would be landing in an hour. Breakfast was served, crisply crusted croissants and delicious coffee, and then they were on the ground, invited to debark.

It was with a weird sensation of freedom that Lucy proceeded to the exit, where the smiling crew members wished her a *bonne journée*, and she stepped out of the plane only to be greeted by an elegantly dressed, very tall, very handsome young Frenchman. "Madame Stone?" he inquired.

"*Oui*," chirped Lucy.

"And Monsieur Stone?"

Bill nodded.

"I am Charles Sangnier from the Devonshire Hotel, so please follow me and I will escort you through arrivals to the waiting limousine."

Lucy and Bill shared a glance. “Great,” said Bill.

“*Merci*,” added Lucy.

“You’re very welcome,” said Charles, leading the way. “Elizabeth said her parents deserve VIP treatment.”

Hearing this, Bill gave Lucy an *I told you so* look.

Chapter Four

Carole, who was debarking right behind Lucy and Bill, watched with amazement as a guy looking like a young Antony Blinken in a beautifully tailored suit and oozing tact greeted the Maine couple and escorted them down the jetway. How come this obviously ordinary middle-class couple from Hicksville rated what was obviously VIP treatment? Here she was, struggling with a carry-on as well as her oversized purse and Frank-O's jacket, which he'd left behind in his seat, and Lucy and her husband just breezed off the plane ahead of everyone to be met by some sort of diplomat.

"Did you see that?" she asked Frank.

"What?" he asked, charging straight ahead, as if there were a prize for the first person off the jetway.

"That couple from Maine," she explained, puffing to keep up with him. "They were met by a fancy-looking guy. A diplomat or something."

"They must know somebody. That's how things work the world over, not just in Providence. It's connections, and you'd be surprised at the folks who've got them. Every high-flyer has a mom who wears gym shoes and elastic-waist pants."

"Speak for yourself, Frank," said Carole, amused by this description of his mother. Her mother, on the other hand, wouldn't dream of stepping out of the house without doing her hair and makeup and dressing in a chic outfit.

"Dad's right, Mom," said Connie, as they reached the terminal and paused to wait for Frank-O. "These days you can't tell the billionaires from everybody else. A lot of our high-net-worth clients make a point of dressing down. They don't want to be identified as wealthy because it can open them up to all sorts of risks: theft, kidnapping, even hostility."

Carole was close to reaching the end of her patience with Frank-O, who was strolling along, bopping to whatever weird music he was getting in his earbuds. "Uh, Frank-O, do you think you could give your poor old mother a hand?" she asked, grabbing his arm.

"Whuh?" he asked, blinking as if waking from a dream.

Frank had definitely had enough and yanked out one of his son's earbuds. "Help your mother," he snarled. "Can't you see she's carrying your coat? And those big bags?"

"Oh, sorry, Mom," he said, quickly taking his jacket and her carry-on bag.

"We're not in first class anymore," growled Frank, stopping in the middle of the busy airport thoroughfare and planting his feet, looking for the sign pointing the way to the baggage area. "We gotta get our bags and then we gotta go through immigration, just like everyone else."

This was the part of traveling that Carole hated, standing by the baggage carousel and watching as all those bags rolled past, bags that always seemed to belong to someone else. But the travel gods were cooperating today and her Louis Vuitton bags and Frank's Samsonite were among the first out of the chute, quickly followed by Frank-O's duffle. Connie didn't have a checked bag. She had brought only a tiny carry-on suitcase, which Carole thought was a shame; she was entitled to two bags thanks to the first-class ticket. Carole guessed that the tiny bag was probably filled with practical black wrinkle-proof travel outfits. She'd have to encourage Connie to add scarves or maybe lend her some of her stuff, otherwise everyone in Provence would think she was in mourning.

Once they'd got the bags on the rolling cart, which Frank-O was assigned to push, they proceeded to immigration, where there was quite a long line. Not good, thought Carole, noticing Frank's tapping foot as he studied the officers in their glass booths. None were smiling, a few were checking their watches, and at precisely nine o'clock, several of the booths were closed. The previously serious immigration officers were now smiling and chatting with each other as they drifted away, oblivious of the crowd and probably intending to enjoy some very small cups of very strong coffee, which they would sip slowly.

"Can you believe it?" growled Frank. "Look at all these people, and instead of opening more booths they're closing them."

"It's the French way," said Carole. "There's nothing we can do about it, so don't make things worse, okay?"

"What me? Make things worse? How exactly would I do that?"

"You know," said Carole, whispering. "Don't be confrontational. Just try to go with the flow. No comments, no sighs. Remember, France is not the USA and they don't have to let us in."

"That's right," added Connie. "They don't only do facial recognition, you know. They're trained to look for signs of stress that could indicate some sort of evil intent, like a terror attack."

"I'll give you evil intent," snarled Frank, "if this line doesn't start moving soon."

The line did move, and the family was admitted, although Frank's interviewer had a few extra questions that definitely tried Frank's patience. Carole watched, fingers crossed, hoping he wasn't going to be escorted to one of those little rooms where they go through your bags and ask the same questions over and over. She let out a huge sigh when the officer stamped Frank's passport and the gate lifted, allowing him entry into France.

They hadn't been able to get a connecting flight to Marseille; the apologetic travel agent back in Providence had told them that Easter was a particularly busy travel time in France, so that meant they would have to grab a taxi to take them to the Gare de Lyon. There they would transfer to the high-speed TGV train. "Only three hours," the travel agent had trilled. "Why that's almost as fast as the plane, anyway."

What the travel agent hadn't foreseen, however, was the traffic tie-up outside the terminal. Nothing was moving, it was gridlock. No one was going anywhere, anytime soon, not even Lucy and Bill Stone, who Carole spotted sitting in a Mercedes limo, trapped between a bus and a delivery truck.

"What now?" asked Frank-O.

"Let's go back inside and get some grub," suggested Frank. "Maybe things'll be moving after we get a decent breakfast."

"*Bonne idée*," said Carole, smiling at her husband. Frank could be a handful, but when the going got tough, he generally got going in search of his next meal.

Chapter Five

"Is the traffic always like this here at the airport?" Lucy didn't want to complain, but they'd been trapped in the traffic jam for at least half an hour and she was eager to see her daughter.

"No, Madame," answered the chauffeur. "There is a general strike in Paris. The streets are packed with marchers, the garbage is piling up, and the Metro is barely operating."

"Oh, my," said Lucy, with a little sigh. She'd been thrilled to be greeted by the charming Charles, who'd magically arranged for their bags to be collected and whisked them through immigration and into the limo, but who had not been able to make the traffic move. He'd left them once they were safely in the limo, probably off to greet some other favored guests of the Devonshire Hotel.

"We're in no hurry," said Bill, relaxing back into his seat and taking Lucy's hand. "We're on vacation and I'm not going to let a little traffic spoil it."

Lucy squeezed his hand. "If we were home, I'd probably be taking out the garbage, or cleaning the bathrooms."

"Ah, we're moving," announced the driver, as the car inched forward.

"I can't wait to see Elizabeth," confessed Lucy, with a big smile. "My baby is having a baby."

The traffic may have begun to move, but there were plenty of stops and starts on the way to Elizabeth and Chris's apartment, past streets that were blocked with protesting strikers and piled with bags of garbage. The driver finally pulled up in front of a large wooden gate marked with their house number. An intercom was fastened to the wall beside it.

"Do you have the code?" asked the driver.

"*Oui*," replied Lucy, reciting the four numbers Elizabeth had given her.

The driver hopped out and typed the numbers on the keypad. The wide door swung open and he drove on through into a large courtyard, surrounded on three sides by three- and four-story apartment buildings. Lucy was admiring the pots of blooming spring bulbs when a door opened, and Elizabeth popped out. Lucy leapt out of the car and hugged her daughter, then stepped back to study her, noting with approval that she was glowing with health. Her short dark hair was beautifully styled, her cheeks were rosy and had filled out a bit, which became her. Chris followed her, tall and handsome as ever, and there were more hugs and exclamations while the chauffeur unloaded the bags. Then the limo departed, and they all climbed up a very old and crooked set of stairs into the young couple's apartment.

"Charming," enthused Lucy, taking in the French windows with checked curtains that overlooked the courtyard, the bright red sofa, the cozy rug, the shelves of books, and the tiny kitchen. She and Bill were seated in the living room, supplied with big glasses of mineral water.

"You've done a great job decorating," she continued. "It's so French."

"We like it," said Chris, wrapping his arms around Elizabeth's waist and patting her little baby bump.

"How are you feeling?" asked Lucy. "Morning sickness?"

"Not anymore, Mom. I'm five months along."

Lucy glanced again at the baby bump that was still barely showing. "Really? Five months?"

"Truly. And the doctor is very pleased with my progress."

"That's wonderful," said Lucy, remembering how she felt like an elephant during her four pregnancies. It had been a struggle to get up from sitting, even pushing a cart around in the supermarket had been difficult, and she had barely managed to squeeze behind the steering wheel of her car. Maybe it was something in the water in France, she decided. Even pregnant French women didn't get fat.

"We can hardly wait," said Chris. "Elizabeth's going to be a great mom."

Elizabeth looked up at Chris, beaming. "You're going to be a great father."

"Ahem," said Bill, clearing his throat. "I suppose you're still planning to go ahead with this solidarity pact thing? Instead of getting married?"

"It's what most people here do nowadays," said Chris. "Hardly anyone goes to church so it doesn't make sense to have a church wedding."

"It's really the same, pretty much. We will have the same legal rights and obligations," added Elizabeth.

"But you're okay with giving up your American citizenship?" pressed Bill.

"Well, the pact is only for French citizens. One partner has to be a French citizen . . ."

"And I need to retain my American citizenship for my business. My clients, they're all high-level Americans doing business in France, and they expect me to have a U.S. passport."

"Well, I don't like it," said Bill, scowling.

"I understand," said Chris. "It's natural, you want what's best for Elizabeth, but so do I. You can count on me to take care of Elizabeth and the baby."

"Well," began Bill, with a shrug. "I guess that's all right then. Is it going to be a boy or a girl?"

"We've decided to wait until the baby's born," said Elizabeth. "It will be a surprise."

"A wonderful surprise," said Chris.

"But I want to go shopping for baby things," complained Lucy. "They have such cute little outfits here."

"You can buy white, or yellow, or green," said Elizabeth. "But I don't think you want to do it here in Paris."

"What do you mean? Why not? The stores here are fabulous."

"It's impossible right now in Paris, Mom, with the strike and all. A lot of the stores are closed. Actually boarded up. It's chaos."

"It did look pretty bad on the way from the airport," admitted Bill. "There was garbage everywhere, lots of graffiti."

"So I've made arrangements for you to stay in Provence. The Cavendish chain has a place there, the Château de Ventoux. It's lovely and you'll be very comfortable. You'll love Provence—there are all these adorable little towns, filled with charming shops and restaurants, and L'Isle-sur-la-Sorgue is nearby."

"The town with the famous flea market?" asked Lucy, who'd seen it featured in design magazines and had always wanted to go.

"That's right," said Elizabeth, smiling. "And Chris and I will come down in a few days and join you for Easter."

"Well, I guess that will be all right, then," said Lucy, already anticipating the flea market.

Chapter Six

The Gare de Lyon in Paris was crowded and noisy, there was no one to help with their bags, and when they got to the ticket window they discovered there'd been a mix-up and they didn't have first-class tickets.

"*Dépêchez-vous*," advised the man behind the ticket window, pointing to the large clock on the wall. "*Dix minutes*," he added, tapping the watch on his wrist.

"The train's leaving in ten minutes," said Carole, "We're on track *onze*, eleven, eleven." Then they were dashing through the station, boarding the train just as the conductor was blowing his whistle for the last call. The car was crowded with people and the luggage rack was already full, so they moved on to the next car, and the next, looking for four seats together. In the end, they had to sit singly, after Frank and Frank-O rearranged the luggage rack and crammed in their largest suitcases. Carole ended up holding her carry-on bag in her lap, sitting several rows behind Frank. It was better this way, she told herself, since she didn't have to listen to his complaining.

They were all tired and grouchy when they finally reached Marseille, where they taxied over to the airport and joined a long line of people who were sweating in the sun at the single car rental outfit. When it was finally their turn, they took the Peugeot 2000, an antique for sure, but they were in no position to argue.

"Can you believe it, they rent twenty-year-old cars?" muttered Frank. "And it wasn't cheap, either."

"There were a lot of people, they're probably running out of cars," suggested Connie, as they straggled through the lot, looking for their car.

"Brat!" exclaimed Frank-O, pointing out a sleek white sedan. "It's the model, 2000, not the year," he continued, pointing to the silver numerals on the car's rear. "Can I drive?"

"No," said Frank. "You load the bags while I familiarize myself with the controls."

"My mother sent us directions to her place," said Carole, seating herself beside Frank and digging into her purse.

Frank started driving toward the parking lot exit. "Looks like the exit only goes to one road, so I guess we'll take it."

Carole had found the printout of her mother's message, which Polly had written herself, drawing on her own unreliable memory. "I think we need to look for the A7," said Carole, struggling to decipher her mother's confusing directions as they drove through crowded city streets.

"I'm hungry," said Frank-O.

"Shhh," said Connie, who had her phone plastered to her ear. "I've got a work call."

"Can you believe these drivers?" exclaimed Frank, braking hard as a tiny little Smart car cut him off.

"Maybe there's a map in the glove box," said Carole, but she found it empty.

"Waze, Mom," suggested Frank-O. "Use Waze. It'll tell you the closest restaurants, too."

"I see the A7," said Frank, hitting the gas. "*Nord*, right?"

"Yeah, Dad," sneered Frank-O. "Unless you want to end up in the Mediterranean."

"If you know what's good for you, you'll shut up," said Frank, as the feminine voice of Waze advised, "Exit left onto the A7."

Frank-O was still complaining about being hungry when the Waze voice informed them an hour and a half later, "You've arrived at your destination."

The gate in the stone wall surrounding the *mas* was open, and Frank drove through the narrow opening while Carole craned her neck, eager to see her mother's new home. It was a classic French farmhouse, built of stone with blue shutters, surrounded by trees. Frank parked beneath a pollarded plane tree, and they all climbed out, stretching. In the distance, Carole spotted numerous hills, a mountain, and miles and miles of vineyards. Odd-looking black-and-white birds fluttered around the base of the tree, making whooping sounds.

"We're not in Kansas anymore," offered Connie, actually smiling, and shrugging out of her jacket. "And so warm. I didn't realize Provence would be this warm."

"Not just warm, hot and dry. Like in *Manon of the Spring*," said Frank-O.

"What's he talking about?" grumbled Frank, shaking his head.

"*Bienvenue, bienvenue*," trilled Polly, appearing in the open doorway. "You're finally here!"

"Finally," said Carole, giving her tiny mother a big hug, noticing she'd let her hair go natural, giving up dye for a streaky silver look. Chic as ever, Polly was wearing a lacy white tunic, slim black Capri pants, and black espadrilles.

"Where's my favorite grandson?" trilled Polly, rising on tiptoes to give Frank-O a big hug. "Handsome as ever." Turning to Connie, she hugged her, then studied her face and gently ran a loving hand along her jawline. "And here's *ma chérie*, Connie, even more beautiful." Turning to Frank, she grabbed his shoulders and subjected him to three *bisous*, air kisses, which she claimed was the Provençal way.

"This joint got a bathroom?" demanded Frank, and Polly led the way inside, pointing him up the stairs that filled the central hall.

"This is my housekeeper, Mathilde," she said, pointing out a plump woman wearing an apron who was standing at the kitchen sink. Polly introduced her family members to Mathilde, speaking in French, and the housekeeper responded with a shy smile, head bent and staring at the floor. "She doesn't speak English," offered Polly, leading them across the tiled hall to a large living-dining room. A long table and chairs were arranged in front of the open glass sliders, and a sofa and armchairs were gathered in front of an open fireplace.

"Your rooms are upstairs," she added. "Carole, you and Frank are on the *première étage*, across from my room. The kids' rooms are one flight up, and there are bathrooms on each floor." She paused, taking in their tired expressions. "What can I get you? Something to drink?"

"*Non, merci*," said Carole, realizing she was exhausted. "I could use a nap."

"Righto, get yourselves settled," suggested Polly. "When you're refreshed, we will go to Benoit's place. He's invited us all for dinner." She gave herself a little squeeze and giggled. "I can't wait for you to meet him."

An hour or so later, Carole woke up, finding herself alone in the simply furnished bedroom that contained only a double bed with nightstands, an armoire, and a chair with a rush seat. The window was closed and shuttered, so she got up and opened both, taking in the view of vineyards and mountains. Stepping into the hall, she found the suitcases were standing just outside the door, and wondered who had brought them up. She couldn't see Frank doing it, or Frank-O, for that matter. It must have been Mathilde, she decided, thinking the woman was too old to be lugging other people's suitcases around. She stopped in the bathroom, washing her hands and dabbing a bit of water on her face, then headed downstairs, intending to thank Mathilde. She found the kitchen empty, however, and her family gathered in the living area.

"Sleeping Beauty's finally awake," said Frank, looking up from an English language newspaper.

"Did you have a good rest?" asked Polly.

"Yes, I did," said Carole. "Is that the *New York Times*?"

"We get it here," said Polly. "I was in town this morning so I picked it up for Frank." She paused. "Well, if you're all ready, Benoit is waiting for us."

Getting nods all around, Polly led the way, walking right by the Peugeot and her car, a Renault. "Aren't we driving?" demanded Frank-O, as if he'd never heard of any other form of transportation. "In this heat?"

"No need," said Polly, pointing out a gap in the wall that enclosed the property. "Benoit lives next door."

Figures, thought Carole. Only her mother, well into her sixties, would have the good luck to move in next to an eligible French bachelor. A bachelor who was very well off, indeed, if the rather large diamond she'd noticed on her mother's ring finger was any indication.

"Lovely ring," she said, taking her mother's hand.

Polly shrugged. "I told him it wasn't necessary, I mean, at my age and all, but Benoit insisted."

"I can't wait to meet him." Carole was indeed eager to see her mother's fiancé for herself.

"Well, you won't have long to wait, because it's just through here." They followed Polly through the gap in the wall, as well as through a hedge on Benoit's side, and found themselves on a spacious patch of scraggly grass. The house was more modern than Polly's *mas* and much larger, with big windows and a flat roof. Unlike Polly's home, it included a large open garage that housed several vintage autos in various states of restoration.

Carole studied the place curiously, noticing the house didn't have much in the way of character. There was no garden in the front, just a stone path that led to the main door. That door opened as they approached, revealing a tall, slender man dressed in jeans and a faded green T-shirt, with longish hair and a stylish three-day beard.

"Polly!" He grabbed her hands and wrapped her in his arms, delivering a deep, passionate kiss. "And this is your family!" As Polly introduced them, he grabbed each one by the shoulders and delivered the three *bisous* Polly had said were the Provençal tradition. He rather lingered over Connie, Carole noticed, not sure that she approved.

"A tour?" he suggested, indicating the open garage.

"Yeah!" exclaimed Frank-O, who had been studying the cars inside. "You've got a mini in there?" he asked.

"A *deux-chevaux*," exclaimed Benoit proudly, leading the way. The car was tiny, and the seats were missing, along with a couple of wheels. "When it's finished I will give it to Polly."

"It's a classic," said Polly, beaming at him.

More like a death trap, thought Carole, who drove a huge Porsche SUV in Providence. But maybe drivers were more considerate here in France. Or not, she added, thinking of Frank's complaints about French drivers.

She wasn't much interested in the cars Benoit was restoring, but Frank-O and Frank seemed quite impressed. Finally leaving the garage, they discovered that Benoit's property was extensive and included olive and cherry trees, a small vineyard, a *potager*, or vegetable garden, and a rabbit hutch. There was also a shaded dining area and a swimming pool. "So private," whispered Polly, "no swimsuit needed."

Carole groaned. "TMI, Mom, TMI."

"I see you've got chickens," said Frank. "Do you get *beaucoup* eggs?"

"*Non, non*," moaned Benoit, shaking his head, launching into a barrage of French, which Carole translated. "He says they are very lazy, they eat a lot but they don't lay any eggs. Mathilde suggested he put a dummy egg in the nest, to inspire them, but so far they haven't got the message."

"Does Mathilde also work for you?" asked Carole.

"She worked for Benoit first," said Polly. "He introduced us. He said she wanted more work, and he knew I needed a housekeeper so he recommended her. She is a very good housekeeper."

Benoit was still talking and Polly laughed, then translated. "He says Mathilde is a good housekeeper but she doesn't seem to know much about chickens. He's still not getting any eggs and the dummy egg is gone, too. He thinks the hens are hiding it somewhere."

"Maybe they need a rooster," suggested Carole.

Even with his limited English, Benoit picked right up on that. "Ah, *l'amour*."

"So what are we having for dinner?" asked Polly. "*Un omelette?*"

"*Non, poulet.*" Benoit laughed.

"One of your chickens?" asked Connie, horrified.

Benoit didn't reply, but ushered them inside to the dining room, where a first course was waiting for them. "The French call this cake," explained Polly, "but it's savory. Stuffed with olives." Benoit was already opening a bottle of wine.

"It's his own wine," said Polly. "From his vines."

While Benoit began filling their glasses, Polly turned to Frank-O. "Will you put something on the stereo? It's in the next room."

"Sure thing," said Frank-O, hopping to his feet. When he returned, a classic Rolling Stones album was playing. "You've got some collection," said Frank-O, complimenting him. "Are you a big rock fan?"

Benoit sat down and took a sip of wine. "*Absolument*," he said.

"He's seen and heard them all at concerts," offered Polly.

"Even the Stones?" asked Frank-O.

"*Bien sûr*. I know Mick."

"Really? What's he like?" asked Frank-O.

Benoit gave another of his shrugs. "*Un type*. He's okay."

My, my, thought Carole, Benoit is turning out to be a very interesting fellow.

Chapter Seven

"So how do we get from here, Paris, to this Château de Ventoux?" asked Bill the next morning, as they ate a breakfast of coffee, croissants, and yogurt that came in adorable little ceramic pots. They'd spent the night on the red couch, which was a sleep sofa.

"This yogurt is delicious, and I love the pot," declared Lucy.

"You can keep the pot for a souvenir," said Elizabeth.

"Back to the problem at hand," said Bill. "How are we going to get to the château?"

"You could rent a car and drive," said Elizabeth.

"How far is it?" asked Bill.

"Um, Chris, how far do you think it is from Paris to Mazan?"

"Less than six hundred kilometers, say about three hundred fifty miles."

"That far?" Lucy was horrified.

"About six hours, Lucy," said Bill.

"If I were you, I'd fly to Avignon and rent a car at the airport to drive to Mazan," advised Chris.

"Another flight?" moaned Lucy, who had jet lag and really just wanted to go back to bed, but maybe not on the uncomfortable sleep sofa.

"It's best," said Elizabeth, agreeing with her partner. "I'll get you tickets."

Thanks to her skills as a concierge, Elizabeth soon had them booked on a noon flight, and by two in the afternoon they were driving through beautiful Provençal countryside and charming villages in a sporty little Mercedes-Benz convertible equipped with GPS, also arranged for them by Elizabeth.

"This is like *Two for the Road*," said Lucy, naming a favorite movie. "I'm Audrey Hepburn and you're Albert Finney. We're college kids again, spending our summer vacation touring Europe."

Bill smiled. "Don't forget, their cute convertible burst into flames, they had all sorts of mishaps, and when they hit middle age their marriage was in trouble."

Lucy refused to concede; she might not look much like Audrey Hepburn but she felt like her, or at least like the part she was playing in the film. "They made up at the end," she said, smiling.

The drive went quickly and Mazan, they discovered, was every bit as charming as Elizabeth promised, with winding streets dotted with trees, a café with a shaded terrace, and a handful of shops and restaurants. And the Château was extremely luxurious, with modern furniture arranged in rooms that had been carefully restored to their eighteenth-century grandeur. Crystal chandeliers tinkled, massive doors swung silently on antique hinges, sunlight streamed through enormous windows.

"It seems they've done quite a bit with the place since the de Sade family lived here," said Lucy, plopping down on the king-size bed and stretching.

"Or maybe they've carefully restored the dungeon, blood stains and all," teased Bill.

"Nope. It's now a spa," said Lucy, waving a brochure

in his direction. "I think a nap followed by a massage might be just the thing for my jet lag."

"No. No napping. We've got to power on. Let's go for a walk and explore the town."

"Really?"

"Yeah. There's a *bureau de tourisme* just across from here. Let's see what they advise."

"Okay," sighed Lucy, swinging her legs off the bed and standing up. "Onward and upward."

"That's the spirit," said Bill.

A young man in the tourist bureau had lots of good ideas. It wasn't at all far to L'Isle-sur-la-Sorgue and its famous flea market, which would actually be taking place the very next day, on Sunday.

"That's one day planned," said Lucy. "But what's of interest in the town?"

"*Le cimetière*, um, I think it is ceremony in English?"

"Ceremony?" wondered Lucy. "Cemetery. I love cemeteries. Where is it?"

"Follow the road to the café, there's a passage beside the café that leads up the hill to the cemetery."

"That sounds fun. Thanks," said Lucy.

"Just be sure to watch out for the *loups-garous*," advised the young man in a helpful tone of voice.

"Werewolves?" demanded Lucy. "Are there really werewolves?"

"Not so much of a problem since they built the chapel," he replied. "But boars do come down from Mont Ventoux occasionally."

"We'll be careful," said Lucy, convinced he was teasing them. "*Merci et au revoir.*"

Lucy and Bill enjoyed the short walk through the town, noting various shops such as a newsagent and a bakery that also offered sandwiches. "We could have a picnic," suggested Lucy.

"With wine," suggested Bill.

A few old men were seated on the café terrace when they passed. They continued through a narrow walled passage that led to a rather steep climb on up to the open cemetery gates. Once inside, they noticed the cemetery was well kept and dotted with trees; there were a number of very old sarcophagi that seemed to be Roman relics, the more recent graves were covered with trinkets and colorful ceramic flowers.

"That's a good idea," said Lucy. "They don't fade, like real flowers."

A little road circled through the cemetery and they followed it, Lucy occasionally attempting to translate the tributes to beloved ones. In the rear they found the chapel, but when Lucy tried the door it was locked.

Finally completing the circuit, Lucy commented that she hadn't seen any *loups-garous*.

"No werewolves, not even a boar," said Bill. "Why don't we celebrate with a drink in the café?"

"Good idea," said Lucy, leading the way to a little table in a shady spot. The waiter took their orders, beer for Bill and rosé for Lucy, and delivered them promptly.

"You know," observed Lucy, after taking a sip of rosé, "I feel like I've stepped into a movie, or a book. This is exactly what people expect France to be like, and it really is. There's no McDonald's, there's no CVS, not even a Starbucks."

"I saw a big supermarket in that town we passed through, Carpentras," said Bill.

Lucy's eyes lit up. "We've got to go."

"For picnic stuff?"

"Yup. But I also want French toothpaste, and skin lotion, oh and magazines . . ."

Lucy's shopping list was interrupted by a loud female voice.

"Well as I live and breathe, if it isn't Lucy Stone!"

Lucy turned and saw Carole Capobianco, the woman from the plane, along with another, older woman. "Lucy, imagine seeing you here, in Mazan! Lucy Stone, meet my mom, Polly Prendergast."

Chapter Eight

Carole couldn't believe it. Here she was in this teeny little French town finding someone she knew. An American, and when Americans encountered each other in foreign places, well, it was practically their patriotic duty to stick together.

"We met on the plane," she explained to Polly, plopping herself down in the chair next to the crunchy granola husband with his backwoodsman's beard. "But I thought you guys were staying in Paris," she asked. "How'd you end up here?"

Realizing that her mother hadn't joined them at the table, but was hovering awkwardly behind her, waiting for an invitation, Carole pulled out a chair. "Take a load off, Polly. Lucy and I are like old friends, right, Lucy? There's nothing like a transatlantic flight for getting to know someone."

While her mother got settled, Carole studied Lucy and Bill. Something was going on with them, she decided, picking up a bit of a vibe. Maybe she'd interrupted something; maybe Lucy and Bob or Bill, or whatever his name was, weren't getting along. But Lucy finally managed to pull herself together enough to give them a lukewarm greeting. "Imagine meeting you here. And so nice to meet you, Polly."

"Polly's my mother," explained Carole, turning to the husband, who really didn't seem too happy. She put it down to jet lag, or maybe they'd been fighting about something, and Carole decided they'd better make it short, maybe just one drink. She looked around and spotted a waiter, leaning casually against a wall, and waved at him. "Garçon!" He glanced at her, nodded, beginning a slow walk toward them.

"What can I get you?" he asked.

But instead of ordering another beer, the husband pushed his chair away from the table. "Well, it's been nice but I think we ought to get going," he said, but Lucy stopped him before he could stand up, placing her hand on his arm.

"You should try the rosé, it's the regional wine and it's delicious," said Lucy. She smiled at her husband. "Bill thinks it's for girls, he's sticking to beer."

So I was right, thought Carole, it was Bill. Of course. An all-American, white-bread sort of name. Though he looked more like a whole-grain sort of guy.

"You can't go wrong with rosé in Provence," offered Polly.

"Okay," said Carole, turning to the waiter. "Another beer for the gentleman and three rosés, *s'il vous plaît.*"

The waiter nodded and strolled off into the café.

"I don't know what's the matter with that waiter, he's got some attitude," Carole said, making herself comfortable and resting her arms on the table. "Some cute town, huh? Polly's got a place here, a *mas*, just outside town. But Mazan is hardly a big tourist attraction. How'd you guys end up here?"

"The plan was to stay with our daughter in Paris but

what with the general strike and all, Elizabeth thought we'd be happier here."

Carole thought she heard a hint of disappointment in Lucy's tone.

"But she and her partner, Chris, will be joining us in a few days, so I'm looking forward to that."

"She's pregnant, right?"

Lucy immediately perked up. "Yeah. She's got the cutest little baby bump, but I am worried a bit about her having the baby here. In France, I mean."

Polly chimed right in. "No worries. France takes very good care of moms and babies. It's a lot safer to give birth here than in the U.S."

"Good to know," said Bill as the waiter arrived with their drinks on a round tray.

"So where are you staying?" asked Carole, burning with curiosity. "Doesn't seem like there's much choice in this little town. No Four Seasons, for sure."

"That's where you're wrong," offered Polly. "A lot of people rent villas to vacationers, and there's the five-star Château de Ventoux. I've been hoping we'll all have dinner at the restaurant there one night. They have a fantastic chef who's getting a lot of attention."

"That's actually where we're staying," said Lucy. "We're eating there tonight."

Carole sipped her rosé and pondered this surprising bit of information. What were these obviously very middle-class people who lived in some Podunk town in Maine doing in a five-star château? Those places didn't come cheap, she knew only too well because they'd stayed at some Relais & Châteaux place the last time they were in France and Frank had practically had a coronary when he got the bill. She really wanted to get to the bottom of this fascinating situation, but she could hardly come right out and ask them if they were millionaires or billionaires. "So does this château live up to its reputation?" she finally asked.

"Well, if it were up to me, I'd rather be staying with Elizabeth in her apartment in Paris, but all things considered, the château is lovely." She glanced at her husband and smiled. "They have a spa and I've booked a couples massage."

"What?" exclaimed Bill, suddenly coming to life.

"You'll love it," said Lucy. "The concierge said everyone does."

Carole decided she'd better reconsider her previous assumptions; there was more to this woman than she'd thought. She remembered how the couple had been met at the plane by that guy in the suit and then she'd seen them in that limo. Like Frank had said, they definitely had connections. The daughter? Or maybe it was the guy, the baby's father? "Tell me about your daughter," she began, in what she hoped was a tactful sort of way. "How does Elizabeth like living in Paris?"

"Oh, Elizabeth's very independent. Always has been. She's been here for, what, ten years?" she asked, turning to her husband.

"About that, I guess."

"And didn't you tell me she's going to be a single mom? One of these modern girls?" That was pretty tactful, she thought. No judgment. A lot of women were going their own way these days, spurning marriage in favor of maintaining their independence.

"Oh, no," said Lucy. "At heart Elizabeth is very traditional. I'm actually kind of surprised she and Chris are going with the solidarity pact."

"So no church wedding?"

"We-e-ll," began Lucy, chuckling and dragging the word

out. "We almost had one of those." But before she could explain, Bill slapped a twenty euro bill down on the table and stood up. "Time for us to go, Lucy, if we're going to have that massage."

"Too bad," said Carole. "Just when we were getting to know each other."

"We must get better acquainted," said Polly, surprising Carole. "You must come for dinner at my place. I want to hear all the news from America, what's really going on, not the French version!"

Carole expected a polite refusal, but she was wrong. "We'd be delighted," said Lucy. "You can leave a message with the details for us at the Château."

"I will, but let's plan on tomorrow night. Around seven?"

"Looking forward to it," said Lucy, definitely not speaking for both of them. The husband, Bill, looked about ready to murder her.

"I'll give the details to the concierge. Do you need directions?"

"No, just the address. Our rental car has GPS."

A top-of-the-line rental car with GPS, a five-star hotel, what was going on here? The more she learned about this couple, the less things added up, decided Carole. She was determined to get to the bottom of this puzzle.

"We're just outside of town, easy to find," said Polly. "*À bientôt.*"

"*À bientôt*," replied Lucy.

Carole watched as they left the terrace and crossed the road, walking and talking together. That must be some conversation, she guessed, studying their body language. The husband had been quiet at the table, but now he seemed to have a whole lot to say.

Chapter Nine

Dinner at the Château was not a success, admitted Lucy, who had hoped a delicious meal would make up for Bill's displeasure when Carole and her mother crashed their table at the café and, even worse, the fact that she'd accepted Polly's dinner invitation. Unlike the couples massage, which much to her relief he had actually enjoyed, the dinner hadn't gone over very well. She'd loved the beautiful dining room, which glittered with mirrors and chandeliers and windows that overlooked the garden; the beautiful linens and plates, and the discreet service from waiters who tiptoed around and whispered to you. But that wasn't the sort of thing Bill enjoyed; he liked a comfortable place where you didn't have to sit up straight and mind your manners but could relax and enjoy a beer with a hearty meal.

Hearty was not what you could call the servings at the Château, where the descriptions on the menu were larger than the portions. The asparagus appetizer, for example, was described as coming with a coulis containing numerous ingredients but turned out to be a single stalk of asparagus with a dab of salmon-colored cream on the side. On the way to Mazan, Lucy remembered passing fields and fields of asparagus. There were even hand-painted signs offering *asperges* for sale at roadside stands. There was no lack of available asparagus to explain the single stalk, bent as it was into a dramatic Z shape. It was perfectly cooked, but still, one stalk? Bill hadn't been able to get over it, he thought it was hysterically funny.

He wasn't all that amused, however, when his lamb entrée turned out to be similarly tiny in size. "No wonder they're all so skinny," he said, downing the entire piece in one bite and emptying the bread basket onto his plate. "I've got to get through the night," he said, reaching for the butter.

But the skimpy dinner had actually worked in her favor, thought Lucy, because Bill was now much more amenable to Polly's invitation. "They're Americans, right, so I think there's a chance we'll get a square meal," he said, as they drove through town to the *mas*.

"I guess the whole family will be there," said Lucy. "It should be interesting."

"I admit, I was surprised when you were so quick to accept their invitation."

"I couldn't help myself. I've been obsessed with France ever since Elizabeth moved here, well, actually before that, it started when I took French in seventh grade. I'm certainly not fluent, but I love the language, even though I make a mess of it. But I can read it and I'm a sucker for the pretty photos in magazines and the big glossy design books. I used to suspect that it was all romanticized and photoshopped but now here we are and it's all true. The photos don't lie. And when Polly invited us to her *mas*, well, I couldn't pass up a chance like that. Even if the Capobiancos are a bit, um . . ."

"Crass? Pushy? Rude?"

"Yeah, but the word I've been thinking is 'connected.'"

Bill's eyebrows shot up. "Like the mob?"

"Duh, Bill. They're from Providence and he's in plumbing."

"Point taken." He paused, carefully turning through the gateway. "Anybody we need to have offed?"

Lucy laughed. "I'll think about it," she said, as he parked the car beside the others beneath a tall plane tree. Lucy looked around, her heart actually skipping a beat. The *mas* was right out of one of her glossy design books, a simple, practical structure made of vine-covered stone with doors and shutters painted the perfect shade of blue. It wasn't pretending to be anything other than it was, and it was perfect. There was even a long table with mismatched chairs set outside for meals *en plein air*, as well as an assortment of easy chairs and even a rusty iron daybed piled with cushions for whiling away long afternoons.

"*Bienvenue*!" sang Polly, appearing in the open door. "Welcome. Come on in."

Lucy didn't have to be asked twice. She presented Polly with a bottle of Irish whiskey, chosen because wine was as plentiful as water in Provence, and some bottles were actually cheaper than some bottled waters.

"Irish, thank you," said Polly, genuinely pleased. "C'mon in and make yourselves comfortable."

They were standing in the hall, which had a floor of square red tiles and featured a curving staircase with a black metal railing that practically made Lucy swoon. Halfway up there was a niche in the curved wall, which held a big vase of lilacs that filled the entry with scent. On one side, she got a glimpse of the kitchen through a partly open door, on the other a large room with a dining table set in front of French doors, left open to the evening breezes.

"No screens?" asked Bill. "You leave the doors and windows open?"

"I know," agreed Polly. "Crazy, isn't it? But there are no mosquitoes. No bugs. A bird occasionally flies in and, realizing its mistake, flies right back out."

"This is lovely," said Lucy, stepping into a room filled with comfy sofas and easy chairs, arranged around a fireplace where a small fire was burning, more for atmosphere than actual heat.

"Thank you. It's not fancy, but it suits me. Now, I think we need some introductions," she said, indicating the people sitting on those sofas and chairs. "You've met my daughter, Carole, and this is her husband, Frank, and my grandkids, Connie and Frank-O."

"Yes, we were all on the plane together. I'm Lucy Stone, and this is my husband, Bill."

"And this," said Polly, with a flourish, as if she were announcing the arrival of the King of Siam, "is my fiancé, Benoit."

Following her gesture, Lucy turned around and saw a tall, rather elegant man in his sixties standing in the doorway, holding a couple of bottles of wine. He was wearing a white scarf around his neck, despite the warm weather; a T-shirt and jeans completed his casual ensemble.

"Benoit, these are our friends from America, Lucy and Bill," said Polly, relieving him of the wine.

"*Enchanté*," he said, grabbing Lucy by the shoulders and delivering three *bisous*, not the usual air kisses, but pressing his face against hers. In America, she thought, it would be cause for a charge of sexual assault, watching with amusement as he did the same to Bill. An equal-opportunity sexual offender, she decided, amused to notice that Bill had accepted Benoit's embrace rather calmly. Meeting his eyes, she got the slightest little shrug.

"No sense waiting, I know Mathilde has everything ready, so *à table*, everyone."

They all seated themselves around the long table, where Lucy found herself next to Benoit. A plump middle-aged woman, presumably Mathilde, appeared carrying a tray of little plates, which she served while Benoit opened a bottle of wine and began pouring. "It's my own," he said, "from my vines."

Lucy took a sip and decided she'd never tasted wine like this. It filled her mouth, like something solid, except it was only a tiny sip. And for the first time she began to understand what people meant when they talked about wine having flavor notes of berry or chocolate, with a lingering finish. "This is absolutely lovely," she said, getting a nod from Benoit.

Bill, however, had gone straight to his first course, which was bits of toast topped with tomatoes and herbs. "Really good," he said, tossing them in his mouth like popcorn.

"Would you like some more?" asked Polly.

Lucy was about to give him a warning shake of the head—she suspected this was only a polite offer as there would be three more courses—but she was too late, as Frank joined in asking for seconds. Mathilde's face was an impassive mask as she refilled their plates, which made Lucy wonder what she was really thinking of these Americans.

"So how do you like Provence so far?" asked Carole. "What did you do today?"

"The flea market!" said Lucy. "In L'Isle-sur-la-Sorgue."

"Good choice," said Carole.

"What did you buy?" asked Connie.

"The question should be, what didn't she buy?" complained Bill, with a sigh.

"Don't mind him. He found some fabulous Laguiole knives, while I found some bits of faience pottery, gorgeous dinner napkins, lavender sachets, dried herbs, some antique silver napkin rings that say *madame* and *monsieur . . .*"

"And that's just the beginning," said Bill. "She hasn't even started on the baby clothes."

"That's right, you're going to have a grandchild," said Carole. "What did you find?"

"The most adorable little onesies. We have nothing like them in the States."

"The French do have the best baby clothes," observed Polly.

"As do the Italians," offered Carole, giving Connie a look.

"I caught that not-so-subtle hint," said Connie.

Benoit had been quiet, so Lucy turned to him, asking if he thought this year would be a good year for the grapes. "As good as the year you made this wine?" she asked.

He gave a shrug. "*Que sera, sera*," he said.

"Like the song," said Lucy.

He looked blank. "Song? *Je ne sais pas . . .*"

"*La chanson*," said Lucy, going on to sing a few bars of the tune.

"Ah, *oui*," he began, launching into a long and complicated explanation with a lot of shrugs and hand gestures, which Lucy didn't understand at all. She caught a few words: *printemps*, which she knew meant spring, and *poulets*, which meant chickens; none seemed to have anything to do with grapes or wine.

"*Poulets?*" she asked. "*Ils vous donnent beaucoup des oeufs?*"

"*Non!*" he exclaimed with force.

Lucy turned to Polly. "There's a problem with his chickens? Are they sick?"

"He doesn't know," explained Polly. "He says they're not laying and he doesn't understand why since it is spring, and that is when the chickens lay the most eggs. But he has none. He's had to buy eggs, which is a catastrophe."

"Oh, my," said Lucy, who indeed knew several people who raised chickens back home and were actually giving the eggs away because they had too many.

Benoit was continuing to complain about his chickens when the second course arrived, an absolutely delicious bouillabaisse that everyone praised. "We're so close to Marseille," said Polly, "I wanted to make sure you got a truly good homemade bouillabaisse, and Mathilde's is excellent."

There was no arguing with that, and the table fell silent as they dug into the heaping bowls that seemed to contain every kind of seafood imaginable, right down to tiny baby octopi.

"My youngest daughter would be very upset about the octopi," commented Bill, popping one into his mouth. "She says they're almost as smart as people."

Benoit muttered something, and Polly smiled. "Benoit says his chickens are smarter than octopi, even smarter than he is."

"*Ce n'est pas vrai*," offered Lucy, enjoying being able to speak a bit of French. "*C'est impossible.*"

Benoit continued his rapid-fire French, none of which Lucy could catch but which seemed to amuse Polly very much. When he paused, to scoop a clam out of its shell, Polly explained. "He even put out a dummy egg, that's a trick that's supposed to fool the chickens into laying, but he says even that has disappeared. He thinks the chickens hid it, that they're mad at him and that's why they won't lay."

"If you ask me, I bet somebody is stealing his eggs and didn't realize the dummy was a fake."

"*Ah*," said Benoit, intrigued by the idea. "*Un voleur! C'est possible.*"

Chapter Ten

Looking around at the animated faces gathered at the table, Carole thought that her mom really knew how to throw a party. Everyone was having a great time, due in large part to Polly's gracious management of the seating. She'd put Frank at the foot of the table, with Connie on one side and Bill on the other, and wisely placed Frank-O at the other end of the table, near Benoit and Lucy. That arrangement fostered lively conversation, and also made it less likely that Frank and Frank-O would come to blows, as they had done at the Feast of the Seven Fishes last Christmas. It was always best to get those two seated as far apart as possible, as neither one was mature enough to behave in a civilized manner.

Personality conflicts aside, Carole was terribly proud of her attractive kids. It was so lovely to see Connie finally relaxing, probably due to the wine. Whatever it was, she looked especially lovely tonight in the candlelight. And Frank-O! It wasn't every kid who could carry off dyeing his hair blue, but on Frank-O it looked good. He had great bone structure, he was tall, and he managed to look buff despite shunning all types of exercise. Maybe it was working on his sculptures that kept him in shape. And he was having a great time talking with Benoit. The two had really hit it off and were managing to communicate in a sort of Franglais, mixing English and French to get their ideas across.

The success of a dinner party depended in large part on the food, and here Carole had to give her mother credit. Not that she'd done the cooking, but she had chosen the menu and Mathilde was a terrific cook. A terrific all-around housekeeper, for that matter, even though she thought she worked for her mother only part time. When she'd asked where she'd found a miracle like Mathilde, Polly had said it was through Benoit. The woman worked for him, too, in a sort of shared arrangement. She hadn't been at the *mas* long enough to figure out how it worked exactly, but all the parties seemed happy enough with it, whatever it was. She thought a dinner party like this must be some sort of overtime for Mathilde, but Polly never skimped when it came to entertaining.

The bouillabaisse was divine, she thought, spearing a last piece of lobster with her fork and popping it in her mouth, savoring the flavor and wondering how Mathilde had managed to preserve the unique flavors of each ingredient at the same time combining them in this delicious mélange. It must be some secret technique, she thought, reflecting that whenever she made a complicated dish with lots of ingredients she ended up with a sort of mush. Oh, well, she thought, taking a sip of Benoit's delicious wine, she'd never claimed to be a cook, and in Providence you didn't have to be since there were so many fabulous restaurants. And thanks to Frank, she certainly didn't have to watch her pennies. Take the lobster ravioli at Venda, so easy and hard to beat!

Frank loved to eat and his manners weren't always the best; his appetite got the better of him. If he liked something, like the first course tonight, he wanted more. He didn't understand the way the French took time to enjoy each course; it wasn't about quantity for them, it was all about quality. Take tonight, when Frank joined Bill in asking for seconds of that first course, which raised Benoit's eyebrows. And he'd really plowed through that bouillabaisse, going back for seconds before Mathilde had finished dishing out firsts for everyone. She knew that Polly found her husband boorish, but she loved his big appetite, which included a lot more than food. Frank never let her down in the bedroom, she could always count on him to satisfy in that department.

Bill, on the other hand, was a big guy, too, but he was a lot more sensitive to the vibe in the room. He'd quickly realized his mistake with the seconds, and afterward she'd noticed him observing the others for cues and checking in frequently with his wife, catching her eye and getting an approving nod or a cautionary little shake of the head. Lucy was definitely a puzzle; she wondered if she'd ever figure her out. She was smart, that was for sure, and she seemed comfortable in any situation despite coming from what appeared to be rather humble circumstances. She never fumbled over what fork to use, in fact, when Frank had used his fingers to pop those toasts into his mouth, Lucy had picked up the correct knife and fork and eaten hers in the French style. She herself thought the French took this stuff a bit too far, like when they used knives and forks to eat pizza, but when in France! That was something Lucy just seemed to know. And take the way she was conversing with both Benoit and Frank-O, which had to be rather challenging considering the difference in their ages and outlook, not to mention the language barrier. But she was holding the attention of both. Just look at the way they were smiling at her over their empty plates.

All the plates were empty, thought Carole, with a start.

Conversation was certainly a big part of a dinner party, but it seemed that people had not been eating for rather a long while and were now running out of conversation. Where was Mathilde? Why wasn't she clearing the table in preparation for the salad course? She caught Polly's eye, and Polly rose, excusing herself. Noticing that the fire had gone quite low, she asked Frank-O to put another log on, then left the room.

Conversation faltered without Polly, and Carole felt she should fill in as hostess, so she turned to Bill and asked if they had any plans yet for tomorrow.

"I believe Lucy wants to go to a place called Fontaine-de-Vaucluse, is that right?" he said, stumbling over the French name.

"*Mon amie a un magasin . . .*" began Benoit, smiling broadly, when they heard a sudden, piercing shriek.

Chapter Eleven

Lucy didn't hesitate. Hearing Polly's cries she immediately got to her feet and headed for the kitchen. As a newspaper reporter back home in Tinker's Cove, she'd frequently covered car crashes or other accidents, as well as crimes. This, she realized the moment she saw Mathilde's body lying on the floor, was no accident. This was obviously murder, indicated by the red marks on her neck. Two thumbprints on either side of her neck were clear evidence that she'd been strangled.

But maybe she was still alive? Polly was on her knees, performing chest compressions, muttering the Bee Gees song "Staying Alive." Aware that she was in a crime scene, Lucy's first impulse was to glance around the kitchen, looking for evidence. A large bowl of salad was on the table, along with a stack of salad plates. A cherry clafoutis had just come out of the oven and was cooling on the counter. The only sign of violence was a potted plant that had been on the windowsill, now lying smashed on the floor. Had the assailant come in through the window, or made a hasty exit?

"*Arrêtez,*" said Benoit, placing his hands on Polly's shoulders and pulling her away from Mathilde. *"Elle est morte."*

Polly resisted, continuing the compressions, and the song,

which struck Lucy as surreal. Mathilde wasn't staying alive, she was obviously staying dead.

"Polly, c'est fini."

Polly raised her head and looked at Benoit, then burst into tears.

"What's going on?" demanded Carole. She was standing in the doorway, which was now crowded with everyone else. "Did she fall? We must call the rescue."

"*Non*," said Benoit. "We must call the police."

"This is a crime scene," said Connie, using her lawyer voice. "We all need to go back in the other room and wait for the police."

"That's right," said Lucy, standing by the door. "There may be evidence here left by the killer."

Polly was still on her knees, apparently in shock, but when Benoit offered his hand, she took it, and he pulled her to her feet. Once upright, she collapsed against him, and he guided her out of the room. The group began shuffling back across the hall, making way for them; Frank stepped forward and wrapped his arms around Carole, drawing her into the other room. Connie positioned herself behind Lucy, indicating she should leave, and once she did closed the kitchen door, making sure it was secure. Then the two continued across the hall to join the others in the salon; Benoit remained in the hall, calling the police on the landline.

Nobody sat back down at the table, where the dirty dishes and half-drunk wineglasses remained, abandoned, along with the crumpled napkins. Benoit had seated Polly in one of the armchairs and was standing protectively beside her; Carole was seated on the arm of that chair, holding her mother's hand. Frank was standing by the open French door, as if standing guard; Connie stood beside him, staring out toward the mountains and setting sun. Frank-O was unable to settle and was moving around the room, checking out the bookshelf, studying a painting hanging on the wall, flipping through a magazine before tossing it back onto the coffee table. Bill led Lucy to the sofa, where they sat together.

"Are you okay?" he asked, giving her hand a squeeze.

"I'm worried."

"Why? This has nothing to do with us."

"No, Bill. We were here, we're involved, whether we like it or not."

Chapter Twelve

"How could this happen?" asked Connie, turning back to face the others in the room. "We were all here. How could someone get into the house and strangle poor Mathilde?"

"We were pretty lively, and loud," said Frank-O. "Everybody was focused on the table, right. We were all looking at each other."

"But if someone entered the hall, we would have noticed," said Polly.

"I suppose the killer could have slipped in through the door," suggested Bill. "It would only take a second or two to cross the hall and enter the kitchen."

"Polly, you were seated facing the hall," said Lucy. "Did you see anyone?"

"No. But I was focused on my guests. I remember looking out at the mountains, thinking we might catch the sunset. Frank-O is right, I probably wouldn't have noticed someone in the hallway."

"Marching right into the house would have been risky for the killer, though," said Lucy, thinking out loud. "There was a broken flowerpot on the floor beneath the window. Maybe the killer came in that way."

"I don't think so," said Connie. "Entering through the

window would have been too risky. It's awkward to climb through a window, it takes a bit of time to maneuver your legs through. Mathilde would have been able to call for help, or even escape the kitchen. I think it's more likely the killer left through the window."

"Maybe it wasn't all that risky, maybe it was someone Mathilde knew," said Lucy. "Maybe it wasn't a planned killing but an argument that got out of control."

"Wouldn't we have heard an argument?" asked Polly, turning to Benoit.

"*Pas Mathilde*," said Benoit, shaking his head. "She was always very quiet. *Comme une souris*."

"Like a little mouse," said Lucy, suddenly remembering a door under the stairs. "Is there a back door?" she asked. "From the hall?"

Polly shook her head. "That's a closet."

"Could the killer have waited there?"

"Possibly," admitted Polly. "But the house was never empty today. We were coming and going, but not all at once. Someone was always here. And it's a big yard, a long drive, the approach to the house is quite exposed. I don't see how someone could have gone unnoticed."

Lucy was beginning to think that Connie was right, that Mathilde might well have known her killer. Given Benoit's comment that she was quiet as a mouse, perhaps she was also secretive. Her work meant that she would inevitably learn a lot about her employers, but that relationship wasn't necessarily reciprocal. She may not have shared much information about herself.

Lucy turned to Polly and asked, "How well do, I mean *did*, how well did you know Mathilde?"

"Not well at all. In fact I've only had her for a couple of weeks. Benoit recommended her to me."

"What about you, Benoit? Did you know her well?"

"*Bien sûr*," he began, speaking rapidly in French.

When he finished, Polly translated. "He often goes into town for coffee in the afternoon, and one day he encountered Mathilde leaving the crèche, and since his former housekeeper was quitting, he asked Mathilde if she knew anyone who might do the job and she said she was interested. She said she didn't like working at the *crèche*."

"Did she say why? Was she trying to get away from someone there?" asked Lucy.

Polly answered. "When I interviewed her I did ask why she left the *crèche* and she said there was too much work in too few hours, and they didn't pay well. I also got the feeling she found it a bit chaotic, what with all the children."

Lucy had plenty more questions, but the sound of an approaching siren caught everyone's attention. Moments later, an ambulance and a police car arrived.

Chapter Thirteen

Carole wasn't happy about getting involved in what appeared to be a murder; she wanted out. In particular, she wanted to go home. She thought longingly of her beautiful apartment overlooking the Woonasquatucket River back in Providence, where her little dog Poopsie was living the life of Riley, thanks to Mom and Big Frank. They both loved Poopsie and Poopsie adored them.

Right now, nervously awaiting the arrival of the police, Carole wanted nothing more than to be sitting with Poopsie beside her, her little pink nose resting lightly on her thigh. Carole could almost feel the little dog's warmth, could imagine her chest rising and falling with each breath, could practically feel her silky fur as she gently scratched her favorite spot, just behind her ears. She and Poopsie could sit like that for hours; it was amazing the way dogs could just fall asleep whenever they didn't have anything else to do. While Poopsie slept, Carole sometimes watched TV, sometimes read, but sometimes she just chilled, doing nothing at all except enjoying the moment.

That's kind of what she was doing now, just trying to empty her mind and not get crazy with anxiety. She knew that Frank was pretty much always ready to explode and that would not be good, not in France, where you were presumed guilty and they'd throw you in jail for looking at a cop crosswise. She was going to have to keep him calm, and that was not going to be easy. She noticed he was jiggling his leg, never a good sign, and that Maine woman, Lucy, wasn't helping the situation with her questions. "Did you know her well? Did you see anyone in the hallway?" Honestly, if her mother knew the woman was going to get killed, she would never have hired her. And if she'd seen an intruder enter the house while they were eating dinner, she'd certainly have mentioned it. All those questions were making her wonder what exactly Lucy was up to.

"Is your wife a cop back in Maine?" she asked the husband, Bob or Bill, why couldn't she get his name straight. Probably because it was vanilla, like the guy.

"No," he replied, with a scowl, which she thought indicated he wasn't very happy about all the questions, either. "She's a reporter for our local newspaper." He scratched his beard. "She's covered a few murders."

The rescue squad had finally arrived, about time if you asked her, but nobody hurried in France, not even for emergencies. Remember how they'd taken hours to get Princess Diana to the hospital after that crash? And, of course, the cops had come, too. Now the fun would really begin.

Benoit, bless him, greeted the EMTs at the door and pointed the way to the kitchen, and the corpse. The cop followed, only one, and she was a woman, looking very official and trim in her uniform. Benoit, dirty old man that he was, greeted her with a big smile. They exchanged a few words, the EMTs joined them, there was a lively discussion in French. The EMTs departed, leaving the body, the lady officer made some calls, then she said something to Benoit and he brought her into the salon.

"I am Charlotte Castaigne, *une gardienne de la paix avec la police municipale de Mazan*. I am sorry for your trouble, but the entire house is now a crime scene. I have referred the incident to the *Police Nationale*, who will take over the investigation. In the meantime, I will need your names and contact information."

"And after that, what happens. Do we stay in the house?" asked Connie.

"We're dinner guests, can we leave?" asked Bill.

"*Non, non*," she said, holding up her hands. "*Patience, s'il vous plaît*. You will remain here, in this room, until the investigators arrive. Also the, what you call, crime scene investigators. CSI."

"And when will that be?" demanded Frank.

Uh, oh, here we go, thought Carole, placing a warning hand on his arm.

"Impossible to say. When they arrive, they arrive."

Carole could feel Frank's arm tensing, but he didn't say anything, just gave one of his disapproving snorts. Tragedy averted, for now.

"I think the best thing is for everyone to make themselves comfortable," said Connie.

"But what about our dinner?" Benoit asked the officer. "We did not have our salad."

"*Dommage*," said the officer, genuinely apologetic. "I saw it in the *cuisine, et aussi, le dessert, le clafoutis aux cerises*."

Figures, thought Carole. A woman was dead, murdered, but to these Frenchies the real tragedy was missing the salad course. Not to mention, the cherry pancake for dessert.

The officer seated herself at the table and began studying her phone. The others also seated themselves, Connie and Frank-O at the table, along with Benoit. The Mainers were sitting on the couch, Polly had taken an easy chair and Frank was manspreading, taking up the entire loveseat. Frank-O took out his phone, as did Connie, but they got a warning look and a figure shake from Officer Louise. *"Non, non."*

Frank, believe it or not, was snoring. It seemed that slightly overweight husbands with sleep apnea could also fall asleep whenever and wherever, just like Poopsie.

With nothing to distract Carole, her gaze wandered over the other captives. Polly was dabbing at her eyes, but Carole wasn't sure if she was crying over Mathilde's murder or the social disaster that the dinner party had become. Probably the latter. Connie was probably searching her brain for whatever she knew about French law and the rights of American citizens. Frank-O, only God knew what went on in that brain of his. As she watched, he turned to Benoit and said something, but Benoit didn't reply. He was looking over toward the open French door, and Carole swore he was trying to figure out if he could escape through it, without the officer noticing. He'd actually started to raise himself from his chair when her head snapped around and she stared at him. Arrested with a look, who knew? Benoit picked up a spoon from the table and began fidgeting with it, tapping it against the table.

The officer put down her phone and stood up. "I have a message from the *Police Nationale*. They will not be able to come tonight."

"What the hell?" growled Frank.

"I am to secure the *rez-de-chaussée*, that it to say, this floor of the house. Everything is to be left as it is. Those of you who are in residence here may retire to your rooms upstairs. Those not in residence may depart, after providing me with their information. Is this clear?"

Benoit was on his feet, headed for the door, when she stopped him. "Monsieur, your details, please."

He turned, reminding Carole of a kid who'd been caught with his hand in the cookie jar. "Benoit Thibodeau, I live next door." He pointed.

"Bien. Téléphone?"

He rattled off some numbers, which the officer noted down. "You may go."

And like that, he was off like a shot.

Chapter Fourteen

"Wow," said Bill, starting the car. "That was quite a party."

"Surreal, wasn't it? Like one of those murder mystery games."

"Except the killer wasn't one of the partygoers. Nobody left the table."

"I don't think that will stop the police from considering all of us suspects," said Lucy.

"Do you think so?"

"As foreigners, I think we're top of the list." They were approaching the town now, where the only signs of life were the lighted windows in the apartments above the shops. "A murder is the last thing you'd expect in a place like this. It's such a sweet little town."

"Well, don't forget we're staying in a château once owned by the Marquis de Sade."

"Only his family, Bill. Not the marquis himself. And besides, they say he really didn't deserve his reputation."

Bill didn't agree. "There must be something to it. They named an entire perversion after him. It's not johndoeism, it's sadism."

Pulling into the parking area at the château, which was deeply shaded and not well-lit, Lucy felt the hairs on the back of her neck rise. Getting out of the car she glanced up at the château, with its neat rows of windows, now all shuttered for the night. "See no evil," she whispered to herself.

"Did you say something?" asked Bill, putting the car keys in his pocket.

"Not really. It's these shutters, the way they close them at night. If you're inside, you can't see out, you can't see the stars and the sky. And nobody outside can see in, either. It just makes me wonder what really does go on in these houses, when the shutters are closed tight."

"You don't have to shut them if you don't want to," said Bill, as they crossed the parking lot to the château.

"I tried that, the first night, but the maid came in while you were in the shower and insisted on closing the shutters and the windows, too. She was horrified they were open, it's like they're worried about the night vapors or something."

Bill slipped his arm around her waist and pulled her close. "Maybe it's the werewolves."

Next morning, the first thing Lucy did when she got out of bed was to open the windows and the shutters. She took a moment to check out the weather, and to breathe the fresh morning air. Back home in Maine, they had screens on all the windows, which they kept open all summer. Even in winter, she'd been known to crack a window at night, just to get some air.

"Are you still fussing about the shutters?" asked Bill, coming out of the bathroom.

"I don't understand it."

"It's the way they do things," he said with a shrug.

"I guess I have to give up my dream of moving here," said Lucy. "I'm too much of a fresh-air fiend."

"I'm a breakfast fiend," said Bill, nibbling the back of her neck.

"I'll get dressed," said Lucy, slipping out of his embrace.

Since the weather was nice, they opted to have breakfast on the terrace. The maître d' had seemed to consider it an odd choice and, as it happened, none of the other guests joined them outside. "It's much too lovely to stay inside," said Lucy, as the waiter set a table for them.

Coffee, croissants, yogurt, and fruit were served, followed by the arrival of a middle-aged man wearing a rumpled suit.

"I am Lieutenant Yves Hugues from the *Police Nationale*," he told them, standing at attention and speaking perfect English. "I have a few questions for you."

"Make yourself comfortable," invited Bill, indicating an empty chair.

"Would you like coffee?" asked Lucy.

"*Merci*," he said, as Lucy signaled the waiter to bring another cup. The lieutenant had no sooner gotten his coffee than he helped himself to a croissant, adding a big dollop of strawberry jam. "This place is known for the croissants," he said, by way of explanation. "*Formidable.*"

"Yogurt? Fruit?" offered Lucy.

"*Non, merci. Ça suffit.*"

Once the business of the croissant was out of the way, the lieutenant signaled the waiter for more coffee, and then got down to the serious business of the day. "I understand you were a guest of Madame Polly Prendergast last night, and there was some unpleasantness."

"Yes," said Lucy. "The housekeeper, Mathilde, was killed."

"Terrible." He took a swallow of coffee. "Do you remember what was served at dinner?"

Lucy and Bill shared a glance. "Of course," began Lucy. "The first course was toast with tomatoes and herbs . . ."

"Ah, with olives?"

"Yes."

"And after . . ."

"A bouillabaisse."

"With lobster?"

"Yes. Lobster and other seafood."

"And the saffron, sometimes there is too little, sometimes too much?"

"No. Just right."

"And the salade?"

"We didn't get to the salad. There was a delay after we'd all finished the bouillabaisse and Polly went to see what the trouble was and that's when she discovered Mathilde's body."

The lieutenant acknowledged the seriousness of the moment. "Most distressing."

Lucy and Bill nodded in agreement, not quite sure if he was concerned about the loss of the salad course or the discovery of the body.

"And you all were at the table the whole time? No one left after the bouillabaisse was served? That was the last time you saw the poor Mathilde?"

"We were all at the table. The killer must have come in from outside."

"Perhaps Mathilde knew the killer," suggested Bill.

"He came and went like a spirit," said the lieutenant.

"So it seems," said Lucy.

"And you are Americans? Do you know Madame Prendergast from America?"

"No. We met her daughter, and her family, the Capobiancos, on the plane, when we were coming over."

"And you wished to continue the acquaintance?" suggested the lieutenant.

"Not really, we went our separate ways at the airport. But as it happened, we ran into them at the café here in town. That's when Polly invited us to dinner. We never met them before the flight."

"And why are you here in Mazan? We do not get many tourists here."

"Well, we were supposed to stay in Paris, with our daughter, but because of the strike and all the disruption she suggested we would be happier here, at the Château."

"And how long are you staying?"

"Ten days in total. We're hoping our daughter and her fiancé can join us here for the weekend."

"Your daughter is an ex-pat, living in Paris?"

"She works for the Cavendish Hotel. She's a concierge."

"Ah. I believe the Château is part of that chain?"

"Yes. That's how she was able to make the arrangements for us."

"Very nice for you," he suggested.

"It's lovely, but I would rather be with my daughter. She's expecting a baby."

"My felicitations," he said, removing his napkin from his lap and placing it on the table. "At this point, I do not think you will have to delay your departure, but I must ask you for your passports."

Lucy's heart sank, remembering an earlier visit to Paris when their travel plans were completely upset due to a murder. "How long will you need the passports?" she asked anxiously.

"Unfortunately, I cannot say how long this investigation will take."

"But surely, once you verify our identities and the fact that we have no connection whatsoever to Mathilde, or Polly, or the Capobiancos apart from a casual acquaintance, well, then you can return the passports, right?"

"That is not the policy," he said. "I will need the passports."

Bill got up. "I'll get them," he said.

Lucy remained with the lieutenant, fuming over this new situation. This was supposed to be a vacation, a family reunion, but now it had turned into an involuntary confinement. She was beginning to sympathize with Marie Antoinette, imprisoned in the Conciergerie. But unlike poor Marie, she didn't have to worry about the guillotine.

"This is very unfair," she said.

"Not so terrible," countered the lieutenant, glancing about the terrace, the garden, the pool.

Lucy was about to say something she probably would have regretted, but was prevented by Bill's timely arrival, passports in hand. "Here you go," he said, presenting them to the lieutenant.

"*Merci*. I do not need to remind you that you should not attempt to leave the area." He straightened his jacket. "But I think you will have a pleasant time, seeing the sights."

"Right," growled Lucy. Watching his departure, and thinking over their conversation, which was mostly about last night's dinner, she came to the conclusion that the investigation might take rather a long time. In fact, Mathilde's murder might never be solved, if it was left to the likes of Lieutenant Yves Hugues.

Seeing her expression, Bill furrowed his brow. "No, Lucy, this has nothing to do with us. Don't even think about investigating on your own."

"I wouldn't know where to start," she said, already considering a few possibilities. "Any plans for the day?"

"I thought I'd check out the gym," he said. "Want to join me?"

"No. I think I'll take a little walk around town. Maybe pick up a newspaper."

He chuckled. "Well, that seems harmless enough."

"Don't worry," said Lucy. "Like I said, even if I wanted to investigate, I wouldn't know where to start."

Chapter Fifteen

Carole didn't sleep well. Frank hated it if she tossed and turned and he could become quite grouchy if his sleep was disturbed. She didn't want to risk waking him out of his bear-like slumber, so she simply remained flat on her back, taking deep yoga breaths and trying to empty her mind. Good luck with that! Bits of memories, fragments, kept popping into her head, growing into complicated scenarios. Point of view, that was the phrase Frank-O was always using, claiming that's why he preferred sculpture. Two-dimensional paintings limited the viewer's point of view, but a three-dimensional sculpture required the viewer to move around, exploring all the sides. It opened, rather than limited, the viewer's point of view.

It seemed to Carole that everyone at the table had been focused on the table, and the people around it. Definitely a limited point of view. If this shadowy killer, whom she pictured as a vague black shape in the hallway, had actually entered through the wide-open front door, it was unlikely that anyone at the table would have noticed. Polly had been seated at the head of the table, looking toward the door, but she would definitely have been focused on her guests. She was a consummate hostess, concerned about keeping the conversation light and lively, making everyone comfortable.

These wide-open doors were a problem, thought Carole. The French were so weird, they either shut the house up tight with shutters, or they left everything wide open. Living in Providence, in a luxury apartment building, Carole was very conscious of security. They were wealthy and everybody knew it thanks to Frank's success with the Bye-Bye Toilet, the low-flow fixture that produced a high-income flow. As much as she loved wearing designer clothes and the gorgeous jewels that Frank gave her whenever he felt guilty about . . . well, she wasn't going to follow that train of thought, not tonight! The fact remained, however, that their lifestyle made them attractive targets for thieves, and she sometimes felt as if she had a target on her back as she went about the hunting and gathering that was her main occupation. That was one reason why she loved having Poopsie. Nobody got near her when she was out with Poopsie. Nobody stepped into the elevator with her, nobody crowded her on the sidewalk. There were the dog lovers, for sure, who exclaimed about Poopsie's good looks and tried to pet her, but Poopsie's raised lip and snarl were clear warning that she was not to be trifled with. Whenever she was out with her person, Carole, she was on guard.

The Esplanade complex had pretty good security; you needed a special fob to open the doors or enter the garage. The lobby was manned 24/7 by a concierge, and the building was well staffed with helpful maintenance workers who kept their eyes out for anything unusual. Each apartment door was equipped with a peephole, a security chain, and a dead bolt lock; Frank had of course upgraded, swapping out the original lock with a fancy obsidian model from Serbia or Turkmenistan, someplace where they took security very seriously.

But here in Provence, she had to admit it, they'd let their guard down. It was all so pretty and quaint, it was easy to forget the people working in those vineyards were mostly transients, single men from northern Africa. They were at the bottom of the social order, dropped off at different vineyards every morning and bossed around all day in the hot sun, doing whatever it was they did to make the grapes grow. She'd noticed them just the other day, wearing big hats and covered head to toe against the sun, sitting on these weird chairs on wheels, slowly working their way down the rows of vines and trimming off the excess growth. They talked in their foreign tongue while they worked, sometimes they sang. It didn't seem like much fun at all and they probably had plenty of time to think about . . .

What would they think about? Stealing? Probably. Killing? Maybe, if say Mathilde had somehow been involved with one of the men. Sex? Could be. Men on their own, without women, well, it had been going on long before those Sabine women were attacked and raped. That, she thought, was the most likely explanation. A rape gone wrong. Mathilde must have resisted and got herself strangled. Or maybe she was being punished for infidelity.

Oddly, Carole felt better after she'd figured this out. She yawned, rolled over onto her side, and went to sleep.

Next morning, she woke to Frank shaking her shoulder. "What're we gonna do? There's no coffee."

Carole blinked a few times. "Water. Have some water."

"I need my coffee."

"Take a shower. That'll wake you up. Then we can figure something out."

Frank grumbled and heaved himself out of bed. Carole

remained, wondering how long it would be before the police inspector arrived to question them. Hopefully, not too long, since they wouldn't be able to eat breakfast, or even have coffee, while they were confined to the upper two stories of the house. She heard the shower running and thanked their lucky stars that the bathrooms were upstairs. That lady cop didn't know that, however, when she issued her blanket order determining the entire ground floor was a crime scene and off limits. When you considered how cavalier she'd been, issuing orders before ascertaining whether such confinement actually included sanitary facilities, it was probably assumed that they would make some adjustments to the situation. Besides, this was France, land of *liberté, égalité, fraternité*. Nobody took the rules seriously in France.

Carole got up and knocked on her mother's door.

"*Entrez*," chirped Polly.

Opening the door, Polly found her mother seated against about a dozen pillows, flipping through a magazine and sipping on a mug of coffee.

"Where'd you get that?" she asked, amazed.

"In the kitchen. Where else?"

"But the policewoman . . ."

"My French isn't all that good . . ." began Polly.

"I think she was speaking English."

"I don't remember that," said Polly, turning the page. "Skirts are longer this year."

"Good to know," said Carole, heading downstairs.

Frank felt much better after he'd had his coffee and toast and a couple of fried eggs, but he was restless. He walked around the yard, he kicked the tires on the car, he gazed off at the mountain. "When's that inspector coming?" he asked Carole.

"How do I know? We're supposed to stay here."

"Benoit told me about this big hardware store, brico-something. It's outside Carpentras. I'd really like to see what they've got in the way of plumbing supplies."

"No. You can't go to Carpentras."

Frank-O, who Carole thought was a lot like his father, which was actually the reason why they didn't get along, was also restless. He was bouncing around, listening to something playing on his earbuds. It was driving Frank crazy.

"Can't you calm down?" he growled.

"What?"

"You're jumping all around."

"I don't like being cooped up."

"Well, none of us do," said Carole. "Except Connie. Where is she?"

"She's sleeping in," said Frank-O. "Making up for about five years of lost sleep."

"Bless her heart," said Carole.

"Do you think I could go over to Benoit's?" asked Frank-O. "It's just next door and I've got my phone. You could call me when the inspector arrives."

"I don't think . . ." began Carole.

"Good idea," said Frank, straightening his shoulders. "Let's go."

Polly, who had come downstairs and was standing in the doorway, called after them. "Where are you going?"

"Just next door," said Frank, marching off down the driveway with Frank-O.

"I don't think that's a good idea," said Polly, seating herself beside Carole at the big table under the plane tree.

"You started it," said Carole. "With the coffee."

"The French will excuse anything that has to do with their stomachs, but defying an official order to remain in place is another thing entirely."

Carole nodded. "How are you holding up?" she asked.

"I didn't really know Mathilde," she said, her eyes wandering to the kitchen window, now shuttered. "Do you think the killer came in through the window?"

"It's possible. I think it might have been one of the workers, from the vineyard. Perhaps a rapist."

"I guess that's the likeliest explanation." Polly shuddered. "I thought we were safe here."

"No place is safe," said Carole, reaching for a deck of cards that was on the table. "Gin?"

"Sure."

The two played cards, and chatted, and looked at magazines they'd already read, and checked their watches. The morning dragged on with no sign of the promised inspector. At around eleven, Frank and Frank-O returned, popping through the opening in the wall that separated the two properties.

"Was that opening always here?" asked Carole. "Or is it a secret passage, like in Versailles? So the king could visit his mistress?"

"Benoit made a path so we wouldn't have to go on the road. It was a surprise for me," said Polly.

"Benoit's full of surprises," said Frank-O, plopping himself down on one of the plastic Adirondack chairs that dotted the yard.

"I know," said Polly, with a little Mona Lisa smile.

"He's really into art," continued Frank-O. "He's got a lot of paintings, and he paints himself. Pretty nice landscapes."

"His father was a painter," said Polly.

"He's got a lot of stuff from his family, old watches and stuff," said Frank.

"He's even got Fabergé eggs," said Frank-O. "He said a

lot of Russians came to France because of the revolution and sold off their jewels and stuff."

"He's full of stories," said Polly, rolling her eyes. "I suspect those Fabergé eggs are Fauxbergés."

"You might be right," said Frank, chuckling. "He's actually been using them as dummies to get his chickens to lay."

"That's Benoit for you," said Polly.

Chapter Sixteen

Bill went off to work out at the hotel gym, and Lucy decided to take that walk. It was a lovely sunny morning, perfect for exploring the town. She thought she might pick up a newspaper and take it to the café, where she could read it and enjoy a coffee. It would be a taste of French life, and she almost felt like a local as she walked along the street on the narrow sidewalk. A bakery beckoned and she paused to look in the window, admiring the beautiful fruit tarts, and tempted by the *pain au chocolat*. No, she told herself, French women didn't get fat, because they didn't eat two breakfasts. It would have to be coffee and nothing else.

The newsagent was only a few doors farther along, and she was pleased to discover they had the international edition of the *New York Times*; she bought a copy, folding it and slipping it into her roomy bag. The café was in sight, the terrace was occupied by a handful of people, but Lucy walked right on by. Suddenly coffee and news from America had lost their attraction; why read about things happening far away when there was a crime right here, begging to be investigated? Mathilde had worked at the *crèche*, and she had a grandchild on the way. What would be more natural than to pay a visit and see what a French nursery was like?

The *crèche* was located about a quarter mile from town, along a flat road lined with homes. They were all surrounded by walls, like Benoit's place, but there were subtle differences. Some people had little plaques with their house numbers, others had jazzy metal versions of the numbers, a few simply painted the number on the wall. Some people had solid wood gates, others had fancy metal filigree gates that allowed glimpses of the house and garden inside. A few places were actually mini-farms and had signs offering asparagus or strawberries for sale. You had to ring and ask if you wanted to buy, nobody left their wares out on a table with a coffee can for payment, like at home. And then, before she knew it, she was at the fork in the road that led to the *crèche* and Benoit's house; Polly's place was just a bit beyond.

The *crèche* was housed in a square stucco building with a parking area containing three cars on one side. A walled play area was behind, Lucy could see the top of a jungle gym, but there were no children playing there. Everyone must be inside, so she did as a sign instructed and rang the bell.

"*Oui*?" asked the woman who answered the door, looking rather suspicious. She was trim and energetic looking, probably in her fifties, with a perfectly coiffed head of white hair. She'd noticed that a lot of French women had that look and Lucy wondered if they bleached their hair white, or if they were simply going natural.

"*Bonjour*," she said, remembering her manners. "*Je suis* . . . do you by any chance speak English?"

"Yes. How may I help you?"

"Well, my daughter is expecting a baby and we're looking for a *crèche*."

"When is the baby due?"

"In four months."

"And your daughter lives here in Mazan?"

"Not yet. She's in Paris but is considering a move to a place with fresh air that is less crowded. My husband and I are staying at the Château; she and her partner will be coming this weekend to look at some houses."

This definitely went over well with *la directrice*, who seemed impressed when she mentioned the Château. And, of course, Lucy had followed Elizabeth's instructions about proper dress in France and had added a Pucci scarf, actually a rummage sale find, to her outfit before leaving the hotel. "Come in," she invited, stepping aside. "I am Geneviève Arnholdt, I am the director here."

Lucy entered and was immediately struck with the sense of order and serenity as Madame Arnholdt gave her a tour of the facility. Various rooms were dedicated to the children's ages, each one divided into a play area stocked with age-appropriate toys and a separate sleeping area with cribs and cots. Some babies were sleeping in the cribs, older children were playing quietly with puzzles and blocks, pretending to cook in the toy kitchen, fussing over baby dolls. In one room they were singing an alphabet song, in another the teacher was reading a story to a handful of children seated on the floor.

"Do you have a cook?" asked Lucy, noticing that nobody was cooking up a morning snack, or preparing lunch in the kitchen.

"*Hélas*!" exclaimed Madame, throwing up her hands. "*C'est une catastrophe*! We are at the moment without a cook! The bakery in town is providing cold lunches, sandwiches, and salads until we find a replacement." She shook her head. "It is not easy to find someone, but I am interviewing a couple of candidates this afternoon. As you can imagine, the parents are very unhappy as they expect the usual four-course luncheon."

"I hope it works out," said Lucy.

"These things happen," said Madame, with a dismissive shrug.

"I can't imagine anyone quitting, this seems like a lovely place to work," said Lucy.

Madame shrugged. "But that's exactly what happened."

"I wonder why? Do you have a lot of staff turnover?"

Madame didn't seem to hear, so Lucy pressed the issue. "My daughter will certainly be looking for a *crèche* that provides stability for the children. She would want to know if there are personality conflicts. Was this cook at odds with the other employees?"

"No, that was not the case. I can assure you that we are all professionals devoted to the welfare of the children in our care," said Madame, rather defensively. She clearly did not like Lucy's implications about the staff.

"Perhaps this cook had family problems?" suggested Lucy, taking another tack.

"It's quite possible," admitted Madame tersely.

"It's hard for women to work, especially in the U.S. but also here in France," said Lucy, chattering away. "The children have needs, husbands get resentful if the dinner is late or they don't have clean underwear. My husband is the kindest, gentlest man imaginable, but I know I better keep that sock drawer full, or else! Nothing upsets him so much as running out of clean socks."

Madame smiled. "I think our cook was worried about more than her husband's socks. If she needed to stay a bit late to finish up, she would panic because she didn't want to keep him waiting." She led the way to a door and opened it. "And this is the outdoor play area. You'll notice we have a canopy for shade, plenty of equipment for the children. The floor was done last year with a special safe surface, no more skinned knees!"

Lucy gave an approving nod. "I have to say I am very impressed. At what age do you accept babies?"

"It depends on the baby, and the mother. We like for the baby to have settled into a schedule."

"Very wise," said Lucy, thanking her for her time. "I can't wait to tell my daughter all about your *crèche*. Maybe it's the thing that will convince her to move here, to Mazan."

"I must warn you that there is a long waiting list, so the sooner she applies the better."

"Thank you for the tour. I will pass your advice on to my daughter."

"I look forward to hearing from her," said Madame, leading her to the gate. "*Au revoir.*"

Chapter Seventeen

Maybe it was good karma, maybe just good luck, but Frank and Frank-O had been back for a few minutes before the inspector arrived, not in a police car but in a somewhat battered Renault sedan. He parked alongside the other cars, under the plane trees, and climbed out, straightening his jacket, which was rather rumpled. Studying him, Carole noticed he had a bit of tummy and his hair was thinning. Odd how French women took such care of their appearance but the men did not. There were some, of course, who groomed their stubbly beards and added a scarf, but a surprising number didn't seem to care about how they looked.

"Lieutenant Yves Hugues from the *Police Nationale*," he said, extending his hand to Frank, who was still in the yard, following his return. Frank-O was there, too. Carole, Connie, and Polly had all been sitting outside.

"I would like first of all to go over your movements last night," he said, making eye contact with Frank.

Good luck with that, thought Carole, wondering if the lieutenant was trying to intimidate him. If only he knew the people he dealt with in Providence.

"You lookin' at me?" asked Frank, challenging him.

"Whoever strangled Mathilde had large hands, like yours."

Frank held out his hands, studying them. "Since I've been here these hands have mostly held forks," he said. "You asked about my movements last night, well, there weren't any. I sat at the table, along with everyone else."

"And you?" he asked, turning to Frank-O. "You are a sculptor? You must have very strong hands, no?"

"Never really thought about it," admitted Frank-O. "I do work with my hands, but not to strangle anyone. Like Dad said, I was at the table. I didn't get up until we heard Polly scream."

"I guess I could've killed Mathilde," admitted Polly, joining them. "I was the one who discovered her, and on the TV shows I watch—I love those British mysteries—well, Miss Marple or Inspector Morse would certainly put me at the top of the list of suspects. But you know, in those mysteries the person they suspect first is never the killer." Polly is really pouring it on, thought Carole, noticing the way she batted her eyelashes at the officer.

Lieutenant Hugues was not amused. "But that is fiction, and we are dealing with real life, and a very real death." He paused, letting this sink in. "Now, Madame Prendergast, would you please tell me what you saw when you went to the kitchen. And why did you go into the kitchen?"

"I went to see what was the matter. We had finished the entrée and were waiting for the salad. There was some sort of delay. I thought perhaps Mathilde had run into a problem, perhaps she'd run out of olive oil and didn't know where to find a new bottle, something like that. I never expected to find her on the floor." Polly took a moment, then continued. "I thought she'd had a stroke or a heart attack."

"But you screamed, which brought the others."

"Well, yes. I was shocked. Surprised. It was a natural reaction."

"She immediately started administering CPR," said Carole.

"You did not notice the marks on her neck?" inquired the inspector.

"No. I was doing the chest compressions, trying to remember the words to that song. It's from the Bee Gees. It's the exact rhythm for the chest compressions."

"She means 'Stayin' Alive,'" offered Frank-O. "Which is weirdly appropriate, if you think about it."

The investigator turned to Connie. "And you, you are an *avocat*?"

"I am a lawyer," said Connie.

"And did you notice that Mathilde was the victim of a crime?" pressed the lieutenant, pronouncing the word as *cream*.

"Not at first," said Connie. "I am not at all familiar with crime, well, not this sort of crime. My clients tend to engage in crimes like fraud, insider trading, cheating on taxes, things like that. They don't engage in violent crime."

"But you said 'not at first.' When did you realize Mathilde was the victim of a very violent crime?"

"I wasn't sure what it meant, but I noticed the marks on her neck."

"So, this is what we have so far. You were all eating dinner, dinner cooked by Mathilde. You ate the entrée . . . what was it?"

"Bouillabaisse," said Polly.

"It was satisfactory?"

"Delicious," said Polly. "Nobody killed her because the bouillabaisse didn't have enough saffron."

"It didn't have enough saffron?" Lieutenant Hugues was concerned.

"It was fine. It was very good."

"But then there was a delay," said the inspector, summing up. "The plates were not cleared for the salad, so Madame went to see what was the matter. Madame found Mathilde on the floor, unconscious, and screamed. Then everyone ran to the kitchen. Why?"

"To help," said Carole.

"To see what had happened," said Frank-O.

"A natural reaction. Something had happened, people wanted to know," said Polly.

The investigator nodded. "And now, if I may once again see the scene." He turned to Polly. "Madame, only."

Carole didn't like this. "But it may be very difficult for my mother. I can help support her, I wish to be there for her."

The inspector sighed, but relented. "Two, that is all."

The others scattered, seating themselves either at the big table or in the plastic Adirondack chairs that were scattered about the yard. Carole took her mother's arm and they led the way into the *mas*.

"Did you do the restoration yourself, Madame?" asked the lieutenant, pausing in the hall.

"No. It was already done when I bought the property. I've only owned it a couple of months."

He did not go in the kitchen, but stood in the doorway, leaning in. Mathilde's body was gone; all that remained of her was a chalk outline on the floor. "This is how the kitchen was left last night?"

"I made coffee this morning," confessed Polly. "Actually, I think my daughter cooked some eggs and made toast, too. But as you can see, we were careful not to disturb anything else. The salad is still on the table, the flowerpot is on the floor, and, oh, I made sure not to add to the garbage. On *CSI* they're always very keen to examine the garbage, so we put the trash, the eggshells and whatnot, in a separate bag." Polly picked up a small plastic bag that was resting on the counter, beside the coffeepot, and handed it to Hugues.

He glanced inside, then handed it back. "For me, the question is, how did the killer gain entry?" he said. "No one saw a person enter the hallway, which is clearly visible from the table."

"My son has a theory," began Carole. "POV, or point of view. We were all looking at the table and the people gathered around it."

"Still, very risky. Is there somewhere the killer could have hidden?"

Polly turned toward the closet door, at the back of the hall. "There?" she suggested.

"Ah!" The inspector was at the door in a flash. "Come see."

Polly and Carole peered into the dark, dank space where the vacuum cleaner and other supplies were stored. Following the inspector's gesture, they noticed that the floor was littered with cigarette butts. A wooden box, which had once held kindling, had been upturned, the sticks tumbled out onto the floor. "You think the killer waited here?" asked a shocked Carole.

"I do not know about your housekeeping, but . . ."

"This closet was clean yesterday morning," declared Polly. "We ran out of dishwasher soap and I got a new box, from that shelf." She pointed to a set of shelves filled with household items, a gap representing where the missing detergent had been.

"Then I think the killer came earlier in the day and

waited here, for the chance to kill Mathilde." After delivering that conclusion, the lieutenant thanked them for their cooperation.

"We're happy to help," said Carole. She believed it was always best to make friends with the cops.

"And now I will need all your passports."

"What? For how long?"

"As long as it takes, Madame."

Carole let out a long breath. So much for making friends.

The moment the lieutenant's car turned out of the drive and onto the road, Polly phoned Benoit. "The cop's just left, you're probably next," she warned, speaking in French. "But he thinks the killer hid in the closet, which means you're not a suspect."

The two chatted for quite a while in French, most of which Carole didn't understand. When the call was over, she asked Polly for a recap.

"Benoit says he's already been interviewed and the lieutenant was most sympathetic about his problem with the chicken and suggested that Mathilde was stealing the eggs all along."

"What could those eggs have to do with Mathilde's death? Nobody gets murdered over eggs."

Polly shook her head. "According to Benoit, the lieutenant said dozens of eggs were found in Mathilde's apartment."

"Was it some sort of black market thing? Was she selling them?"

"It doesn't seem so. Just keeping them."

"Was she some sort of egg kleptomaniac?"

"No. Remember I told you she was the one who suggested to Benoit that he could put the Fabergé egg in the nest, to encourage the chickens to lay?"

"The dummy egg."

"Right. And when it disappeared, Benoit thought it had rolled out of the nest, or that the chickens didn't like it and pushed it out. But it seems Mathilde stole it."

"She didn't realize it was a fake? A Fauxbergé?"

"Right," reported Polly. "The cops studied her phone and found it had pictures of the egg, offering it for sale."

"So it's gone," said Carole.

"He says he has a dozen more, all made by his great-grandfather," said Polly. "And the chickens have resumed laying."

"Every cloud has a silver lining," said Carole.

"I can't believe Mathilde was a thief," said Polly, shaking her head. "She never took anything from me."

"Is that why she got killed?" asked Carole. "She got killed over a fake Fabergé egg?"

"She must've ticked somebody off," said Frank, "You cross the wrong person and . . ." He paused, sliding his finger across his neck. "Finito."

Chapter Eighteen

Still puzzled, Carole wandered over to Benoit's place. She found him in the chicken coop, filling the birds' waterer with a hose.

"*Vous avez les oeufs maintenant?*"

"*Oui.*" He showed her a bowl containing what looked like a dozen or more eggs.

"*Et les policiers?*" she asked, hoping he would understand she was asking if they were under suspicion for Mathilde's death.

Benoit turned off the hose and held up his hand, fingers crossed. Next he poured chicken feed into a long metal tray and, leaving the coop, invited Carole to join him for his morning coffee. He stowed the feed bag inside a nearby toolshed, then led the way to his patio, where a French press was already on the table, along with several tiny cups. He pushed down the plunger and filled two cups.

"Delicious," said Carole, politely, after taking a sip. It was espresso, very strong, much stronger than she actually liked.

"*Trop fort pour vous?*" he asked.

"Not too strong," said Carole, politely. Not sure how much he'd understand, she continued in English. "Frank-O told me you have quite a collection of Fabergé-style eggs that your great-grandfather made," she said. "I'd love to see them."

"*Ah, bien sûr*," he said, then drained his cup.

Carole abandoned her cup and followed him into the house, where he brought her into the dining room and went over to a sideboard. He pulled out a drawer, revealing a collection of gilded, bejeweled eggs.

"Your grandfather made these?" asked Carole, picking up a pink-enameled egg decorated with gold and pearls. "They're beautiful."

"*La famille de ma mère était émigrées à cause de la révolution en Russe*," he said.

"*Oui*. Frank-O told me your great-grandfather had worked for Fabergé and it wasn't safe for him in Russia. Anyone connected with the royal family or the aristocracy was considered an enemy of the people."

Benoit nodded and rattled off a whole lot of French, which Carole didn't really understand, but she did get the idea that this great-grandfather was a highly regarded craftsman, who had even repaired valuable clocks at the Louvre.

"He must have been very skilled," offered Carole.

"*C'est vrai*," admitted Benoit, picking up a turquoise egg. "I think," he said, in halting English, "it helped him, uh, re, re . . ."

"Remember," said Carole.

"*Oui*, it was a way to remember his life before, in *Russe*."

"Where did he get the jewels? The gold?"

Benoit gestured, waving his hand over the drawer. "*Faux.*"

"It's a shame they're not genuine Fabergé. Those are worth millions. You could be a very rich man."

Benoit laughed. "The Soviets seized them all." He closed the drawer. "*Je suis content.*"

"Avez-vous les questions de Mathilde? Elle était honnête?" She wondered whether he'd had any suspicions about her honesty.

"Pas de tout." He sighed. *"Mais le mari de Mathilde . . ."* he said, letting the rest hang.

Of course, thought Carole, leaving Benoit and heading back to the *mas*. The husband was probably behind the whole thing; she'd seen it happen before. It didn't take a very big leap of the imagination to picture Mathilde telling her husband all about her new employer, maybe the husband had even targeted Benoit and urged Mathilde to quit the *crèche* to work for him. She might well have told him about the fancy jeweled eggs, and he would have assumed they were genuine. She couldn't steal the Fabergé-style eggs without being immediately suspected so they cooked up the scheme to steal the chicken eggs so that it seemed the hens weren't laying. She could then suggest the idea of a dummy egg, and when it disappeared, no blame would attach to her as Benoit would assume the chickens had rejected it. It was posting the egg on the web, claiming it was genuine, that got her killed. Once the buyer realized the egg was fake . . .

That's when Carole realized she'd let her imagination get the better of her. Why wouldn't the buyer simply return the egg, complaining that it was fake and demanding a refund? Killing the woman wouldn't solve his problem. Unless Frank was right, that she, or more likely her husband, had gotten mixed up with serious criminals. Poor Mathilde, what had she gotten herself into?

She'd hardly known Mathilde, but she'd seemed to be the perfect servant who supplied whatever you needed before you realized you needed it. Meals magically appeared, as did snacks when you felt a bit peckish. There was soap and toilet paper in the bathrooms, the beds were made, the living room tidied. She didn't like to think that Mathilde's home life was not as perfect as the calm and orderly lifestyle she had created for her employer. But perhaps the *mas* was a sort of refuge for her, a safe space that tragically had turned out to be not safe at all.

She was ducking through the opening in the wall when she encountered Frank-O.

"Ooh, you startled me," she said.

"Sorry. I'm just headed over to see Benoit. He told me about this welding technique that I might find useful."

"Welding? Like with a flame?"

"Yeah, Ma, that's how you weld."

"Well, you be careful."

"I will," he said, giving her a peck on the cheek, which she thought was rather weird.

Definitely not the sort of thing he usually did. Or ever did. But maybe it was being in France, maybe the murder had affected him more deeply than she thought.

"Penny for your thoughts," said Polly, as she seated herself at the outside table, beside Connie. Polly had been working on a crossword puzzle, Connie had been working, reviewing some sort of legal stuff on her laptop. Too bad, thought Carole, studying her daughter. The airlines lose luggage all the time, why couldn't they lose that stupid laptop.

"Um, I was thinking about work. Connie does too much, and poor Mathilde, she was a really hard worker, too." She propped her elbow on the table and rested her head on her hand. "Benoit suggested the husband is a bit dodgy. If he was behind stealing the eggs they probably didn't realize they were fakes, made by his grandfather. He actually worked for Fabergé, so he was very skilled."

"But maybe a couple aren't fakes. Maybe the grandfather brought a genuine one with him when he came to France," suggested Polly.

"No way. Benoit says the Communists have all the eggs."

"No, they don't," said Connie. "Two are known to be missing."

"How do you know that?" asked Carole.

"Because I'm working on a case involving the son of a Russian oligarch, Viktor Lysenko, whose son is at Brown. He's trying to sell what he claims is a Fabergé egg to pay the kid's legal fees. He's short on cash because his assets have been frozen due to the Ukraine war."

"Legal fees? What did the kid do?" asked Polly.

"Injured a pedestrian who was, until he was paralyzed from the waist down, a top Hollywood stuntman. He was in Providence, working on that Marvel action flick they're making. He's asking for millions in lost wages, and I don't think we're going to find a jury that's sympathetic to some Russian oligarch's spoiled kid. I'm pretty sure he's going to need a lot of dough."

"Or eggs," said Polly, as a loud bang was heard.

"That sounded like a gunshot," said Frank, suddenly appearing in the doorway and running toward Benoit's place.

Chapter Nineteen

Lucy was just leaving the *crèche* when she heard the bang, a bang that sounded an awful lot like a gunshot. She'd reached the road and was standing across from Benoit's place, wondering why somebody was shooting. Weren't guns largely illegal in France? She knew that some French people were enthusiastic hunters and would certainly have shotguns, even if they were strictly regulated. And this was the country, like Tinker's Cove, where people also hunted deer and turkeys, and occasionally fired a shot to scare off predators on their property. Maybe a fox had gone after Benoit's chickens? And there were tales of those wild boars coming down from Mont Ventoux. Did boars go after chickens?

She was thinking that maybe she ought to go and investigate, especially since Mathilde had been murdered. But she hesitated, thinking that if it was actually the murderer who had fired the shot, and was likely still lurking behind the fence that enclosed Benoit's property, well, that would be stepping into a very dangerous situation. Then she heard female voices, yelling, and turned to look across the road toward the *mas*, where she saw Connie and Carole running across the yard, trailing Frank and screaming at him.

Figuring there was safety in numbers she decided to see for herself what was happening and ran across the street and up the drive to the *mas* just in time to see Connie and Carole disappearing through a gap in the wall. Polly was standing in the driveway, talking on her phone, probably calling the police.

She paused, trying to decide what to do. Should she go to Polly, or should she follow the others through the hedge. The sound of loud voices decided the matter, and she pushed her way through to Benoit's property. There she found Benoit lying on the ground with Carole and Connie leaning over him, a shotgun on the ground beside him. Frank was alert, standing guard.

"What happened?" she asked.

Benoit sat up, shaking his head as if dazed. "*Un voleur a pris mes œufs!*"

"You fired the shot?" asked Carole.

"*Oui.*"

"*Avez-vous*, uh, *recognizez* the thief?" asked Lucy, mixing up English and French. "*Le mari de Mathilde*?" asked Lucy.

Benoit nodded, wincing at the pain.

Carole turned to Lucy. "How'd you know?" she demanded.

"I was at the *crèche*, they told me Mathilde's marriage wasn't happy. I put two and two together and figured her husband was making her steal the eggs." She glanced around, thinking. "It must be something to do with the fake Fabergé," she said. "I think she was stealing the chicken eggs so Benoit would put out the dummy, which I guess they thought was genuine. Does that make any sense at all? What do you think?"

"It's possible the dummy was genuine," said Frank-O, joining them. He was holding an old, yellowed piece of paper.

"*Qu'est-ce que c'est ça*?" asked Benoit, getting to his feet with Connie's help.

"It was in the drawer, under the eggs your great-grandfather made. This is a plan, with the Fabergé stamp, for an egg with a hen inside."

"*Ce n'est pas possible. Les Communistes . . .*"

"There are two missing Fabergé eggs," said Connie.

"And how do you know this?" asked Benoit.

"A legal case I'm involved with. It's true. According to the records, there are two missing Fabergé eggs that the tsar gave to his wife and mother as Easter presents. One had a golden chicken inside, the other had an enormous amethyst."

"So one of my eggs is genuine," said Benoit, amazed.

"Maybe two," said Connie.

"*Mon Dieu.*"

"Mathilde didn't want the chickens' eggs," continued Connie, "she was after the dummy. Or dummies. She figured you'd keep putting out the dummies as long as it seemed the chickens weren't laying."

"Do you really think the husband knew that one of the Fauxbergés was genuine?" asked Carole.

"I'm not sure he cared," said Lucy. "He sounds like a petty thief to me, making his wife steal for him. I think advertising the egg brought them some unwanted attention."

"Lysenko," said Connie.

"Who?" asked Lucy.

"Russian oligarch. It's a long story," said Connie, beginning to explain the case involving Lysenko's son, but Benoit wasn't interested. While she was talking, he picked up his shotgun and started walking away.

"Hey!" demanded Carole. "Where are you going?"

"I'm going to Mathilde's house. I'm going to get my Fabergé egg back."

Chapter Twenty

"I think we should call the police," said Connie.

"I agree," said Lucy. "If Mathilde and her husband are involved with this Russian oligarch . . ." Seeing that Benoit was ignoring her and was getting into his Mercedes, Lucy stopped talking and ran after the car. Benoit stopped the car and waited for the gate to respond to the signal from his remote. She yanked open the rear door and jumped in, followed immediately by Carole.

"Shove over," said Carole, sliding in beside her and slamming the door.

The gate swung open, but Benoit didn't drive through it. "Get out," he said.

"I'm not going anywhere," said Carole, "except with you."

"*Ce n'est pas votre affaire*," he said. "*C'est pour moi et le mari de Mathilde.*"

"Mathilde was killed in my mother's house," said Carole. "My whole family was put in danger. So it is very much my affair."

"Et Lucy?"

"I can help. I have experience in situations like this."

"*Encore, je vous prie . . .*" he began, but seeing them shake their heads, Benoit let out a long sigh of frustration, then shifted into drive. Moments later they were in the center of town, parked in front of a pizzeria.

"What's the plan?" asked Lucy, but Benoit was already out of the car, shotgun in hand, opening a door situated to one side of the pizzeria's entrance.

"He's going in," said Lucy. "I guess we better follow him."

"Wait a minute," said Carole. "I think we should call the cops."

"You do that. I'm following Benoit."

"*Merde*," muttered Carole, as Lucy got out of the car. She followed, phone in hand, dialing 911 as she stepped into a dark hallway that contained little more than a staircase. A door at the top of the stairs was ajar. Realizing that her call wasn't going through, 911 didn't work in France, she whispered to Lucy, "911 isn't working."

"999," hissed Lucy, already halfway up the stairs.

Carole punched in the number and followed Lucy to the door, which opened directly onto the stairs. Lucy was reaching for the knob when she quickly reared back, the sudden barking of a dog startled her, almost knocking her down the stairs.

"What the . . ." hissed Lucy, as Carole showed her the phone. "I hit the wrong button. It's Poopsie," explained Carole. "I Skyped her last night and I saved it."

The door was now open and they were confronted by a large man dressed in black; looking behind him she glimpsed a couple of others holding Benoit. "Oh, *pardon*," said Lucy, thinking their goose was well and truly cooked thanks to that stupid dog. And her brainless owner. "*Je vous dérange*, I don't mean to disturb you. I think I have the wrong address, I'm from the U.S. and I'm looking for . . ."

"Madame DeFarge!" said Carole, pretending she didn't

see the gun sticking out of the guy's waistband and stepping back and down a step. "She is my mother's cousin. We're doing our family tree."

"Do you know of the DeFarge family?" asked Lucy, following Carole's approach and playing dumb American tourist while stepping down.

"No DeFarge here," said the man, as the siren of a cop car was heard. He suddenly grabbed Lucy's arm and started pulling her inside. She screamed and felt Carole grab her around the waist, jerking her backward and causing them both to tumble down the stairs. Lucy found herself at the bottom, with Carole on top of her. They were lying there, stunned, when the door to the outside was yanked open and two police officers politely helped them to their feet.

"Upstairs!" said a dazed Lucy, trying to point and discovering her arm wouldn't work and hurt like hell.

"They're armed," added Carole.

"How many?" asked one of the cops.

"Three and one hostage," said Lucy.

The cop was talking rapid-fire French into his phone, presumably calling for reinforcements. The next thing Lucy knew, she was sitting at one of the tables on the terrace outside the pizzeria but didn't recall how she got there. She remembered falling down the stairs, which explained why she felt sore all over, but nothing seemed to be broken. Carole was beside her, holding her head.

"Are you okay?" Lucy asked.

"I must've hit my head," Carole said, as an ambulance arrived. The cop conferred with the EMTs, pointing to Carole and Lucy.

The EMTs approached and then ushered the two women into the ambulance as the tactical units arrived. The ambulance began to move, they heard shots, and Lucy turned toward the rear windows of the ambulance. As they were driven away she saw the team, decked out in riot gear, beginning their assault. She was drifting into unconsciousness when she heard Carole, whispering into her phone, "Good doggie, Poopsie. You caught the bad guys."

Easter morning found the two families, including Elizabeth and Chris, as well as Benoit, gathered at the Château's restaurant for a holiday feast. "I thought I was doing the right thing, getting you out of Paris," said Elizabeth, in an apologetic tone. "I never suspected Mazan would be dangerous."

"Well, if your mother had minded her own business . . ." began Bill.

"I am absolutely fine," said Lucy, giving Carole a big smile. "Just a few bruises and a dislocated shoulder. A small price to pay for helping my friends."

"And don't forget, it's because of us and Poopsie that the police caught those Russian gangsters," said Carole, who had an enormous bruise on her forehead.

"Which led to the arrest of Viktor Lysenko," added Chris. "One of my contacts told me he'd been looking for those missing Fabergé eggs for years, killing dozens of people in the process."

"Poor Mathilde," said Benoit sadly. One side of his face was badly bruised.

He continued, speaking with some difficulty, and Polly translated. "He says he's sure she didn't want to, it was her husband who made her do it. Then when the Russians showed up, they killed her. Maybe they thought she would go to the police, or maybe it was to pressure her husband, they're not talking. Those butts the police found in the closet were Russian and they matched the DNA to one of the two guys. After they got Mathilde out of the way, they went after the husband, he was tied to a chair and bloody when Benoit got there. They wanted the Fabergé egg but he wouldn't tell them where it was. That's when Lucy and Carole arrived . . ."

"We were worried you were going to get in trouble," said Carole.

"So you stepped right into the middle and nearly got yourselves killed," said Frank. "Not smart."

"We saved the day," insisted Carole, never one to back down.

"I wish she'd asked me for help," said Polly, her brow furrowed in concern. "I would have encouraged her to leave what seems to have been an abusive relationship."

"I'm not sure Mathilde was quite the victim you think she was," said Lucy. "She must have told her husband about the eggs in the first place, and she could have refused to steal the chickens' eggs. For that matter, she could have stayed with her job at the *crèche*. Getting hired by Benoit was probably the first step in a scheme to steal as much as she could."

Polly shook her head. "No, Lucy. You didn't know her. I think that between her job at the *crèche* and then working for me and Benoit, she was beginning to want more independence. She was perhaps realizing that she didn't need her rotten husband anymore and she could support herself." She turned to Benoit. "*Que pensez-vous vis-à-vis Mathilde?*"

Benoit paused, gently patting his swollen lip. When he began speaking, Polly translated. "He says he is grateful to Mathilde because if it wasn't for her, he would never have suspected that one of his great-grandfather's eggs was a genuine Fabergé, smuggled out of Russia."

"I woulda liked to have met that great-grandfather of

yours," confessed Frank. "Sounds like a guy who knew what was what, if you get my meaning, and looked out for number one."

"I do," sighed Carole, turning to Benoit. "So what are you going to do with the egg?"

There, in the middle of the table, was an ivory egg decorated with a cross-hatch of gold filagree studded with pearls and precious jewels. Beside it was a diminutive gold basket, containing a carved amber chicken that fit neatly inside the egg.

"It was made for the tsar's mother, Empress Maria Feodorovna," said Connie.

"There's a bit of damage. The hinge is broken," said Frank-O. "I bet it was sent back to the Fabergé atelier for repairs . . ."

"And that's when my great-grandfather liberated it from the Soviets."

"The long-lost Egg with Hen in Basket," said Connie. "So, Benoit, what are you going to do with it?"

"Keep it," said Benoit.

"I suspect there will be a long legal battle over that little hen," cautioned Connie.

Benoit raised his champagne glass. "*Aux armes, citoyens*!" he said. "I will fight for my patrimony."

"*Aux armes, citoyens*!" they all chimed in, raising their glasses in a toast.

Epilogue

A year later, Lucy was back in Boston's Logan Airport waiting for her suitcase to appear on the revolving luggage carousel. Although she was physically in the airport, her mind was still in Paris, where she'd just visited her adorable granddaughter, Anais.

Anais was now eight months old, and Lucy was convinced she was already showing signs of being an exceptionally gifted child. Not only could she sit, but she was crawling and even trying to pull herself up to stand. These physical milestones were impressive, but it was her budding personality that Lucy found so enchanting. Anais was a cheerful little spirit who laughed at everything and especially loved it when her *mami* played peekaboo and made funny faces. Her smile revealed a budding little tooth, but she didn't seem to be bothered by teething, having settled into a routine that included sleeping through the night.

So while Lucy watched the suitcases roll by, she was thinking of how lovely little Anais smelled, especially after her lavender-scented bath. She was a little snuggle bunny who loved cuddling with her grandmother, tucking her head under Lucy's chin. She remembered the softness of her golden hair and the amazing silkiness of her unblemished skin. She was already missing her *petit ange*, her little angel, and was wondering how soon she could manage to get back to France, when she heard her name.

"Lucy! Yoo-hoo! Lucy Stone!"

Lucy turned around, and who did she see barreling toward her but Carole Capobianco, obviously just off a flight but fresh as a daisy with perfect makeup and hair, and wearing a comfy designer track suit. "Hi! Imagine meeting you here!" said Lucy, turning to grab her suitcase which had finally appeared.

"So you were in Paris!" said Carole, glancing at the sign indicating the flight. "Oh, right! I bet Elizabeth had her baby! Boy or girl?"

"Um, a little girl. Anais. She's eight months old."

"Already! My goodness, how time flies! Do you have photos?"

Well, of course she did. She had a phone, after all. "Um, sure," she said, yanking up the handle and plopping her carry-on on top of the wheeled suitcase. "Do you want to see?"

"Of course I do! If she's anything like her mom, she's gorgeous."

Lucy could feel her defenses dropping, just as they had when she first met Carole last spring. "So where have you been?" she asked, noticing the enormous pile of suitcases Carole was pushing on a rolling cart. "France?"

"No. I was in Italy," said Carole, as they moved to a quieter part of the bustling luggage area. "My mother has really gotten into this genealogy thing, and she wanted to visit Matera, the town where her great-grandparents lived in Puglia." She laughed. "Wouldn't you know, the place was known as the shame of Italy, but it's improved. Now there's all these expensive cave hotels."

"You stayed in a cave?" asked Lucy, opening her photo file and passing the phone to Carole.

"We did," said Carole, swiping through the photos. "You're so lucky! She's adorable."

Lucy smiled and nodded. "And very bright, too."

"Of course! She's got your smarts."

"Well," said Lucy, turning pink with pleasure. "I guess I can take some credit."

"Of course you can!" She returned the phone. "If only my Connie would get on the ball." She rolled her eyes. "She's finally got a boyfriend, but she insists they're not serious."

"Well, it's been a long and winding road with Elizabeth, that's for sure," said Lucy, as they headed toward immigration. They were at the tail end of the crowd of passengers; Lucy's suitcase had been the last off the plane. They chatted about their families as they made their way, walking slowly down the long hallway dotted with posters advertising regional attractions.

Suddenly, Carole shrieked, "That's Frank!" and dashed ahead, her mules clattering against the tiled floor.

Lucy followed her pointing finger and saw it was indeed Frank, pictured from the chest up and wearing a hard hat, posed in front of a rehabbed industrial building. A banner above proclaimed in big letters "Providence Rising."

"Wow," said Lucy, suitably impressed. "Do you want me to take a photo?"

"Sure," said Carole, handing over her phone and arranging herself in front of the poster. Lucy snapped the photo and showed it to Carole, who nodded in approval. "You know what?" she suddenly said. "Why have a photo when I could have the real thing?"

Next thing Lucy knew, Carole was peeling the poster out of its frame and rolling it up. She tucked it between a couple of suitcases on the trolley and gave it a push.

"I think you'll get in trouble," said Lucy, shocked and amazed.

"No, I checked. Nobody saw me," said Carole, as they entered the large arrivals area where people were standing in a long, winding queue. "I guess this is where we part ways," said Carole, "unless you have Global Entry?"

"I don't," said Lucy, as Carole engulfed her in a hug.

"Well, you take care now. Don't be a stranger."

"Right," said Lucy, stepping between the cordons and getting in line. She watched as Carole rolled off toward the Global Entry sign, produced an ID, and was waved through by the immigration officer.

"Uh, ma'am," said a male voice.

Lucy turned to see a uniformed officer accompanied by a small beagle, who was sniffing her luggage and wagging its tail. "Oh, cute dog," she cooed. "I bet he's smelling the French chocolate in my suitcase."

" 'That's probably it," said the officer, as another joined him. "But we'll still need to examine your luggage. Come this way, please."

The search revealed nothing at all incriminating, only rather a lot of clothing that could do with a wash and three chocolate bars. Free to go on to her connecting flight to Portland, Lucy called Bill to let him know she'd landed safely.

"I've missed you," he said, and she quickened her pace.

"Me too," she answered, smiling. "I'll be home soon."

Dear Reader,

You might very well be wondering what on earth Carole Capobianco is doing in a Lucy Stone mystery? If you're familiar with the thirty-plus other books in the Lucy Stone Mystery Series, you know that Lucy's almost always been a lone operator, solving the most challenging murder mysteries. Through the years I've been writing about her, Lucy and I have grown quite close and I have come to admire her strength and intelligence, even though I have to admit I sometimes think she's a bit uptight. She's definitely a good girl. Like me, Lucy went to Sunday school every week as a child, sang in the church choir, and was a Girl Scout. That sort of upbringing has an effect, and Lucy has a somewhat Puritanical sense of right and wrong.

It was when my husband's work took us to Providence, RI, for a year that I discovered a way of life that was quite different from the way folks behave in Massachusetts, where I live, and in Maine, the setting for the Lucy books. I found Providence absolutely fascinating, not least because of its connection to organized crime. Those days are gone but not forgotten, and visitors today can take a Crime and Cuisine walking tour any weekend. The late former mayor Buddy Cianci is fondly remembered, even though he went to jail twice, and was actually reelected after his first felony conviction, only to be convicted a second time. I haven't actually seen it, but they say his portrait still hangs in city hall.

In Providence I was also struck by some of the women I observed, freewheeling gals who strutted around in high heels, spent a lot of money on hairdos and nails, and drove big SUVs like maniacs. They were very different from the women in my town in Massachusetts, where Skechers and roomy sweaters are the norm, and comfort is prized over glamour. I found myself intrigued by this difference and began writing *A Matter of Pedigree*, featuring Carole Capobianco, along with her mischievous puppy, Poopsie.

As I wrote *A Matter of Pedigree,* the first book in the Carole and Poopsie series (which is now in bookstores and online retailers everywhere), I found I really enjoyed Carole's more flamboyant and assertive attitude. I have great plans for Carole, we're going to have terrific adventures together, and you're invited along for the ride.

But don't worry, Lucy isn't going away any time soon. The plan is to alternate the two series, a Lucy Stone mystery one year, a Carole and Poopsie mystery the next, so they will both be appearing in new books. The next Lucy Stone mystery, *Countdown to Christmas Murder*, will be published later this year. I'm really excited about this new challenge, and ever grateful for the encouragement and support from my editor, John Scognamiglio, and the team at Kensington.

But what about Poopsie? you might ask. Well, there was a real Poopsie, her name was Sylvie, and I loved her dearly even though she was a very naughty dog. I like to think she's romping in doggy heaven, but I wouldn't bet on it.

Sincerely yours,
Leslie Meier

DEATH BY ANOTHER EASTER EGG

Lee Hollis

Chapter One

Hayley Powell stood at the entrance of her bustling restaurant, Hayley's Kitchen, soaking in the lively scene. The place was packed tonight—people laughing, forks clinking, waitstaff rushing between tables with plates heaped high with her pre-Easter specials. It was everything she had ever dreamed of when she opened the place, but tonight, as she watched, she could not shake the anxiety bubbling in her stomach.

Every spring, Easter rolled in like a bunny on a sugar high, bringing a mix of sweet nostalgia and, in recent years, the slightest hint of dread. After all, it was only two years ago that the Bar Harbor Easter Bunny, a well-loved local named Raymond Dobbs, had dropped dead right after sampling an indulgent peanut butter egg. It had turned out to be murder—a shock for the whole town, and one Hayley had never fully recovered from.

She didn't even like peanut butter anymore.

Well, that wasn't entirely true.

But every time she popped a handful of Reese's Pieces, the memory of poor Raymond crept into her mind.

So this year, she was determined that Easter would go off without a hitch.

And, for the most part, tonight seemed to be running

smoothly . . . until she spotted her hostess Betty frantically flipping through her reservation book, her face paler by the second.

Hayley weaved her way over, expertly dodging servers balancing trays. "Betty? What's wrong?"

Betty looked up, eyes wide with panic. "Hayley, I don't know how this happened, but I . . . I think I overbooked. We're at least six tables short."

Hayley bit her lip. Well, that explained why every available nook and cranny was filled with diners. Even the bar was elbow to elbow.

"All right, don't panic," she said in a calm, steady voice, though her heart thudded in her chest. "Let's just keep things moving, and we'll make it work. We've handled busy nights before."

But just as she was about to move on to the next minor crisis, her phone buzzed in her apron pocket. It was Todd, one of her newer waiters who had failed to show up for his shift earlier. She frowned and answered, and his voice, rough and scratchy, came through the line.

"Hey, Hayley, I'm so sorry . . . I'm not gonna make it tonight. I think I have the flu."

"I wish you had called me sooner. It's a madhouse here tonight, Todd."

"I know, I took some NyQuil earlier thinking I might feel better, but I dozed off and just woke up. Sorry."

"That's okay, feel better."

Hayley felt the anxiety creep up another notch. One less server meant more work for everyone. Still, she pasted on a bright smile and hung up, already forming a new plan. She would jump in herself, take a few tables, and lend Betty a hand with seating arrangements.

Tonight was going to be chaotic, sure, but nothing she couldn't handle.

Right?

As she made her way to a couple waiting to be seated, she glanced toward the kitchen, where her chef, Kelton, was waving her down.

"Hayley!" he called, his usual cheerful expression noticeably absent. "We're out of the Easter ham special. I don't know what happened—we're not even halfway through the night!"

Hayley closed her eyes for a second, then forced herself to smile. The ham had been a big draw tonight, but she had other dishes, and she wasn't about to let something like that derail the whole evening. "No worries, Kelton," she called back. "I'll talk to the tables, let them know we'll be improvising a bit."

With a pep talk prepared, she turned and spotted a familiar face at Table 12—Emma Lane, a young reporter with the *Island Times* who had joined the paper recently. She was dining with her boyfriend, Alex Matthews, a quiet, bespectacled guy Hayley had met a few times. Hayley's husband, Bruce, who also worked at the paper as the resident crime reporter, had said nice things about her and about her focused and ambitious work ethic.

"Emma! Hi!" Hayley said, slipping into her warm, welcoming hostess mode.

"Hey, Hayley!" Emma greeted her with a grin. "I'm really looking forward to trying the Easter ham. I heard it's amazing."

Hayley grimaced. "Oh, I'm so sorry. We're fresh out. But I can whip you up something special—you just name it."

Emma's face fell briefly, then brightened. "How about surprising me? I trust you."

Alex, who was studying the menu intently, looked up. "And I'm, uh, still vegan," he reminded Hayley with an apologetic smile.

"Not a problem," Hayley assured him, mentally cataloging her options. "How about a spring veggie medley with cashew cream? And Emma, you're in for something special from Hayley's secret stash."

"Oh, and don't forget the cocktail!" Emma added, laughing. "I need something to help me unwind from this crazy week."

Hayley winked. "Rose Kennedy, am I right?"

Emma nodded gratefully. "Yes, but tonight I'm in the mood for something more exotic."

"You got it. On the house. Alex?"

"Bar Harbor Ale, if you have it."

"Fully stocked. At least we won't be running out of that tonight."

She darted back to the bar, where her bartender, Kim, was already crafting something fresh and colorful for Emma. Hayley put together a quick plan for their meal, mentally patting herself on the back for turning things around despite all the chaos.

As she moved through the dining room, Hayley noticed that things were starting to calm down. Tables were beginning to clear out, and Betty looked less frantic as she directed a few stragglers to their seats before the kitchen closed.

Maybe they were finally past the worst of it.

In the kitchen, she assembled Emma's surprise meal—a delicate seafood risotto with fresh herbs and lemon zest, just the right touch for a spring evening. She plated it with care and brought it out herself, setting it down with a flourish in front of the young reporter, who was almost finished with her cocktail.

Emma clapped her hands in delight. "Wow, Hayley, this looks incredible!" Emma said, her eyes widening at the vibrant dish.

"Only the best for you two," Hayley replied, grinning.

For a moment, Hayley felt the knot in her stomach loosen. The rush was nearly over, and the restaurant buzzed with the happy hum of satisfied customers. Easter might actually turn out to be drama free this year, and Hayley was relieved. She turned to head back to the kitchen when she heard a strangled sound from behind her.

Emma.

Hayley whipped around just in time to see Emma drop her fork and lurch forward, clutching her throat. Her face twisted in pain, and she seemed to be gasping for air. Alex was at her side, frantically patting her back, but Emma was already collapsing, her body slumping over the table, her plate of risotto tilting dangerously close to the edge.

"Emma!" Hayley shouted, rushing over, her heart pounding. "Someone call 911!"

Betty ran to the phone, her face pale as she punched in the numbers, while the restaurant descended into chaos. Diners turned, gasping and murmuring, as Alex tried to shake Emma awake. But her face had gone slack, her skin an unnatural shade of gray.

It felt like hours, but the paramedics arrived within minutes. Hayley stood frozen, watching as they assessed Emma, her heart thudding as a horrible thought began to creep into her mind.

This could not be happening again.

Not here.

Not to her restaurant.

After a few agonizing minutes, one of the paramedics looked up, his expression grave. "I'm sorry," he said softly, shaking his head. "She's gone."

Hayley staggered back, her hand clapping over her mouth.

How?

She had just served Emma, chatted with her, laughed with her. And now she was . . . gone?

The police arrived shortly after, sealing off the restaurant. Hayley's brother-in-law, Sergio Alvares, Bar Harbor's chief of police, made his rounds, questioning everyone.

Hayley stood back, next to Betty, trying to stay out of the way, but overheard snippets—suspicions of food poisoning, whispers of foul play.

Her worst nightmare was unfolding all over again, and she was powerless to stop it.

Lieutenant Donnie, Sergio's second-in-command, ambled over and pulled Hayley aside, his notepad at the ready. "Hayley, can you tell us exactly what was in that dish?"

"Oh, come on, Donnie, you don't honestly think . . . ?" Her voice trailed off as Donnie looked at her, waiting for an answer.

Hayley's mind raced as she rattled off the ingredients, each word catching in her throat. She knew every single one by heart. There was nothing dangerous in the dish—nothing that should have caused this.

"I-I can't imagine what happened," she stammered. "It's just a simple seafood risotto. I've served it a thousand times."

But her explanation didn't seem to ease Donnie's suspicions, and Hayley felt her stomach churn.

The police were already looking at her restaurant as the source of Emma's sudden death, and the unthinkable was happening.

Somehow, her Easter nightmare had suddenly come back to life.

Chapter Two

The morning sun crept over Bar Harbor, casting a soft light on Hayley Powell's windshield as she pulled into the small parking lot behind the *Island Times* office. It was a bright day, but the news hanging over the town felt like a storm cloud. Emma Lane's sudden death last night had stunned the community, and the small newspaper's staff was reeling. Hayley could see it on Bruce's face as he sat in the passenger seat, uncharacteristically silent, staring out the window.

"You ready for this?" she asked softly, hoping to inject a little bit of encouragement.

Bruce shook his head, still staring at nothing in particular. "Not really," he admitted. "Emma . . . she was so young. It just doesn't feel real."

Hayley placed a comforting hand on his arm. "I know. But they'll need you in there today. Sal's going to be leaning on you to help make sense of everything."

Bruce gave her a sad, appreciative smile before gathering his things and heading inside. Hayley watched him disappear through the doors, her heart heavy. She had not even had time to process what had happened, not truly. All she could focus on was the growing cloud of suspicion over her restaurant. Everyone knew that Emma's last meal had been at Hayley's Kitchen, and the rumors were already spreading.

It was not long before her phone buzzed. The Bar Harbor grapevine was swift and unforgiving, and the texts and calls had started trickling in. Friends, regulars, even acquaintances—all asking the same question: Is it true that Emma died because of something she ate at Hayley's Kitchen? Each one felt like a small jab to the gut, and Hayley's stomach twisted with each new ping.

She turned her phone off, deciding she would deal with the rumors later, and walked toward the newspaper's front door. She didn't know exactly why she felt the need to be here today. Lately she would always file her food and cocktails column "Island Food & Spirits" from home, rarely venturing to the office. Maybe it was loyalty to Bruce and the team, or maybe it was just her own way of coping. But whatever the reason, Hayley felt she couldn't just go back to her restaurant and pretend everything was fine.

Inside, the office was somber, the usual chatter replaced by hushed voices and anxious glances. As she wandered through the back bullpen past reception, passing a few desks, Hayley noticed the paper's editor-in-chief, Sal Moretti, sitting in his office, head in his hands. She had known Sal for years, back from her days as the office manager. Blustery, a bit gruff, and always loud—Sal was hardly ever one to show much emotion. But today was different. He looked up, eyes red-rimmed, and let out a long sigh.

"I hired her, you know," Sal murmured when he saw Hayley, his voice a mix of disbelief and sorrow. "Emma . . . she had so much potential. She was sharp, curious. Just a kid, really. And now . . ."

He trailed off, shaking his head. Hayley sat down across

from him, feeling her own eyes prick with tears. She had never seen Sal this vulnerable.

"I'm so sorry, Sal," she whispered.

"We need to know what happened, Hayley," he continued, then cleared his throat. "I don't care what it takes. We're going to get to the bottom of this, even if the cops don't want us snooping around. People need answers, and that's our job."

"Absolutely," Hayley agreed, glancing over at Bruce, who was watching from the doorway. "I'll do whatever I can to help. I don't know what's going on, but I know my food didn't kill Emma."

Bruce walked over, nodding. "The police are being tight-lipped, but we'll know more after the autopsy, or at least that's what I'm hearing."

Sal's gaze hardened. "Good. They'd better find out, and fast."

The tension was palpable. Hayley could see that everyone felt the pressure, especially Bruce, who was already fielding calls and jotting down notes with a strained expression. She squeezed his shoulder reassuringly before deciding to leave. If she wanted to help him—and protect her own reputation—she would have to do more than just sit around and provide moral support.

The moment she stepped outside, her mind started racing. She needed information, and if there was anyone in town who might have it, it would be Sabrina Merryweather. She was the county coroner now, but Hayley still remembered the high school days when Sabrina had been a snippy cheerleader and Hayley had been, well . . . not. They had managed to move past that, though Sabrina could still be a bit of a "mean girl" now and then. Hayley knew Sabrina would be the one conducting Emma's autopsy, and if she could just find a way to get a few details, it might calm some of the rumors swirling around.

Hayley grabbed her phone and dialed one of her BFFs, Liddy Crawford, Bar Harbor's very own Queen of Real Estate. Liddy had mentioned that Sabrina was looking to buy a summer home on Lake Sebago to escape the crush of tourists on weekends during the busy summer season at Acadia National Park. She explained the plan quickly to Liddy, outlining the whole "just so happening" to stop by Sabrina's office with photos of potential lake houses. Liddy, always up for a bit of intrigue, was immediately on board.

A little while later, they found themselves walking into Sabrina's office. The coroner greeted them with a somewhat weary smile, her eyes flickering with interest as Liddy pulled out a folder filled with real estate listings. Hayley watched, waiting for the right moment as Sabrina flipped through the photos, talking animatedly about her dream of a peaceful lakeside escape.

"Now, Sabrina," Hayley interjected lightly, "have you even had time to look at any properties? I imagine you've been a little . . . occupied?"

Sabrina's expression cooled slightly, and she glanced at Hayley. "Busy is an understatement. I assume you're asking about Emma Lane?"

"Everyone's talking," Hayley said carefully. "I'm sure you understand why I'd want to know what happened. After all, she was at my restaurant right before she . . . well, you know . . ."

Sabrina's gaze softened a bit, though she hesitated. "I can't give away specifics, Hayley. I've been reprimanded before for sharing autopsy details when I shouldn't have."

"Oh, come on, Sabrina," Liddy chimed in. "This is Hayley we're talking about."

Sabrina threw her a look. "Especially Hayley. Do you

know how many times I've talked out of school *specifically* to Hayley? She's the whole reason I got into trouble in the first place. I wouldn't be surprised if this visit was designed to corner me into confessing what I know about Emma Lane's death!"

Hayley managed a surprised gasp. "*What*? That's the most ridiculous thing I've ever heard!"

Sabrina cocked an eyebrow. "Is it?"

Hayley knew she had been exposed. "Okay, I understand why you would feel that way, but this time is different, Sabrina. My livelihood is at stake. Something like this could drive my restaurant out of business!"

Sabrina sighed, her resolve slipping. "Okay. Look, I shouldn't be telling you this, but . . . the preliminary results show signs of acute thallium toxicity. It's absorbed through the skin. It was . . . it was awful."

Hayley's eyes widened, her heart hammering.

Thallium?

That was serious—and terrifying.

Just then, Hayley's phone buzzed. It was Bruce. She stepped out of the room to answer, her pulse racing. "Hey, what's going on?"

"Hayley, I just got a tip from one of my sources that Sergio just brought Alex in for questioning," Bruce whispered urgently.

Hayley knew that source had to be Sargeant Earl, the most chatty and gossipy officer who worked at the Bar Harbor Police Department. Bruce had spent years cultivating a relationship with him in order to garner fresh information coming out of the station.

"My source . . ." Bruce continued.

"You mean Earl."

"You know as a journalist I can't reveal my sources."

"Come on, Bruce, everyone knows it's Earl."

"Okay, Earl. Earl says Alex gave Emma an Easter basket with treats from Mrs. Bittersweet's Candy Shop on Mount Desert Street, and . . . a bottle of perfume in an Easter egg-shaped container he bought for her. According to the autopsy results, she died from—"

"Acute thallium toxicity."

There was a pause on the other end of the phone.

"How did you know that?"

"Not important."

"Okay, fine. Thallium is water soluble. If it was mixed into perfume . . ."

Hayley's stomach turned. "You think the thallium was in the perfume?"

"That's the suspicion," Bruce confirmed. "And it makes Alex look pretty bad right now."

Hayley quickly thanked him and hung up, her mind racing. She relayed the information to Liddy, who gasped in horror.

"I need to go to the station," Hayley said, grabbing her purse. "If they're questioning Alex, I want to be there. I'll call you later!"

"Go!" Liddy cried.

When Hayley arrived at the police station, she saw Alex sitting in the waiting area, looking devastated. His eyes were red, and he seemed almost dazed, staring off into space as though he could not process what was happening.

"Alex!" Hayley called gently, moving toward him.

He looked up, his face contorting with grief and frustration. "Hayley, I swear—I didn't do anything to hurt Emma. That basket was just a gift, a little something special for Easter. The perfume . . . it was just *perfume*!"

"I believe you," Hayley said softly, placing a reassuring hand on his arm. "Tell me everything. What did you say to the police?"

Alex took a deep breath, looking desperately around as though searching for someone who might listen, who might understand. "I told them everything. The basket was just filled with her favorite things—some chocolates, a little perfume egg I thought was cute. I didn't even pick it out specifically! I just grabbed something that looked nice. That's it."

Hayley nodded, her mind churning. She could see the pain in Alex's eyes, the genuine sorrow over Emma's death.

She wanted to believe him.

He seemed too shaken, too heartbroken to have done anything so malicious.

But by the time she returned home, Bruce called with an update that sent a chill down her spine. The CSI lab in Bangor had tested the perfume bottle. Someone had mixed a high dose of thallium with the perfume. The case against Alex was building fast, and it didn't look good.

She hung up, sitting on the edge of her couch, her heart heavy. All the evidence pointed toward Alex, but something just did not sit right. If Alex had truly cared about Emma, there's no way he would've put poison in that perfume bottle. And where would he get his hands on thallium? It didn't make sense.

No, there was something more to this story, and Hayley was determined to uncover it. She couldn't sit by and watch an innocent man get caught up in the aftermath of a tragedy. Whatever had really happened to Emma, Hayley was going to find out—even if it meant peeling back some dark layers hidden beneath the town's picture-perfect Easter festivities.

Chapter Three

Hayley found herself standing outside the modest blue cottage that Alex and Emma had recently started calling home. She took a deep breath, trying to shake off the chill in the early morning air and the strange feeling in her stomach. Alex had agreed to let her visit this morning, though she could tell he was hesitant. His shock over Emma's death had turned him into a shell of himself, and Hayley felt a pang of sympathy as she knocked on the door.

Alex opened it slowly, his face hollow and his eyes red-rimmed from what had probably been a sleepless night. "Thanks for coming," he mumbled, stepping back to let her in.

"Of course," Hayley replied softly, trying to tread lightly in her words and actions. "I can't imagine what you're going through, Alex. If there's anything I can do . . ."

He gave a half-hearted nod as he looked to the ground. The only spark of life in him seemed to come when a large Maine coon cat padded into the room and rubbed affectionately against his legs. Alex bent down and scratched the cat's head, his expression softening just a bit.

"This is Lucky," he said, forcing a faint smile. "He

was . . . he was Emma's, but he's been sticking by me since everything happened. I think he knows."

Hayley smiled, leaning down to give Lucky a quick scratch behind the ears. "Animals have that instinct. They can sense when we're upset."

Lucky purred in response, then trotted over to a spot by the window, curling up and keeping an observant eye on the two of them.

"Alex," Hayley started, keeping her tone gentle, "I don't believe you had anything to do with this. And I think the police are jumping to conclusions too quickly. I'd like to see if there's anything here that could help clear your name."

He nodded, still looking lost, but he seemed to appreciate the gesture. "You can look through her office," he said, gesturing toward a small room down the hallway. "She spent a lot of time in there, working on her articles. Maybe you'll find something . . . I don't know."

Hayley gave his arm a reassuring squeeze before heading down the hallway. The office was small and neat, with a simple desk facing the window, stacked with papers, notebooks, and a laptop that sat open but powered off. Hayley slid into the chair, took a deep breath, and reached for the mouse, bringing the desktop computer to life. The login screen appeared, prompting her for a password.

"Do you know her password?" Hayley asked, glancing back at Alex, who had leaned against the doorway.

He shook his head. "She was careful with stuff like that. Never shared passwords. Not even with me."

"Worth a shot," Hayley said. She tried a few basic guesses: "Emma123," "BarHarbor," "IslandTimes." None of them worked. She sighed, drumming her fingers on the desk in thought.

Just then, she felt a nudge at her elbow. Lucky had jumped onto the desk, purring and rubbing against her arm, as if trying to offer her some support.

"Lucky," she murmured thoughtfully, a smile tugging at her lips. On a hunch, she typed his name into the password field.

The screen flickered, and she was in.

"Bingo," she muttered, feeling a small triumph as she navigated through Emma's files. There were drafts of various articles, notes on local events, and email threads with editors and sources. But after a bit of searching, one particular folder caught her eye: "Confidential."

After opening it, Hayley scanned through a series of documents and files, her pulse quickening as she read. Emma had clearly been working on something big—an exposé involving a scandalous affair between a married town councilwoman, Madeline Petty, and an anonymous local man. And it didn't end there. According to Emma's notes, Madeline had allegedly received undeclared gifts from a wealthy donor who wanted her to vote in his favor on certain town matters.

Hayley leaned back, processing the information. If Emma had been digging into this story, it was possible she had uncovered something—or someone—who did not want their secrets exposed.

She shut the computer down and turned to Alex, who was petting Lucky, his fingers absently ruffling the cat's fur. "Alex, thank you. This is . . . helpful. I think Emma was onto something bigger than just her usual article topics. Do you mind if I print out a few files?"

"Be my guest," Alex said, eyeing her curiously.

"It might be nothing, but I'll let you know," she said as the printer started spitting out papers.

Alex looked up, his expression a mix of grief and confusion. "I knew she was passionate about her work, but I had no idea she was digging into something that could be dangerous."

"Sit tight," Hayley advised, scooping up the papers from the printer tray and patting his shoulder. "I'll do my best to find out what happened to her."

With a final nod, she left, feeling the weight of what she had learned pressing on her. If Councilwoman Madeline Petty had known about Emma's story, she might have been desperate enough to silence the young reporter. It was a disturbing thought, but Hayley couldn't shake the possibility.

The town office was bustling with activity when Hayley arrived, but her goal was clear. She marched down the hallway and knocked on the door of Councilwoman Madeline Petty's office, her mind whirling with questions.

"Come in!" came a curt voice.

Hayley opened the door to find Madeline seated at her desk, her expression pinched and tense as she glanced up. "Hayley Powell," she said coolly, her eyes narrowing. "What brings you here?"

Hayley didn't waste any time. "I wanted to ask you about Emma Lane."

Madeline's expression flickered with something Hayley couldn't quite read—surprise, perhaps, or annoyance. "I was sorry to hear about what happened to the poor girl . . . at your restaurant." She paused to let that last comment land. "What about her?"

"Emma was working on a story," Hayley began, watching Madeline's reaction closely. "A story involving an affair . . . well, with you and a local man."

"Who is this supposed paramour of mine, if you don't mind me asking?"

"Well, she doesn't say a name exactly . . ."

"Art and I have been happily married for fifteen years. We don't cheat on each other," Madeline said forcefully.

Art Petty was the town treasurer.

Hayley took a deep breath. She had saved the best for last. "She also mentioned some undeclared gifts you've been receiving. Care to comment on that?"

Madeline's face went pale, but she recovered quickly, her expression hardening. "That's absurd," she snapped. "Emma was known for digging up unfounded rumors and spinning them into stories. I assume she had no sources to back up any of those claims, which is why nothing ever went to print. It was just . . . talk."

"Talk, or something more?" Hayley pressed, leaning forward. "Because if Emma had evidence, maybe someone wanted to make sure that story never saw the light of day."

Madeline's gaze darkened, her jaw tightening. "I had nothing to do with that girl's death, if that's what you're implying. And if you're here to spread baseless accusations, I suggest you leave."

Hayley stood, holding her gaze. "If Emma's story was just a rumor, as you say, then there should be nothing to worry about. But I think you know more than you're letting on, Madeline."

"You should leave the investigative reporting to your husband and focus your attention on saving the reputation of your restaurant, if you ask me."

Without another word, Hayley turned on her heel and left the office. Madeline's reaction had been telling; she was clearly rattled, and Hayley's gut told her that the councilwoman was definitely hiding something.

That evening, Hayley and Bruce arrived at Chief Sergio's house, which had a breathtaking view of the Maine coast, for a quiet gathering. Sergio and his husband, Hayley's brother Randy, were hosting tonight and in exchange Hayley and Bruce would have them over for dinner on Friday. Sergio and Randy were warm and welcoming, but Hayley noticed the tension lingering in Sergio's eyes. After some small talk and a few sips of wine while Randy retreated to the kitchen to check on his roast, Hayley brought up the investigation, hoping to get some answers.

"Sergio, any updates on Emma's case?" she asked, trying to sound casual.

Sergio hesitated, exchanging a quick glance with Bruce. "The investigation is ongoing," he replied, his tone cautious. "But we're still focusing on Alex. He's our primary suspect."

Bruce raised an eyebrow. "Why? Hayley said Alex seemed devastated. It doesn't make sense that he'd hurt Emma."

Sergio sighed, clearly torn. "We found evidence on Emma's social media that she was planning to break up with Alex. There were some private messages on her phone to a few of her friends, ones that suggested she was . . . less committed than he might have thought. And then there's the perfume bottle."

Hayley frowned. "So you think Alex knew she was planning to leave him and poisoned her out of . . . revenge?"

"We're not jumping to conclusions," Sergio said quickly. "But it's certainly a possibility we can't ignore."

Hayley's mind whirled. She could not believe that Alex—heartbroken, grieving Alex—would plot something so sinister. But if the police were convinced he had motive, he was in serious trouble.

"Hayley," Sergio said gently, breaking her train of thought. "I know you're close to Alex, but you have to understand that we're just following the evidence."

She nodded, though her heart ached with frustration. She had promised Alex she would find the truth, but it felt like every clue was leading the police further down the wrong path.

Later, as she and Bruce walked home, Hayley confided her suspicions. "I can't help but think Madeline had something to do with this. Emma was onto her, Bruce. She was digging into the councilwoman's secrets, and Madeline looked ready to break when I confronted her."

Bruce gave her a thoughtful look. "If Madeline knew Emma was working on that story, she might've felt threatened. But would she go so far as to poison her?"

"People have done worse to protect their reputation," Hayley muttered.

Bruce nodded. "You're probably right. But if the police are convinced it's Alex, then it's up to us to prove otherwise, and we're going to need more than a few notes on her computer to do it."

Hayley sighed, her heart heavy with the weight of it all.

Chapter Four

Hayley stepped into the *Island Times* office early the next morning, carrying a bag of warm, fresh bagels from her restaurant. She knew the office would be buzzing with the latest on Emma Lane's murder, and she hoped the bagels might help break the ice. The staff had been on edge since Emma's death, and she suspected there was a lot more going on beneath the surface than anyone was letting on.

"Bagels!" she called, placing the bag on the small table near the kitchenette. Clara Banks, the new office manager, turned and gave her a weak smile.

"Thank you, Hayley," Clara said, her voice barely above a whisper. She looked exhausted, her hair slightly disheveled, a few papers clutched tightly in her hands. Clara had started working at the *Island Times* just a few weeks ago, and it was clear she was still struggling to find her footing. Hayley remembered those early days well—trying to keep up with Sal, who was as unpredictable as a Maine thunderstorm.

Sal had been going through office managers like Henry VIII went through wives.

"How are you holding up, Clara?" Hayley asked gently,

grabbing herself a bagel. "I know things can be a little hectic around here."

Clara sighed, casting a wary glance through the bullpen at Sal's office door. "I'm trying, Hayley. But Sal . . . he's so . . . so . . . demanding. Every time I think I have something figured out, he barks at me for doing it wrong." She wrung her hands, her voice dropping to a fearful whisper. "Yesterday morning, he actually yelled at me because I forgot to stock the fridge with cream cheese."

Hayley couldn't help but laugh, though she quickly covered it with a cough. "Sal can be a bit of a bear, I know. But trust me, he's more bark than bite. Underneath that gruff exterior, he's really just a big ole softie."

As if on cue, Sal appeared in the doorway of the back bullpen, his eyes zeroing in on the bagels. "Finally, breakfast," he grumbled, heading straight for the table. "Clara, where's the cream cheese?"

Clara froze, her face paling. "Oh, I'm so sorry, Sal—I forgot again. I'll go get some—"

"Forgot?" Sal's voice boomed, his face turning a shade of red. "Clara, I told you about this yesterday! How many times do I have to say it? Bagels need cream cheese!"

Clara looked like she might cry, mumbling an apology before hurrying toward the restroom, her steps quick and shaky.

Hayley shot Sal a glare, crossing her arms.

"Sal, really? Was that necessary?" she chided.

Sal looked taken aback. "What? I need my cream cheese!"

Hayley shook her head. "She's new and she's trying. Cut her some slack. Not everyone can read your mind, you know."

He huffed but did not respond, shuffling back toward

his office with a plain bagel. Once he was gone, Hayley settled back in, looking around the office and wondering who she could talk to about Emma's work. She had a strong hunch that something in one of Emma's articles had set off the chain of events that led to her murder.

But who could she ask?

As she pondered this, a couple of local reporters, Dave and Sarah, along with the paper's photographer, Johnny, approached the bagels. They were all new since Hayley's tenure as office manager so she did not know any of them that well. She had only met them at last year's *Island Times* office Christmas party since she habitually filed her food and cocktails columns from home. They greeted Hayley, and she quickly steered the conversation toward Emma.

"I know Emma was working on some big stories," Hayley said, keeping her tone casual. "She was so dedicated. I can see why Sal thought so highly of her."

Dave raised an eyebrow. "Yeah, Sal was her cheerleader. Saw himself in her, or something like that. But she had a way of getting under people's skin, you know?"

Hayley leaned in, curious. "Really? I thought everyone liked Emma."

Sarah snorted. "Well, most people did. But, let's just say she could be . . . intense. She was young and ambitious, sometimes a little too ambitious. Some people thought she was overstepping."

"Like who?" Hayley asked, trying not to sound too eager.

Johnny chuckled. "You might not want to hear this, Hayley, but . . . Bruce, for one, didn't exactly love working with her. He felt like she was always stepping into his territory. He's been with the *Island Times* forever, and then here comes Emma, all fired up, and he felt a little sidelined."

Hayley's jaw dropped. "Bruce? *My* Bruce?"

"Yep," Dave confirmed, nodding. "I heard him complaining to Sal about it more than once. Said he didn't appreciate her attitude, that she was trying to outshine him. I wouldn't say it was hostile, but . . . there was definitely some tension."

Hayley's mind reeled. She hadn't known Bruce felt this way. Was it possible his frustrations with Emma had gone deeper than she had realized? And worse, if others at the office had noticed, then that meant Bruce might now be on the police's radar as a suspect. And the last thing she needed now was her husband under suspicion of murder. The thought was ridiculous.

She thanked the group for the insight, doing her best to mask her concern, but her mind was racing. She would have to talk to Bruce. And if the police had picked up on the rumors, she knew Sergio would soon be looking into him too, despite the fact he was family.

That evening, Hayley found herself setting the table with extra care. Sergio and Randy were coming over for dinner, it was her and Bruce's turn to host, and she knew the conversation could quickly turn uncomfortable. She hadn't told Bruce about what she had learned at the paper, nor did she intend to—at least, not until she could make sense of it herself. But a part of her worried that Sal or one of the reporters might mention it to Sergio, and the last thing she wanted was for her husband to be blindsided.

Just as she finished arranging the place settings, her phone rang.

It was Sal.

"Hayley," he said, sounding agitated. "I just wanted to give you a heads-up. I, uh, might have slipped to Sergio that Bruce wasn't exactly Emma's biggest fan. I didn't mean to, but it just came up out of the blue."

Hayley's heart sank. "Sal, are you serious?"

"I didn't mean any harm," he insisted. "But now Sergio's curious, and I thought you should know."

Hayley thanked him and hung up, feeling a wave of dread. This dinner was going to be harder than she had imagined.

A few minutes later, Sergio and Randy arrived. Hayley greeted them warmly, doing her best to hide her anxiety, and they settled into light conversation over drinks and appetizers.

Bruce seemed relaxed, blissfully unaware of the potential storm brewing.

But as they sat down for dinner, Sergio finally broached the subject. "So, Bruce, I've been hearing a lot of interesting things around the office lately," he said with a playful smile, though his eyes were keen and watchful. "It sounds like you and Emma . . . how do you say it . . . did not exactly see nose to nose?"

Bruce blinked, clearly confused. "Didn't see . . . *nose to nose*?"

Hayley jumped in, hoping to deflect. "Sergio, I think you mean they didn't see eye to eye."

"Yes, yes, that's it!" Sergio grinned, though his expression quickly grew serious. "So, Bruce, it seems there were . . . tensions? Feelings of competition?"

Bruce shot Hayley a bewildered look. "I—well, I mean, Emma was ambitious. But I never held that against her."

Hayley held up a hand, cutting off any further questioning. "Sergio, come on. This is outrageous. You're talking to your friend and brother-in-law, not a suspect."

Sergio gave her an apologetic look but persisted. "Hayley, you know how these things work. I have to ask questions. Everyone's talking, and Bruce . . . well, he was heard complaining."

Bruce finally seemed to realize the gravity of the situation, his face going pale. "You can't be serious. I'm actually a suspect now?"

Randy, sensing the tension, placed a hand on Sergio's arm. "Sergio, maybe now isn't the time."

But Sergio was not easily deterred. "Bruce, it's just part of the investigation. It doesn't mean anything. But when people start mentioning someone's name, I have to look into it."

Hayley could see the distress on Bruce's face and quickly jumped in. "Bruce may have felt sidelined, but he didn't want anything bad to happen to Emma."

Bruce shot her a look. "*Sidelined*? Who have *you* been talking to?"

Hayley ignored the question keeping her focus on Sergio. "This is all just office politics, Sergio. Nothing more."

Bruce nodded vehemently. "Exactly. I may not have liked feeling outshined, but Emma's death . . . it was a shock to me, just like everyone else."

The awkwardness hung in the air as they all ate in silence. Eventually, Randy suggested they take dessert to go, sensing that no one was in the mood to linger any longer.

After their guests left, Bruce turned to Hayley, his face stricken. "How could anyone think I'd hurt Emma? I didn't even realize people thought I was upset with her. I just . . . I was a little frustrated, that's all."

Hayley took his hand, giving it a reassuring squeeze. "I

believe you, Bruce. And I promise, I'll find out who really did this. You don't need to worry."

Same promise she had made to Alex.

But she wasn't exactly brimming with confidence.

Bruce nodded, though his expression was still filled with confusion and hurt. Hayley watched him, her heart aching, vowing to uncover the truth no matter what it took.

Chapter Five

Hayley adjusted Leroy's leash as they strolled through Bar Harbor's quaint streets, enjoying the mild spring air. Leroy, her trusty shih tzu, trotted alongside her, his nose twitching with every new scent. The town was bustling, decked out with pastel-colored decorations and bunny-shaped banners for Easter, making her heart lift despite the grim events of the past few days. She wanted to focus on a simple errand today, something far removed from murder investigations and town gossip.

Hayley was heading for Bittersweet Confections, a cozy, old-fashioned store where she knew she would find the perfect chocolate Easter bunny for Bruce. With his sweet tooth, Bruce would not be able to resist the rich, creamy chocolate that Mrs. Bittersweet, a local treasure, had perfected over the decades.

As she pushed open the door, a soft chime tinkled overhead, and the unmistakable aroma of chocolate filled her senses. Hayley sighed in appreciation, a temporary escape from her worries.

"Hayley Powell!" Mrs. Bittersweet emerged from behind the counter, her face lighting up in recognition. Though in her seventies, Mrs. Bittersweet was as spry as ever, her small frame practically buzzing with energy. Her white hair was styled in a neat bob, and she wore a lavender apron decorated with Easter eggs and bunnies. "Always lovely to see you, dear. And look at you, Leroy! My, what a handsome boy."

Leroy barked happily, his tail wagging as he took in the sweet surroundings.

"Good to see you too, Mrs. Bittersweet," Hayley replied with a smile. "I'm in desperate need of one of your special chocolate bunnies. Bruce has been dropping hints about it for weeks now."

"Oh, Bruce does have a sweet tooth, doesn't he?" Mrs. Bittersweet chuckled, already bustling to jot down the order. "I'm absolutely swamped with Easter orders, but I promise I'll have it ready for you in time."

Hayley watched her, hesitating for a moment before deciding to introduce the topic that had been weighing on her mind. "Thank you so much. And Mrs. Bittersweet . . . I don't mean to bring up something so sad, but I can't stop thinking about poor Emma Lane."

Mrs. Bittersweet's cheerful expression dimmed as she pressed a hand to her heart. "Oh, Hayley, isn't it just terrible? That poor girl. To be poisoned by her own boyfriend, no less. It's unthinkable."

Hayley frowned, lowering her voice. "You know, there was some kind of toxic substance in that perfume bottle. Apparently, it was in the basket you put together."

Mrs. Bittersweet's eyes went wide, and she shook her head adamantly. "Oh, heavens, Hayley! I had no idea. Alex brought that perfume in with him. I thought it was a sweet touch and simply followed his instructions. I just added the chocolates and packaged it all up. I wouldn't know the first thing about fancy perfume."

Just then, the bell over the door chimed again, and Mrs. Bittersweet's nephew, Lance, walked in, his aunt's chocolate lab, Truffle, trailing behind him. Truffle immediately trotted over to Leroy, sniffing him with intense curiosity. The two dogs seemed to hit it off instantly, darting around the shop as though they had known each other for years.

"Oh dear, those two will be underfoot in no time," Mrs. Bittersweet said with a laugh, watching the dogs with fond exasperation. "Go on, you two! Play outside!"

She opened the back door, letting Truffle and Leroy bolt into the backyard, barking excitedly as they chased each other around. Hayley turned her attention to Lance, who had been lingering in the doorway, clearly nervous.

Mrs. Bittersweet patted his shoulder proudly. "Hayley, have you met my nephew Lance? He's recently come down from Caribou to help me run the shop. I'm getting too busy to manage it all on my own these days."

Lance gave a stiff, awkward smile, his gaze shifting to the floor. "Hello," he mumbled, his cheeks turning slightly pink.

"Nice to meet you, Lance," Hayley said, observing him closely. He was tall and lanky, with dark hair that hung over his eyes, giving him a somewhat timid appearance. When Mrs. Bittersweet mentioned Emma's name, though, she noticed a subtle change in his posture—he stiffened, his gaze darting toward his aunt and then away again.

"You didn't know Emma Lane, did you?" Hayley asked, curious about his reaction.

"No, no . . . not really," Lance said, stammering slightly. "I mean, maybe I saw her . . . once or twice. But I didn't know her."

Mrs. Bittersweet looked surprised. "But didn't you ask about her that day Alex came in for the Easter basket?"

Lance's face flushed a deeper red, and he fumbled with the hem of his shirt. "I . . . I don't really remember. Maybe I asked about her in passing, just to be polite," he said hastily, averting his eyes. “Excuse me, I should get back to work.”

Before Hayley could ask anything else, Lance turned and hurried into the back room, leaving her with more questions than answers.

Mrs. Bittersweet watched him go, shaking her head with a fond smile. “That boy. So shy, bless him. He’s a hard worker, though. Right now, he’s working on those chocolate eggs for the town’s Easter egg hunt. A huge order, let me tell you.”

Hayley smiled and nodded, but her mind was already racing. Lance’s reaction to her questions about Emma seemed a bit too guarded. She had a feeling there was something more to the story, and she was determined to find out what it was.

“I should get going, Mrs. Bittersweet,” Hayley said, standing up. “Thanks for taking Leroy off my hands for a bit.”

“Anytime, dear! You know we’re dog people around here.” Mrs. Bittersweet laughed, patting her apron. “I’ll have your bunny ready in a few days. And, oh, let me just make sure Truffle hasn’t buried any of his ‘treasures’ in the yard.”

As she opened the back door to call for Leroy, Hayley noticed her little dog trotting back inside with something in his mouth. She leaned down to see, and her eyes widened—it was a large gnawed bone.

Mrs. Bittersweet’s face paled as she quickly reached down and took it from Leroy. “You naughty boy, Truffle! He’s always burying things all over my yard, Hayley,” she explained, shaking her head. “Bones, bits of raw meat . . . you wouldn’t believe the mess he makes. I would hate for Leroy to choke on it.”

Hayley nodded, her curiosity piqued. “Well, he certainly

seems to have quite a stash. I guess he takes after his owner with a taste for all things delicious."

They laughed together, but Hayley's mind was already working through new questions. The gnawed bone was odd, and it struck her as peculiar that Mrs. Bittersweet didn't seem curious about where Truffle had found it. But she brushed it off for now, said her goodbyes, and left the shop.

Once she was outside, Hayley pulled out her phone and called Alex.

"Alex, I just had an interesting conversation at Mrs. Bittersweet's shop," she said, keeping her tone casual.

"Why am I not surprised?" he replied, though there was a weariness in his voice.

"Do you know her nephew Lance?" Hayley asked. "He seemed . . . well, he seemed uncomfortable when Emma's name came up."

Alex hesitated. "I don't know him very well, but Emma . . . she thought he was strange. She ran into him a few times when we were hiking out near Witch Hole. She said he gave her the creeps, made her feel . . . I don't know, uneasy. But I thought she was just being paranoid."

Hayley's interest piqued. "What kind of vibes did he give off?"

"The kind that makes you want to keep your distance," Alex replied. "Emma said she wanted to stay clear of him, but I thought she was overreacting. Guess I should've paid more attention."

Hayley thanked him and hung up, the pieces of the puzzle starting to shift in her mind. Lance's awkwardness, his reluctance to admit he knew Emma, and Mrs. Bittersweet's insistence on hiding any trace of Truffle's "buried treasures"—it all pointed to something, though she could not yet see the full picture.

As she walked back to Hayley's Kitchen, she pondered her next steps. Perhaps Lance's strange behavior and Emma's unease around him were not coincidental.

One thing was certain: the more she dug, the more unsettling this case became. And Hayley was not one to leave a mystery unsolved, even if it meant crossing a few lines to get the truth.

Island Food & Spirits by Hayley Powell

I still can't help but get a little nostalgic and misty-eyed around the holidays, especially now that my children are grown and off living their own lives. Easter is no exception. This year, as I often do, I pulled out one of my treasured photo albums filled with memories of Gemma and Dustin when they were young, sweet, and still living at home.

That's when I came across a picture of me, smiling at the camera, holding two rabbits. My kids still think those were a friend's bunnies, but the true story is one I've kept to myself—until now.

It was my first Easter after my divorce, and for the first time, Gemma and Dustin were spending the holiday with their father. I was sitting at my desk at the *Island Times*, feeling sorry for myself, when Janis Jones burst in waving a piece of paper in the air. She needed to place an ad to sell two rabbits because her poor Dougie had suddenly developed a severe allergy.

Noticing my gloomy mood, Janis sympathized, saying she'd be devastated if Dougie wasn't home for Easter. Then she lit up and declared she had the perfect solution to cheer me up: two soft, furry bunnies to keep me company. And wouldn't it be a wonderful surprise for my kids when they returned home? Hook, line, and sinker—I was sold.

Janis delivered the bunnies, along with all

their accessories, and I had to admit they were adorable—though much larger than I expected. I named them Dottie and Diane and decided they needed plenty of exercise. An hour later, I was questioning my decision as I chased them around the house, trying to keep them from chewing on cords and papers.

The next morning, I went down to the laundry room and was greeted by Dottie hopping to the front of the kennel. But Diane? Nowhere to be found. Peering inside, I moved some hay around and froze. Diane wasn't alone—she had TEN tiny baby rabbits snuggled beside her.

Three things became clear: (1) I had been completely suckered into taking a pregnant rabbit, (2) I wanted to strangle Janis Jones, and (3) I needed to act fast before my kids saw them and convinced me to keep them all.

Then I noticed Dottie nibbling at my leg with a self-satisfied expression. That's when it hit me—Dottie was actually a Dougie.

Panicked, I did what any rational person would do in a crisis: I called my brother, Randy. He rushed over, assessed the situation, and then called his husband, Sergio, claiming there was an emergency at my house. Sergio arrived with sirens blaring and was not amused to find out that the "emergency" was a rabbit explosion. I heard him mumble something about a boiling pot, which I chose to ignore.

Randy also summoned my BFFs, Liddy and Mona, citing an emergency. They arrived breathless, only to find themselves facing twelve rabbits in my laundry room. We started calling everyone we knew, hoping to find homes for them. But even though it was Easter, no one wanted a rabbit.

Just as I was about to resign myself to a life overrun with rabbits, Liddy remembered a Realtor friend whose daughter was involved with a 4-H club. A few phone calls and a promised lunch later, Diane, Dougie, and their family would be going to Brewer and their new home at a school farm.

Crisis averted, I collapsed onto the floor as Dougie hopped into my lap for a snuggle. The words "Maybe a couple wouldn't hurt" had barely left my mouth when a chorus of "NO!"s echoed around the room. I came back to my senses just in time to see Dougie happily gnawing on a lamp cord.

My kids never knew how close they came to being rabbit owners that Easter. The only bunnies they got were the stuffed ones I picked up at Walmart for their Easter baskets. And what did I learn from all this? Not much—because the next year, I found myself dealing with a stray mama cat and her six newborn kittens. But that's a story for another time.

Reminiscing about past Easter chaos has worked up my appetite. If you're looking for a delicious cocktail and an easy, make-ahead breakfast casserole for Easter brunch, I've got you covered!

Chocolate Egg Martini

Ingredients

2 ounces vodka
1 ounce chocolate liqueur
Splash of cream
Chocolate shavings

Fill a shaker with ice and add the vodka, chocolate liqueur, and cream.

Shake well. Strain into a martini glass.

Sprinkle the chocolate shavings on top. Enjoy!

Sausage and Hash Brown Breakfast Casserole

This easy casserole can be prepped the night before, making Easter morning stress-free!

Ingredients

1 pound pork breakfast sausage
10 eggs
1½ cups whole milk or half-and-half (2% milk works too)
1 teaspoon salt
1 teaspoon pepper
½ teaspoon garlic powder
1 (30 ounce) package frozen shredded hash browns, thawed
2 cups shredded cheddar cheese

Preheat oven to 375°F. Grease a 9 × 13 inch baking dish.

Brown the sausage in a skillet over medium heat, breaking it into small pieces. Drain grease.

In a bowl, whisk together the eggs, milk, salt, pepper, and garlic powder.

Layer the hash browns, cooked sausage, and cheese in the baking dish.

Pour the egg mixture over the top. (If making ahead, cover and refrigerate overnight.)

Cover the dish with foil and bake for 40 minutes. Remove the foil and bake another 20 minutes.

Serve as is or with a splash of hot sauce. Enjoy!

Wishing you all a Happy Easter filled with love, laughter, and—most importantly—no unexpected baby bunnies!

Chapter Six

The sun was beginning to dip below the horizon when Hayley pushed open the door to Randy's bar, Drinks Like a Fish. After the chaotic week she had endured, a night out with her best friends, Liddy and Mona, was exactly what she needed to decompress.

"Hayley!" Randy called from behind the bar, his face brightening as he spotted her. He wiped his hands on a bar towel, then approached her with a tray piled high with crispy fried clams. "Here—consider this my peace offering. I feel terrible about how that dinner went down the other night, with Sergio going hard at Bruce like that."

Hayley gave him a reassuring smile, though she was still troubled. "Thanks, Randy. I know it wasn't your fault. Sergio's just doing his job, but I can't believe anyone would seriously think Bruce could kill anyone."

Randy nodded, glancing over his shoulder at a table of patrons who were calling him over. "Well, I know he didn't mean to hurt Bruce. Enjoy the clams. I'll be back in a sec."

Hayley popped a clam into her mouth, savoring its salty fried crunch, her mood lifting ever so slightly. As she glanced around the bar, she noticed a table by the window where the three young *Island Times* staffers—Dave and Sarah, and Johnny—were having beers and an animated conversation. They had not noticed her at the bar, so she subtly leaned closer, her ears pricking up when she realized they were talking about Bruce.

". . . I mean, I really don't know why Sal insists on keeping him around, he's practically a dinosaur in that office," Dave scoffed, then took a swig of his beer. "No wonder he felt threatened by Emma. Generation X versus Generation Z, am I right?"

"Right?" Sarah laughed. "He's been acting so weird ever since she died. He won't even acknowledge he's a suspect. I mean, Sal should probably have him work from home. Who knows who might be next if he gets angry."

Johnny snickered. "He's like Bruce Banner from *The Incredible Hulk*—one wrong move, and pow."

Hayley felt her jaw clench, irritation simmering inside her. She grabbed the tray of mugs Randy had set out as refills for their table, deciding to deliver them herself. As she approached, the laughter at the table died down, and the three staffers looked up in surprise, their faces turning various shades of red.

"Here you go," she said, setting the mugs down with a forced smile. "And while I'm at it, maybe I should remind you all that Bruce has supported each of you since you started. He's dedicated years to the *Island Times*, and he deserves a lot more respect than what you're giving him now."

They stared at her, chastened. Sarah spoke up first, her voice a little shaky. "Hayley, we didn't mean any harm. We're just . . . frustrated. We all want to find out who killed Emma, but there's so much pressure, and . . . no leads."

Hayley softened, understanding their frustration, though her anger hadn't fully dissipated. "I get it. But think before you judge him so quickly. We all know Bruce is innocent, and your jokes could end up making things worse for everyone."

She took a deep breath, letting go of her irritation and deciding to pivot. "Have any of you heard of Lance? He's Mrs. Bittersweet's nephew, and I think he knew Emma."

Dave and Sarah exchanged blank looks, but Johnny perked up. "Actually, I've seen him around. I remember the last time I saw Emma—she was leaving the office and was talking to someone who had been waiting for her on the street."

Sarah sat up in her chair. "I remember that guy. Tall, kinda weird acting, looked like he lacked social skills."

"Yeah, that's the one," Johnny confirmed. "I didn't think much of it, but when I stopped by Mrs. Bittersweet's shop to pick up candy for my cousin's kids, I saw the same guy working there. It had to be him."

Hayley leaned forward, her interest piqued. "Did Emma look upset?"

Johnny shrugged. "Not that I could tell. But I only saw them for a second before I had to leave to cover the high school football game."

Just then, Hayley noticed that Dave and Sarah had gone quiet, their gazes shifting uncomfortably. She followed their line of sight and felt a chill go down her spine. Lance was at the bar, his expression hard as he looked in her direction. He ordered a drink from Randy, but his eyes never left her.

Hayley turned back to the table, lowering her voice. "Do you think he heard us?"

All three nodded, looking sheepish and worried. Dave muttered, "Oh, yeah. No doubt about it. He definitely heard everything."

Hayley's stomach dropped.

Not good.

Just then, Liddy and Mona burst through the door, bickering as usual.

"Don't be mad, Mona," Liddy cooed, waving at Randy, who was behind the bar.

"I'm not mad," Mona barked.

"You didn't say a word the whole way here. You're mad at me," Liddy noted.

"I'm not mad," Mona insisted. She turned to Randy. "Do I look mad, Randy?"

Randy nodded. "Yes, Mona, you look mad."

"Okay, yes, I'm mad!" Mona howled, spinning back to Liddy, her arms crossed. "Because you make us late every single time we go anywhere together."

"Relax, Mona. We're not *that* late," Liddy shot back with a grin.

"Hayley said let's meet at six thirty. It's already ten to seven!"

"It's not my fault you had to try three times to parallel park your truck," Liddy sniffed.

Mona shook her head, frustrated. "I try to do a nice thing. I say, 'Hey, Liddy, I'll pick you up on the way, give you a ride to the bar,' and what happens? You keep me waiting outside your house twenty minutes while you do god knows what!" Mona huffed.

"Fifteen minutes," Liddy corrected her.

"It's still fifteen minutes! When you do that, it's like you're saying your time is more valuable than mine."

"Exactly, Mona, what's your point?"

Mona shook her head and turned to Randy. "I need my beer, Randy! Pronto!"

Mona and Liddy's familiar banter lifted Hayley's spirits, and she went over to them at the bar. Randy delivered their usual—Liddy a Cosmopolitan, Mona a Budweiser on draft—and they immediately dug into the fried clams.

Hayley leaned in, keeping her voice low. "Do you know anything about that guy sitting on the other side of the bar . . . Lance?" She nodded subtly in his direction.

Mona raised an eyebrow, thinking. "He's Mrs. Bittersweet's nephew, right? If I remember right, I think his dad was the brother of her ex-husband Dewey."

"Yeah," Liddy interjected. "But Lance's real last name isn't Bittersweet. It's Dratch. Dewey Dratch is the ex-husband. Mrs. Bittersweet's real name is Marion Dratch. She just goes by 'Bittersweet' because, well, Marion Dratch doesn't exactly scream 'chocolate empress,' does it? It's all about building the brand, I guess."

"Interesting," Hayley said, filing that detail away. "And whatever happened to Mrs. Bittersweet's ex-husband?"

Mona shrugged. "Beats me. But my parents used to know Dewey and Marion. They said Dewey took off ages ago. Apparently Marion was always on his case, a real henpecker. Eventually, he just packed up and left town. He couldn't take her nagging anymore."

Liddy nodded. "Moved up to Aroostook County, last I heard. That's where he was from originally."

Hayley turned to Mona. "Do Bubba and Jane still keep in touch with Dewey?"

Mona shrugged. "Not that I know of, but only they could tell you."

Hayley's mind raced, wondering if there was more to this family story than met the eye. "Do you think your parents would know more?"

Mona grinned. "Why don't we go ask them? They're having dinner right now up at Side Street Café."

Liddy's eyes widened. "Wait. Your father has agreed to

actually eat out at an actual restaurant? I think I just saw a pig fly past the window."

Mona chuckled. "It's their wedding anniversary, so Ma insisted they do something special. I can hear him complaining about the menu prices as we speak. Want to go crash their meal?"

Hayley did not hesitate. "Let's go."

They paid their tab and waved at Randy, who looked bewildered as they filed out the door. Hayley was all too aware of Lance's hard stare as they left.

At Side Street Café, Hayley, Liddy, and Mona found Mona's parents, Bubba and Jane, tucked into a corner booth finishing their meals. Jane beamed as they approached, but Bubba gave a good-natured groan.

"Oh, great. I suppose I'm picking up the bill for these three jokers too now?" he muttered, though there was a glint of affection in his eyes.

"Dad, it's on us," Mona assured him, though Bubba kept a watchful eye on the menu prices as they pulled up extra chairs.

"Nearly thirty bucks for a friggin' lobster roll. Highway robbery! And twenty-eight dollars for a barbecue dinner? What does it come with, the Hope Diamond?"

"Enough, Bubba," Jane said with a snort. "It's my one night out a year. Don't ruin it with your constant whining!"

Liddy plucked a menu off the table and quickly perused it. "I'm starving. How about I order the artichoke spinach dip for the table?"

"Why stop there? Go on. Get the Harbor Wings and Bangin' Shrimp to boot. I'll just extend the credit on my Mastercard!" Bubba wailed. "I'm not drowning in real estate commissions like you, Liddy. Me and Jane live on a fixed income."

Liddy put down the menu. "Never mind. I can eat when I get home."

"Dad, please!" Mona admonished. "Hayley wants to ask you and Ma a few questions."

"Actually," Hayley said, leaning in, "I need your help with something. Do you remember Dewey Dratch?"

Bubba perked up. "Of course! Dewey and I used to go fishing together at Eagle Lake. He was a good friend, but his wife, Marion, was always riding him. He finally had enough and left her. Never heard from him again after that."

Jane nodded. "Marion was devastated. Never remarried. She threw herself into that shop and never looked back. She doesn't talk about him much, though. It's still a sore subject apparently."

"Interesting," Hayley murmured, piecing together what little she knew. "So she lost touch with him completely?"

Jane sat back, trying to remember. "Far as I know, yes. Marion built herself a little empire with that shop. When Dewey left, she focused on her business and nothing else."

The waiter stopped by the table. "Would you like anything else?"

"Just the bill, thanks," Bubba said too quickly.

"I don't even get a dessert on my anniversary?" Jane asked.

"I thought you wanted to cut down on sweets," Bubba said innocently.

"Bubba Butler, you are this close to sleeping on the couch tonight," Jane hissed. But then she glanced at the waiter with a smile. "That will be all, thank you."

The waiter set the check down on the table, and Bubba muttered some more about the prices as he reluctantly pulled out his wallet slowly, hoping someone would intervene before the waiter came back for his card. He was in luck.

Liddy snatched up the bill. "My treat! Happy anniversary!"

Jane scoffed. "Oh, Liddy, you don't have to pay for our anniversary dinner! We can—"

Bubba interrupted her. "Jane, if someone wants to do something nice, it's rude to deny them that pleasure!"

"Cheapskate," Jane muttered under her breath, then turned to Liddy. "Thank you, dear, that's very generous of you."

Hayley felt a rush of gratitude for their insights, but she was still left with more questions than answers about Lance's place in all this.

As the three friends left Side Street Café, Hayley parted ways with Liddy and Mona, waving them off as they headed home. "Night, guys," she called, stepping onto the quiet street.

The evening air was cool and still, and Hayley's thoughts drifted as she walked alone through the town square, past the Congregational church, and then down Ledgelawn toward home, the dim glow of streetlights casting long shadows on the pavement. She'd gone only a few blocks when she noticed something unsettling—a shadowy figure was following her.

She kept her pace steady, forcing herself to stay calm, but the hairs on the back of her neck prickled. The figure was tall and moved with a distinct gait. Hayley resisted the urge to glance over her shoulder, instead keeping her eyes focused straight ahead, quickening her pace slightly. She could hear footsteps matching hers, staying just close enough to keep her on edge.

Her heart raced, but she forced herself to keep her wits. She turned onto Glenmary Road, her own street, hoping the familiar path would give her a sense of comfort. But the shadow persisted, staying just out of reach.

Finally, she couldn't take it anymore. She stopped and spun around, ready to confront whoever was following her—but the street was empty. The figure had vanished into the shadows, as though they had never been there.

She let out a shaky breath, relieved but still wary. She turned back to continue walking, but in her distraction, she collided with a solid figure, letting out a scream before she realized who it was.

"Hayley! It's me!" Bruce's familiar voice cut through her fear, and she sagged in relief, clutching his arms.

"Bruce!" she gasped, her heart still racing.

She heard a bark and looked down to see Leroy at her heels, Bruce gripping the leash.

Hayley sighed with relief. "I thought . . . I thought someone was following me."

He wrapped his arms around her, his voice filled with concern. "I finished up work and stopped by Drinks Like a Fish to join you and the girls, but Randy said you all left in a hurry, so I drove home to wait for you and decided to take Leroy out for a walk. I didn't mean to scare you."

She took a shaky breath, her pulse gradually calming. "I think someone was tailing me, but I don't know who. He just disappeared."

Bruce glanced around, his expression turning serious. "Let's get you home. Whoever it was, they're gone now."

They walked the rest of the way hand in hand, Hayley comforted by his presence. Leroy trotted a few feet ahead of them. But Hayley's mind was still racing, her thoughts swirling around Lance, Mrs. Bittersweet, and the shadowy figure who had vanished into the night.

Chapter Seven

The scene was organized chaos at the annual Easter egg hunt at the Emerson Conners Middle School field. Families and children of all ages roamed the grounds, their excitement palpable as they gathered for one of the town's biggest spring events. Hayley and Bruce held hands as they strolled, taking in the sight of children darting across the field, baskets in hand, as they searched for brightly colored eggs hidden in tree branches and behind bushes and nestled in swings and on top of ladders on the recess playground.

"It's a shame Eli couldn't make it this year," Hayley sighed, thinking of her grandson. "He's growing up so fast. I'd have loved to watch him scramble for eggs again."

Bruce gave her hand a gentle squeeze, smirking. "I don't know, Hayley. The last time we brought Eli to the Easter egg hunt, we stumbled across a dead body. I think I can go without that kind of excitement again this year. Especially given the current situation."

Hayley rolled her eyes. "Come on, Bruce. Everything's going to be fine today. We're here to enjoy ourselves—no drama, no mysteries, just a nice, normal Easter event."

Bruce chuckled, casting a wary glance around the field

as if double-checking for any suspicious figures lurking nearby. "Normal would be nice for a change."

They continued their stroll around the field, Hayley scanning the crowd for a glimpse of this year's Easter bunny. Since Raymond Dobbs, the usual bunny, had passed away, the town had been relying on volunteers. Last year, Art Petty, the town treasurer, had donned the bunny suit—though that had ended in disaster when he had suffered a claustrophobic panic attack halfway through the event. This year, no one knew who would be taking on the role.

Just then, a flash of white caught Hayley's eye, and she nudged Bruce, pointing toward a grumpy-looking Easter bunny in an oversized costume, surrounded by a small group of children. But instead of the usual cheerful demeanor expected of someone playing the Easter bunny, this one was gruffly shooing kids away from his Easter basket.

"Hey! Stop grabbing candy from my stash!" he growled, swatting a boy's hand. "Keep your grubby little hands to yourself! You're supposed to be hunting for eggs, not bugging me for mine! Go on! Get out of here!"

The children stared at him in shock before scattering, and Hayley couldn't help but laugh.

"That's got to be Sal," Bruce muttered. "Who else would volunteer to be the Easter bunny and act as if he's in a hostage situation?"

"I can't believe anyone could actually convince him to do it," Hayley marveled.

As they watched, the bunny grudgingly posed for a few pictures with reluctant children, his arms stiff as they clung to his legs. When Hayley and Bruce approached, the bunny looked at them, his head cocked slightly as if he were trying to play dumb.

"Hello there, Mr. Easter Bunny," Hayley greeted with a smirk. "You wouldn't happen to be Sal Moretti under that suit, would you?"

The bunny's ears twitched, and he grumbled in a low voice, "I don't know what you're talking about."

Hayley chuckled, nudging Bruce. "Come on, Sal, you're not fooling anyone."

"Nobody else was available. I can't believe I agreed to do it. Worst mistake of my life. Other than trying that keto diet once Roseanna insisted I try. What a nightmare!"

Hayley and Bruce laughed and continued walking through the crowd, catching sight of Madeline Petty and her husband, Art, lingering near a display of Easter baskets set up for the town's charity auction. Madeline, who organized this event in her role on the town council, had a faintly uncomfortable look, glancing around as if she wanted to be anywhere else. When Hayley waved at her, she turned away sharply, pretending not to notice.

But Art spotted them and eagerly waved them over. "Hayley! Bruce! Great to see you two."

Hayley exchanged an amused glance with Bruce as they walked over. Art, a genial man in his forties with a robust laugh and a love for ice fishing, did not seem to notice his wife's reluctance. He grinned broadly, shaking Bruce's hand with enthusiasm.

"Bruce, you excited for ice-fishing season?" Art asked, his eyes lighting up. "They're predicting some nice fat trout this year."

Bruce matched his enthusiasm. "I can't wait. I'm getting my gear together already and it's only spring."

As the men dove into fishing talk, Hayley kept her gaze on Madeline, who was clearly panicked. Hayley could sense she was dreading a possible mention of her recent affair, the one Emma Lane had uncovered in her investigation. Hayley leaned in slightly, pretending to be casual.

"I don't know how you find time to do all you do, Madeline," she teased, watching Madeline's face turn pink.

"Ah . . . yes, well, it's, um . . . it's quite the balancing act," Madeline stammered, her eyes darting nervously. She cleared her throat and gave Hayley a strained smile. "Would you like to see the Easter baskets for the auction? Some of them are quite beautiful."

Before Hayley could reply, Madeline grabbed her arm and practically dragged her away from Art and Bruce. Once they were out of earshot, Madeline's friendly demeanor vanished, replaced with desperate pleading.

"Please, Hayley," Madeline whispered, her voice tight. "I'm begging you. Don't say anything to Art. He doesn't know . . . about the affair. And it's over now. I love my husband, and I don't want to hurt him."

Hayley folded her arms, keeping her tone measured. "Madeline, your marriage is none of my business. But the man you were seeing is definitely a person of interest in Emma's case. You need to stop protecting his identity."

"He had nothing to do with Emma's death, I promise you. So just forget about him," she pleaded, desperate.

"This isn't something I can just ignore, Madeline."

Madeline's face crumpled, and tears welled in her eyes. "Please, Hayley, don't drag him into this. He would never do anything to hurt Emma. You have to believe me."

Hayley shook her head gently. "I'm sorry, but I need to get justice for Emma. She was working on an exposé that was going to ruffle more than a few feathers, especially yours, and now she's dead. If you want to protect Art from getting hurt, I suggest you tell the police the truth."

Madeline's expression hardened, and her voice rose in a defensive tone. "Come on, Hayley. Everyone in town is acutely aware that Emma died while eating *your* food. Your restaurant's reputation is at stake. This is all just self-serving. And I've heard the rumors. People are talking about Bruce. Don't pretend you're not trying to steer attention away from him, too."

Hayley's patience thinned. "I love my husband just as much as you love yours, Madeline, and I'll do whatever it takes to protect him. But don't mistake my motives—I'm here for the truth of what happened to Emma."

Just then, Bruce and Art returned, Bruce looking concerned as he glanced at Madeline, who was hastily wiping her eyes. She forced a bright smile, linking her arm with Art's.

"Time to go, dear," she said briskly, steering her husband away without another word.

Bruce frowned, watching them go. "What was that about? She looked like she'd been crying."

Hayley sighed, looping her arm through his. "Just a conversation she didn't want to have. But I think she knows more about Emma's death than she's letting on."

They were about to leave when Hayley's phone buzzed. It was a text from Mrs. Bittersweet:

Truffle misses Leroy! How about a playdate?

Hayley glanced at Bruce apologetically. "I know we had plans, but I think I need to follow up on this. Mrs. Bittersweet might have more useful information."

Bruce looked almost relieved. "Honestly? That's fine by me. I'll go home, crack open a beer, watch a game, and forget about being a murder suspect for a few hours."

They left the Easter egg hunt and drove home. After exchanging a quick kiss, Hayley put a leash on Leroy and headed toward Mrs. Bittersweet's Chocolate Shop, the little dog trotting eagerly beside her.

* * *

The shop was busier than ever, bustling with customers as chocolate bunnies and eggs flew off the shelves. Hayley spotted Mrs. Bittersweet behind the counter, her usual sweet smile in place, her fingers fidgeting with the ribbon on a large Easter basket.

Leroy, upon seeing Truffle, immediately perked up, wagging his tail and giving a happy bark. The two dogs were clearly delighted to be reunited, sniffing and playfully circling each other.

"Thank you for bringing Leroy over, Hayley," Mrs. Bittersweet said, though her tone was a little too bright, her eyes darting toward the Easter baskets with a strange unease. She seemed especially cautious with the baskets, adjusting them with delicate precision.

"No problem," Hayley said, watching her carefully. "It's nice to see Truffle and Leroy getting along so well. Maybe they can run around in the backyard again?"

Mrs. Bittersweet's smile faltered, and she shook her head quickly. "Oh, no, no. Not today. As you know, Truffle has a habit of making a mess back there. Hold on. I'll be done with these in a jiffy."

Hayley watched Mrs. Bittersweet continue to fuss over the baskets. Just then, Lance emerged from the back room, looming behind her with an intense look that made Hayley's skin prickle. He didn't say anything, but his presence felt unsettling, like a silent shadow.

"Lance, keep an eye on the shop for me," Mrs. Bittersweet said, giving him a quick nod. She grabbed her coat and motioned to Hayley. "Shall we take the dogs for a walk?"

Hayley nodded, feeling her curiosity piqued. They strolled down to Agamont Park, just left of the public pier by the Atlantic Ocean. The dogs darted around happily, chasing each other and fetching tennis balls. After a few minutes, Hayley decided to approach the topic that had been nagging at her.

"So, Mrs. Bittersweet, I was wondering about your husband, Dewey," she said gently. "I've heard bits and pieces, but I'd love to hear more about him from you."

Mrs. Bittersweet's expression turned somber, and she looked away. "I don't talk about Dewey much. He . . . he left me a long time ago, without a word. I tried dating again, but I never found anyone I could trust. I built this shop because it gave me purpose—a reason to move forward."

Hayley nodded, sensing the raw emotion beneath her words. "I can't imagine how hard that must have been."

Mrs. Bittersweet's tone softened, but her words held a faint bitterness. "Heartbreak does funny things to a person, Hayley. It changes you."

They walked in silence for a few moments, but Mrs. Bittersweet quickly shifted the conversation, eyeing Hayley with a hint of suspicion. "Speaking of change, I've heard you've suddenly taken quite an interest in my nephew, Lance."

"You have?"

"Yes. Lance tells me everything. You seem rather obsessed with him."

Hayley raised an eyebrow. "I would hardly call it an obsession. I just think he might know something about Emma's death, and I need to be thorough."

Mrs. Bittersweet's demeanor shifted, her usual sweetness taking on a sharper edge. "I don't appreciate your baseless speculation about Lance and what he might or might not know, Hayley. He's a sensitive boy, and I won't have you recklessly gossiping about him all over town."

"Sensitive boy?" Hayley repeated, surprised. "Mrs. Bittersweet, he's in his late twenties."

Mrs. Bittersweet's eyes flashed, and for a moment, her warm exterior cracked. "He's had a difficult life, and I won't have you meddling in it."

Hayley held her ground, refusing to back down. "If Lance has information about Emma, that's not just my business—it's the whole town's. We all deserve to know the truth."

Mrs. Bittersweet's mouth pressed into a thin line, her gaze icy. "Maybe it's time you started minding your own business, Hayley."

It sounded like a threat.

Mrs. Bittersweet smiled again, letting her words hang in the air.

As they stood in tense silence, Hayley couldn't shake the feeling that Mrs. Bittersweet knew more than she was letting on, just like Hayley suspected with Madeline Petty.

And it was also becoming clear that, beneath her sweet facade, Mrs. Bittersweet was not so entirely sweet after all.

Chapter Eight

Hayley sat at her kitchen table the next morning, cradling a cup of coffee as she stared at her laptop. The conversation with Mrs. Bittersweet the day before lingered in her mind. Mrs. Bittersweet's sudden shift from sweetness to irritation was not just unsettling—it was suspicious. And Hayley couldn't shake the feeling that Dewey Dratch's disappearance might be the key to unlocking the truth behind Emma Lane's murder.

Bruce, sitting across from her with his tablet, looked up. "Still thinking about Dewey?"

Hayley nodded. "It just doesn't add up, Bruce. Everyone assumed he went back to Aroostook County after leaving Mrs. Bittersweet, but if that were true, someone up there would have heard from him."

"Why don't you check?" Bruce said, taking a sip of his coffee. "Look up the Dratch name and see who's still around."

Hayley took his advice, typing "Dratch Aroostook County" into a search engine. A few results popped up, but only one seemed relevant: a woman named Malibu Dratch. Hayley raised an eyebrow at the name and decided to call her.

After a few rings, a gruff voice answered. "This is Malibu."

"Hi, Malibu," Hayley began, doing her best to sound cheerful. "My name's Hayley Powell, and I'm trying to find information about Dewey Dratch. I understand he might have been related to you?"

Malibu sighed audibly. "Dewey Dratch, huh? Heard the name, but never met him. If he came back up here after leaving wherever he was, I sure didn't see him. And trust me, I'd know."

Hayley frowned. "You'd know?"

"Thanksgiving, Christmas, birthdays . . . the Dratches were a loud, volatile bunch," Malibu said, her voice dripping with disdain. "Fistfights, screaming matches, the works. If Dewey had shown up, he'd have been right in the middle of it."

"That sounds . . . colorful," Hayley said, unsure how to respond.

"Yeah, well, most of them are dead now," Malibu continued. "Good riddance, if you ask me. Worthless losers, the whole lot of 'em. I kept the name because my maiden name's Barbie. Malibu Barbie. My parents thought it was hilarious. Explains my outlook on life, don't you think?"

Hayley bit back a laugh. "It does sound . . . unique."

"That's just what I need as a woman in her fifties, kids making fun of me all over again, laughing and pointing. I'm too old to put up with that nonsense. No way, no how. I'll die a Dratch!"

"But you're certain Dewey never came back to Aroostook County?"

"Positive," Malibu said firmly. "If he's not dead, he's somewhere else entirely."

After thanking Malibu, Hayley hung up and turned to

Bruce. "That's odd. If Dewey didn't go back home, where did he go?"

Bruce frowned, putting down his tablet. "Let's see what the internet has to say." He typed "Dewey Dratch" into the same search engine and scrolled through the results. "There's a Dewey Dratch on social media, but he's a teenager in Billings, Montana, who's into cosplay. Definitely not our guy."

"So he just disappeared," Hayley murmured.

Bruce leaned back in his chair, his brow furrowed. "If everyone assumed he left without a word, maybe they didn't look too closely. What if something happened to him?"

Hayley's mind raced. "What if Emma wasn't just working on the city council scandal? What if she was also investigating what happened to Dewey Dratch?"

They sat in silence for a moment, the implications sinking in. Hayley felt more certain than ever that Emma's death was tied to something bigger than anyone realized.

After dropping Bruce off at the *Island Times* office, Hayley was about to drive to her restaurant when she heard someone calling her name. She looked in her rearview mirror and saw Dave, Sarah, and Johnny running out of the building, waving her down.

Hayley put her window down as they approached. "Hey, guys. What's going on?"

The two young journalists and photographer looked sheepish, but Sarah spoke up first. "We just wanted to say we're sorry for what we said about Bruce at Drinks Like a Fish the other night. It was unprofessional, and we all feel terrible."

Dave nodded. "Yeah, we were out of line. And we want to help you find out who killed Emma."

Hayley hesitated. She was used to working alone, and the thought of dragging a trio of Gen Z reporters into her investigation was not exactly appealing. But they seemed earnest, and she couldn't deny that extra help might be useful.

"I don't know . . ." she began, but Johnny cut her off.

"We really want to learn the ropes of investigative journalism. Bruce has been a mentor to all of us, and this feels like the right way to repay him."

Hayley sighed. "Fine. But if you're serious about helping, I need someone to tail Madeline Petty. She knows my car, so I can't do it."

Johnny grinned. "I've got a van. She'll never know I'm there."

Hayley looked doubtful. "Isn't your van . . . a little beat-up?"

"Rustic charm," Johnny said with a wink. "My dad gave it to me as a graduation present. She may not look pretty, but she gets me around."

It was official.

Hayley was now den mother to a Scooby gang.

That evening, Hayley found herself crammed into the back of Johnny's old van, wedged between a pile of crumpled fast-food wrappers and a stained sleeping bag. She had brought food from her restaurant, but the thought of eating in such a dirty space made her stomach churn.

"This is disgusting," she muttered, glaring at Johnny.

"Welcome to the glamorous world of journalism," he replied cheerfully, turning up the music on the van's ancient stereo.

Hayley cringed at the noise, realizing she didn't recognize any of the obscure bands Johnny was playing. She felt every bit her age surrounded by these enthusiastic twenty-somethings.

They parked across the street from the Petty house and waited, Hayley trying to ignore the smell of stinky socks and a strong gas odor most likely from a leaky fuel line. Remarkably, her three stakeout partners appeared totally oblivious.

When Madeline's husband, Art, left their house for his weekly poker game, only a few moments passed before Madeline emerged from the house and made a beeline for her car, which was parked in the driveway. She looked like a woman on a mission. After she backed the car out onto the street and peeled away, the team sprang into action. They followed Madeline's car, Johnny's erratic driving making Hayley nauseated as she was tossed around in the back of the van from his hairpin turns and swerves.

"Do you even have a license?" she snapped after a particularly sharp turn.

"Of course," Johnny said, looking offended.

After a few tense minutes, they hit pay dirt. Madeline's car pulled up to a modest house, one that looked remarkably familiar to Hayley, because she had been here before. When Madeline stepped out of her car, she was greeted at the door by a man.

Hayley's breath caught when she realized who it was.

Alex.

Emma Lane's boyfriend.

Madeline and Alex embraced briefly before he pulled her inside, the door shutting firmly behind them.

"Holy . . . ," Sarah whispered, staring wide-eyed out the window.

Hayley leaned back against the van, her mind racing. This changed everything.

Alex was not just Emma's grieving boyfriend; he was the man Madeline had been having an affair with. And now, more than ever, Hayley was certain they were connected to Emma's murder.

She turned to the group, her expression grim. "We need to figure out what's really going on here. And fast."

Chapter Nine

Hayley pushed open the glass door of Nature's Nook, the only health food store in Bar Harbor. The faint scent of eucalyptus and lemongrass greeted her, mingling with the hum of a soft indie playlist piping through the overhead speakers. Shelves were stacked with neatly arranged boxes of herbal teas, colorful jars of organic honey, and an array of vitamins and supplements that all promised to change your life.

She spotted Alex in the middle of an aisle, crouched down and stocking jars of almond butter on a lower shelf. His slumped shoulders and slow movements screamed exhaustion, and Hayley almost felt bad for what she was about to do.

But Emma Lane's death was too important to tiptoe around.

Grabbing a bag of chia seeds as a prop, Hayley approached with what she hoped was a casual smile. "Hey there, Alex. Didn't know you worked here."

Alex glanced up, startled, then quickly masked his surprise with a wary frown. "Hayley. What are you doing here?"

"Trying to eat better," she replied, shaking the bag of

chia seeds for emphasis. "Figured I'd start with some superfoods or whatever you call this stuff."

Alex's brow arched skeptically as he stood, brushing his hands off on his khakis. "Really? I've read your columns. You're more butter, sugar, and carbs than kale smoothies and avocado toast."

Hayley sighed, dropping the act and putting the bag back on the shelf. "Fine, you caught me. I'm not here for chia seeds. I'm here to talk about Madeline Petty."

Alex froze, his jaw tightening. "I don't know what you're talking about."

"Sure you don't," Hayley said, folding her arms. "I saw her at your cottage last night. If you're not having an affair with her, then what was it about? I don't see you two traveling in the same social circles."

Alex's face flushed red, and his eyes darted toward a middle-aged woman lingering nearby with a basket full of quinoa and plant-based protein powder. "Can we not do this here?" he hissed. "Come on. Outside."

The back of Nature's Nook was nothing more than a small delivery area, cluttered with pallets of boxes labeled *organic* and *gluten-free*. A couple of seagulls squawked from a dumpster nearby. Alex leaned against the brick wall, crossing his arms tightly over his chest.

"You're *spying* on me now?" he asked, his voice sharp with accusation.

"I'm trying to find out what happened to Emma," Hayley replied evenly. "Someone put poison in her perfume. If it wasn't you, maybe it was the woman you were sneaking around with behind her back. She could have gotten jealous, wanted you all to herself, and was willing to do whatever it took to eliminate the competition."

"This isn't a telenovela, Hayley! Stuff like that doesn't happen here in Bar Harbor."

"You'd be surprised. Okay then, enlighten me."

Alex flinched, running a hand through his disheveled hair. "I swear, it wasn't like that. Emma and I were having problems. She was so obsessed with her work that it felt like I didn't even exist anymore. I'd spend my nights alone with Lucky, trying to convince myself that things would get better, but they didn't."

"So you turned to *Madeline*?" Hayley pressed.

Alex sighed, his shoulders slumping. "I started volunteering at the town office. I thought getting involved in local politics might give me some direction. Keep me busy. I don't get a lot of inspiration from this assistant manager job."

"And that's how you came to meet Madeline?"

"The clerk in charge of interns assigned me to her office. Madeline . . . she's this confident, powerful woman. She made me feel important at a time when I felt invisible at home. I just got caught up in it. We were working late one night, we both reached for a file at the same time, our hands touched, we just kind of looked at each other, it had been building up for weeks . . ."

"And one thing led to another, as they say."

"Yeah, I'm not proud of it. But it didn't mean anything, Hayley. It was just a stupid mistake."

"Did Emma know?"

"No. She never knew," Alex said firmly.

"She was investigating Madeline. You were having an affair with her. How could she not find out? I did with very little effort, I might add."

"I'm positive she didn't have a clue. It was over by the time Emma was poisoned. I had already quit the internship and was picking up more hours here at the store. There was nothing to find out at that point."

"Did Madeline end it?"

"No, it was me. I broke up with Madeline as soon as Emma told me she wanted to try again. She was my whole world, Hayley. I never stopped loving her."

"How did Madeline react?"

He shrugged. "I don't know. She seemed okay with it. We were both always worried we were going to get caught. I'm guessing she was as relieved as I was that it was over and done with and we could stop taking risks."

"If what you say is true, and it truly is over with Madeline, then why on earth was she at your place last night?"

"She's panicking," Alex admitted. "Ever since you started asking her questions, she thinks someone's going to find out about the affair and it'll ruin her career. She came over to talk, but I told her she needs to let it go. We both agreed to keep our distance from each other and not make any further contact."

Hayley studied him closely, watching for any signs of dishonesty, but Alex seemed genuine. "Do you think Madeline could have had anything to do with Emma's death?"

Alex shook his head vehemently. "No. Madeline wouldn't . . . she couldn't. And I swear, I didn't even know Emma was working on a story about her. If I had, I would've told her everything."

Hayley exhaled, feeling the tension in her chest ease slightly. "I want to believe you, Alex. For Emma's sake."

"I loved her, Hayley," Alex said, his voice cracking. "I still do."

That evening, Hayley was in her kitchen, preparing a light and healthy dinner for herself and Bruce. She had promised to cut back on their indulgent meals for a while—after all, both of them had been making noises about needing to lose a few pounds. Tonight's menu was roasted salmon with lemon and dill, steamed asparagus, and a quinoa salad with fresh herbs and a light vinaigrette. She had been inspired by her visit to Nature's Nook earlier in the day and didn't want to leave without buying a few items.

Leroy sat nearby, his small body tense with excitement as he waited for anything edible to fall from the counter. "No salmon for you, buddy," Hayley said, tossing him a baby carrot as a consolation prize.

As the salmon sizzled in the oven, Leroy's ears perked, and he let out a sharp bark. Hayley glanced out the window above the sink, squinting into the darkness of the backyard. For a moment, she thought she saw a shadow moving near the fence, but when she looked again, it was gone.

"Probably just a raccoon," she muttered to her dog, turning back to the salad. But Leroy, who was up on his hind legs in the dining room, staring out the window, barked again, this time louder, and Hayley felt a prickle of unease. She wiped her hands on a towel, grabbed a flashlight, and stepped outside.

The air was crisp and quiet. Hayley scanned the yard, her flashlight beam sweeping across the fence. Nothing seemed out of place—except for a familiar pink delivery truck parked near the street.

"Mrs. Bittersweet's truck?" Hayley said to herself, frowning.

What was it doing here?

The sound of footsteps on gravel made her spin around, but she saw no one.

"Bruce?"

She had been expecting him home at any minute.

She could see Leroy still watching from the dining room window, paws on the sill.

Her pulse quickened, and she hurried back inside, locking the door behind her.

Just as she returned to the kitchen, Leroy barked again, this time at the front door. Hayley turned and froze. Standing on her porch, glaring through the window, was Lance.

Her heart raced as she grabbed a meat mallet from the counter and marched down the hallway. She flung the door open and glared at him. "What are you doing here?"

Lance flinched, his gaze darting nervously. "I-I'm making a delivery," he stammered, holding up a large wicker basket wrapped in cellophane. "Aunt Marion . . . I mean, Mrs. Bittersweet wanted to apologize for snapping at you the other day. She made this for you."

Hayley eyed the basket warily. It was filled with an assortment of goodies: the large chocolate bunny she had ordered for Bruce, scented candles, a bottle of her favorite wine, and other treats. "You couldn't just leave it on the porch?"

"I didn't want it to get stolen," Lance said, his voice shaky. "I went around back to see if there was a safer place, but then I saw you were home."

Hayley hesitated before taking the basket. "Thanks. Tell Mrs. Bittersweet I appreciate it."

Lance lingered, his unsettling gaze holding hers. "You're welcome," he said finally, before retreating to the truck.

Hayley didn't close the door until she saw him drive away.

Bruce arrived home a few minutes later, letting out an exaggerated groan as he kicked off his shoes. He spied the gift basket, which she had left on the living room coffee table. "I walked home. That means I'm entitled to some chocolate bunny, right?"

"Not until the weekend," Hayley scolded, playfully swatting his hand away. "We're trying to be good, remember?"

Bruce held up his hands in mock surrender. "Fine. I'll wait." But as he turned toward the living room, Hayley caught the slight smirk on his face and suspected he was crossing his fingers behind his back.

As they ate dinner, Hayley filled Bruce in on her conversation with Alex. He listened intently, nodding thoughtfully as he cut into his salmon. "So Alex admits to the affair. That doesn't clear him. If anything, it gives him motive."

"Or it gives Madeline motive," Hayley countered. "Alex told me she's terrified of the affair coming out and becoming public knowledge."

"And Lance?" Bruce asked, setting his fork down. "What's his deal?"

"I don't know yet," Hayley admitted. "But I think Mrs. Bittersweet is protecting him for some reason. And I need to find out why."

The case was getting more complicated by the minute, but Hayley was determined to get to the truth—no matter how many secrets she had to uncover.

Chapter Ten

Hayley pulled open the door of Bittersweet Confections and was immediately greeted by the warm scent of caramel and chocolate. It was so inviting, it almost made her forget why she was here.

Almost.

"Mrs. Bittersweet?" Hayley called, stepping inside.

The bell above the door tinkled cheerfully, but the mood in the shop was anything but.

". . . You can't keep ignoring it, Marion!" Les Dobbs's voice boomed from the back of the shop.

Hayley froze in the doorway, her hand instinctively reaching for the strap of her purse. She had never heard Les raise his voice before. Normally, he was as mild as a bowl of unsalted mashed potatoes.

Mrs. Bittersweet's voice, shrill and defensive, shot back. "I told you, Les. I'll handle it!"

"Handle it? You've been saying that for weeks! The whole neighborhood stinks. It's disgusting!"

Hayley peeked around a towering display of Easter baskets and saw Les standing with his arms crossed, his face as red as a boiled lobster. Mrs. Bittersweet, with her arms akimbo and flour dusting her apron, looked just as furious.

"Don't you dare take that tone with me, young man," Mrs. Bittersweet snapped.

"Young man?" Les sputtered. "I'm *sixty-three*!"

"Still young enough to mind your own business!" she shot back.

"It is my business when your leaking septic tank ruins the air in my backyard," Les growled. "You either get a plumber out here or—"

"Or *what*?" Mrs. Bittersweet cut in. "You'll stop buying my peanut butter fudge? *Please*." She picked up a cellophane-wrapped tray of fudge and held it out with a syrupy smile. "Let's not fight. Here. A peace offering."

Les swatted the tray aside, sending it skidding across the counter. "I don't want your fudge, Marion! I want you to fix your septic tank!"

With that, he spun on his heel and stormed past Hayley, muttering something under his breath about hiring lawyers.

Mrs. Bittersweet spotted Hayley standing awkwardly near the entrance. For a brief moment, her expression shifted—wide eyes, tight lips, a flicker of something like fear—but she quickly smoothed it over with a saccharine smile.

"Well, if it isn't Hayley Powell! What a pleasant surprise." She wiped her hands on her apron and approached, ignoring the ringing bell as Les slammed the door behind him.

Hayley forced a smile, deciding to play it cool. "Hi, Mrs. Bittersweet. I just stopped by to thank you for the lovely Easter basket. It was such a thoughtful gesture. Especially with all those little extras you included."

"You're very welcome, dear," Mrs. Bittersweet said, her tone warm but slightly brittle. "I do love to spread a little sweetness around the neighborhood."

Hayley glanced toward the door. "Everything okay?"

Mrs. Bittersweet waved her hand dismissively. "You know how it is. Some people have nothing better to do than complain. Now, what can I get you? A box of truffles? A slice of fudge, perhaps?"

"No, I'm all set," Hayley said, her curiosity burning. "I should let you get back to your evening. I just wanted to stop by and say thanks."

Mrs. Bittersweet beamed. "You're too kind. Now, give my regards to Bruce, will you?"

"Will do," Hayley said, but as she left the shop, the exchange with Les replayed in her mind. She spotted him stomping toward his house across the street, his hands still balled into fists.

"Les! Wait!" she called.

He stopped, turned, and threw up his hands. "*What?*"

Hayley glanced over her shoulder to make sure Mrs. Bittersweet was not at the door listening, then lowered her voice. "Why do you think she's so reluctant to let anyone poke around her backyard? I mean, it's just a septic tank, right?"

Les snorted. "Who knows? Maybe she's got a dead body buried back there."

Hayley laughed nervously, but the joke hit too close to home. Images of Truffle digging up bones flashed through her mind, and suddenly Mrs. Bittersweet's resistance seemed a whole lot less innocent.

By the time Hayley got home, the house smelled faintly of takeout, and Bruce was sitting at the kitchen table, an innocent look plastered on his face as he carefully peeled the pink foil from the large chocolate bunny Mrs. Bittersweet had made specially for him.

"Bruce!" Hayley's voice was sharp as a knife.

He froze, mid-peel. "What?"

"You promised to wait until the weekend!" She marched over and snatched the bunny out of his hands.

"It's not like I ate it," Bruce said defensively.

"Not *yet*," Hayley muttered, cradling the bunny protectively. "You have no self-control. And don't think I don't know you've been snooping around the house for hidden sweets. You're worse than a kid looking for Christmas presents!"

Bruce raised an eyebrow. "And what are you up to, exactly?

"What do you mean?"

"I saw you going into Mrs. Bittersweet's shop when I picked up my Thai takeout."

"I was just thanking her for the Easter basket."

Bruce smiled skeptically. "Oh, please. Sneaking around, asking questions . . . I know that look, Hayley. You're plotting something."

"I am not," she said, avoiding his gaze. She marched over to the coatrack to retrieve Leroy's leash. "I'm going to take Leroy for a walk."

"I already did."

"Well, like us, he's getting a little pudgy. Some extra steps will do him a world of good."

Bruce folded his arms. "If you're going to poke around Mrs. Bittersweet's place, I'm coming with you. No way are you getting yourself into trouble alone."

Before Hayley could protest, the police scanner crackled to life.

"Possible break-in reported at Cool as a Moose gift shop on Main Street. Unit responding."

Bruce sighed and grabbed his coat. "Of course. I'm sure their son just tripped the alarm again, but duty calls." He turned to Hayley. "Now promise me you'll stay away from Mrs. Bittersweet's shop."

Hayley plastered on her best innocent smile. "Cross my heart."

Bruce gave her a long look before heading out the door.

Of course, just as he had done when promising to steer clear of the chocolate bunny until the weekend, Hayley had crossed her fingers behind her back.

As soon as he was gone, Hayley darted to the basement, carrying the Easter basket. She shoved it onto the highest shelf, muttering, "Not that it'll stop him for long."

Then, with Leroy's leash in hand and her scarf wrapped snugly around her neck, she slipped out into the cold spring night.

Hayley crouched low behind the wooden fence across the street from Mrs. Bittersweet's shop, shivering in the brisk night air. Leroy sat obediently beside her, his leash looped around her wrist, his tail wagging ever so slightly as he sniffed the April breeze.

The shop's front windows were dark, but Hayley knew better than to assume the house above it was entirely still. She pulled her scarf tighter around her neck, her breath condensing in the chilly air, and whispered to Leroy, "We just have to wait a little longer."

Her patience paid off. After several minutes, the side door of the shop creaked open, and a tired-looking Lance stepped out. He was wearing a thick jacket and a Boston Red Sox cap, and the set of his shoulders suggested he had had enough of whatever the day had thrown at him.

"He's going to Drinks Like a Fish," Hayley muttered to Leroy as they watched Lance pull out his keys, climb into the shop's pink delivery truck, and drive away. "Probably needs a stiff drink after dealing with his aunt all day."

Once Lance's truck disappeared around the corner, Hayley turned her attention back to the second-story window. A faint light glowed from within, and soon enough, Mrs. Bittersweet appeared, her face partially obscured by a layer of cold cream. She stood at her vanity, dabbing carefully at her cheeks with a tissue, her fluffy pink robe hanging loosely around her shoulders.

Hayley waited, her nerves buzzing as she kept her eyes on the window. A few moments later, the light flickered off, plunging the upstairs into darkness.

"It's now or never," she murmured, giving Leroy a quick pat on the head.

They crossed the street quickly, and Hayley guided Leroy to the back of the shop, her steps cautious and deliberate. The stench of sewage grew stronger with each step, thick and putrid, making her wrinkle her nose. She kept low, her heart pounding, and made her way to the section of the yard where Truffle had previously unearthed that suspicious-looking bone.

"Stay quiet, Leroy," she whispered, crouching down as she began brushing away dirt with her gloved hands.

Leroy, however, was distracted. His ears perked up, and he sniffed the air excitedly, his tail wagging faster. Before Hayley could stop him, the doggie door on the back of the house flapped open, and Truffle bounded out with a joyful yelp.

"Oh, no," Hayley muttered.

Truffle spotted Leroy immediately, and with a delighted bark, the two dogs began chasing each other around the yard. Leroy tugged his leash from Hayley's wrist, and she stumbled forward, nearly falling face-first into the dirt.

"Leroy!" she hissed, scrambling to her feet. "Come back here!"

The dogs ignored her, barking and yipping as they raced

in wide, gleeful circles. Leroy's leash dragged behind him, tangling briefly around a bush before whipping free again.

Truffle barked louder, egging Leroy on, and the two animals seemed determined to make as much noise as possible.

Hayley lunged for Leroy's leash, but her foot caught on a loose root, and she went sprawling to the ground. Her hands sank into the damp soil, and as she pushed herself up, she felt something hard beneath her palm.

She paused, her heart skipping a beat.

A bone.

This one was large, far too large to belong to an animal. Hayley stared at it for a moment, her pulse racing, before quickly wrapping it in her scarf.

"Truffle! Shut up!" Les Dobbs's angry voice bellowed from the other side of the fence.

Hayley froze, clutching the bone tightly.

Leroy and Truffle paused their game momentarily, their tails wagging, but Truffle let out another excited bark.

"Truffle!" Mrs. Bittersweet's sharp voice cut through the night as the upstairs light snapped on.

Hayley's breath caught in her throat. She pressed herself against the side of the house, her back to the wall, as Mrs. Bittersweet's window creaked open.

"Truffle, what's gotten into you?" Mrs. Bittersweet called, leaning out the window. Her pink robe glowed faintly in the moonlight, and the cold cream on her face gave her an eerie, ghostly appearance.

Leroy panted loudly beside Hayley, and she pressed her hand over his snout, trying to keep him quiet.

Truffle, oblivious to the tension, barked happily and wagged his tail.

A rustling noise caught everyone's attention. From the shadows near the fence, a squirrel darted out, its bushy tail twitching as it scurried along the fence line.

Mrs. Bittersweet groaned. "A squirrel? Really, Truffle? You're waking up the whole neighborhood over a squirrel?"

Les's voice erupted again from the other side of the fence. "Control your dog, Marion, or I will!"

"Mind your own business, Les!" Mrs. Bittersweet snapped before slamming her window shut.

Hayley exhaled shakily, her heart hammering in her chest.

Truffle, however, wasn't done. The dog continued sniffing around, barking intermittently as if he could sense something was amiss.

"Come on, Leroy," Hayley whispered, tugging him gently toward the gate. She moved as quickly and quietly as she could, her every nerve on edge, the bone wrapped tightly in her scarf.

When she finally slipped through the gate and into the safety of the alley, she let out a shaky breath, clutching the bone as if it were evidence in a case she had not yet fully understood.

She knew one thing for certain: This bone was not an animal's. And if her instincts were right, Mrs. Bittersweet's backyard held more than just a septic tank problem.

Island Food & Spirits
by
Hayley Powell

I just love flipping through my old photo albums—every picture holds a memory that feels like it happened just yesterday. And some? Well, some are just too hilarious to ever forget. Case in point: an Easter celebration from years ago that turned into the most chaotic, side-splitting holiday disaster (or masterpiece, depending on how you look at it) in Bar Harbor history.

Randy and Sergio had decided to throw a grand Easter brunch and egg hunt party at their gorgeous oceanfront estate. But let's be real—they were more excited about the egg hunt and the elaborate dessert buffet than the kids were. My brother and Sergio are just big kids at heart, and if I didn't keep them in check, they'd be spoiling my kids rotten all year long. We compromised on holidays and birthdays, but even then, my living room often looked like a toy store explosion.

The day before the big event, they recruited my kids, Gemma and Dustin, to help dye dozens of hard-boiled eggs. By the time the kids got home, they couldn't stop chattering about the prizes for the most eggs found and—most important—the ice-cream sundae bar. I was lucky to get them to bed that night!

The next day, Randy and Sergio had truly outdone themselves. Their outdoor space looked like the Easter bunny himself had worked overtime—pastel colors everywhere, adorable stuffed rabbits, and helium-filled balloons tied to every available post. After indulging in a delicious brunch, my best friends, Mona and Liddy, and I grabbed our cocktails and settled into lawn chairs to watch the kids prepare for the big egg hunt. The sun was shining, the ocean was sparkling, and the seagulls were crying overhead. "This is the perfect day," I sighed, raising my glass in a toast.

Then the chaos began.

Sergio, being his dramatic self, kicked off the hunt with his police-issued bullhorn. The kids took off squealing with excitement, baskets in hand. But just as the laughter filled the air, the screeches of the circling seagulls grew louder. One swooped down, snatched an egg, and took off.

Mona let out a yelp. "Did you see that?!"

Before we could answer, more seagulls dove from the sky, snatching eggs from the lawn, baskets, and—horrifyingly—a small child's hand! Suddenly, the joyful egg hunt turned into a scene from Alfred Hitchcock's *The Birds.* Kids were screaming, parents were running, and the gulls were relentless. And then, as if things couldn't get worse, some of the seagulls lost their grip on the eggs midflight, sending the eggs plummeting to the ground. Eggs were splattering everywhere—on the rocks, on the grass, and in one unfortunate case, bouncing right off Randy's head.

"Hayley, it's an egg-plosion!" Randy yelled, trying to duck the incoming fire.

Through tears of laughter, I managed to shout back, "No, it's an egg-vasion!" We collapsed onto the lawn, gasping for breath as eggs rained down around us.

Just when we thought it couldn't get any worse, there was a sudden, deafening bang. Silence. The seagulls scattered. We turned to see Sergio, looking smug, with a starter pistol in his hand.

"Situation under control," he declared.

As order was restored, the kids happily settled down with their ice-cream sundaes, and we adults refilled our cocktails.

Raising my glass to Randy, I grinned. "Eggscellent party, brother dear." And once again, we collapsed into laughter.

To celebrate Easter without an unexpected egg-vasion, try these delicious recipes.

Easter Brunch Punch

A refreshing, fruity cocktail perfect for sipping while watching an egg hunt (preferably minus the seagulls).

Ingredients

2 cups raspberry vodka
3 cups strawberry juice
3 cups pineapple juice
2 cups lemon-lime soda
½ cup sliced pineapple
6 strawberries, sliced
1 cup raspberries
2 limes, sliced

The day before, freeze the fruit and chill the rest of the ingredients.

On the day, mix the chilled juices and vodka in a punch bowl. Add ice.

Right before serving, gently mix in the lemon-lime soda. Add the frozen fruit.

Ladle the punch into glasses. Cheers!

Sheet Pan Omelette

A simple way to make a delicious, customizable omelette without standing over the stove.

Ingredients

1 Tablespoon butter
½ pound bacon, cooked and crumbled
1 cup chopped baby spinach
4 green onions, chopped
1½ cups shredded cheddar cheese
12 large eggs
½ cup milk or half-and-half
1 teaspoon salt
1 teaspoon pepper
1 teaspoon granulated garlic
1 teaspoon onion powder
Hot sauce, to taste (optional)

Preheat oven to 350°F. Grease a 15 × 10 inch jelly roll pan with the butter.

Add the bacon, spinach, green onions, and half the cheese evenly to the pan.

In a bowl, whisk the eggs, milk, salt, pepper, garlic, onion powder, and hot sauce. Pour this mixture over the cheese in the pan.

Sprinkle with the remaining cheese.

Bake for 20 minutes. If still jiggly, bake 5 more minutes until set.

Slice into squares and serve with toast or fresh fruit. Enjoy!

Wishing you an egg-straordinary Easter with plenty of fun, food, and hopefully fewer seagulls! Cheers!

Chapter Eleven

Hayley stepped out of her front door, her shoulder bag slung casually over one arm. The bone, still wrapped tightly in her scarf, was snugly in her bag but was too long not to be sticking out. Leroy wagged his tail from behind the screen door, watching her leave.

"Be good, Leroy," she said absently, her mind racing. She needed to get to Mount Desert Island High School to see Calvin Kramer. If anyone could confirm what she had found in Mrs. Bittersweet's backyard, it was him.

As she turned to lock the door, a Bar Harbor Police cruiser pulled into her driveway.

Hayley's heart skipped a beat.

Sergio.

The officer stepped out of the car, his uniform crisp, his expression a mix of curiosity and suspicion. He adjusted his belt as he approached, his dark eyes narrowing slightly.

"Morning, Hayley," he said, his tone friendly but cautious.

"Morning, Sergio." Hayley forced a smile, discreetly tightening her grip on her bag.

"What's that you've got there?" Sergio asked, nodding toward the bulging bag with a large object wrapped in wool in plain view.

She was not prepared to clue him in on the bone until she was sure it belonged to a human. Hayley's mind raced. "This?" She patted the bag and laughed nervously. "It's, uh . . . a ham!"

"A *ham*?" Sergio raised an eyebrow.

"For the restaurant," she added quickly, her smile widening.

"Wrapped in a scarf?"

Hayley blinked. "It's . . . very cold ham."

Sergio tilted his head, clearly unconvinced. "Right. Anyway," he said, dropping the subject but not the suspicion in his tone, "I came by to update you on the case."

"Case?" Hayley said, feigning innocence.

Sergio gave her a pointed look. "Emma. We're intensifying our focus on Alex."

Hayley frowned. "Why? What's changed?"

"Word got out about Alex's affair," Sergio said. "A town employee came forward. They told us they witnessed . . . let's say, inappropriate behavior during Alex's time at the town office. Apparently, you and Madeline Petty were also overheard discussing it a few days ago."

Hayley winced. "Okay, yes, I knew about the affair. But I wasn't hiding it, Sergio. I just . . . I wasn't sure it mattered."

Sergio crossed his arms. "You weren't sure it mattered? You don't think that's relevant to the investigation?"

"I didn't want to make baseless accusations," Hayley said defensively. "You've always told me a million times not to jump to conclusions."

"Still," Sergio said, his tone firm, "you should have come to us when you found out. That's practically obscuring justice!"

"Obstructing justice?" Hayley offered.

Sergio nodded. "Yes, that."

Again, English?

Sergio's second language.

Hayley sighed. "I'm sorry, Sergio. I just . . . I wanted to be absolutely sure before saying anything. Besides, I don't think Alex is guilty. In my heart, I know he didn't do this."

Sergio's expression softened slightly. "Hayley, Alex had the most to gain from Emma's death. And don't forget, he was the last one to handle that perfume bottle."

"No, he wasn't," Hayley said quickly.

Sergio frowned. "What do you mean?"

"Mrs. Bittersweet was the last person to handle it," Hayley said. "She's the one who prepared the Easter basket for Emma."

"Mrs. Bittersweet?" Sergio said skeptically. "Why would she have any reason to harm Emma?"

"I don't know," Hayley admitted. "But I'm going to find out. Trust me."

Sergio eyed her warily. "You won't let this go, will you?"

Hayley shook her head. "Not until I have answers."

With a sigh, Sergio stepped back toward his cruiser. "Just don't do anything reckless, Hayley."

"Me? Reckless?" Hayley gave him her most innocent smile. "Never."

Sergio rolled his eyes and moved his cruiser so that Hayley could back out of her driveway. As soon as he was gone, she climbed into her car and set off for the high school.

Hayley stepped cautiously into Mount Desert Island High School's biology lab, instantly hit by the smell of formaldehyde and the unmistakable tang of adolescence. Calvin Kramer stood at the front of the room, wearing a lab coat that had seen better days, his hair sticking up in its usual tousled style.

The students were gathered around lab tables, latex gloves on, scalpels in hand, and fetal pigs pinned to dissecting trays in front of them.

"All right, folks," Calvin said with his trademark humor. "Today we begin our grand exploration of the pig. Or, as I like to call it, Pork Anatomy 101. If you feel queasy, there's a trash can in the corner. If you feel guilty, talk to the ethics department. If you feel fascinated, you might just have a future in science."

A girl with dark braids at the nearest table raised her hand. "Mr. Kramer, I can't do this. It's wrong to carve open a living thing."

Calvin smiled patiently. "Well, first of all, it's not living, Keisha. The pig is deceased. Second of all, this is how we learn. You'll see the organs, the systems, the miraculous design of life itself."

Keisha scowled. "You know what I mean. It's still *wrong*."

Her lab partner, a lanky boy with glasses, rolled his eyes. "Keisha, it's dead, okay? It doesn't care what you do to it."

"*You* don't care," Keisha shot back. "*I* care."

Calvin stepped in before it could escalate further. "How about this? You observe while your partner does the cutting. Deal?"

Keisha crossed her arms. "Fine. But I'm not touching that scalpel."

At another table, a boy suddenly gagged and his face turned pale. He lurched out of his chair and stumbled toward the trash can, emptying his breakfast in a dramatic heave. The sound was enough to make half the class groan and turn away from their pigs.

Calvin clapped his hands once. "Okay, who wants to be a hero? Matt, take your buddy to the nurse's office."

The boy named Matt reluctantly stood, hoisting his queasy lab partner to his feet. "Come on, Jake. Try not to hurl again on the way, cause if you do, I'll be next!"

"Thanks, Matt," Calvin said, as Jake muttered a weak groan.

Hayley could not help but smile as she watched from the doorway. The chaos reminded her of her own days in high school, though Calvin's freewheeling teaching style was definitely more entertaining than anything she remembered.

The bell rang, and the students hurried to clean up and head out. Calvin called after them, "Read chapter twelve tonight! Reflection paper due tomorrow. And no, you can't write about how gross this is."

Once the last student left, Calvin turned toward the door and spotted Hayley. His face lit up.

"Well, well, Hayley Powell in my humble lab! To what do I owe the honor?"

Hayley stepped inside, smiling. "Thought I'd drop by and see what my favorite biology teacher is up to."

Calvin chuckled. "Still dissecting pigs, as you can see. But let's not talk about me. How about you? Still writing witty columns and solving crimes in your spare time?"

Hayley grinned. "Something like that. Actually, I have a favor to ask, if you don't mind."

"Anything," Calvin said warmly. Then his expression turned sheepish. "But first, can I just say thanks again? For being so nice at the last high school reunion?"

"Oh, Calvin," Hayley said, waving it off. "That was years ago."

"Still," he said, rubbing the back of his neck. "I was drunk, I blurted out my whole 'I had a secret crush on you' thing, and you could have laughed in my face. But you didn't."

Hayley smiled fondly. "I was flattered. And honestly, I

kind of suspected. I remember you trying to hold my hand when we walked to the bus stop every morning. Fourth grade, maybe?"

Calvin laughed, his cheeks reddening. "Wow, busted. So"—he leaned on his desk—"what brings you here?"

Hayley set her bag down on the table and pulled out the scarf-wrapped bundle. Calvin's humor evaporated as he watched her unwrap it to reveal the bone.

His eyes widened.

"Is that what I think it is?"

"You tell me," Hayley said, pushing it toward him.

Calvin picked it up carefully, his face growing more serious by the second. "It's human," he said after a moment. "A femur, to be exact."

Hayley's stomach tightened. "I was afraid you'd say that."

"Where did you get this?" Calvin asked, his tone low.

Hayley hesitated. "I can't say just yet. But I need you to keep this between us for now."

Calvin gave her a long look before nodding. "You've got my word."

At the Bar Harbor police station, Hayley unwrapped the bone once more and laid it on top of Sergio's desk.

"You're not going to believe this," she said.

Sergio leaned forward, his expression skeptical but intrigued. "Try me."

Hayley took a deep breath. "I think this belongs to Dewey Dratch. I don't believe he left town like everyone says. I think his wife, Marion, aka Mrs. Bittersweet, killed him and buried him in the backyard. Which is where I found this."

"You were digging around in Mrs. Bittersweet's backyard? That's trespassing, Hayley."

"Technically, no. Our dogs are friends. We had a late-night playdate and I just happened to stumble across this . . ."

Sergio raised an eyebrow.

"While digging around in her backyard," Hayley admitted. Then she slapped her hands on his desk. "She did it, Sergio. I know it."

Sergio stared at her, his jaw tightening. "That's . . . a serious accusation, Hayley."

Before Hayley could respond, the front door swung open, and Sergeant Earl and Mona walked in, laughing about something as they carried to-go cups of coffee. Earl's smile vanished as his eyes landed on the bone.

"Is that what I think it is?" Earl asked, his face going pale.

"It's a human bone," Hayley confirmed.

Earl swayed on the spot, his eyes fluttering. "I think I need to—" He did not have the chance to finish his sentence before collapsing backward, his coffee cup flying out of his hand.

Mona darted forward, catching him just before he hit the floor. She shook her head, rolling her eyes. "My dashing brave hero," she deadpanned.

Hayley bit back a laugh as Sergio sighed, pinching the bridge of his nose. "All right, Hayley, I'll send it out for DNA testing. But even if it is Dewey Dratch, we'd need something to compare it with."

"Like DNA from a relative," Hayley said quickly. "What about his nephew, Lance?"

Sergio crossed his arms. "You think Lance would willingly help us prove his uncle was murdered?"

"No," Hayley admitted. "But if anyone can get him to, it's me."

Sergio gave her a skeptical look. "Just don't do anything crazy, Hayley."

Hayley grinned. "When have I ever done anything crazy?"

Mona snorted. "Do you want that list alphabetically or chronologically?"

Chapter Twelve

The smell of leftovers still lingered in the kitchen as Hayley finished loading the dishwasher. Bruce had disappeared somewhere upstairs after dinner, leaving Hayley to clean up while trying to ignore the familiar gnaw of worry in her stomach.

She was heading out soon to Drinks Like a Fish to meet Liddy and gather DNA from Lance, but her instincts told her she needed to keep tabs on Bruce first. Sure enough, just as she grabbed her coat, she heard the sound of rummaging from the hallway closet.

"What are you doing?" she called, leaning against the doorway.

Bruce's voice came back muffled. "Looking for something."

Hayley smirked. "Let me guess. The notorious chocolate Easter bunny?"

Bruce poked his head out of the closet, a pair of socks in one hand and a guilty expression on his face. "What? No. I'm looking for, uh, a missing sock."

Hayley raised an eyebrow. "You mean the sock you conveniently misplaced after I hid that Easter basket?"

"I'm not looking for the basket," Bruce insisted, though his eyes darted suspiciously toward the stairs.

Hayley sighed. "Fine. Here's the deal. If you can find it, you can eat it. But no hints from me. Consider it a scavenger hunt. At least you'll get some exercise."

Bruce grinned. "Challenge accepted. I'll start with the attic."

"Good luck with that," Hayley muttered under her breath as she grabbed her bag. She knew she had bought herself some time. The basket was hidden in the basement, and it would take Bruce all night to search every nook and cranny of the house.

Hayley swept into Drinks Like a Fish and noted that the crowd was strictly locals—fishermen swapping tales at the bar, a group of retirees huddled around a dartboard, and Liddy waving at her as she stood next to a table near the back, where Earl and Mona sat together.

"Look at them!" Liddy cooed as Hayley approached. "Aren't they adorable?"

Mona shot her a warning glare. "Don't make me clock you, Liddy. You'd be well advised to leave us be."

Earl beamed. "I think it's sweet. Hey, Mona, let's take a selfie."

Mona groaned, dragging her palm down her face. "No, Earl. We don't need to broadcast our relationship all over social media."

"But you're beautiful," Earl insisted. "I want the whole world to know I scored such a wonderful girlfriend."

Liddy leaned in, smirking. "Come on, Mona, say something nice to the guy."

Mona rolled her eyes and finally muttered, "Yeah, you're alright too, Earl."

Liddy clutched her chest dramatically. "What a poet! True love! I think I'm gonna cry."

"Would you shut up?" Mona growled, though the faintest of smiles tugged at her lips.

Hayley cut in. "Liddy, focus. We've got a job to do." She nodded toward the bar, where Lance sat nursing what looked like a rum and Coke.

"Right," Liddy said, suddenly all business. "Leave him to me. You're looking at the queen of distraction."

Hayley watched as Liddy adjusted her sweater and sashayed over to Lance, her confident smile beaming.

"Lance!" Liddy said, sliding onto the stool next to him. "This is one of my favorite songs! Dance with me!"

Lance blinked at her, confused. "There's no dance floor here."

"Oh, come on," Liddy insisted, grabbing his arm. "It's a slow song—classic 1980s. We don't need a dance floor. Just you, me, and the magic of Lionel Richie."

Before Lance could object, Liddy tugged him off the stool. The bar erupted in chuckles and whistles as Liddy spun him around near the jukebox, swaying dramatically to the music.

Meanwhile, Hayley edged closer to the bar. Lance's glass was sitting within arm's reach, still wet with condensation. She reached for it, but just as her fingers brushed the rim, Randy's voice boomed from behind the bar.

"Hayley Powell! Are you trying to steal my glassware?"

Startled, Hayley fumbled the glass. It slipped from her hands and shattered on the floor. The bar erupted in laughter.

Hayley forced a sheepish smile. "I'll pay for that."

"You bet you will," Randy said with a grin, handing her a broom and dustpan.

While she cleaned up, Liddy pulled Lance closer, one

hand on his shoulder and the other dramatically clutching her chest.

"Oh, Lance," she said, loudly enough for everyone to hear. "You have such strong arms. Don't you think I'm the best dancer you've ever met?"

"Uh . . ." Lance muttered, his face reddening as Liddy leaned in and kissed him lightly on the lips.

Hayley seized the moment. With Lance thoroughly distracted, she darted toward his coat hanging on a nearby chair and rummaged through the pockets. Her fingers brushed something soft—a crumpled napkin. She pulled it out and unwrapped it, finding a wad of used chewing gum inside.

Perfect.

After pocketing the gum, Hayley shot Liddy a thumbs-up.

Liddy instantly released Lance with a dramatic sigh, and whispered his ear, "Thanks for the memories."

Then she returned to the bar.

"I owe you one," Hayley whispered.

"You owe me ten," Liddy said, grinning.

The aroma of freshly brewed coffee filled the kitchen as Hayley leaned against the counter, sipping from her favorite mug. She glanced at the clock on the wall and shook her head. It was late enough that Bruce should have been in his office working on his column, but instead, muffled noises filtered up from the basement.

Hayley set down her coffee and walked over to the basement door, calling down, "Bruce? What are you doing down there?"

"Nothing!" came his suspiciously quick reply, followed by a loud thud and a muttered curse.

Hayley smirked. "That doesn't sound like nothing. Let me guess—you're still looking for the basket with the chocolate bunny."

"Nope," Bruce said, though his tone was defensive. "I'm, uh . . . reorganizing the storage bins."

"Uh-huh," Hayley said. "You realize I know you better than that, right?"

As Hayley descended the basement stairs, mug still in hand, she saw Bruce crouching near a stack of boxes, rummaging through one labeled *Holiday Decorations*. He straightened up, brushing dust off his jeans. "You're always saying the basement's a mess. I'm being productive."

"You're digging through tangled Christmas lights looking for a chocolate bunny," Hayley said, raising an eyebrow. "Just admit it."

Bruce put on his best innocent face. "Who, me? I told you, I'm not looking for the bunny. I gave up that mission last night."

Hayley leaned against the banister. "Fine. You don't have to admit it. But you're never going to find it."

"Oh, I'm going to find it," Bruce said with a grin, resuming his search. "And when I do find it, I'm eating that damn bunny. Fair and square. Just like you promised."

"*If* you find it," Hayley corrected. She took another sip of her coffee and watched as Bruce pulled another box off the shelf. "You know, I could just tell you where it is."

"Not a chance," Bruce said, now flipping through an old stack of magazines. "The hunt is half the fun."

Hayley chuckled. "Okay, Sherlock. But don't blame me if you end up buried under a pile of decorations."

"I'm being careful," Bruce said, though the precarious wobble of a stack of boxes nearby suggested otherwise.

Hayley shook her head, amused, and started back up the stairs. "Good luck, Bruce. You're going to need it."

She knew he was very close to finding it.

In fact, he was standing right in front of the shelf where she had hidden it behind some boxes.

As she hustled back up to the kitchen, she heard the faint crackle of the police scanner on the counter. She paused mid-sip when a voice came through, clear and urgent.

"All units, report of a trespasser at Bittersweet Confections."

Hayley's stomach dropped. She set her mug down and grabbed her coat, her heart already racing. She called down to Bruce. "I'm heading out!"

"Where are you going?" Bruce called from the basement.

"Mrs. Bittersweet's shop," Hayley called back. "There's something happening over there."

Bruce popped his head around the basement door, a box of tangled string lights in one hand. "Want me to come with you?"

"No," Hayley said quickly, forcing a smile. "You keep looking for that bunny. I'll be back soon."

Bruce gave her a mock salute, but as Hayley rushed out the door, her mind was already racing. Something told her this was more than just a trespassing incident. She had a bad feeling in her gut, and it was rarely wrong.

Hayley arrived at Bittersweet Confections to find the small candy shop's usually inviting atmosphere in chaos. A burly plumber stood outside his van, shouting at a police officer. Les Dobbs was arguing with Mrs. Bittersweet, who clutched her chest dramatically, teetering on the front step like a soap opera heroine in distress.

"I was hired to do a job!" the plumber bellowed, throwing his arms up. "That septic tank is a disaster waiting to happen!"

"You were trespassing!" Mrs. Bittersweet shrieked. "I don't care what he told you, you can't just dig up my property!"

"It's a health hazard, Marion!" Les snapped, his face red. "The whole street stinks because of you!"

"I'll have you arrested next!" Mrs. Bittersweet cried, pointing a trembling finger at Les.

Hayley stepped forward, her gaze narrowing on Mrs. Bittersweet. She looked pale and frightened as if she was consumed with worry.

"Are you okay?" Hayley asked, trying to cut through the noise.

Mrs. Bittersweet turned to Hayley, clutching her chest with one hand and fanning herself with the other. "Hayley, dear, I feel faint. All this excitement—it's too much for an old woman."

"Where's Lance?"

"He's out making a delivery. When I saw that strange man poking around in my backyard, it gave me such a start. I almost had a heart attack. I can barely catch my breath!"

"You should sit down," Hayley said, guiding her into the shop.

Inside, Hayley helped Mrs. Bittersweet into a chair behind the counter. The air smelled faintly of chocolate and caramel, but there was an undercurrent of something sour—the same smell that had been wafting from the backyard the night before.

"Do you need your blood pressure medicine?" Hayley asked, glancing toward a cabinet near the back of the shop.

"Yes, dear, it's in the bathroom," Mrs. Bittersweet said weakly, dabbing at her forehead with a lace handkerchief. "In the vanity. Top shelf."

Hayley headed toward the bathroom, her eyes scanning the shop as she went. The pristine candy displays and cheerful pastel decorations suddenly felt eerie in the dim light.

When she reached the bathroom, she opened the mirrored vanity and quickly spotted a small bottle of blood pressure pills. But as she grabbed it, her gaze caught on a drawer below the sink, left slightly ajar. Curiosity got the better of her. She nudged it open and froze.

Inside was a small, unlabeled dark bottle that was half full of tablets. She opened the bottle and poured a couple pills into the palm of her hand. They had a symbol. TI. A quick google search on her phone confirmed what she had already suspected.

TI was the symbol for thallium.

Emma had died from acute thallium toxicity.

She had just found the murder weapon in Mrs. Bittersweet's bathroom. She had most likely crushed the pills into a powder and put it in the perfume she wrapped in the Easter basket that Alex had ordered for Emma.

Hayley's breath hitched as she put the pills back in the bottle and marched with it back out to the front of the shop.

Mrs. Bittersweet noticed the dark pill bottle. "Those don't look like my blood pressure meds, dear."

She held up the bottle. "They're not. What is this?"

Mrs. Bittersweet's eyes widened for a fraction of a second before she composed herself. "Oh, that? It's a poison."

"I know that. Why do you have it?"

"For rodents. I can't have mice running around my

shop, can I? The health department would shut me down in a heartbeat."

"Rodents?" Hayley said, her voice sharp. "People don't normally use thallium to kill rodents. And why were you hiding it in your bathroom?"

Mrs. Bittersweet faltered, her face flushing. "I-I didn't mean to hide it. I must have forgotten that I put it there."

Hayley's eyes narrowed. "Forgotten? Or were you hoping no one would find it?"

Mrs. Bittersweet's hands shook as she waved her handkerchief. "I don't know what you're accusing me of, Hayley, but—" She stopped suddenly and looked at Hayley, her eyes narrowing in what almost seemed like concern. "Why haven't you tried that bunny I sent over to you and Bruce? You'd love it. My best chocolate yet."

Hayley blinked. "What?"

"The bunny I put in your Easter basket with all those other goodies," Mrs. Bittersweet said quickly. "I just thought you would've enjoyed it by now. It's been a couple of days. You don't want it going bad."

The words hung in the air like a fog.

"Since when does chocolate go bad after a couple of days, and why would you ask me that now?"

"You offer a kind gesture, you just want it to be appreciated. If you don't like it, I can make you something else."

Suddenly, everything clicked into place. The bottle of thallium, Mrs. Bittersweet's defensive behavior, and her fixation on whether Hayley had eaten the chocolate bunny she had personally prepared.

Hayley's stomach churned.

Mrs. Bittersweet had spiked it with the thallium.

It wasn't meant to be a treat, but a silencer.

"You *poisoned* it," Hayley said, her voice barely above a whisper.

Mrs. Bittersweet's eyes darted toward the door. "I don't know what you're talking about."

"You wanted to stop me from investigating Emma's death, Bruce too," Hayley said, her voice rising. "You knew we were getting too close. That bunny wasn't a gift. It was a death sentence."

Mrs. Bittersweet stood suddenly, her chair scraping against the floor. "Now, Hayley, you're making wild accusations. I would never—"

But Hayley was already backing toward the door. "*Bruce*," she whispered, the realization hitting her like a punch to the gut. "Bruce is at home. He's been looking for that basket all morning."

Mrs. Bittersweet opened her mouth, but Hayley did not wait to hear another excuse. She bolted out of the shop, her heart hammering in her chest.

Hayley raced to her car, fumbling with her phone as she slid into the driver's seat. She dialed Bruce's number with trembling fingers.

"Come on, Bruce," she muttered as the phone rang. "Pick up."

It went to voice mail.

"Bruce, don't eat the bunny! Call me back as soon as you get this!"

She hung up and sent a flurry of texts in all caps as she sped down the road.

DON'T EAT THE BUNNY.

I'M ON MY WAY HOME.

CALL ME NOW.

There was no response.

Her hands gripped the wheel so tightly, her knuckles

turned white. The road blurred as her mind raced through worst-case scenarios. If Bruce had already found the basket, if he had eaten even a single bite of the poisoned chocolate . . .

Acute thallium toxicity.

It kept ringing in her ears.

"No," she said aloud, shaking her head. "He's fine. He has to be fine."

But as she reached the house, the silence loomed like a shadow.

And Bruce still was not answering his phone.

Chapter Thirteen

Hayley's car screeched into her driveway, her tires kicking up gravel as she barely managed to shift into park. Heart pounding, she flung the car door open and sprinted toward the house, shouting Bruce's name before she even reached the front door.

"Bruce! Don't eat that bunny!" she yelled, bursting inside.

She stopped short in the dining room, where Bruce sat at the table with a cup of coffee in one hand and the remnants of the chocolate bunny in the other.

Half of it was gone.

"Oh, my God," Hayley gasped, her voice shaking. "You ate it!"

Bruce frowned at her, confused. "Yeah? I told you I'd find it. It was in the basement behind the toolbox. Good hiding spot, by the way."

"Bruce," she interrupted, her voice frantic, "Don't panic, but you've been poisoned!"

Bruce blinked, his expression shifting from confusion to alarm. "*What?*"

"Get up!" Hayley ordered, yanking his arm. "We're going to the hospital!"

"What are you talking about?" he asked, still holding the bunny as she dragged him toward the door.

"There's no time to explain!" she shouted, shoving him out the door.

Hayley's car roared down the road as she gripped the steering wheel, her heart pounding. Bruce sat in the passenger seat, clutching the half-eaten chocolate bunny and looking thoroughly alarmed.

"I feel fine!" Bruce protested, bracing himself as the car swerved sharply around a corner.

"You don't know that!" Hayley snapped, her knuckles white against the steering wheel. "Poison doesn't always hit you right away!"

Ahead, the mail truck pulled into the intersection, its driver blissfully unaware of the speeding car. Hayley honked wildly and swerved, narrowly missing the truck.

"Watch it, Hayley!" Bruce yelped, clutching the door handle.

"Don't distract me! I'm saving your life!" she shouted, swerving again to avoid a chipmunk that had wandered into the street.

Bruce groaned, leaning his head back. "If the poison doesn't kill me, I'm sure your driving will."

Hayley ignored him, focused on weaving through traffic. A neighbor stepped into the crosswalk, waving a cheerful hello, only to jump back as Hayley's horn blared.

"Sorry, Doris!" Hayley yelled out the window as she sped past.

By the time they reached the hospital, Bruce was gripping the edge of his seat, his face pale. Hayley skidded to a stop in the drop-off zone, barely remembering to put the car in park before leaping out.

"Let's go!" she ordered, pulling Bruce along.

The hospital staff moved quickly, though they exchanged confused glances at Hayley's frantic explanation about poisoned chocolate. Dr. Cormack and Nurse Tilly entered the exam room shortly after Bruce was settled, both struggling to keep straight faces.

"Poisoned chocolate bunny?" Dr. Cormack asked, arching an eyebrow.

"It's not funny!" Hayley snapped. "You don't know what that woman is capable of!"

"Mrs. Bittersweet?" Nurse Tilly asked, her voice tinged with amusement. "The little old lady who makes fudge? Are we talking about the same person?"

"She poisoned Emma Lane," Hayley insisted. "And she tried to poison me and Bruce to stop us from investigating!"

Bruce groaned. "I told you, I'm fine. I don't feel anything."

"Not *yet*," Hayley muttered darkly.

Dr. Cormack chuckled as he finished checking Bruce's vitals. "Well, he's in perfect health. No symptoms of poisoning, no abnormalities. I think we can safely say the bunny is just chocolate."

Nurse Tilly smirked. "Maybe next time don't hide chocolate so well. It seems to cause unnecessary drama in your house."

Bruce gave Hayley a triumphant look.

She, however, remained unconvinced.

Later that day, Hayley stormed into Sergio's office. He was already sitting behind his desk, looking exasperated.

"You're not going to believe what happened," Hayley started. "Bruce ate—"

"I already heard," Sergio interrupted. "Everyone in town's

talking about how you thought Mrs. Bittersweet poisoned your husband with a chocolate bunny."

"She did poison Emma, and I still think she killed her husband!" Hayley insisted.

Sergio sighed. "Hayley, do you have any actual evidence? Because right now, you're just making accusations."

"I found pills in her bathroom drawer," Hayley said. "They had a strange symbol on them—thallium. It's a *poison*!"

"Do you have these pills?" Sergio asked.

Hayley winced. "No. I was in such a rush to save Bruce that I left them behind."

"Well, you're in luck," Sergio said dryly. "Mrs. Bittersweet came here after you ran out. She explained the whole situation and handed over the pills. Turns out, they're a harmless thyroid medication."

"She could've switched them! Besides, when I asked her about them, she told me it was rat poison, not thyroid medication. So she's lying about something!" Hayley said.

"Maybe the containers look similar," Sergio suggested.

"I doubt it!"

Sergio gave her a long look. "You're grasping now, Hayley. And there's more. The DNA test came back."

Hayley leaned forward. "And?"

"No match," Sergio said. "The bone doesn't belong to anyone related to Lance."

Hayley stared at him, stunned. "But . . . how? I was so sure."

Sergio shrugged. "It could've been there for decades, long before Mrs. Bittersweet and her husband even bought the place."

Hayley felt as if the rug had been pulled out from under her.

She'd been so certain.

And yet . . .

"I still think she's guilty as sin," Hayley said quietly.

"Well, stay away from her," Sergio warned. "You've caused enough trouble for one week."

Hayley nodded.

But as usual when Hayley was on a mission, his advice went in one ear and right out the other.

The bell above the door of Bittersweet Confections jingled brightly as Hayley stepped inside. The warm, familiar scent of chocolate and caramel greeted her, but it did little to calm the knot twisting in her stomach. Behind the counter, Mrs. Bittersweet was delicately arranging a tray of candied almonds. Her expression froze when she saw Hayley.

"Well, if it isn't Hayley Powell," Mrs. Bittersweet said, her voice as sweet as ever, though her hands trembled slightly as she adjusted the tray. "What brings you back, dear? Come to accuse me of something else?"

Hayley forced a smile, holding her hands up in a gesture of surrender. "No accusations. I actually came to apologize."

Mrs. Bittersweet's eyebrows lifted. "Oh?"

"I overreacted," Hayley said, stepping closer to the counter. "Accusing you of trying to poison me and Bruce with that Easter bunny in the basket you sent over . . . it was irrational. There's no excuse. I'm sorry."

Mrs. Bittersweet relaxed slightly, her tight smile softening. "Well, I can't say it wasn't upsetting, but I appreciate you coming by to clear the air. I know your mind tends to run wild with all these . . . murder theories."

Hayley cracked a half smile. "It's an occupational hazard, I suppose. But I also wanted to apologize for something else."

Mrs. Bittersweet's smile faltered. "And what would that be, dear?"

Hayley hesitated, studying the older woman carefully. "For sneaking into your backyard the other night. I shouldn't have done that. Digging up the yard, finding that bone . . ."

Mrs. Bittersweet stiffened. Her hand, mid-reach for another tray, froze in the air. Slowly, she straightened and turned to face Hayley fully, her expression carefully neutral. "What bone?"

"You know exactly what bone," Hayley said evenly, watching her carefully. "The one I had tested for DNA."

Mrs. Bittersweet's face paled. She put down the last bonbon with trembling fingers and turned to face Hayley fully. "You *tested* it?"

Hayley nodded slowly. "Yes, I did. And while I was at it, I grabbed something else." She leaned back casually, her voice steady but sharp. "A wad of chewing gum from Lance. Had his DNA tested too."

Mrs. Bittersweet's hands gripped the counter as a faint sheen of sweat appeared on her forehead. "You . . . what? His DNA?"

Hayley tilted her head, her tone growing sharper. "Yup. Test just came back. Should we take a look and see what the results are?"

Mrs. Bittersweet's face crumpled, her sweet facade slipping. "You already know, don't you?" she whispered, her voice breaking.

Hayley smiled faintly. "I do. It's a match." She lied with the confidence of a seasoned sleuth, her eyes locked on Mrs. Bittersweet's every reaction.

The older woman gasped softly, her hand flying to her

mouth. "I knew this day would come," she muttered, almost to herself. "I knew it couldn't stay buried forever."

Hayley's heart raced.

Her bluff had worked.

The bone was Dewey's.

Before Hayley could press further, Mrs. Bittersweet snapped back into focus, her eyes narrowing. "I didn't mean for things to go this far," she said, her voice trembling. "But that perfume . . . it wasn't supposed to kill her, just make her sick enough so she'd stop—"

The door to the back room creaked open, cutting her off. Lance stepped into view, his towering frame filling the doorway. His dark eyes scanned the room, locking on Hayley.

"What's going on?" Lance asked, his voice low and cautious.

Mrs. Bittersweet flinched, but Hayley held her ground. "I was just explaining to your aunt that a test with your DNA matched the bone I found in her backyard. The bone belongs to Dewey."

Lance's brows furrowed as he crossed his arms over his chest. "That's not possible."

Hayley tilted her head. "Oh? And why's that?"

"Because I'm adopted," Lance said flatly, his gaze boring into hers. "My DNA wouldn't match Dewey's. Aunt Marion doesn't even know, do you?"

Mrs. Bittersweet's mouth opened in shock, but no words came out. Her gaze darted between Lance and Hayley, her mask of control slipping further by the second.

"So the bone could belong to anyone," Lance continued, his tone steady. "You're obviously bluffing."

Hayley felt her pulse quicken. Lance's revelation threw her off, but it explained why it was not a match. And she couldn't ignore the panic in Mrs. Bittersweet's expression moments before.

It was not about Lance.

It was about Dewey.

"Even if the DNA doesn't match Lance," Hayley said, her voice sharp, "I know that bone is Dewey's. You've practically admitted it."

Mrs. Bittersweet's composure snapped. Her sweet, grandmotherly demeanor dissolved into cold fury. "You don't know *anything*," she hissed.

Hayley stood, her heart pounding. "I know enough. Enough to take this to Sergio. You killed Dewey, didn't you? And Emma. You poisoned her because she found out."

Mrs. Bittersweet's eyes blazed with anger. "You can't prove any of this!"

"I'll find proof," Hayley said firmly. "If you'll pardon the expression, I'm like a dog with a bone. I won't let this one go."

Mrs. Bittersweet's lips curled into a thin smile, but her eyes betrayed her desperation. "I'm so sorry to hear that. Lance," she said softly, her tone laced with menace, "be a dear and lock the door."

Hayley's breath hitched as Lance moved to the front door, his movements deliberate. The click of the deadbolt echoed through the shop, sending a shiver down her spine.

"You're not going anywhere," Mrs. Bittersweet said, her voice calm but icy. "You've meddled enough in my affairs, Hayley Powell."

Lance stepped forward, his imposing figure blocking the exit as Hayley's mind raced. She had walked right into the lion's den, and now she was trapped.

Chapter Fourteen

Hayley's heart pounded in her chest as Lance stood in front of the door, his arms crossed, his imposing frame blocking any hope of escape. Mrs. Bittersweet hovered nearby, her once-sweet demeanor replaced by a cold, calculating glare.

"You should've left well enough alone, Hayley," Mrs. Bittersweet said, her voice steady but laced with venom.

"Mrs. Bittersweet," Hayley said, trying to keep her voice calm despite the panic clawing at her insides. "You don't have to do this. Whatever you're planning—it's not too late to stop this madness."

Mrs. Bittersweet let out a soft, humorless laugh. "Stop? After everything you've uncovered? You've left me no choice, dear."

Hayley's eyes darted to Lance. He stood stiffly by the door, his expression unreadable. Her pulse quickened. Was he going to help his aunt . . . or her?

"You're just as guilty as she is, Lance," Hayley said, taking a step back. "If you help her now, you're an accomplice."

Lance's jaw tightened, but he didn't respond.

Mrs. Bittersweet moved toward the counter, her hands

steady as she reached for something in a drawer. Hayley's breath caught when she saw her pull out a heavy metal spatula with a serrated edge.

She pointed it toward Hayley, her eyes dark and dangerous as she readied it as a weapon.

"Lance," Hayley said, her voice rising with urgency. "You don't have to do this. You don't have to help her."

For a moment, Lance didn't move. His gaze shifted between Hayley and Mrs. Bittersweet, his brow furrowed deeply.

Finally, he let out a slow breath.

"I didn't come here to help her," he said, his voice low but firm.

Mrs. Bittersweet turned sharply toward him, her expression twisting in confusion. "What are you talking about?"

Lance's eyes locked on his aunt, and for the first time, Hayley saw a flicker of determination in his expression. "I came to Bar Harbor to find out the truth. About Uncle Dewey."

Mrs. Bittersweet froze. The spatula trembled slightly in her hand. "The truth? What are you talking about? Dewey left. He ran off and abandoned me."

"No," Lance said, his voice rising. "He didn't. I've been suspicious for a while, but when that reporter, Emma, contacted me, she raised too many questions. Questions I couldn't ignore."

"*Emma*?" Mrs. Bittersweet repeated, her voice faltering.

"Yes, Emma," Lance said. "She called me up in Aroostook County, asking questions about Uncle Dewey. About what kind of man he was, how he treated people. She told me she suspected foul play, and it made me think about all the things that never added up. Why Dewey would leave without a word. Why you never seemed interested in finding him."

Mrs. Bittersweet's face hardened, her grip tightening on the spatula. "She was trying to ruin everything."

"She was trying to find the truth," Lance said. "And so was I. When I got to town, I tried contacting Emma, but she refused to talk to me. She thought I was loyal to you, Aunt Marion, and she was afraid I would tip you off about the story. I kept trying to reach out, but she threatened to call the police and accuse me of stalking her, so I backed off and got a job here at the shop so I could do my own investigating."

"You came here to *spy* on me?" Mrs. Bittersweet spit out, aghast.

Hayley seized the moment. "You killed Emma because she knew too much. You poisoned her before she could publish her story, didn't you?"

Mrs. Bittersweet's eyes darted toward Hayley, her expression wild. "She wouldn't leave it alone! She was going to ruin me—ruin everything!"

Lance took a step forward, his voice cold. "And what about Dewey? Why did you have to kill him?"

Mrs. Bittersweet's lips trembled. For a moment, her gaze softened, but it quickly hardened again. "He was going to leave me," she spat. "After everything I did for him, after all the years I stood by him. He deserved what he got."

Lance's fists clenched, and he stepped between Hayley and his aunt. "You're not hurting anyone else. This stops now."

Mrs. Bittersweet's eyes blazed with fury. "You nosy, annoying bitch—" She lunged toward Hayley with the spatula raised, but Lance moved quickly, grabbing her wrist and twisting it just enough to make her drop the utensil.

"My, what a potty mouth you have, Mrs. Bittersweet. It certainly is a far cry from your sugary sweet reputation," Hayley noted.

"Get in the pantry," Lance said through gritted teeth, dragging her toward the back of the shop.

"Let go of me!" Mrs. Bittersweet shrieked, struggling against his grip.

But Lance was stronger. He opened the pantry door and pushed her inside. Before she could react, he slammed the door shut and turned the lock.

From inside, Mrs. Bittersweet pounded on the door, her voice muffled but furious. "You'll regret this, Lance! Let me out right this minute!"

Hayley stared in stunned silence as Lance leaned against the door, breathing heavily.

"Call the police," he said, his voice steady but strained. "Don't worry. She's not going anywhere."

Hayley fumbled for her phone, her hands trembling as she dialed Sergio's number. When he picked up, she wasted no time. "Sergio, get to Bittersweet Confections as soon as you can. I've got Mrs. Bittersweet locked in her pantry. She just confessed to killing Dewey Dratch and Emma Lane."

Sergio's response was quick and sharp. "Stay there. Don't let her out. We're on our way."

Hayley hung up and looked at Lance. For the first time, he seemed to relax slightly, though his face was still tense with emotion.

"I didn't know, I swear," Lance said quietly. "I didn't want to believe it. But I couldn't let her hurt you."

Hayley placed a hand on his arm. "Thank you, Lance. For doing the right thing."

They stood in silence as the sounds of sirens grew closer, the weight of the moment settling over them. In the pantry, Mrs. Bittersweet's furious shouts continued, but Hayley felt a strange sense of relief.

The truth was finally out, and justice was on its way.

Chapter Fifteen

The house was alive with laughter and the clinking of glasses as Hayley carried a platter of glazed ham to the dining room. The Easter table was laid out with her favorite holiday dishes: scalloped potatoes bubbling with cheese, honey-glazed carrots, fresh asparagus, and fluffy homemade dinner rolls. The centerpiece, a cheerful arrangement of tulips and daffodils, brightened the room with spring colors.

Bruce was busy uncorking a bottle of wine, the scent of roasted garlic mingling with the floral arrangement. Hayley allowed herself a moment to breathe. For the first time in weeks, Bar Harbor felt peaceful again.

Sergio and Randy were already seated at the table, deep in a spirited debate about who had the best lobster roll in town. Mona and Earl sat on the far side, with Mona rolling her eyes as Earl gently patted her hand.

Hayley smirked, sidling up to Mona. "Still planning to break up with him tomorrow?"

"First thing in the morning," Mona said firmly. "No sense dragging out the inevitable. It's got to be done."

Hayley arched an eyebrow. "Uh-huh."

"I mean it," Mona insisted, but the tiniest hint of a smile betrayed her resolve.

Earl, blissfully unaware—or perhaps too smitten to care—beamed as he passed her the butter. "More butter for my beautiful girl?"

Mona sighed. "Fine. Maybe I'll wait until the next holiday, which is what, Memorial Day?"

Bruce leaned in with a knowing grin. "You're not breaking up with him. None of us believe it."

Randy raised his glass. "To Earl! The most persistent man in Bar Harbor."

"To Earl!" Sergio added, smirking, as Mona groaned.

Just then, the doorbell rang. Hayley wiped her hands on her apron and hurried to answer it. When she opened the door, she found Lance standing there in a crisp suit and tie, his hair neatly combed. He looked every bit the part of someone ready for Easter service rather than a casual family dinner.

"Lance," Hayley said, surprised. "I'm so happy you could come join us today. And you look very nice."

"Thanks," Lance said with a shy smile. "I didn't know how fancy this would be."

Hayley chuckled. "Well, you overshot it a bit, but come in. You're just in time."

As Lance stepped inside, Liddy entered from the kitchen, carrying a platter covered with a suspicious-looking cloth. Her eyes widened when she saw Lance. "Well, well," she said, giving him an appraising look. "If I'd known you were going to dress like this, I might've tried harder."

Lance's cheeks turned pink. "You're looking great too," he said, a little too eagerly.

Hayley shot Liddy a warning glance and whispered, "Don't lead him on."

Liddy raised an eyebrow. "Who's leading him on? In case you hadn't noticed, the boy cleans up real nice."

Hayley shook her head and ushered Lance into the dining room, where he took a seat near Liddy, clearly pleased by the arrangement.

Dinner was a lively affair, with everyone digging into Hayley's carefully prepared meal. The ham was a hit, the scalloped potatoes disappeared almost instantly, and even the picky eaters cleaned their plates.

"I have to say," Sergio said, leaning back in his chair, "this might be the best Easter dinner I've ever had."

"High praise from the guy who usually eats microwave burritos at the station," Randy teased.

"Hey, they're good burritos," Sergio shot back, earning a round of laughter.

Mona, who had been quiet for most of the meal, finally leaned over to Earl. "The ham's good, isn't it?"

Earl's face lit up. "Not as good as you, Mona."

Mona rolled her eyes again but didn't bother hiding her smile this time.

Hayley stood, holding a chocolate bunny. "Bruce," she said with a grin, "this one's for you. I promise I didn't get it from Mrs. Bittersweet this time. I made it myself. And before you ask—no, you can't eat it until after dinner."

Bruce feigned disappointment, holding out his hands. "But I'm starving!"

"You just ate two plates of ham," Hayley said, smirking as she handed him the bunny.

Liddy leaned over to Lance. "You see what she puts up with? That's true love."

Lance chuckled, his gaze lingering on Liddy. "Maybe I'll stick around Bar Harbor a little longer."

Hayley caught the exchange and muttered under her breath, "Oh, boy."

As the night wound down, Hayley finally allowed herself to relax with a glass of her signature Cottontail Margarita. The tart, citrusy flavor was a perfect complement to the warmth of the evening. She leaned back in her chair, watching her friends and family talk and laugh around the table.

It had been a harrowing few weeks, but now, with Mrs. Bittersweet behind bars and Bar Harbor safe again, Hayley felt a sense of calm settle over her. The mysteries were solved—for now—and life could return to its cozy, chaotic normal.

Bruce leaned over, clinking his glass against hers. "Another case closed," he said with a smile.

Hayley nodded, smiling back. "Here's to a peaceful spring."

"For now," Bruce added, grinning.

Hayley laughed, knowing he was probably right.

Island Food & Spirits
by
Hayley Powell

Every year, I look forward to planning and cooking Easter dinner for my family and friends. It's a tradition that brings me joy—until, of course, life decides to throw a wrench into my well-laid plans. That's exactly what happened a couple of years ago, and it turned into one of the most memorable (and unconventional) Easters we've ever had.

It all started when I was debating between making ham or lamb when my brother Randy called. He and Sergio had found a last-minute deal on plane tickets and would be heading to Brazil to visit Sergio's family. I wished them a great trip, but I was disappointed. Then my BFF Mona called to say she was driving her parents to Boston because her mother had revoked her father's driving privileges after a road rage incident. As if on cue, I heard Mona's brakes screeching and her yelling at some poor driver, making me suspect it would be a very long trip for the Butler family.

Next, Liddy rang to say that her dad Elmer's husband, Rocco, was playing piano at a fancy New York hotel's Easter brunch, and she'd be tagging along for a weekend of shopping. (You don't have to ask Liddy twice when shopping is involved!)

Then my kids called to say they were swamped with work but promised a summer visit. And just like that, for the first time since we got married, Bruce and I were alone for the holiday.

When I broke the news to Bruce, I expected him to be just as sad as I was—but to my shock, he was practically giddy. He explained that we could do anything we wanted. No fancy meal, no expectations—just us and whatever we felt like eating. Suddenly, I was excited too. We were like two kids running wild in Mrs. Bittersweet's candy shop, making a grocery list that started with chocolate donuts and ended with pizza rolls, hitting every frozen aisle delight in between. Bruce grabbed the list and ran out the door before I could come to my senses.

Easter morning, I woke to bright sunshine and the smell of bacon and coffee. I glanced at the clock—it was past ten a.m.! I hadn't slept in that late in years. I pulled on Bruce's Led Zeppelin T-shirt (holes and all) and a pair of his boxers and headed downstairs. There was Bruce, belting out classic rock tunes while plating up crispy bacon and chocolate-glazed donuts. I grabbed a donut, added a piece of bacon on top, took a big bite, and sighed. This was going to be a great day.

After a long walk with Leroy to make room for more food, we settled in for our much-anticipated John Wick marathon, accompanied by gin cocktails and pizza rolls. But just as the first movie started, there was a knock at the door.

"Hayley, answer the door—it's us!"

I opened it to find Randy and Sergio, looking sheepish. Their flight had been canceled until the next day, and instead of staying in Bangor with nothing open, they decided to crash at our place. Randy had bet on lamb, Sergio on ham—both were stunned when I told them the menu consisted of pizza rolls. Their disappointment made me laugh, but of course, I invited them in, grabbing more pizza rolls from the freezer.

Then came another knock. Mona stormed in, griping about terrible drivers. Apparently, her road trip had been cut short when her father made an unfortunate hand gesture—directed at none other than Reverend Jim from her mother's church. That did not go over well, and her mother demanded they turn around immediately. Mona, always one to make the best of things, showed up at our place demanding ham or lamb. Instead, she got pizza rolls.

Bruce sighed and went to mix more gin cocktails, just as yet another knock came. He didn't even need to guess—it was Liddy. Her trip had been canceled due to a bout of food poisoning in her family. Seeing our ridiculous spread of frozen delights, she grabbed a drink, shrugged, and joined the party.

As I watched my unexpected guests dig in, Bruce gave me a warm smile and whispered, "Hayley, when I said 'I do,' it wasn't just to you."

So here's to good friends, last-minute plans, and the best Easter we never saw coming. And just for you, I'm sharing the gin cocktail we all enjoyed that day, plus one of my family's favorite quick and delicious breakfast taco recipes.

Bruce's Favorite Gin and Tonic

Ingredients

2 ounces gin, your favorite
3 ounces tonic water
1 cinnamon stick
Orange peel

In a glass with ice, add the gin and the tonic and give it a mix. Garnish with the cinnamon stick and orange peel. Serve and enjoy!

Hayley's Breakfast Tacos

Ingredients

1 pint grape tomatoes, quartered
½ sweet onion, diced
1 lime, juiced
½ cup cilantro, chopped
6 large eggs
2 tablespoons cream (or milk)
1 tablespoon butter
16 ounces grated sharp cheddar cheese
8 small flour tortillas (or corn, if you prefer)
1 avocado, cubed
Kosher salt and pepper

In a bowl, mix the tomatoes, sweet onion, lime juice, cilantro, salt, and pepper.

In another bowl, whisk the eggs with cream. Melt the butter in a skillet over medium-low heat. Add the egg mixture to the skillet, and cook the scrambled eggs to your liking. Set aside on a plate.

In the same skillet, sprinkle some of the shredded cheese in a circle roughly the size of your tortilla. Place the tortilla on top, then add more of the cheese on the upside. Let the cheese crisp around the edges.

Add some of the scrambled eggs, tomato mixture, and avocado. Fold in half with a spatula. Now repeat with remaining tortillas, cheese, and filling mixture.

Serve with a squeeze of lime and extra toppings of your choice.

Happy Easter from my crazy, wonderful family to yours!

AN EGGY WAY TO DIE

Peggy Ehrhart

Acknowledgments

Abundant thanks to my agent Evan Marshall, and to my editor at Kensington Books, John Scognamiglio.

Chapter One

"The children certainly did a thorough job." Bettina Fraser surveyed the wide lawn, where a few people who weren't children roamed about, peeking under the shrubbery that bordered the expanse of delicate grass.

"I only found two leftovers," Pamela Paterson said, holding out a basket containing a pair of gaily decorated eggs, "though there are probably still a few tucked away in hidden places for the raccoons to find."

"Our most successful Easter egg hunt yet, wouldn't you say?" The voice came from a pleasant-looking middle-aged woman advancing toward them from the kiddie playground at the edge of the park. She too was carrying a basket, a basket that held a single egg. "It was under the merry-go-round," she added. "Quite thoroughly hidden."

No introduction was needed, since Marlene Pepper was well known to both Pamela and Bettina.

"The children were adorable," Marlene went on, having stationed herself at Bettina's side. "All dressed up in their Easter outfits, and so excited about their finds."

"Their moms will be making lots of deviled eggs this week, I suspect," Pamela commented.

"I should have thought to run your deviled egg recipe in the *Advocate* this past Friday," Bettina said, "instead of

Ellen Weatherby's eggs Benedict, but she's been such a pest about getting herself featured in 'Cook's Corner.' "

The three women were silent then, gazing at the lawn. What Bettina and Marlene were thinking, Pamela had no idea. She herself was remembering when her daughter Penny had been among the excited children turning out after lunch on Easter for Arborville's annual Easter egg hunt.

"Why is Midge Raymond poking around way out there?" Bettina inquired suddenly, pointing toward a stand of trees beyond the tennis courts. "Nobody hid any eggs that far away."

But as they watched, Midge emerged from among a cluster of blossoming trees, her expression completely at odds with the placid beauty of the setting. Lest, at a distance, any puzzlement remain about her state, she uttered a scream so intense that it was ear-piercing even at a distance of at least two hundred feet.

"What on earth—" Bettina set out across the lawn. In dressing for the morning's event, she had foregone the fashionable high heels that were her usual footwear in favor of bright red sneakers. Pamela could barely keep up with her as she sped over the grass.

Marlene Pepper brought up the rear, and they arrived at the stand of trees just as additional egg-hunt volunteers converged from other directions. Midge was still standing in the pose she had struck as she uttered the scream, stiffly at attention, with her hands poised as if to clutch her head.

"Don't—" she stuttered, then tried again as one arm gestured spasmodically behind her. "Don't go in there. It's too awful!" She focused on Bettina. "What should we do?"

As the sole reporter for Arborville's weekly newspaper, and in that capacity the liaison to the town's police department, Bettina was seen as something of an authority when it came to matters of public safety.

Bettina straightened her spine. "First of all," she said, "what on earth . . ."

But Pamela had already disobeyed Midge's warning. Stepping among the trees, whose blossoms filtered the sunlight in a way that lent the scene a delicate pink glow, she was startled—despite the warning—to discover a woman's body sprawled on the pale spring grass. The woman was attractive, nicely dressed, though in an ensemble more suited to partying than an Easter morning outing, and seemed merely to be sleeping. What made the scene disturbing, however, were the raw eggs. They were everywhere, apparently the helter-skelter result of an egg-hurling frenzy.

Viscous, deep orange yolks, intermingled with translucent whites, were smeared on tree bark and puddling on the ground, where ridges of grass had been dislodged, perhaps by a struggle, to expose muddy dirt. Pieces of eggshell, large and small, littered the area, some clinging to the oozing remains of their contents. In some places, shells and contents both had been trodden into the soil.

This was a crime scene, Pamela knew, and she knew better than to disturb anything in any way. She'd already erred in that regard, just by stepping as close to the body as she had. But something lay on the ground next to the woman, something like a note. It had fallen face up, perhaps as the woman was attacked, but then her body had landed on it so only part of its message was visible.

Pamela leaned over as far as she could, mindful of the difficulty she would have explaining smears of raw egg on her clothing if she were to lose her balance and fall. As she strategized the angle from which she could most readily study the note, which was anchored by the woman's left shoulder, she could hear voices drawing closer.

Bettina's voice was recognizable among the tangle of voices, but then a male voice asserted itself, suggesting that the police had been summoned. No wailing siren had heralded their arrival because the park where the Easter egg hunt had been held shared a parking lot with Arborville's library and its police station.

Balancing at a precarious angle, Pamela stared at the note. The only words she could make out were "Bunny Cuddle," but part of the small page was taken up by a sketch. She circled the body, being careful not to step too close. Viewed from another angle, the sketch seemed to be a map, featuring an open space, rectangles that could be tennis courts, scalloped circles that could be an aerial view of blossoming trees, and a parking lot complete with little ovals for cars.

The voices were nearly upon her now. Instead of walking toward them, Pamela edged backward, threading her way among the trees and emerging onto a patch of grass. Then she made her way around the stand of trees and crept up next to Bettina. The police officer who had responded was burly Officer Keenan, and he was currently focused on Midge Raymond.

"It's a frightful sight," Pamela whispered to Bettina. "There are raw eggs everywhere. No wonder Midge was horrified."

The other egg-hunt volunteers were standing off to the side, conferring nervously and clearly interested in the proceedings. Officer Keenan left off talking to Midge and ventured in among the trees, returning quickly with his phone already out.

"Everyone step back," he commanded, reinforcing the words with shooing gestures.

"She wasn't just screaming about eggs, was she?" Bettina leaned close to Pamela.

"No." Pamela shook her head. "Someone has been—"

But Pamela was interrupted by Officer Keenan's words, spoken into his phone: "Send backup. There's a body near the tennis courts, and tell Clayborn."

Bettina's features, normally plumped by good cheer, sagged and her hazel eyes widened. "Who?" She addressed the question to Pamela.

Pamela shook her head spasmodically. Her attention was not on Bettina, however, but on the small procession en route from the police station. In the lead was Officer Sanchez, Arborville's only female officer, with her sweet heart-shaped face and tidy black bun. Following her was boyish Officer Anders, usually tasked with making sure that the children crossing Arborville Avenue on their way to the grammar school arrived at the other side safely. Bringing up the rear was Detective Clayborn, his nondescript sports jacket flapping open to reveal his pudgy midsection.

As she watched, another figure fell in behind them, but at a distance. The figure, a bulky figure dressed in denim overalls topped by a canvas jacket, had just emerged from an ancient Mercedes parked in a space near the edge of the lot. The group in the lead drew closer and Detective Clayborn strode ahead, responding to the gestures of Officer Keenan and slipping in among the blossoming trees. Officer Keenan accompanied him. Partially obscured by tree trunks, they could be seen moving about, bending over, and straightening up.

Meanwhile, Officer Sanchez and Officer Anders stationed themselves between the stand of trees and the onlookers, who had by now been augmented by Wilfred Fraser, the owner of the Mercedes.

"Dear wife!" he exclaimed, extending a comforting arm and pulling Bettina to his side. "What on earth has happened? I came out for a quick errand at the Co-Op and had no idea I'd happen upon . . ." With his free arm he gestured toward the officers positioned at attention a few yards away. He repeated the question: "What on earth has happened?"

It was Pamela who spoke. "It's a crime scene, I think. A body . . . in there." She nodded toward the trees. "Bettina and I and the other egg-hunt volunteers were tidying up, looking for stray eggs the children didn't find, and all of a sudden Midge Raymond screamed . . ."

Her explanation was cut short. Detective Clayborn had reappeared. "Get statements from these other people," he directed, speaking to Officer Sanchez. "And you, Keenan," he went on, "get the CSU here."

He himself focused again on Midge Raymond, dipping beneath the lapel of his jacket to retrieve a small notepad and pen. Pamela remarked, as she often did in the presence of Detective Clayborn, the tightening around the eyes that transformed his nondescript features when there was detecting to be done.

Pamela and Bettina waited their turn to describe to Officer Sanchez the lead-up to Midge Raymond's scream—the innocuous task of checking for stray eggs. When Officer Sanchez focused on her, Pamela admitted that she had peeked in among the trees to see what had provoked Midge's scream, though she didn't admit she had gotten close enough to the body to notice, let alone read, the enigmatic note.

After Bettina finished giving her statement to Officer Sanchez, she lingered with an eye on Detective Clayborn.

Pamela suspected Bettina had a reason for lingering, and her suspicion proved correct.

"Yes, Ms. Fraser?" Detective Clayborn's manner suggested that he too knew why Bettina was lingering. His eyes had tightened to the point that he was nearly squinting.

"The usual time tomorrow morning?" Bettina inquired brightly. "I know the readers of the *Advocate* will appreciate staying abreast of this case in their own town newspaper."

Detective Clayborn grunted. "The next issue of the *Advocate* won't be out until Friday. By then the case will be solved."

Undeterred, Bettina responded, "Nine a.m. sharp then."

Bettina's reporting zeal appeared to have displaced her initial distress. As she and Wilfred turned toward the parking lot, she seemed positively jubilant, and Pamela fell into step beside them. She and Bettina had arrived together in Pamela's serviceable compact, but Bettina would be carried home in her husband's ancient Mercedes. The two vehicles would be headed for nearly the same destination, however, because the Frasers' house and Pamela's faced each other across the street.

On their way out of the parking lot, they passed a large silver van with the sheriff's logo on the side.

The drive to Orchard Street was a short one. Pamela normally walked when she had errands in town, as Arborville's few blocks of commercial district plus library-park-police complex was known. But Bettina had insisted that they drive to the Easter egg hunt, despite her comfortable shoes.

Barely five minutes had passed before Pamela was turning left into the driveway of her hundred-year-old wood-frame house with its clapboard siding, and the Frasers were turning right into the driveway of their even older Dutch colonial. No sooner had Wilfred helped Bettina out onto the asphalt of the driveway, however, than he reclaimed his seat behind the steering wheel and set off up Orchard Street again.

"Where's he going?" Pamela called, heading toward where Bettina was standing.

"Eggs!" Bettina said. "He forgot to get eggs. That was his Co-Op errand but he got sidetracked. He only remembered when I told him what you said you saw: Raw eggs everywhere. Anyway . . ." Bettina paused. "He's still cooking Easter dinner tonight, obviously, and you're still invited, and the eggs are for a soufflé. Come about six."

Pamela thought about the eggs at the crime scene as she crossed back to her own house. They had been remarkable eggs. The yolks were so *orange*.

Chapter Two

Stepping across her threshold, Pamela was greeted by a furry welcoming committee. Could the cats have been wondering why her absence had stretched longer than they expected? Even Precious, the aloof Siamese, had left her perch on the top platform of the cat climber to join Catrina and Ginger on the thrift-shop carpet that covered the entry floor. All three cats gazed at her with eyes that seemed accusing, and as soon as Pamela made a move in the direction of the kitchen, they spun around and trotted before her, checking back to assure themselves that she was indeed following.

Though it was early for their dinner, Pamela obligingly fetched cans from the cat food cupboard, choosing liver paté for Catrina and Ginger to share from their communal bowl and Pick of the Catch for Precious, who preferred seafood. She couldn't help glancing at Richard Larkin's kitchen window as she stood at the counter with the can opener. He was away, far away in Iceland, lecturing at the university on sustainable architecture. She could have accompanied him but had demurred. She'd been struggling ever since to understand why. She had marked his return date on her calendar the day he left, and she still remembered the kiss with which he had taken his leave.

An hour remained until it was time to cross the street and join the Frasers for dinner. Pamela climbed the stairs to her office, where she checked her email. No messages from celine.bramley@fibercraft.com lurked in her inbox, and it appeared that even her boss, who seemed never to rest, had taken Easter off. As associate editor of *Fiber Craft* magazine, Pamela had been able to work from home long before that was an option for so many people. The arrangement had been most welcome long ago, when she was a young widow with a child to raise on her own.

She crossed the hall to her bedroom and opened the door to her closet. Changing into another outfit for dinner would result in only the most minimal alteration to her appearance. Pamela had settled on a simple uniform of sorts long ago: jeans and a sweater, usually hand-knit, in chilly weather, and jeans and a casual blouse in warm weather. Bettina had long since given up urging her friend to take advantage of her enviable height and slenderness by choosing more adventurous styles. The sweater she had topped her jeans with that morning was forest-green in tone and lacy in texture, suited to a spring day or evening. No need to change. She closed her closet door and headed back downstairs.

Bettina, on the other hand, had put considerable thought into the ensemble she wore as she opened the Frasers' door to admit Pamela that evening. A dress sewn from glossy pink fabric in a fit-and-flare style hugged her ample curves, and pink kitten heels echoed the dress's pale hue. She had accessorized the dress with a triple strand of oversize pearls and matching earrings. The dress and pearls contrasted strikingly with Bettina's scarlet hair, described even by her as a color not found in nature.

"I'm just trying to forget about what happened this afternoon," she said before even greeting her visitor. "Tomorrow when I talk to Clayborn will be soon enough to remember the experience."

"We don't know who the victim is yet . . . ?" Pamela stepped into the Frasers' welcoming living room, where a flickering fire acknowledged that nights in early April could still be chilly. The large shaggy dog slumbering on the comfortable-looking sofa added to the coziness.

"Welcome, welcome, welcome," came Wilfred's voice from the arch that separated the living room from the dining room. "I'm just about to open a bottle of champagne, so let's all congregate in the kitchen."

"'All' just means the three of us," Bettina clarified. "The Arborville children and grandchildren are in Boston with the Boston children and grandchild." The "Arborville children" were actually Wilfred Jr. and his wife, and the "Boston children" were the Frasers' other son, Warren, and his wife.

As she and Pamela moved toward the dining room and the kitchen beyond, she added, "And we're missing Rick of course, too." She halted and seized Pamela's arm. "You could be there in Iceland with him, though. I still don't see why you refused."

"It's all so new, Bettina," Pamela said. "These things take time."

"You've *had* time . . ."

Pamela hadn't meant to frown, but her expression—whether frown or something else—had the effect of silencing Bettina. Neither spoke as they stepped into the kitchen, where they were greeted by competing aromas.

The Frasers' house was the oldest house on Orchard Street, built by the Dutch family who owned the apple orchard that ultimately gave the street its name. Little by little the apple trees were replaced by other houses, houses that were themselves now old. When the Frasers bought the house as newlyweds, they added a spacious kitchen. A high counter separated the cooking area from a roomy space furnished with a scrubbed pine table and chairs, and suited for casual meals. Sliding glass doors looked out onto a patio and the lawn and shrubbery beyond.

Three champagne flutes from Bettina's Swedish crystal set were lined up on the high counter. One of the competing aromas was clearly ham. The air was warm with the rich, salty, smoky evidence that a ham was in the process of being baked.

The other aroma was both sharper and mellower, and it was emanating from the tiny, pillowy squares of golden-brown puff pastry arranged on a sage-green platter near the champagne flutes. In the center of each puff pastry square was a jammy caramel-colored splotch topped by a few crumbles of pale cheese.

"Caramelized onions," Wilfred announced in response to Pamela's unspoken question. "And goat cheese. Try one!"

Pamela needed no urging.

The little treats were still warm, and the flaky puff pastry yielded easily to the teeth, with the sweetness of the caramelized onions set off by the tang of the goat cheese. After sampling one of his own creations, Wilfred busied himself with the champagne.

He twisted off the wire cage that anchored the bulbous cork in place, tilted the bottle away from his audience, and gently twisted the cork until it eased from the bottle's neck. A sharp pop and a puff of vapor indicated that the cork had come free. Soon the three crystal flutes resembled columns of pale gold topped by silvery foam.

Pamela and Bettina chatted while Wilfred, champagne at hand, returned to his cooking, and soon it was time to proceed to the dining room and settle around the table.

Upon retirement, Wilfred had become the family cook, but Bettina still enjoyed the ritual of setting the table with the linens and tableware she collected. In preparation for the Easter feast, she had chosen a cloth in an elegant cream color that set off the sage green of her pottery set. The napkins were a spring-like print that combined shades of green, peach, and cream. An arrangement of peach and gold tulips in a low bowl was centered between the pewter candleholders.

Soon Wilfred arrived with the ham, which he set near his place with a ceremonial flourish. A second trip brought Potatoes Bettina, a dish of his own invention, which involved slicing potatoes into thin rounds, arranging them in concentric circles, and roasting them to a golden brown with the addition of much melted butter. Finally a dish of Swiss chard, sautéed just to a pleasing limpness, appeared.

Once Wilfred had furnished plates with ample slices of the ham, deep pink and glistening, and the side dishes had been passed, he raised a fork to command attention and uttered his customary "Bon appétit!" Pamela and Bettina raised their forks too, and knives, and for the first few minutes no sound was heard but for the scrape of cutlery on plates and inarticulate murmurs of appreciation. Words like *delicious* and *amazing* took the place of murmurs, and gradually the conversation began to flow into comfortable channels.

The first topic was the doings of the Frasers' Arborville granddaughter, Betty, up in Boston but adorable in her Easter dress, Bettina was sure. Gardens were on people's minds, with pansies just now available at the garden center but herb seedlings a ways off. And of course Penny's doings, away at graduate school in Illinois, came up for discussion.

Second helpings were urged, accepted, and eaten, whereupon salad was served—a salad so interesting that it provoked a conversational detour. Like Potatoes Bettina, it was dish original to Wilfred. He had based it on lettuce and carrots, which thoughts of the Easter bunny brought to mind. But he had slivered the carrots, and blanched them to remove some of the crunch and bring out the sweetness. The carrot slivers had been tossed with torn butter lettuce and candied pecan halves, and the whole thing dressed with sesame oil and balsamic vinegar.

Only when the dessert was served did the conversation veer away from quotidian topics to touch upon the decidedly un-quotidian discovery made at the conclusion of the Easter egg hunt. Pamela hadn't intended to bring it up. The body found in the stand of trees near the tennis courts would undoubtedly provide fodder for endless conversations in the days to come, conversations that would surely involve her, and Bettina, and even Wilfred. For this one evening, the three had seemed united in an unspoken agreement to carry on as if the meal climaxed an Easter day as normal as any might be.

But then Wilfred served dessert, a lemon soufflé. It came to the table in a tall, straight-sided baking dish, with its tawny pouf rising a few inches above the fluted rim. Smiling a smile of intense satisfaction, he allowed time for admiring gazes before he picked up a serving spoon, plunged it into the soufflé's center, and transferred a portion, in an airy drift of yellow, to a serving plate. The first serving went to Pamela, the next to Bettina, and the third to Wilfred. A hearty "Bon appétit" was the invitation to commence.

Pamela raised a spoonful of the soufflé to her mouth. The scent of lemon reached her nostrils before the taste registered, infusing a substance so delicate in texture that no sooner had it touched her tongue than it seemed to melt away.

Mostly a soufflé was eggs, she knew, and Wilfred seemed to read her mind.

"Yes," he said. "I should have double-checked my recipe in advance. It called for many more eggs than I anticipated and that was the reason for my last-minute dash to the Co-Op."

"Well worth it," Pamela responded. "The soufflé is delicious."

It was such a *pale* yellow though. Egg whites beaten stiff were what made a soufflé airy, but yolks were included too, she was sure.

"The eggs . . ." she said suddenly, turning to Bettina, who sat at the foot of the table. "You didn't see them, but the raw eggs thrown around the . . . body . . . had *orange* yolks, the most amazingly *orange* yolks."

"Free-range." The voice was Wilfred's. "The color of the yolk comes from what the hens eat. Hens that are allowed to roam freely eat all kinds of things, but hens farm-raised for their eggs don't eat as rich a diet."

"The Co-Op has good eggs, though," Bettina commented. "We've always enjoyed them."

"They come from farms where the hens have nice lives." Wilfred nodded. "At least that's what the Co-Op egg man claims. But good as the Co-Op eggs are, they don't compare with real free-range eggs."

Free-range, Pamela reflected as she lifted another spoonful of soufflé to her mouth. Someone intent on murder had access to a large supply of free-range eggs and, for some reason, decided to fling them around the murder site.

Sitting at her kitchen table on Monday morning, with coffee at hand in a wedding-china cup and whole-grain toast on a wedding-china plate, Pamela turned her attention to the front page of the *County Register*. The dramatic headline, EASTER EGG MURDER SHOCKS ARBORVILLE, was no surprise. It had been legible through the plastic sleeve that encased the paper as she picked it up from her lawn. Now she read the article, which appeared under the byline of Marcy Brewer, who frequently reported on Arborville doings.

According to Marcy, the body found in the stand of trees near the tennis courts was that of forty-year-old Arborville resident Ellen Weatherby. Volunteers helping with the town's annual Easter egg hunt had come upon it while cleaning up after the hunt ended at three p.m. Ellen had been the author of the soon to be released *Eggotist's Cookbook*. The cause of death appeared to be manual strangulation, though the medical examiner's report would not be available for some days. From the condition of the body, it was estimated that she had been dead no more than three hours when the body was found, and evidence of a scuffle suggested that she had been killed in that same spot. The large number of raw eggs at the crime scene were a curious feature. Here Marcy editorialized to remark on the gruesome fact that the murder must have taken place while the children of Arborville were searching for gaily decorated hard-boiled eggs.

Pamela had been sipping her coffee as she read. Having finished the article, she picked up a piece of toast and turned the page. In the spot where her kitchen cupboards met at a right angle to form a corner, the three cats were still crouched over their bowls, oblivious to all but the pleasures of breakfast. Pamela focused then on her own breakfast too, and set Part 1 of the *Register* aside in favor of Lifestyle.

* * *

"You didn't tell me that the body was Ellen Weatherby!" Bettina's tone was accusing, though any genuine anger was neutralized by the gesture that accompanied the words. Bettina had arrived on Pamela's doorstep bearing a white cardboard bakery box, and she handed it to Pamela as she stepped across the threshold. The pastel green of her pants and jacket ensemble echoed the pale tint of the spring foliage just starting to appear.

"I know I'm early, but I hope there's coffee," she added. "Clayborn had nothing at all to tell me beyond what Marcy Brewer already put in the *Register*."

"There can be coffee," Pamela led the way across the entry floor into the kitchen. En route they passed Catrina, curled into a compact oval and enjoying the sun that warmed that spot on the thrift-shop carpet every morning.

Talking as she worked, Pamela set water to boil in her kettle, spooned coffee beans into her grinder, and slipped a fresh paper filter into her carafe's filter cone.

"I didn't know the body was Ellen Weatherby," she said, "not until I read Marcy's article, and I still don't really know who Ellen Weatherby is."

"She's an egg influencer," Bettina replied. "She's all over YouTube, and she's been sending me recipes to put in the *Advocate* every week. Surely you've seen those."

"I guess I didn't connect the name in Marcy's article with the recipes"—Pamela shrugged—"and I certainly had no way of knowing what she looked like."

The kettle summoned Pamela with a whistle, and she tipped it over the filter cone. Steam rose as the boiling water saturated the dark grounds, releasing the spicy aroma of brewing coffee. Meanwhile, Bettina had set out wedding-china cups, saucers, and plates, and transferred the cut-glass sugar bowl and the cream pitcher, to which she added a large dollop of heavy cream, to the little table.

"I didn't get the crumb cake," she announced as Pamela brought the carafe to the table and took a seat, "but I got something almost as good." She tugged at a string end to loosen the bow atop the bakery box and folded the top flap back to reveal doughnuts iced with pink icing and sprinkled with multicolored sprinkles.

With a doughnut on the plate before her and her cup full to the brim with the black coffee she preferred, Pamela watched Bettina add sugar and cream to the beverage in her own cup, coaxing it, as was her custom, into a sweet and pale state.

"Marcy's article may have identified the victim," she said after Bettina had sipped her coffee and indicated with a smile that it met her requirements, "but it didn't include all the details of the crime scene."

"No?" The doughnut in Bettina's hand paused midway to her mouth.

"There was a note."

"A note?" Bettina reared back, doughnut still in hand. "You didn't tell me about the note, only the raw eggs." She leaned forward. "What did the note say?"

"Bunny Cuddle." Pamela suppressed a giggle. "That's all I could make out. It was on the ground, half hidden by . . . Ellen's . . . shoulder. But there was a map too, something like a little hand-drawn map showing an open space that could have been the lawn, the parking lot, the tennis courts, and the stand of trees."

"Someone was inviting her to an assignation!" Bettina's carefully shaped brows rose and her eyes opened wide. "And then they killed her! The police must have found the note if it was sitting right out there for you to see. That's a giant clue." She lowered the doughnut, still intact, to her plate. "Clayborn certainly didn't mention any note to me—

and if he'd told Marcy, that detail would have been on the front page of the *Register* this morning, guaranteed!"

"It's definitely a clue." Pamela nodded. "It could be a very important clue, and maybe that's why he's not revealing it. Sometimes the police keep crucial details from the public if letting the killer know what they know might give the killer an advantage." She nodded again. "That's what they do in the British crime shows, anyway."

Bettina had no sooner picked up her doughnut again than a melodic trill, very faint, reached them from the entry.

"My phone." Bettina rose, still holding the doughnut. "I think."

She darted through the kitchen doorway and returned in a moment holding her phone near her ear and frowning as she listened. Pamela could hear a tinny voice but couldn't make out what the voice was saying.

"Of course, yes," Bettina murmured when the voice ceased speaking. The doughnut was resting on the wedding-china plate once again, the color of its pink icing echoing the roses that edged the rim. "She *would* have wanted that, and you're thoughtful to get in touch." She paused and the tinny voice resumed. When it was Bettina's turn to respond, she said, "I *do* know where it is and, in fact, I'm very close."

A few pleasantries were exchanged—at least Pamela assumed the tinny voice's closing comments were as cordial as Bettina's—and the phone, its screen darkened, was set on the table.

"I'm going to eat this doughnut before I say another word," Bettina announced, and the action that followed made good on the promise.

Pamela had been enjoying the leisurely back and forth

of nibbling her doughnut and sipping her coffee, appreciating the interplay between the crumbly cake-like interior of the doughnut and its sugary icing, set off by the hot and bitter coffee. She was curious, though, about the call, and abandoned both doughnut and coffee when Bettina wiped her fingers on her napkin and prepared to speak.

"That was Ellen's neighbor," she explained. "Corinne Charters. Ellen was very conscientious about getting her weekly recipe into the *Advocate*—I can testify to that—and Corinne is sure that Ellen would have wanted the recipe she had prepared for this coming Friday to appear."

"Is she suggesting that we try to make contact with Ellen by consulting a medium, or . . . ?"

"Of course not." Bettina laughed. "Corinne has the recipe. She was the 'tester,' and Ellen always asked her to follow the recipe just as it was written, to make sure anyone making it would get the result the recipe promised."

"Did she say what the recipe was?"

"Deviled eggs. Very timely, though I imagine she puts her own spin on them. Anybody who knows how to cook knows how to make deviled eggs—not to say that yours aren't special."

"It sounded like you told her you'd come by . . ." Pamela picked her doughnut up again.

"I did," Bettina responded, "and you're invited, but I haven't even tasted my coffee yet, and there are two doughnuts left."

"No more for me." Pamela stretched out a hand in a "halt" gesture as Bettina folded back the top flap of the bakery box.

"That's why you're thin and I'm not," Bettina remarked cheerfully as she transferred a doughnut to her plate.

Chapter Three

"I suppose we're driving," Pamela said a short time later as they proceeded toward her front door, past the spot in the entry where Catrina still slumbered in the patch of sunlight. Her tone was teasing.

"I'm not like you," Bettina responded, "walking everywhere, even to the Co-Op and back, with bags of groceries." She extended a foot, shod in a pump that echoed the pastel green of her suit. "I think I can manage half a block though, even in good shoes."

Corinne Charters lived in the stately brick apartment building at the corner of Orchard Street and Arborville Avenue. Apartment 4A, Corinne's apartment, was just to the left as the elevator doors opened on the fourth floor, right next to an apartment whose door was crisscrossed with yellow crime-scene tape.

"They're gone now," Corinne commented as she swung her door open in response to Bettina's light tap. Bettina and Pamela were both studying the crime-scene tape. "But they were here for ages yesterday evening, and a few of them came back for a bit this morning."

She was a tall woman, taller than Pamela, with a shapely figure that offset the impression made by her unstylish gray-blond hair. She was wearing jeans, a flannel shirt unbuttoned over a cotton turtleneck, and clogs.

"Come in, come in." She reinforced the invitation with a beckoning gesture, and they stepped into a living room whose furnishings seemed chosen more for utility and economy than for style.

"It's right here," Corinne said after introductions were out of the way. She pointed at a sheet of paper lying on the coffee table. "Excuse the oil spots. Ellen's version of deviled eggs uses olive oil instead of mayonnaise, and I got a little sloppy while I was working."

Bettina picked the recipe up and handed it to Pamela. "You're the cook," she said. "What do you think?"

Before Pamela could respond, though, Corinne cut in. "Mediterranean, I'd say. There's not that much you can do to deviled eggs—unless of course you want to just veer off and stuff the egg-white halves with tuna, or crab, or avocado, or whatever . . . but then I wouldn't really call it a deviled egg."

"Sounds good." Bettina nodded. "Especially crab, or maybe shrimp . . ."

"Don't you dare steal my ideas!" Pamela was startled by Corinne's serious tone, and she stared at the woman.

"Oh!" Corinne laughed, as if to neutralize the effect of her curt admonition. "I should have mentioned—I'm a cookbook author too, but my book's scope is much broader than just eggs."

"Are you working on a project right now?" Ever willing to be sociable, Bettina offered an encouraging smile.

"I certainly am!" Corinne smiled back, but the smile faded when she said, "I didn't get the advance I was expecting, but hopefully after the book comes out the royalties will make up for that."

"What else besides eggs?" Bettina was always interested in food and seemed eager to hear more about the cookbook project, but Corinne's response took the conversation in a different—though egg-related—direction.

"The *Register* mentioned raw eggs at the scene where Ellen's body was found," she said. "I suppose the eggs will help the police in tracking down the killer?"

"The eggs were a curious detail"—Bettina nodded—"though of course Ellen *was* an egg influencer."

"Somebody making a point . . ." Corinne shrugged, her shoulders jerking upward and then relaxing once again.

"Yes," Bettina murmured. "But what was the point?"

She glanced at Pamela with an expression that suggested she was ready to leave. Corinne noticed the glance and intuited its meaning.

"Something else," she said quickly, "before you go." She reached over and picked up a shopping bag from the sofa. "I know you're a knitter, Bettina, from hearsay. Everybody in Arborville knows about Bettina Fraser from the *Advocate*."

She thrust the bag toward Bettina, who intercepted it with a carefully manicured hand, peeked inside, and looked up to comment, "Yarn."

"Ellen was a knitter, too," Corinne explained. "A real Martha Stewart, with the cooking and the crafts. She always had a knitting project going for some boyfriend or other, and I guess these are the leftovers from the projects. I don't know why she thought I'd want them, though I used to knit a bit. Maybe you'll have a use for them, or Pamela—or you can pass them along."

Bettina handed the bag to Pamela, who stood for a moment with the recipe in one hand and the bag in the other.

Then she folded the recipe and tucked it into the bag, feeling her way among the many balls and partial skeins of yarn.

"There's certainly a lot of it," she commented.

"Ellen went through a lot of men." Corinne's tone was matter-of-fact. "She was certainly enjoying her freedom since her divorce, so it was a good thing she was a fast knitter." She scrutinized Bettina's face, then Pamela's, before she went on, perhaps to determine whether they'd be shocked by her next utterance.

After a moment, though, she added, "Let me just say it's a good thing this building is old and the walls are solid plaster, well insulated. Otherwise I'd have had some interrupted sleep, being right next door . . ." She smiled to herself and nodded, rocking back and forth. "I'm just as glad to have put all that behind me."

Bettina began to edge toward the door and Corinne took the hint. "You've got the recipe?"

Pamela felt down into the bag again and fingered the folded paper. As she did so, her fingers encountered something else that wasn't yarn, something bulky, hard, and kind of lumpy. She grasped it and pulled it up from the bag's woolly depths. Extracted, it was revealed to be a cellophane package of Jordan almonds—glossy almond shapes sugar-coated in assorted pastels.

"Oh, those!" Corinne chuckled. "They were an Easter gift from Ellen and I can't stand the things. Please take them!"

"I'm sure Clayborn interviewed Corinne," Bettina observed as they stepped off the elevator into the building's lobby. "She knows a lot about Ellen. There's an ex-husband in the picture and lots of boyfriends since then, it sounds like. Ellen cared enough for them to knit them sweaters, but then got bored with them, or . . . ? Plenty of suspects, I would think. Men resentful at being tossed aside."

"The note, though . . ." They'd reached the heavy door that separated the lobby from the building's landscaped front yard and the sidewalk beyond. Pamela waited until they were outside to go on. "The note at the crime scene, which I'm sure the police found, seemed to be inviting Ellen to an assignation. Why would she want to rendezvous with someone she'd tossed aside?"

"Good point," Bettina murmured faintly, but she seemed distracted. She'd been creeping along slowly as they approached the sidewalk, focusing not on the path ahead but on the overstuffed shopping bag that dangled from Pamela's hand.

"Ninotchka's!" she exclaimed suddenly, coming to a halt. "Fancy, fancy, fancy!"

Pamela held the bag out at arm's length. It was pink, a shade of pink that could only be described as . . . suggestive, with the word "Ninotchka's" scrolled across the side in a typeface that seemed both elegant and teasing. Below, smaller letters in the same script spelled out "because you know you're worth it."

Bettina laughed. "It might just as well say 'because you want to spend more on lingerie than most people spend on their mortgage.'"

"The yarn came from Ellen," Pamela observed. "I suppose the bag came from her, too. The egg influencer business must be quite lucrative."

"She might not have been the one who actually paid for the goodies from Ninotchka's." Bettina added a pitying look that suggested Pamela was unacquainted with the ways of the world.

"Boyfriends!" Pamela said. "Plying her with expensive lingerie. But then they did get sweaters in return . . ."

"We'll give the yarn to Nell." Bettina reached for the bag and peeked inside to examine the contents. "There's enough here for a whole zoo full of those animals she likes to knit for the children at the women's shelter. She'll be delighted."

Back at home, Pamela tidied the kitchen and then climbed the stairs to her office, settling at the desk where her computer monitor slumbered. She had checked her email first thing that morning and found a message from her boss at *Fiber Craft*. Files for three articles were attached, with instructions to read them and advise whether they were suitable for publication in the magazine. Their short titles, strung across the top of the email message, were "David's Closet," "Fashion in the Abstract," and "Flag Redesign." She opened the first, whose full title proved to be, "What Was in King David's Closet? Royal Purple Fragments Offer a Hint."

The article, by a textile historian named Agnes Strathmore, described a recent discovery made by an Israeli archeological team. She had been called in as a consultant to analyze one of their finds, fragments of vivid purple cloth that, from the context in which they were found, appeared to be at least three thousand years old. She had confirmed the archeologists' hunch that the color was an example of the royal purple long associated with elite status and created by an arduous process involving a substance derived from the bodies of mollusks. The location of the find, together with the dating of the fragments, suggested a link between them and biblical references to "garments of purple" worn by such figures as David and

Solomon. Photos of the purple fragments illustrated the article, testifying to the fact that they were indeed purple and that they were indeed fragments.

Pamela pushed her chair back from her desk and closed her eyes after reading the final page and studying the photos. The article's author was certainly qualified to handle her subject, and the article was scrupulously documented, including a citation of the archeological journal in which the archeologists who made the find had reported their discovery. In a sense, though, the article submitted to *Fiber Craft* was redundant. The findings had already been reported in the *Bulletin of Biblical Archeology*, published by the Free University of Utrecht.

On the other hand, readers of *Fiber Craft* most likely did not also read the *Bulletin of Biblical Archeology*. They might not encounter this material anywhere else, and the author had been sure to emphasize the find's relevance to textile studies. Pamela opened a new file, titled it "Evaluations," and wrote a brief paragraph recommending that "What Was in King David's Closet?" be published.

The evaluations weren't due back till the end of the week, and one article was enough for one day, she decided. Besides, her stomach was reminding her that, even though her breakfast had been augmented by the pink-iced doughnuts delivered by Bettina, she was quite ready for lunch.

Bettina was in her element, and chic as ever in black-and-white checks, her flared skirt and cropped jacket complemented by black patent pumps and a matching handbag. It was Tuesday afternoon, and she was covering an event at the Arborville library, a book talk given by a local author who was an authority on butterflies. At the moment Bettina was interviewing the author as attendees milled about nibbling on cookies and sipping coffee or tea. Pamela had been happy to accept Bettina's invitation to accompany her to the event. She was interested in butterflies and had been trying to encourage them to visit her yard. Spring planting season was at hand, and she'd been eager for tips on plants they favored.

As she lingered off to the side, enjoying her coffee and the buzz of conversation, she noticed a small red-haired woman who looked to be in her forties. The woman stood out from the crowd in that her expression and manner would have suited a person who had just sat through a lecture on some looming catastrophe, whereas the book talk had been a celebration of the joy that butterflies bring to life, not to mention their important function as pollinators.

The woman seemed to sense Pamela watching her, and she began to edge through the crowd, moving in Pamela's direction. She reached Pamela's side after a minute or two, but remained silent. Pamela mustered her social smile, turned to the woman, and heard herself say, "Interesting topic, isn't it?"

"I was hoping to have a word with Bettina," was the woman's response.

"She'll be finished in a bit, I'm sure." Given that her attempt at small talk had been ignored, Pamela felt justified in focusing on her coffee in silence.

Bettina *was* finished in a bit, and she headed toward where Pamela was standing, tucking the phone with which she had been recording her interview into her handbag. The red-headed woman stepped forward to intercept her as she approached.

"Shannon!" Bettina greeted her. "Wonderful talk, wasn't it?"

"I suppose." Shannon spoke so quietly that Pamela could barely make out the words. "Do you have a minute?"

Shannon was shorter than Bettina, and slender, and her hair was a paler shade of red—more natural-looking, some might say. As she leaned toward Bettina, she seemed almost as unsubstantial as her confiding whisper.

"Of course!" Bettina said. Shannon's distress was plain to see, and Bettina's expression shifted instantly to concern. She eased an arm around Shannon's narrow shoulders and drew her toward the doorway that offered an escape from the bright, noisy room.

The book talk had taken place in the community room on the lower level of the library. The doorway opened to a hall with a ramp at one end that led to an exit. With Pamela following, Bettina and Shannon proceeded along the hall, up the ramp, and through the exit, stepping onto a concrete path that bordered the library's rock garden.

Sandstone rocks surrounded a patch of earth already abloom with daffodils. The garden was furnished with a pretty wooden bench that commemorated a beloved librarian. The April day was mild enough to make sitting outside tolerable, and Bettina guided Shannon to the bench. It was a roomy bench, with space for three people or even four, but Pamela sensed that Shannon was seeking a private tête-à-tête with Bettina.

Accordingly, Pamela strolled across the parking lot to where additional benches offered a resting spot. These benches faced the kiddie playground, and some were occupied by women alternating between chatting and monitoring the children who spun on the merry-go-round or lined up to take a turn on the slide. Pamela's back was to the library, and she resisted the urge to twist around and try to guess from gestures and facial expressions what Shannon's urgent business with Bettina might be. Instead, she let her mind wander back to the days when she had occupied perhaps this very same bench while watching a very young Penny explore the kiddie playground's attractions.

So lost was she in her memories that Bettina's greeting came as an unexpected interruption. A moment later Bettina had settled next to her, sighing as she made herself comfortable. Pamela had no need to inquire why Shannon had been so eager to confer with Bettina. The sigh modulated into a murmured, "Poor thing."

"*Ummm?*" That was all the encouragement Bettina needed.

"I know you'll be discreet," she said, "or I wouldn't share what Shannon told me . . ." She paused. "Though actually it's relevant to our experience Sunday after the Easter egg hunt, as well as what we learned from Corinne, so even if you *weren't* discreet . . ." She paused again. "Anyway . . ."

It seemed that Shannon's husband, Dwight Silverthorne, had been questioned by the police concerning Ellen's murder, and because Bettina reported on police doings (as well as almost everything else that took place in Arborville) for the *Advocate*, Shannon thought Bettina might have some insight into the implications.

"The thing is," Bettina explained, "she had suspected he was straying, and we know from Corinne that Ellen got up to all kinds of things."

"What made her suspect?"

"He was inattentive, and suddenly there were 'work emergencies' that kept him out late, and her birthday came and went without even a card, where in the past he always bought her fancy lingerie."

"Ninotchka's!" Pamela exclaimed. "He was still buying fancy lingerie, but just not for Shannon."

"Something to think about." Bettina nodded and the lively tendrils of her hair quivered.

"Something to think about," Pamela agreed. "But he hasn't been arrested."

"Not yet, anyway."

They made their way back to Orchard Street then and parted at the end of the Frasers' driveway, but not before agreeing that they would drive to the Knit and Nibble meeting at Nell's house that evening in Pamela's car.

Chapter Four

The sun had not yet set, though to the west the horizon was stained coral and gold, when the Bascombs' front door swung open to reveal Harold Bascomb. Pamela and Bettina stood on a small porch at the top of steps that zigzagged up a slope planted with azaleas and rhododendrons whose leaves were just reviving after the winter cold.

"Come in, come in, come in," he urged. Harold and his wife, Nell, were in their eighties, but Harold's hearty voice and vigorous manner belied his years. "Everyone else is here, even Roland—though he insisted on checking and double-checking the parking signs to make sure the Porsche is in a legal spot."

Harold ushered them into the slate-floored entry, which gave a view of the living room, with its high beamed ceiling and natural stone fireplace. A small fire burned in the fireplace, adding to the welcoming effect of the pleasant room.

The group's youngest members, Holly Perkins and Karen Dowling, sat side by side on a chintz-upholstered loveseat, one of a pair that flanked the fireplace. Across from them, Roland DeCamp sat alone on the other, his fingers already busy with his knitting needles, and his lean face intent. Next to him on the loveseat was the elegant leather briefcase that he used in place of a knitting bag.

The long sofa that faced the fireplace was empty at the moment. Nell had popped up from her seat there and was beckoning the new arrivals. "Plenty of space here," she said. "Come and join me."

Harold, who was not a knitter, retreated toward the kitchen, and Pamela and Bettina accepted Nell's invitation. For a few moments, the only sounds were the crackling of the fire and low murmurs as Holly and Karen chatted. Pamela and Bettina were silent as they extracted their projects from their knitting bags.

Bettina was partway through a dress for one of her granddaughter's dolls. The yarn was pale pink, and the lacy stitch was challenging enough to require frequent references to the instructions. Pamela was nearly finished with a sweater intended for Penny, whose birthday was in May, though as far as wearing it went, that would have to wait till cooler weather.

It was a simple, close-fitting cardigan knit from navy-blue yarn, but it was modeled on a warm-up jacket, with a zipper instead of buttons. It featured deep ribbing at the bottom edge and cuffs, and a ribbed collar that could function as a turtleneck when the cardigan was zipped up. The zipper was waiting in reserve to be sewn in as the last step. Only one piece was left to complete, and Pamela set to work, the half-finished sleeve dangling from her left-hand needle as she maneuvered the right-hand needle into position for the first stitch.

Near Pamela's feet, tucked against the sofa, sat the shopping bag of yarn leftovers. Nell had seemed eager to get back to her knitting as soon as Pamela and Bettina took their seats on the sofa. Rather than distract her with the gift of leftovers now, Pamela would wait until eight o'clock, when by long tradition the knitters set their work aside to nibble a sweet treat provided by the evening's host. She was happy now to focus on her knitting, adding one row and then another and another to the in-progress sleeve.

So deeply engrossed was she that she reacted with a start when Bettina nudged her.

"Pamela? Pamela?" came a voice from one of the loveseats, though it took her a moment to identify its source. "Pamela?" the voice, which was Holly's voice, repeated.

"Eggs," Bettina clarified. "We've been talking about eggs."

"Dyeing them," Holly added, "and decorating them. It's so much fun, all those different colors, but you end up with dozens of hard-boiled eggs. What do you do with them then?"

Looking at Holly, it was clear that she was a person to whom the artistic possibilities of egg decoration would appeal. Abundant raven hair accented with a streak of bright crimson set off a glowing complexion, expressive eyes, and full lips tinted with the same crimson hue. Dramatic earrings, like tiny chandeliers, dangled from her earlobes.

"Devil them, of course," Bettina said, "and that was my advice, and since nobody makes better deviled eggs than you, Pamela . . ."

It seemed that Holly had come prepared for just such a suggestion. She bent forward and tugged a capacious black leather tote from under the coffee table.

"Here they are," she announced. She stood up as she hefted the tote, which was clearly heavy.

"I can't take them all," Pamela protested. She leaned past Bettina toward where Nell sat. "Nell," she said. "You hate to waste food. Surely . . ."

"We have our own." Nell laughed. "The Easter bunny was very good to the Bascomb household."

"Well . . . all right." Pamela stood up, reached for the tote, and stowed it on the floor near the shopping bag. "I'll devil them, but I won't keep them all." She addressed Holly. "You can pick some up during the week. I'll let you know when."

She surveyed the room. No one was knitting except Roland, and it was getting on toward break time anyway. She picked up the shopping bag and stepped closer to Nell.

"Here's something for you that I . . . we"—she glanced at Bettina, who was sitting next to Nell—"Bettina and I . . . hope you *will* take." She tilted the bag to display its contents more clearly. "Lots and lots of yarn, leftovers, all kinds and all colors. For your elephants, or donkeys, or teddy bears, or whatever."

Nell set her work down—it looked to be one of her elephants, judging by the oval shape that was forming on her needles.

"Why, yes," she responded, taking the bag onto her lap and pulling out a partial skein of fuzzy green yarn. "I'm always happy to use up leftovers."

Holly had left her seat and was perched on the end of the sofa next to Nell. "Amazing!" she murmured, reaching into the bag and coming up with a ball of yarn the color of orange sherbet and then three more in varying shades of turquoise, and a skein of fuchsia. "Beautiful!" she went on. "It's like yarn in all the Easter egg colors."

Karen had joined Holly at Nell's side. Quiet and pretty and blond, Karen was as different from Holly as might be imagined, but they were the best of friends. She too began examining the contents of the bag, commenting on the variety of colors and the high quality of the yarn.

"You're both welcome to take some home with you"—Nell gave each a fond smile—"but only on condition that it comes back to me in the form of animals for the children at the shelter."

"I'll do one," Holly said, scooping up a ball of yarn the color of bubble gum, and Karen echoed her, choosing pale yellow.

Nell began gathering up the various balls and skeins that had been strewn here and there.

"Where did this bounty come from?" she inquired as she tucked the last ball back into the bag.

Pamela let her eyes meet Bettina's. They hadn't planned an answer for this question, and Nell was known to disapprove of letting shocking town events become fodder for idle chitchat.

"It belonged to someone who didn't want it," Pamela said, "and that someone gave it to someone else who also didn't want it, and so that someone else gave it to us."

"Does the first someone have a name?" Holly inquired, her gaze lively. "She's an awfully busy knitter."

"She *was* . . ." Bettina whispered to Pamela.

Holly's hearing was sharper than Nell's. "*Was*?" she inquired, "As in, she doesn't have a use for all this yarn because she's . . ."

"Why she didn't want it doesn't matter," Bettina said. "It's found a good home, and the elephants or whatever will make a lot of children very happy."

A curious sound interrupted the conversation then—the sound of a throat being purposefully, though perhaps unnecessarily, cleared. The sound emanated from the loveseat where Roland sat alone.

"Does anyone care," he inquired when he was satisfied all eyes were focused on him, "that it's eight o'clock? Or, having dispensed with knitting, shall we also dispense with nibbling?"

"We never dispense with nibbling!" Bettina announced gaily. An amused glance at Pamela conveyed both her glee at Roland's so-typically-Roland reaction and her gratitude that he'd provided a distraction from Holly's curiosity.

"Even if the evening's nibble is broccoli bars?" Harold had appeared at the end of the hallway that led to the Bascombs' kitchen.

"Harold?" Nell twisted sideways from her spot on the sofa to regard her husband. "What are you talking about? People have made fun of my broccoli bars enough times that I'd never serve them to Knit and Nibble."

"New Year's resolution, my dear." Harold smiled. "Healthful eating. Don't you remember?"

Nell was on her feet now, with a fond smile that mirrored Harold's, though hers was only a hint. "We're over three months into the new year," she said, "and I've noticed no change at all in your eating habits."

"I've got the coffee going, and water for tea." Harold took a few steps back toward the kitchen. As he retreated, he could be heard to say, "And I stopped by that Italian bakery in Meadowside this afternoon . . ."

The treat Harold had fetched from the Italian bakery was a far cry from broccoli bars. Coffee and tea were served with help from Holly and Karen, and the six knitters gathered around the coffee table. Harold entered, bearing a splendid creation featuring ricotta, mini chocolate chips, and candied orange peel in a pasta frolla crust.

"It's an Italian Easter pie," he explained as he took up a knife and prepared to serve it.

Seven dessert plates from Nell's china set, which dated from the long ago start of her marriage, sat at his elbow.

Each plate was furnished with a wedge of pie and handed round, and soon forks were raised in unison. A unanimous *yum* greeted the first taste, Pamela's *yum* loud among them.

The taste and texture were like cheesecake, though not quite as sweet and not quite as creamy. The bittersweet chocolate chips, the piquant orange peel, and the sweet and flaky crust added variety.

As the wedges of pie dwindled to nubbins and crumbs, and only traces of coffee or tea remained in the depths of the china cups, lips and tongues were freed to converse once again. Holly had clearly been pondering the backstory of the yarn leftovers that had made their way into Nell's hands.

Nell had vacated her spot on the sofa in order to perch at the end of one of the loveseats, close to the hearth, where Harold was sitting. Holly now slipped into Nell's old spot, next to Bettina. Speaking so low that Pamela, on the other side of Bettina, could make out only a few words, she seemed to be inquiring whether the yarn had come from someone recently deceased.

Bettina's nod of assent was barely perceptible.

"It didn't come from that egg influencer, did it?" Holly's voice was louder.

"It might have," Bettina whispered, with a glance toward Nell. "How did you know?"

"She's on TikTok. I watch her sometimes. She talks about everything, not just recipes. A few weeks ago, she was showing off some yarn she had bought—Easter egg colors, she called it. She was really looking forward to Easter."

"Looking forward to Easter." The phrase struck Pamela. Had Ellen been anticipating something more than the traditional eggs and bunnies and feasting, a something that hadn't turned to be at all what she expected?

Roland was stirring, consulting the impressive watch that lurked beneath the cuff of his flawlessly starched shirt. The shirt, and the discreetly patterned tie, complemented the pinstripe suit that was Roland's habitual garb, befitting his job as a corporate lawyer.

"It's a quarter after eight," he announced after a pause, perhaps delaying the announcement until the second hand of his watch made the time exact. "I don't know about the rest of you, but I plan to resume my knitting." With that, he took up the project, with its dangling bobbins and four double-pointed needles, that was his latest argyle sock.

"I have to admit," Bettina said as she and Pamela made their way down the steps that zigzagged from the Bascombs' front porch to the curb, "that I didn't get as much knitting done tonight as I could have, but Roland is certainly a spoilsport."

"Nell liked the yarn, and I don't think she overheard what Holly was saying." They had reached the spot where Pamela's serviceable compact was parked. She unlocked the passenger-side door.

"Ellen was looking forward to Easter." Bettina lowered herself into her seat.

"Looking forward to what in particular, I wonder," Pamela murmured as the car pulled away from the curb. "An assignation with Shannon's husband, lent a special hint of naughtiness by its being outdoors and coinciding with the town's Easter egg hunt?"

"It doesn't surprise me that he might be involved in this," Bettina said. "I've met him and he's very flirtatious."

"Bettina!" Pamela laughed. "*You're* flirtatious. Just

because a person is flirtatious, that doesn't mean they're a killer."

The next morning, after she and the cats had breakfasted, Pamela climbed the stairs to her office, sat down at her desk, and let her mouse roam freely on its mouse pad until her monitor awakened. Of the two articles remaining to be evaluated for *Fiber Craft*, "Fashion in the Abstract" and "Flag Redesign," she chose "Fashion in the Abstract."

The article proved to be about the French-Ukrainian artist Sonia Delaunay, whose early career coincided with the rise of abstract art in the early decades of the twentieth century. Her relevance to the readers of *Fiber Craft* was that, rather than using traditional artistic tools such as paint and paper to convey her fragmented and abstracted vision of reality, she first used cloth. And most interestingly, the fragmentation was literal. She designed garments made of patchwork—abstract shapes in dramatic colors cut and pieced together. Only later did she render those same shapes as abstract designs on paper.

The article was illustrated with photographs of actual garments, such as a close-fitting ankle-length dress that would have made the wearer resemble an ambulatory crazy quilt, and a man's waistcoat that would have greatly enlivened a formal ensemble.

Pamela wrote an enthusiastic recommendation that the article be published. She noted, as the author had, that Sonia Delaunay deserved to have her work considered apart from that of her husband, the painter Robert Delaunay, who had often seemed to eclipse her.

Pamela had just completed her evaluation and closed her evaluations file when the phone rang, awaking Ginger, who had been slumbering in Pamela's lap.

"Come over for lunch" were the first words she heard.

The caller was not hard to identify, and the next words confirmed Pamela's guess. "Wilfred came home from the Newfield farmers market with rye bread and pastrami, both from New Jersey farms. I tried your other phone but it went to voice mail. I suppose you're working."

"I was just finished," Pamela said.

Five minutes later, she entered the Frasers' kitchen to find Bettina staring at a smart phone. She rotated her hand to display the small screen to Pamela, saying, "Trevor Brant. He lives in Arborville. Wilfred thinks I should interview him for the *Advocate*."

The photo showed an attractive youngish man standing behind the counter of a farmers market stall. Above him, a banner announced "Trevor's Farm Fresh Free-Range Eggs." The words were bracketed by images of happy-looking chickens.

"He's not there every day," Wilfred said. "He does a few other farmers markets too, and he has a subscription service where people can sign up to have eggs delivered weekly or whatever."

"Did he know Ellen?" Pamela inquired.

"Actually, he did. He tried to enlist Ellen in the free-range cause and was hoping she would use the *Eggotist's Cookbook* to proselytize for it, but she refused."

"Maybe Detective Clayborn should interview *him*," Pamela suggested. "There's a motive right there, and the yolks of the broken eggs at the crime scene were definitely that free-range color."

"I'm not sure a person would kill someone just because she wasn't a free-range devotee." Wilfred was holding his phone now and gazing at the photo. "He's so closely associated with free-range eggs that it would be kind of dumb to kill Ellen and then decorate the crime scene with them."

"Besides," Bettina added, speaking to Pamela, "the note you saw suggested Ellen had gone there to meet a romantic interest."

Wilfred fingered his phone until the screen went dark. The parcels from his farmers market errand had remained on the table, identifiable by their aromas—dark and yeasty with a hint of caraway for the loaf shape, and peppery for the parcel wrapped in butcher's paper. He picked them up and headed for the counter to launch the sandwiches.

Chapter Five

Thursday morning, Pamela and Bettina were finishing up a leisurely brunch at Hyler's Luncheonette, lingering over the remnants of the waffle and sausage combo that could only be had if one arrived before eleven a.m. Instead of one of the burgundy Naugahyde-upholstered booths, they had chosen to sit at a table near the floor-to-ceiling windows that looked out on the sidewalk.

"A little more coffee?" inquired the server, and without waiting for an answer she tipped her carafe and dark liquid splashed into Pamela's mug.

Bettina's mug was refilled too, requiring that Bettina perform the sugaring and creaming operation necessary to transform the dark liquid into the sweet and pale concoction she preferred. While she was busy with sugar packets and the cream pitcher, Pamela enjoyed the passing scene. A young mother pushed a stroller with one hand and led a toddler with the other. A dog walker waited while her furry charge sniffed the base of a tree. Three teenage boys walking abreast suddenly broke ranks to let an elderly woman pass. And here came an attractive youngish man who somehow looked familiar.

"Bettina." Pamela was whispering, though she didn't

know why. Bettina looked up from stirring her coffee. "Isn't that Trevor Brant?"

At this point he had passed by, so identification would be imprecise, though he was jacketless and the sweater he was wearing was very distinctive.

"I don't think he was wearing that sweater in Wilfred's photo"—Bettina squinted after the retreating figure—"but I've definitely seen it somewhere before."

"You've seen the *yarn*," Pamela said. "We both have."

"Ellen's yarn leftovers!" Bettina exclaimed.

Trevor was still in view, though Pamela had to swivel in her chair to see him. The sweater was a simple pullover, but it featured broad horizontal stripes knit mostly in shades of blue and green. Deep turquoise was juxtaposed with grass green, lime, and sage, and the contrast was dramatized by narrow stripes in fuchsia, orange, and yellow.

After he turned the corner and vanished, Bettina sampled her coffee. A longer sip and a moment of reflection led to her saying, "This complicates things."

Pamela nodded. "Spurned love is a much stronger motive than lack of appreciation for free-range eggs."

"But if she'd spurned him, why would she respond to a note inviting her to a tryst?"

"Could the note have been from someone else, and he somehow knew she'd be showing up there to meet the other person . . . ?" Pamela lifted her own replenished mug and tilted it to her lips. "*Oo-or* . . ."—she drew the word out, willing the caffeine to do its work ". . . Trevor forged a note in the style of whoever Ellen was currently involved with . . ."

"Who knows what goes on in the mind of a killer?" Bettina shook her head, setting her earrings in motion and suggesting puzzlement. The earrings were large amber teardrops that harmonized with the peachy shade of the floppy silk bow visible between the lapels of her chic camel blazer.

"In any event"—resolution replaced puzzlement—"whatever the explanation, the sweater suggests he's got the motive, or at least was involved with her at some point. As far as means and opportunity go, she was strangled. No exotic murder weapon there. And the venue for the crime was a public park, open to anyone. The eggs are just the icing on the cake, better than fingerprints or footprints."

"Shannon would certainly be relieved to know that the police had a much more likely suspect than Dwight."

"And I'm going to make sure that happens." Bettina opened her handbag, which had been dangling from her chair back, and took out her wallet. "Here," she said, handing Pamela a few bills. "This should cover most of it." Her chair scraped against the floor as she pushed away from the table and stood up. "I'm off to see Clayborn. Meet me by my car."

Just to the left of Hyler's, a narrow passageway offered a shortcut from Arborville's commercial district to the parking lot that served the police station, the library, and the park where the Easter egg hunt had taken place. Bettina's car waited in that lot.

The stand of trees by the tennis courts came into view as Pamela emerged from the passageway, and she noted that the crime-scene tape still marked it as off limits. Despite the proximity of the courts to the crime scene, a lively tennis game was in progress.

Bettina was nowhere to be seen, and so Pamela strolled over to the rock garden outside the library and settled onto the memorial bench. She was happy to daydream and enjoy the bright day, and was almost disappointed when Bettina came into view.

Bettina, however, clearly *was* disappointed, with no *almost* about it. She ambled slowly across the asphalt, her scarlet-coiffed head drooping. Even the bow at the neck of her blouse seemed dispirited.

"They've arrested Dwight Silverthorne," she announced with no preamble, and before even sitting down.

As if to invite company, Pamela moved over, though there was already plenty of room beside her on the bench.

"He has no fashion sense," Bettina went on in a disgusted tone, "but we already knew that."

"Dwight Silverthorne?" Pamela turned to regard her friend. "You might have known that, but I've never met the man."

"Clayborn, I mean." Bettina stamped a foot. "You've seen how he dresses, so of course the fact that Trevor Brant owns a sweater that is so clearly the handiwork of a murder victim known to cast off men . . . well, as rapidly as she might cast off a . . . a . . . *sleeve* she's finished knitting—" Bettina paused to take a breath. "That means nothing at all to him. He's probably even color blind."

"What about the connection with the free-range eggs and the orange yolks at the crime scene?"

"He doesn't know anything about food, either. He's never even heard of the Newfield farmers market."

On the drive back to Orchard Street, a glum silence reigned until Bettina had turned into the Frasers' driveway and the Toyota had come to rest next to Wilfred's ancient Mercedes.

"Shannon will probably call me," Bettina murmured, slumped in her seat as if she'd lost the will to move, staring at nothing in particular. "I don't know what to tell her."

Still staring, and in the same despondent murmur, she added, "Ellen's funeral is tomorrow."

"I don't see any reason to go," Pamela said. "Do you?"

"I should, for the *Advocate*."

With that, they parted ways and Pamela crossed the street to her own house. The meal of waffles and sausages guaranteed that she wouldn't be hungry again for a very long time so, upstairs, she settled into her desk chair and opened the *Fiber Craft* file labeled "Flag Redesign."

Flags, it appeared, were as subject to the whims of fashion—though "whims" was perhaps not quite the right word—as any other artifact produced by humans. The author of the article described himself as a retired civil servant and amateur vexillologist, a word that owed its first half to the Latin word for *flag*.

He pointed out that as logos associated with products had become more streamlined, realistic images on flags, such as trees, buildings, or animals, had come to look dated—not to mention that they'd always been hard to decipher from a distance. Modern flag design might reduce a pine tree, for example, to an elongated green triangle with a glimpse of trunk that was no more than a small brown square.

More fraught was the modernization of flags that incorporated state seals into their design. First of all, details on state seals were difficult to make out from a distance, and if they had lettering, the lettering made no sense when the reverse side of the flag was viewed. More important, though, states whose flags featured state seals were among the first states united into what became the United States, and the seals often celebrated the conquest and subjection of Native Americans. Redesign involved completely rethinking appropriate symbolism for the state.

"Pictures," Pamela whispered to herself, "why don't you have pictures?"

She skimmed the article again and then opened her evaluations file. "The author should resubmit with illustrations," she wrote, after praising the article's topic and the author's expertise. She suggested that the article, if resubmitted with satisfactory illustrations, be included in a possible midsummer issue with a patriotic theme.

Friday morning brought the *Register*, and the *Advocate*. The former had nothing new to report on the Easter egg murder, and Bettina's article in the latter was, at this point, decidedly old news—though devotees of Arborville's weekly had been known to say "better late than never" about the *Advocate*'s coverage of town events both big and small. After breakfast and a pleasant browse through both newspapers over coffee, Pamela looked over her evaluations of the three articles and sent them on their way to Celine Bramley. That task completed, she crossed the hall to her bedroom to ponder the contents of her closet.

She'd agreed to accompany Bettina to Ellen Weatherby's funeral—and she had to admit she was curious to see who the mourners might be. She'd enjoyed more than one BBC mystery in which the funeral of a deceased man brought out a crowd of women, each startled to realize that she had been only one among many romantic conquests. Would Ellen's mourners skew heavily toward male?

Bettina would be chic in black with pearls, she knew, as she reached for brown slacks and a wool jacket whose brown and black stripe picked up the shade of the slacks. In the bathroom, she combed her dark hair, which usually hung loose to her shoulders, and corralled it with a wide barrette at the nape of her neck.

* * *

Ellen had had a brother and sister-in-law in Timberley, and they'd arranged the funeral at their own church, a stately red-brick structure with a Victorian air, far removed from Timberley's bustling commercial district. It featured its own graveyard, a vast expanse of pale grass, interrupted by tombstones, which stretched to a straggling border of trees. The grave into which Ellen's coffin was lowered had been dug in a portion of the graveyard occupied by generations of Weatherbys going back to the origins of the congregation.

Looking around at the people surrounding the gravesite, Pamela recognized Corinne Charters, as well as a number of other Arborville residents known to her by face but not by name. As soon as the minister uttered the last few soothing words of the burial liturgy and a symbolic clump of earth landed on the coffin's surface, Ellen's brother and sister-in-law detached themselves from the group of onlookers. Followed by another couple whom they acknowledged with a nod, they set out across the grass toward the parking lot.

"Snobby," Bettina whispered to Pamela. "The Weatherbys are an old Timberley family. Not all that proud of her, I suspect, but they did the right thing and held the funeral."

"Come along to my place." The invitation came from an attractive man who had been following the burial ceremony most attentively and introduced himself as Ralph Minster. He surveyed the group, which was beginning to disperse. "I was a work colleague of Ellen's, and I've prepared a few snacks and laid in some champagne. I've been putting the word out that everyone who knew her is welcome."

He lived in Arborville, it seemed, and he repeated his address a few times as people keyed it into their phones.

"Work colleague," Bettina commented as she picked her way across the lawn in her black suede pumps, trying to keep up with Pamela's long strides en route to the car. "Where did she work?"

"We might find out if we went to the reception and chatted with Ralph Minster," Pamela responded. "Are you that curious?"

"I'm *hungry*!"

Ralph Minster lived in the section of Arborville the old-timers referred to as The Farm. Long ago it had been a farm owned by the Van Ripers, a family descended from early Dutch settlers. Eventually the Van Riper heirs had realized there was more money to be made selling their land to developers than continuing to farm, and now houses more modern than most of Arborville's housing stock occupied land where vegetables once grew.

As Pamela and Bettina navigated the winding streets and cul-de-sacs of The Farm, so different from the neat grid that marked Arborville's older residential neighborhoods, they realized that Ralph Minster and Roland DeCamp were neighbors. Like Roland's house, Ralph's was an angular split level with a two-car garage that took up nearly half of the house's facade. A cement path bisected the well-groomed yard and widened out into a low porch, where the door was decorated with a fanciful wreath involving pastel eggs and flanked by terra cotta urns planted with multicolored pansies. The door was ajar, which Pamela and Bettina took as an invitation to let themselves in.

Ralph Minster looked past the small group he was chatting with to greet the new arrivals with a cordial wave and a smile. As Pamela had remarked at the burial, he was a very attractive man. Dark hair a bit longer than the norm suggested artistic leanings, large dark eyes gave his well-modeled features a sensitive air, and the smile revealed perfect teeth. He detached himself from the group and advanced to where Pamela and Bettina were standing just inside the front door.

"Welcome, welcome," he said, his voice lively over the buzz of conversation that filled the elegantly decorated room. "I hope you like ham, and champagne."

He gestured toward the dining room, visible through a doorway to the right, where a few people were clustered around a long table helping themselves to the contents of several large platters. "I'm in the midst of a weeklong blog series, 'The Endless Ham,' and I'd already made a lot of food. It seemed a shame not to set it out for people to enjoy."

He was interrupted then by Marlene Pepper, with a neighbor Pamela recognized from the Co-Op in tow. As Ralph allowed himself to be pulled away, Pamela caught the words, "I'd like you to meet . . ." and then Bettina's voice intruded.

"I have no objection to ham," she said, "even though we've been eating leftovers from Easter all week."

Just inside the doorway, a young woman was tilting a champagne bottle over a champagne flute. Several other flutes, already filled with the sparkling golden liquid, sat waiting to be claimed.

Opting to eat first, Pamela and Bettina joined the group exploring the food offerings, which were identified with artistically lettered signs: Mini Quiche Lorraine, Sliced Ham on Beaten Biscuits, Ham Salad on Pumpernickel, and

Ham Turnovers. A large platter featuring raw vegetables suitable for munching offered a counterpoint to the ham.

"So creative" came a voice at Pamela's elbow. She glanced over to see a familiar-looking woman, who noticed the glance and addressed Pamela directly, "It's me, Noddy Gantry from the library. I follow his blog. Do you?"

"I've only just become aware of it," Pamela said.

"The blog is great, and he writes the Table for Two column in the *Register*. It's nationally syndicated." Noddy reached for a mini quiche, with its custardy center and fluted edges baked to a golden brown. "Eggs, however . . ." She studied the little tartlet, as though its appearance had triggered a thought. "When it came to eggs, nobody could compete with Ellen. I often wondered if there was a rivalry there—though when they were together, they were as cordial as can be."

"I guess they knew each other pretty well," Pamela commented, "or he wouldn't be hosting this." She made a gesture that took in the buffet table as well as the people mingling in the living room.

"I get the idea that the New Jersey food world is quite small."

Pamela's plate now held one of each ham offering, as well as a few carrot sticks, a cucumber spear, and a radish. She edged away from the table and waited near the doorway for Bettina to finish making her selections. Bettina added a second turnover to her plate and together they stepped back into the living room.

Most of the other guests had also made the circuit through the dining room and returned with well-supplied plates. On account of that, the buzz of conversation had faded to an occasional murmur, and individual voices stood out more, perhaps, than their owners intended. Ralph had peeked into the dining room, apparently to check on the supply of food and champagne. As he paused in the doorway, Pamela heard a voice, perhaps that of the young woman pouring the champagne, say, "Nice of you to do this, considering . . ."

Ralph glanced behind him but failed to notice that Pamela and Bettina were nearby, then he stepped through the doorway. Barely audible, his voice reached them.

"I thought I owed her something, *considering* . . ."

Chapter Six

"Are you thinking what I'm thinking?" Pamela asked as Bettina maneuvered the Toyota out of the cul-de-sac where Ralph Minster's house was situated.

"The beaten biscuits were amazing?"

"Not quite"—Pamela laughed—"though they were. I was actually thinking that I had kind of expected to see Trevor Brant at the funeral, or at least at Ralph Minster's gathering."

"Why would he come, to either, if Ellen broke up with him?" Bettina braked as a teenager on a skateboard lurched out of a driveway.

"He still wears the sweater she made for him," Pamela said. "Sometimes people go on loving, even after they know they'll never win the person back."

They had reached the cross street that bordered The Farm and led down to Arborville Avenue. Bettina made the turn and then replied, "I take it you've decided he's not a suspect anymore."

"Dwight Silverthorne has been arrested. Remember?"

"That doesn't mean he's guilty," Bettina said. "Clayborn has no idea how distinctive a hand-knit sweater can be, and I'm sure Shannon Silverthorne would much prefer that her husband be cleared and Trevor Brant be arrested."

Startling Pamela, Bettina swerved into the parking lot adjacent to the post office, which they were just passing, and brought the Toyota to a brake-squealing halt.

"He shouldn't be that hard to track down, with the egg business and all." Bettina swiveled around to retrieve her handbag from the back seat and took out her phone. "I'll interview him for the *Advocate*."

Trevor Brant opened his door seemingly unsurprised to have visitors, but his first words were directed to the glossy red-brown chicken that had greeted Pamela and Bettina as they advanced toward the small house. It stood now pecking at a spot near the front steps, but it looked up when he called out, "Hey, Rhoda! Go back to your flock!" He stepped over the threshold and made shooing motions, adding "Get! Get! Go!"

Addressing Pamela and Bettina, he added, "They live out back. I try to keep them away from the road, lest they're tempted to cross." With a flurry of wings and a gobbling cluck, the chicken scurried away.

Trevor's house was located in a pocket of land, still surprisingly rural, at the northeastern edge of Arborville. It had once been farmland, like the Van Ripers' land, but it hadn't been included in the parcel that became The Farm.

"Rhode Island Reds can be very friendly," Trevor said. "I think you'll like their eggs. May I ask who referred you?"

As Pamela recalled from Wilfred's photo and the glimpse of him through Hyler's window, Trevor Brant was youngish and handsome, with a compact athletic build, sandy hair, and striking green eyes. Had his appearance not been enough to identify him, he was wearing the striped sweater that had so clearly been created from the yarn whose left-overs Ellen had passed on to Corinne.

"We're not here only for eggs . . ." Bettina dipped into her handbag and came up with a small rectangular card, which she presented to Trevor, saying, "Bettina Fraser from the *Advocate*. My husband, Wilfred, met you at the New-field farmers market a few days ago, and I know readers of the *Advocate* would be interested in your egg business."

"I love the *Advocate*." Trevor backed up, pulled the door open wider, and beckoned Pamela and Bettina to enter. "I especially love 'Freebees'—such a clever idea, free ads where people can offer free things, because a lot of the people at an age where they want to clear out their excess things aren't internet savvy enough to post them online."

The room they had been invited to enter testified to Trevor's fondness for castoffs. A picturesque but battered pine trunk served as a coffee table, flanked by a small sofa whose worn upholstery was partly hidden by a much-repaired patchwork quilt. A wooden rocking chair and a distressed leather armchair provided additional seating, and a faded carpet covered most of the small room's floor.

Trevor noticed their reaction to his décor and he smiled. "Freebees," he confirmed, "all of it. I scavenge around on trash day too, especially The Farm." He waved them toward the sofa. "Sit down, please. It's clean. It's fine. No bugs. I'm constantly amazed at what people will throw away." He glanced down at the sweater, raised a hand, and stroked the soft-looking wool. "Someone had even put this beautiful sweater out for the trash. Exactly my size too, so it didn't go to waste."

Bettina and Pamela had just lowered themselves onto the sofa, so when Bettina lurched in surprise Pamela felt the cushion beneath her quiver. Trevor, now sitting in the rocking chair, was still talking—though had he been silent, she wasn't sure what she or Bettina might have said in response to the revelation about the sweater.

"And speaking of waste, I saw the article in the *Register* about the eggs at the scene where Ellen Weatherby's body was found." He leaned forward, a movement exaggerated by the motion of the rocking chair, and lowered his voice. "I was disappointed that she wasn't more supportive of the free-range cause as a fellow egghead and all, but I hope the police are working hard to find the killer. Anybody who's as into eggs as she was deserves admiration."

"Do you have any ideas about where the eggs at the crime scene came from?" Bettina inquired in an offhand tone.

"They could be *my* eggs." Trevor compressed his lips into a tight knot.

"How would they have gotten to the crime scene?" Pamela could sense Bettina vibrating slightly. The unexpected comment about the origins of the sweater had reframed the conversation, requiring a new perspective. Pamela felt her head tilt.

Trevor continued, unperturbed. "Kids," he said. "Teenage kids. They sneak around and steal eggs, like an Easter egg hunt for real. My hens don't always lay their eggs in the expected places. Then the kids get up to mischief with the eggs, like Halloween, or Mischief Night, all year round. I suppose they thought it was funny to make a mess with the eggs while the little kids were having their hunt."

Pamela cut in.

"But . . . the body . . . ? The teenage mischief-makers just ignored it?"

"Eggs could have already been there," Trevor said. "Probably were."

* * *

"Do you think the sheriff's crime scene unit thought to compare how long the eggs had been out of their shells, if that's even possible, with the amount of time that had elapsed between Ellen's murder and the discovery of the body?"

Pamela asked the question of Bettina as the two were heading back to Bettina's car, trailed by Rhoda the Rhode Island Red and each carrying a carton containing a dozen free-range eggs. Bettina also carried, on her phone, material and photos for an article on Trevor and his hens. He'd declared himself most appreciative of the publicity, and she'd assured him that the article would appear soon, though she couldn't say when. As a loyal reader, he perhaps already knew that both fans and detractors of the *Advocate* joked that any given issue contained all the news that fit, no more and no less.

"Time of death can be determined within a couple of hours, I think—especially if the body is found soon." Bettina handed her carton of eggs to Pamela and dipped into her handbag for her car keys. "But if the eggs had been thrown around at the same time Ellen was being strangled, and then a few hours had passed, I'm not sure they'd look all that different than if they'd been sitting there out of their shells for a while before she showed up for her tryst."

She unlocked the passenger-side door and circled the car to let herself in on the driver's side. With Pamela holding both egg cartons on her lap, they set off down the rutted road that served Trevor's egg farm.

"I'm glad Clayborn didn't follow up on my lead about the sweater and the free-range eggs," Bettina said when they were well underway. "I liked Trevor, and I'd hate to think of him in Clayborn's clutches."

She slowed down as they approached the intersection where a right turn would take them onto the road that skirted The Farm and sloped down to Arborville Avenue. "And I'm glad you thought to ask him where he found the sweater. I just hope we can find the house. His description was pretty vague."

"On a street with a lot of daffodils, an inflatable Easter bunny, and a basketball hoop on a garage."

"On a cul-de-sac, too," Bettina added.

"Almost every street in The Farm ends in a cul-de-sac."

"He said you drive in that main street and keep forking to the right until you can't go any farther because there's a cul-de-sac and no fork."

A few minutes later, they reached the corner where another right turn led into the twisty maze of streets that made up The Farm. Bettina turned, and after they'd passed a string of pleasant split-levels, each on its large, well-manicured lot, they faced a choice between continuing straight ahead or forking to the right.

"Keep forking to the right," Pamela murmured, and then repeated it when a similar choice loomed a few minutes later. At the next fork, she craned her neck to the right and reported, "Lots of daffodils off that way." Her voice quickened as she added, "Lots and *lots* of daffodils."

The Toyota veered toward the block with the daffodils and seemed to leap ahead when Pamela exclaimed, "I see an inflatable Easter bunny!"

The house with the inflatable Easter bunny, which was pink and at least six feet tall, occupied a lot on the left side of the cul-de-sac toward which they were heading. The house that occupied the lot on the right side featured a garage with a basketball hoop. Between the two houses, on the lot at the center of the cul-de-sac, was a house whose door featured a wreath decorated with pastel eggs. On either side of the door was a terra cotta urn brimming with pansies.

"We've already been here once today," Bettina announced as the Toyota slowed to a crawl.

The observation was scarcely necessary. Pamela was shaking her head as her lips shaped a faint, unsurprised, smile. "It fits together, doesn't it?" She turned to Bettina.

In the few moments before Bettina responded, Pamela could almost hear her brain whirring as, computer-like, it finished processing this new piece of data. If Ellen had presented the sweater to Ralph as a gift from one foodie to another, testimony of a platonic friendship, he'd have had no reason to discard it. But consigning a lovely, personally handmade garment like that to the trash seemed almost a violent act, a forceful rejection intended perhaps as a response to her rejection of him as a romantic interest.

"*Nice of you to do this, considering* . . ." Bettina quoted.

"I overheard that comment, too." Pamela switched from shaking her head to nodding. "Did she mean, considering Ellen broke up with you?"

"Then he said, *I thought I owed her something, considering* . . ."

"And did *he* mean, considering I killed her?"

"This all requires thinking." A crease appeared between Bettina's brows. "Lots of thinking."

Cooking had the same effect on the mind as knitting. It induced a meditative state that allowed questions to percolate, sometimes generating their own answers. Accordingly, after a quick detour upstairs to change out of her funeral outfit, Pamela now stood at her kitchen counter with Holly's colorful eggs before her in a favorite wooden bowl.

Deviling eggs wasn't exactly *cooking*, but she set to work, pleased to be embarking on a task whose every detail she could manage, unlike the unruly puzzle of who killed Ellen Weatherby. It was a shame, though, that the process of deviling the eggs would require sacrificing their decorated shells.

Holly had clearly enjoyed her egg-decorating session. Each egg was different, some with stripes, some with polka dots, some with zigzags, but all glowing with shades like deep pink, sky blue, a tender yellowish-green, and peach and lavender and yellow . . . Pamela picked out a lavender one with polka dots that were tiny flowers and tapped it against the counter, rotating it in her hand, until countless delicate fissures crazed its shell. She pushed the shell, now flexible, aside and the egg within, white and smooth, slipped loose.

Time passed, her thoughts floated free, and the number of decorated eggs in the wooden bowl diminished. Soon the peeled eggs had been sliced in half and made to yield up their golden yolks, and the yolks had been mashed with mayonnaise, salt and pepper, powdered mustard, and a dash of tabasco.

A long-ago tag-sale find, a cookie press, came out of its cupboard when there were eggs to be deviled. It consisted of a hollow cylinder to which a choice of nozzles could be fitted at one end and a pump handle at the other. Pamela screwed a nozzle into place and transferred the mashed yolk mixture to the cylinder, using a rubber spatula to capture every last bit. Then she screwed the pump handle to the other end and applied herself to the enjoyable task of piping the yolk mixture back into the egg whites, one egg half at a time.

But after she had done the first few, she paused. What to do with the completed eggs and how to hand them over to Holly presented a conundrum. Pamela collected deviled egg plates and had many, but typically a deviled egg plate accommodated only twelve egg halves. The deviled egg project had involved nearly two dozen whole eggs, which translated to nearly four dozen half eggs.

After pondering for a bit, she took out her largest cookie sheet and arranged the few completed eggs in the upper left-hand corner. She set to work again, and soon the deviled eggs, in tidy rows of pale ovals with centers like little suns, covered the cookie sheet's surface. Reached by phone, Holly was happy to hear that her eggs were ready and she arranged to stop by the next day—though she made Pamela promise to keep half of them.

Chapter Seven

Bettina's voice carried across the street, but just barely. "I'll be over as soon as I get dressed," she called. It was not yet eight a.m. and Bettina was wearing a fleecy robe in pale blue, with fleecy slippers to match. She pointed toward the just-retrieved newspaper dangling from Pamela's hands in its plastic sleeve. "We have a lot to discuss. You'll see when you read the paper."

Inside, Pamela slipped the *Register* from its plastic sleeve and, still standing in the entry, scanned the front page. The major headline involved a decision in an affordable housing case, but a bit farther down, and in only slightly less bold type, she read, ARBORVILLE MAN CLEARED IN EASTER EGG MURDER. Smaller type beneath added, "Police Remain Puzzled."

She lowered herself into the nearby chair and shook the newspaper out to get a clearer look at the article. Apparently, as Marcy Brewer reported it, Dwight Silverthorne had been cleared because his alibi—he was volunteering at the Haversack women's shelter Easter party—had been verified by numerous people.

Pamela had set water to boil before dashing out to collect the paper, and the kettle was now hooting to announce that the water had more than reached the desired state.

After popping up from the chair, she dashed through the doorway, startling Precious, who was the only cat still eating—then she paused, with her fingers on the kettle's handle. She'd planned on coffee for one, but Bettina was en route.

It was quick work to grind more coffee and add it to the grounds waiting in the filter cone, and to launch the kettle to boil with extra water. To toast or not to toast, though? Bettina's visit would be impromptu, and thus no Co-Op bakery box would accompany her arrival.

Soon the doorbell rang, but not before the aroma of brewing coffee had filled the little kitchen and Pamela had set two places at the table—wedding-china cups and saucers, and small plates too. Pamela stepped to the doorway and through it.

Beyond the front door, and visible through its lace-curtained window, a figure was visible, but it wasn't Bettina. This figure was slender, garbed in a color darker than Bettina's usual vivid tones, and dark-haired. Pamela opened the door to admit Holly.

"Not too early, I hope!" Holly glanced at Pamela's robe and slippers. "Saturdays are always busy, and I'm due at the salon, and I've got to run the eggs back home first."

Before Pamela could answer, another voice spoke from the porch. "Did you read it?" Bettina inquired. She was as yet hidden by the door, which was only slightly ajar.

Holly edged aside as it swung open and Bettina stepped in. Her ensemble, a peach-colored tunic and leggings, contrasted with Holly's close-fitting black leather jacket and matching miniskirt.

"Bettina!" Holly exclaimed. "This is perfect timing. I hope you'll take some deviled eggs home with you. From my share," she added, with a nod at Pamela.

"I didn't come empty-handed"—Bettina displayed a

jar—"even though I know you're perfectly happy with plain toast. Wilfred brought all kinds of goodies home from Newfield on Wednesday. This is blueberry jam made with New Jersey blueberries."

The mention of toast had clearly been a hint, and the coffee aroma, which had reached the entry, was not lost on Bettina. She was heading quite purposefully toward the kitchen.

"There's coffee." Pamela addressed Holly. "And there's going to be toast with blueberry jam."

Holly smiled. "Tempting, for sure."

An extra chair was fetched from the dining room, and an extra place setting of wedding china retrieved from the cupboard, as Pamela worked at the counter preparing toast. Soon the three friends were clustered around the little table, and sociable conversation punctuated the eating of toast and sipping of coffee.

"Shannon Silverthorne must be terribly relieved," Holly commented, licking a bit of the sticky purple jam from a finger. "The police certainly took their time checking up on his alibi, and all the while there were plenty of people who could vouch that he was in Haversack at the Easter party." She took another bite of toast. "In fact, one of my clients at the salon volunteers there, Jan Bowser. She and Nell are great friends. Anyway, she said Dwight Silverthorne did a great job as the Easter bunny. Such a good sport, she said, hopping around for two hours non-stop."

Pamela's coffee cup halted midway to her mouth. She turned toward where Holly sat at the end of the table, and she could feel a crease forming between her brows as she said, "Wearing an Easter bunny costume, I suppose . . . ?"

"I expect so." Holly laughed, displaying her dimple. "Otherwise, how would the children know he was the Easter bunny?"

"Was there a mask?" Pamela inquired as she felt the crease deepen. "And did he keep it on the whole time?"

"Oh!" Holly raised a hand to her mouth, leaving a smudge of blueberry jam on her lips. She gazed at Pamela and her dark eyes widened in amazement. "You are *awesome*!" she whispered. "Is an alibi a real alibi if the person who needs an alibi is wearing a costume the whole time? The police didn't even think of that, but you did." She stood up. "My phone is in my bag and my bag is on that chair in your entry. I'll call Jan right now."

While she was gone, Pamela and Bettina sat in silence, each with ears alert to what could be gleaned from Holly's side of the conversation as it filtered in from the next room. The conversation concluded with Holly saying, "Thank you, thank you, and I'll see you soon," and then she bounced through the doorway.

"Jan talked to him when he arrived," Holly reported, "and she talked to him as he was leaving, but in between, according to her, he was the Easter bunny—totally in character and, yes, the costume included a mask."

She advanced to the table, picked up her cup, and tilted her head back to drain the last few swallows. "And now," she said, "I've really got to go."

Pamela was on her feet then too, and Holly was sent on her way with a third of the eggs in a plastic bin, carefully arranged in layers separated by foil.

Returning from seeing Holly out, Pamela discovered Bettina standing at the counter watching the toaster. "I'm heating what's left of the coffee, too," Bettina commented. "We have a lot to discuss."

"I don't want the killer to be Dwight Silverthorne," she announced a few minutes later, seated once again. A toasted slice of whole-grain bread, glistening with blueberry jam, reposed on a plate before her, and her cup was full to the rose-garlanded rim with coffee sugared and creamed to sweet, mocha perfection. "But," she added, "what an ingenious way to commit a murder and get away with it: Recruit an accomplice to take over as the Easter bunny long enough to dash to Arborville, murder Ellen, return to Haversack, and turn back into the Easter bunny."

"She didn't make a sweater for Dwight Silverthorne," Pamela observed.

"Not as far as we know. Clayborn never revealed the evidence he thought pointed to Dwight's guilt."

"She made a sweater for Ralph, and he said he thought he owed her something."

"*Considering*," Bettina added.

"They definitely had a relationship."

Bettina picked up a toast half, as if to signal that the discussion was over. But before she lifted it to her mouth, she said, "I'm going to tell Clayborn about the bunny costume, even though I know he'll ignore me."

The prospect of being waylaid by Mr. Gilly often caused Pamela to quicken her pace when she approached the stately brick apartment building at the corner of Orchard Street and Arborville Avenue. Mr. Gilly was the super of the building, and if he was outside, which was frequent, he never minded stopping work for a chat, welcome or not.

Sunday afternoon, though, Pamela was glad to linger. Mr. Gilly, a tall and wiry man in his fifties, had paused to greet her, and from the looks of things, some interesting discards were being made available for browsing. Pamela had furnished her house mostly with thrift-shop treasures, hand-me-downs, and scavenged items, and Mr. Gilly had just added a bulging cardboard box to a pile of similar boxes at the curb. A wheeled hand truck stood next to him.

"I hate working on Sunday," Mr. Gilly said, "but there's lots to do." He was clad in his usual sturdy work pants and matching utility jacket. "Her apartment was full of stuff, her brother and sister-in-law don't want it, and nobody could get at it while the crime-scene tape was up." He stooped to reposition the box, which seemed in danger of toppling. "The whole place has got to be repainted by the beginning of next month because the landlord wants to get another tenant in right away."

"That shouldn't be hard," Pamela murmured. "It's a nice building in a desirable location."

Mr. Gilly dipped into a jacket pocket for a pack of cigarettes, chose one, and set it alight, signaling that he was in no hurry to resume his work.

"Sad, this." He gestured at the boxes and Pamela intuited that he was referring not only to the emptying of Ellen's apartment but also to the event that had made that necessary. "She was a nice woman." He gazed thoughtfully into the distance, took a long drag on the cigarette, and exhaled. "Kind of a relief for the landlord, though."

Pamela blinked. "But not a model tenant . . ." she murmured, recalling Corinne's allusion to Ellen's nocturnal visitors.

"Behind on the rent." Mr. Gilly leaned toward Pamela and lowered his voice, though no one was nearby to overhear. "She could be charming, and she kept stringing him along, saying she was expecting a large windfall any day."

The cigarette was diminishing rapidly. Mr. Gilly glanced toward an open door near the area where the building's trash bins were ranged. "I should get back to work," he said.

Pamela stepped toward the repositioned box and lifted one of the flaps.

"Go ahead." Mr. Gilly accompanied the words with an

encouraging wave. "Books, mostly. Help yourself." Wheeling his hand truck before him, he headed for the open door.

Once all four flaps had been folded back, the box proved to contain, as Mr. Gilly had revealed, books. The topmost ones in the box, the few whose covers could be seen, were cookbooks: Moroccan, Scandinavian, Southern French, and vegetarian. Pamela looked beneath them to discover more cookbooks, including an oversize one with a glossy cover featuring a smiling young woman in a chef's toque presiding over an array of pastries. The author was celebrity chef Camille Chartreuse, tall and blond, as glamorous as a supermodel.

Something about the young woman looked familiar though. Could she possibly be . . . ? Pamela checked the publication date of the cookbook to discover it had come out twenty-five years earlier. As if the thought had summoned up the corporeal being, Corinne Charters was approaching, apparently looking to discard a bag of garbage in the trash bins.

She and Pamela caught sight of each other at the same time and both spoke, almost echoing each other's words, with comments to the effect that Mr. Gilly had been busy.

"I'm glad I came along before the trash pickup," Pamela added. "It would be a shame for all these cookbooks to go to waste." She stood up, still holding the oversize one, and turned it to display the cover to Corinne. "Is this one by you?" she asked. "You said you were a cookbook author—but this is really impressive. Camille Chartreuse, Corinne Charters. Why would you change your name with such a promising career underway?"

"I don't know what you mean," Corinne muttered. She left the sidewalk and scurried diagonally across the grass toward the trash bins.

Pamela set the Camille Chartreuse cookbook aside and continued examining the contents of the box. It was so tempting to take *all* the cookbooks home, but the bookshelf in her kitchen was already full to the point of books being tucked behind and on top of other books. Anyway, recipes tended to repeat from cookbook to cookbook, except in the case of those introducing previously unexplored cuisines to cooks unfamiliar with them. For that reason, she set the Moroccan cookbook on top of the Camille Chartreuse cookbook, along with one that offered a culinary tour of the Danube River, and a truly vintage edition of the Fannie Farmer *Boston Cooking-School Cookbook* dating from 1941.

With an armload of books, Pamela resisted the urge to check the contents of the other boxes. Mr. Gilly was heading her way, pushing the hand truck piled with more discards, and she was disinclined to resume chatting with him. Saluting him with a cordial wave and a "thank you," she set off down Orchard Street.

Ellen had been expecting a large windfall—or claimed to be—Mr. Gilly had said. Presumably then her financial difficulties would be solved, at least as far as her back rent was concerned. But how large was large? Pamela wondered, and was cookbook writing really that lucrative? Certainly if the author was famous, like Julia Child or Paula Deen or Ina Garten, but Ellen Weatherby hadn't exactly been a household name, and what kind of market was there for a cookbook focusing only on eggs?

Pamela's mind was so occupied with these questions that she passed her house and only realized where she was when she reached the driveway that served the parking lot of the church next door. She backtracked to her own front walk and had soon deposited the armload of cookbooks on the kitchen table.

The Camille Chartreuse cookbook was lavishly illustrated, with photographs chronicling a jet-setting life lived as a private chef, serving salade Niçoise aboard a yacht anchored in the Mediterranean, or tea and finger sandwiches at a stately home in Bath. The cookbook was organized by type of event: formal dinner, cocktail party, al fresco luncheon, seaside picnic, and the like, with suggested menus—recipes included, of course. A recipe for almond cake sounded especially elegant, and Ellen must have thought so too, because she had marked it with a slip of paper.

What career bump had turned Camille Chartreuse into Corinne Charters, a person who had traded a life rubbing elbows with the rich and famous for a rented apartment in Arborville, New Jersey? And could she, as Corinne Charters, recapture some of her previous glory with the new cookbook project she had referred to?

Pamela left the cookbook on the table and climbed the stairs to her office. No messages from her boss at *Fiber Craft* lurked in her inbox, though the coming week would doubtless bring new assignments. A note from Richard Larkin brought the reminder that he'd be back in Arborville on Tuesday, probably late afternoon, taking into account the time difference between Iceland and New Jersey.

As often happened when Pamela lingered at the computer with her fingers resting on the mouse and no pressing chores calling her away, the mouse began to move of its own accord, Ouija-like, over the mouse pad. First the cursor roamed to the upper corner of the screen, where it chose AccessArborville, the town listserv, from among Favorites.

A quick scan of the postings revealed that someone on Beech Street was giving away a child's desk, and many people objected to the affordable housing decision reported in Saturday's *Register*—though one commenter, in favor of the decision, posted that she felt as if a yolk had been removed from her shoulders.

"Don't you mean yoke?" Pamela whispered to herself. But she had no time to ponder, because the mouse had opened an internet search page, and she discovered that her fingers were suddenly in motion, keying in the words *Camille Chartreuse*.

"Oh, my goodness," she heard herself murmur as article after article presented itself. Only a few minutes of reading were required to understand why the words *Camille Chartreuse* summoned up such a trove of material—and why Camille Chartreuse had now chosen to live, and hopefully publish her new cookbook, as Corinne Charters.

Chapter Eight

"You know I already know this, don't you?" Pamela said with an affectionate laugh.

It was past midday, and Monday morning's *Register* had landed on front lawns shortly after sunrise. The update on the Easter egg murder case—Dwight Silverthorne rearrested—had been startling, but Pamela had had several hours to digest Marcy Brewer's nearly breathless coverage of the new development.

"I'm sure Clayborn was listening to me when I spoke to him on Saturday, even though he hardly let me get ten words out." Bettina stepped across the threshold, advanced into the entry, and added, "Then this morning when I had my usual meeting with him, of course there was no acknowledgment of my help—or should I say Holly's?"

Prepared for the task at hand, she'd tied one of Wilfred's aprons over the stylish aqua linen pantsuit she'd worn for her visit to the police station. The apron reached nearly to her ankles, leaving her aqua kitten heels visible.

Pamela nodded. "Understandable, though. He must be embarrassed at having to admit Dwight Silverthorne's alibi wasn't rock solid, and all the more embarrassed that he didn't figure it out for himself."

"The question of the accomplice is still up in the air,"

Bettina said. "Who took over as the Easter bunny while Dwight was dashing back to Arborville to kill Ellen? But Dwight's back in police custody and might be willing to talk." She headed through the kitchen doorway. "Let's make those cookies. I can hardly wait to show Betty what a good cookie-maker her grandma is."

Pamela followed Bettina through the doorway and gestured toward the counter. A favorite mixing bowl, caramel colored with three white stripes near the rim, waited next to one egg and canisters of flour and sugar. "I've set things out, but first I want to show you something. Dwight might not have needed an accomplice or an alibi, because I don't think he was the killer."

The Camille Chartreuse cookbook, with the glamorous photo of its celebrity chef author on the cover, sat in the middle of the kitchen table. Pamela picked it up and edged next to Bettina.

"Does this woman look familiar to you?" she inquired after Bettina had had a chance to study the photo.

"Not exactly," Bettina said with a twist of the lips like a cross between a smile and a frown. "Should she?"

"She has a different name now, but the same initials, and I think Detective Clayborn should . . ." Pamela's voice trailed off as a musical trill emanated from Bettina's handbag.

"Who could this be?" Bettina murmured, lifting the flap of the handbag and extracting her phone. She glanced at the screen. "Shannon Silverthorne. Of course the poor thing is beside herself. I have to take this."

She lowered herself into one of the chairs that flanked the table. Pamela set the cookbook back where it had been and stepped over to the counter to check on the contents of the caramel-colored bowl. At the moment, half a pound of butter, cut into little pieces, was softening in preparation for being blended with sugar as the first step in the cookie recipe.

Shannon's voice on the other end of the phone was audible only as scratchy static, but Bettina's side of the conversation made its content quite clear. Shannon indeed was beside herself—even more so than one might have supposed, given that Dwight's guilt as a straying husband had never been in doubt. Shannon had apparently forgiven the straying and was convinced that he was innocent of the murder.

Catrina responded to the doorbell's chime before Pamela heard it. The time for basking in the sunny spot on the entry carpet was long gone, but she emerged from the hall that led to the laundry room and made her way across the black-and-white tiled floor, looking back at Pamela as she neared the entry. Pamela joined her in the kitchen doorway and observed an unfamiliar figure waiting on the porch. The doorbell chimed again.

The visitor was Corinne Charters, her unstylish hair and unbecoming jeans-and-flannel ensemble pointing up the contrast with her glamorous younger self in the cookbook photos. She was bearing gifts, but the gifts had strings attached—one string at any rate.

"I got to thinking about that cookbook you showed me," she said, after Pamela had invited her in. The statement, with its offhand phrasing, seemed calculated to distract from a certain intensity in her expression. "I wish I'd thought to ask Mr. Gilly for a chance to look at the discards, but I didn't . . . so"—she thrust a stack of books at Pamela—"I'll trade. Here's Julia Child's *Mastering the Art of French Cooking*, signed by Julia herself, and . . ."

She paused and stared toward the kitchen doorway.

Bettina's voice had suddenly become very loud. "Shannon, Shannon, Shannon," she was saying, "calm down! Dwight isn't guilty, and Clayborn will know that soon enough." After a few seconds of silence, as if Shannon was responding, Bettina went on. "Shannon! I guarantee you! Pamela has figured everything out and there's another, much much more likely suspect, and I will make sure Detective Clayborn follows up."

Pamela was holding the stack of books now. She backed up, slightly off balance, as Corinne's expression became even more intense. Her features froze, all but her eyes, which seemed to enlarge until their gaze exerted a hypnotic pull.

"I see I'm too late," Corinne said, the words coming out in a raspy whisper. "But I can't let the police tie me to Ellen's murder, not with the new cookbook underway, and I certainly couldn't let Ellen reveal that story about my past either. That's why she had to die, and now you have to die."

She lunged at Pamela, who continued to retreat. Pamela felt herself sway, and then she toppled over backward and the books scattered. Her head hit the parquet floor with a thump that resounded inside her skull, but she was still conscious, staring at Corinne bending over her, crouching. She felt Corinne's hands close around her neck. "Cooks develop strong hands," Corinne was saying, "especially if they make pasta from scratch or knead a lot of bread."

"What is going on out here?" The voice came from Bettina, who was stepping through the kitchen doorway. "Corinne Charters! What on earth are you doing?"

Without waiting for an answer, Bettina stooped and picked up the closest book, *Mastering the Art of French Cooking*. She raised it in the air and brought it down on the back of Corinne's head with a solid *thunk*. Pamela felt

Corinne's hands loosen, though they remained in place around her neck. Bettina struck Corinne with the book again, and Corinne's hands loosened enough that Pamela was able to roll out from under her.

Corinne remained in the same position, still crouched on the floor but with Pamela off to the side. Her hands were clasped tightly over her head, her face hidden. Her voice emerged, muffled but audible. "Nobody would buy a cookbook written by a cook whose almond cake had poisoned her employer, and Ellen knew that, so she decided to blackmail me." A convulsive sob interrupted her words, followed by a laugh. "No good deed goes unpunished. I gave that ingrate a recipe for egg mayonnaise to use in the *Eggotist's Cookbook* and she recognized it from the celebrity chef cookbook and figured out that the notorious Camille Chartreuse was actually me."

Bettina slipped into the kitchen and Pamela heard her on the phone summoning the police. In a few moments, she was back, stooping toward Pamela, who was still lying on the floor. Bettina's eyes, normally hazel, seemed darker as she studied Pamela's face.

"Does anything hurt?" she inquired, her expression so serious she barely resembled herself.

"I don't think so." Pamela braced her hands against the floor and boosted herself to a sitting position. She raised a hand to feel the back of her head. It felt smooth, despite the thump with which she had landed when she fell, though she knew goose eggs took a while to form.

Corinne, meanwhile, had not moved. The surge of adrenalin that had propelled her lunge at Pamela seemed to have abated. Perhaps she had intended to dispatch Bettina too, once she finished with Pamela, but the thunk with the book had interrupted her, and she must have realized that with the police on the way anything she might do, other than remaining still, would just make matters worse for her.

Bettina lowered herself into the chair that was the entry's sole piece of furniture. It faced a window that gave a view of the street, and Pamela could see that she was watching intently for the arrival of the police. She was clearly also pondering the revelation that it was Corinne who had murdered Ellen, not Dwight Silverthorne, Trevor Brant, or Ralph Minster.

Without taking her eyes from the street, she asked, "How did she lure Ellen to the spot where she killed her?"

The question was addressed to Pamela, but it was Corinne who answered. Corinne's voice was still muffled, but Pamela thought she almost sounded pleased at the chance to describe her stratagem.

"Ellen wasn't bored with Dwight yet," Corinne said, "and she left his silly love notes sitting out any old place around her apartment. I'd seen them, notably when I was helping her master egg mayonnaise. It was easy to slip a message from 'Bunny Cuddle' into her mailbox."

"What about all the broken eggs?" Bettina inquired.

"A gift from Ellen. Some local guy who raises free-range chickens kept hounding her about promoting his eggs. I thought they'd add a nice touch—sort of a red herring, you might say."

The police were heard before they were seen. Faintly at first, from the top of the street, came a thin wail, becoming louder as it grew into a hiccupping whoop, then a fading to a whimper as the police car nosed into place along the curb. It came to an abrupt halt, both doors opened, and two officers sprang out as if choreographed. Officer Sanchez emerged from the door closest to the curb and she took the lead, sprinting up Pamela's front walk. Behind her came Officer Anders.

Bettina was on her feet and had flung the front door open even before the officers' feet clattered on the porch steps.

"Was it you who reported an emergency?" Officer Sanchez inquired as she approached the door, bobbing her head to look past Bettina. Catching sight of Corinne, who was still crouched on the floor, she added, "Has this woman been injured?"

"Yes!" Corinne reared up onto her knees and clumsily turned to face Bettina and Officer Sanchez, who had stepped into the entry as Bettina withdrew and swung the door open farther. "I *have* been injured, namely, I've been blackmailed." Her skin was flushed from her face-down position on the floor. "Ellen Weatherby was the real criminal, not me. I was just . . . protecting myself, trying to survive. I needed the money that my new cookbook would bring in, but she threatened to reveal all that old stuff to her followers unless I paid her off, paid her a lot."

Officer Sanchez looked at Bettina, who was still clad in the long apron. Puzzlement knotted the officer's pretty lips and widened her dark eyes. Pamela hadn't risen from the floor, and Officer Sanchez shifted her focus in that direction as Officer Anders slipped across the threshold.

Anticipating a question, Pamela scrambled to her feet, bracing herself on the arm of the chair. "I'm fine," she said.

"Not really." Bettina spoke up, pointing at Corinne. "This woman tried to strangle her."

Officer Sanchez turned back to Corinne. "Is that true?"

"Ellen Weatherby was blackmailing me," Corinne repeated.

"She killed Ellen Weatherby," Bettina said. "That was her motive. Blackmail. Dwight Silverthorne is innocent."

Once again, Officer Sanchez focused on Pamela. "Did this woman try to strangle you?" Pamela nodded. "Do you wish to press charges?"

"You do!" Bettina nodded, so emphatically that her scarlet hair quivered. "You do!"

"I have to hear it from the injured party," Officer Sanchez explained.

"Yes," Pamela said. "Yes, I wish to press charges."

"And you witnessed the act?" This question was addressed to Bettina.

Bettina nodded again.

"You'll both need to make a statement at the police station. You can follow me in your own car." Officer Sanchez gestured for Officer Anders to take charge of Corinne, who seemed resigned to her fate.

"It will all come out, I'm sure," Bettina commented as she steered the Toyota along Orchard Street with the police car leading the way. "Corinne seems determined to make it known that Ellen was blackmailing her, and if she talks about that long enough she's bound to veer over to Ellen's murder and incriminate herself. She almost already did, right in front of Officer Sanchez."

She swiveled her head to look at Pamela, and Pamela held her breath as the car approached the intersection with Arborville Avenue. "You're sure you're all right?" Bettina inquired.

"Fine, really," Pamela murmured. "Please, just watch the road and concentrate. You don't want to rear-end a police car."

Once they'd rounded the corner, Bettina returned to the

earlier topic. "What, actually, had Ellen found out about Corinne that gave her material for blackmail? And how did you figure that out?"

"Remember the Jordan almonds that Corinne gave us? She said Ellen had given them to her."

"They were good," Bettina said. "How could anyone not like Jordan almonds?"

"Ellen had a mean streak. Not only was she blackmailing Corinne but she was taunting her about the tragic event that she was threatening to reveal."

"Okay . . ." Bettina pulled over to the curb, despite the fact that they were within two blocks of the police station. "I can't drive safely and listen at the same time if you're going to tease me like this."

Pamela laughed. "Here's the story, which I discovered thanks to a successful internet search after I realized that Corinne Charters used to be the celebrity chef Camille Chartreuse."

"The cookbook you showed me . . ." Bettina whispered. "Corinne was once very glamorous."

"I was looking through the cookbook after I rescued it from some things Mr. Gilly was clearing out of Ellen's apartment, and Corinne came by. She pretended she didn't know what I was talking about and acted very odd when I asked her if she was the author. That's what made me curious. Anyway . . . Corinne, as Camille Chartreuse, had been a private chef to a rich Long Island family. The husband fell in love with her and murdered his heiress wife to claim the wife's money and be free to marry Camille. He poisoned a cake that he'd requested Camille to make, an almond cake to cover up the taste of cyanide."

"And she's out of prison now . . ."

"She was never in prison. She wasn't prosecuted because her lawyers successfully argued that she only baked the cake and wasn't aware of the husband's nefarious plan."

"I feel kind of sorry for her," Bettina said, "except that she tried to strangle you. Her celebrity chef career was really destroyed, and all because an unscrupulous man fell in love with her."

Half an hour later, Pamela and Bettina emerged from the police station and crossed the parking lot to where the Toyota waited.

"You're sure you feel okay?" Bettina inquired once they were seated in the car.

"I'm fine," Pamela said. "She let go of my neck as soon as you hit her with Julia Child."

"Wilfred often says that consulting her cookbooks saved many of his cooking projects from disaster, but who knew that *Mastering the Art of French Cooking* could truly be life-saving?" Bettina turned toward Pamela. "You landed on the floor with quite a thump. I could hear it from the kitchen. Are you *sure* you're okay?"

"Fine, really." Pamela reached up to feel the back of her head. It still felt smooth.

"We didn't make the cookies," Bettina observed as she steered the Toyota toward the parking lot's exit.

"Come over tomorrow and we'll do them," Pamela said. "I still have your apron."

"It's Wilfred's. He's got others, and he's making scalloped potatoes with leftover ham tonight. Eat with us."

Chapter Nine

Tuesday morning's *Register* brought news that must have set the minds of many Arborvillians at ease. A bold headline on the front page announced that another arrest—of the actual killer—had been made in the Easter egg murder case. The article itself, under Marcy Brewer's byline, led with the information that police had been summoned to an altercation at a home on Orchard Street, an altercation that resulted in Arborville resident Corinne Charters confessing to the murder of Ellen Weatherby. The home was that of Pamela Paterson, who had been assaulted by Ms. Charters.

The news was no surprise to Pamela. She had suspected that once Corinne was in the hands of the police, questions about why she had assaulted Pamela would quite naturally elicit information linking her with Ellen's murder. That suspicion had been confirmed the previous evening when Marcy Brewer showed up at the Frasers' front door after failing to find Pamela at home.

Marcy's first stop had been the Arborville police station, where she learned from Detective Clayborn that Corinne Charters, otherwise known as Camille Chartreuse, had confessed to the murder. She relayed this information to Bettina, who answered the door. Pamela and Bettina had been relaxing on the sofa after dinner while Wilfred cleaned up in the kitchen.

"I understand from Detective Clayborn that Corinne Charters was taken to the police station after assaulting Pamela Paterson," Marcy had said, craning her neck to peer past Bettina.

When Woofus began to bark, she retreated a few steps but continued speaking. "Is Ms. Paterson available to clarify what brought Ms. Charters to her house and what provoked the assault?" she inquired. "And can Ms. Paterson clarify the relationship between the assault and Ms. Charters's subsequent confession?" She stepped forward again. "Or can you?"

Bettina had sent Marcy on her way, stating that neither she nor Pamela had anything to add to the information supplied by Detective Clayborn. As the door closed on Marcy Brewer, Wilfred had appeared, depositing three mugs of coffee, cream and sugar, and a plate of lemon bars on the coffee table.

As soon as she had paged through the rest of the *Register*, finished her breakfast, and dressed, Pamela had turned her attention to tidying the house in preparation for hosting the Knit and Nibble group that evening. Now, with the house clean and lunch eaten, she was standing at her kitchen counter. The caramel-colored bowl with three white stripes held the same softened bits of butter from the previous day. The electric mixer sat nearby, as did the canisters of flour and sugar, and one egg, along with vanilla, baking soda, baking powder, and salt. The important extra ingredients that would elevate the recipe beyond mere vanilla sugar cookies were still in the cupboard, but four small bowls were lined up on the table in preparation for the moment when the dough would be divided into four parts.

The doorbell's chime sounded promptly at two o'clock. A few minutes later, with her buttercup-yellow tunic and leggings protected by Wilfred's apron, Bettina was standing at Pamela's kitchen counter with Pamela by her side. Bettina was holding the electric mixer, and Pamela was monitoring the progress of the beaters as they nosed through the butter bits scattered over the interior of the bowl, creaming them into pale yellow smoothness.

Bettina was not monitoring the progress of the beaters. She was looking straight ahead, her gaze aimed at Richard Larkin's kitchen window.

"He's due back today," she said, raising her voice to be heard over the hum of the mixer. "Are you excited?"

Pamela was quite aware that this was the day Richard Larkin was due back. She had awakened that morning with a thrill of anticipation. But instead of responding, she laid her hand atop Bettina's and steered the beaters toward a clump of uncreamed butter bits.

"I know you." Bettina tilted her head to make eye contact. "You like to keep your feelings private. Here's what I think, though. Things were finally getting somewhere, after you—both of you—being so—" She sighed. "I don't know. If I was attracted to a man—assuming I was single, which I certainly don't want to be—and I knew he was attracted to me, I wouldn't tiptoe around. There are plenty of other fish in the sea, as Wilfred would say, and it's a wonder Richard Larkin hadn't picked another fish after all this time, and he even invited you to come to Iceland with him, and if that doesn't mean he's ready to stop tiptoeing and he hopes you'll stop tiptoeing, I don't know what it means."

"Enough." Pamela switched off the mixer with a click.

"No! You need a nudge, obviously, and what is your best friend for, if not—" Bettina had turned quite pink and was panting slightly.

"The butter, I meant." Pamela stifled a laugh. "You've beaten it long enough, so now we'll add the sugar." The distraction of cookie making was very welcome, and Pamela herself had been gazing more often than usual at Richard Larkin's kitchen window.

"Have you at least been emailing back and forth while he's gone?"

"Of course," Pamela said. The emails had in fact been a high point of her day.

"What about?"

"Things . . . what he's doing, what I'm doing. It's still winter in Iceland." She clicked the mixer back on.

Bettina was silent as Pamela tipped the measuring cup over the bowl and let the sugar drift slowly through the whirl of the beaters, where it vanished into the softened butter to form a pale, fluffy cloud. A teaspoon of vanilla streaked the mixture briefly and then it vanished too, along with the egg. Pamela gave Bettina the task of whisking the flour and other dry ingredients together in a second bowl and then stirring vigorously with a wooden spoon as they were combined with the butter, sugar, and egg mixture. Now the caramel-colored bowl held a large, sticky mass of raw cookie dough.

"We could just put scoops of it on a greased cookie sheet and put the cookie sheet in the oven for ten or fifteen minutes and we'd have very nice sugar cookies," Pamela said, "but we're going to do something more festive for the Knit and Nibblers—something inspired by Easter eggs."

She stepped around Bettina and opened a cupboard. She took out a small oblong box and set it on the counter.

"First," she explained, "we have to divide the dough into four equal parts and put each part in its own small bowl."

She transferred the small bowls from the table to the counter, and then, using a rubber spatula, she scooped a quarter of the dough into each of the small bowls.

"Food coloring?" Bettina inquired as Pamela opened the oblong box and took out four tiny plastic bottles.

"We're going to color the dough, like Easter eggs. We can use red, yellow, blue, and green, or we can mix the colors and make purple and orange and . . . whatever."

In the event, drops of color were squeezed onto the lumps of dough, the colors were blended in with much vigorous stirring, and the result was a row of bowls containing purple, yellow, deep pink, and green dough.

"Now here's the really fun part . . ." Pamela smiled.

"Shouldn't we turn on the oven and grease some cookie sheets?" Bettina inquired.

"Not yet."

Pamela opened a drawer and fetched a roll of plastic wrap. She tore off a square piece and smoothed it out on the counter, which had been cleared of all but the four bowls of colored dough. Taking up the bowl of purple dough and a clean rubber spatula, she transferred the dough to the center of the plastic wrap, using the spatula to capture every last bit.

Bettina watched, quite transfixed, as Pamela used the plastic wrap rather than her fingers to coax the dough into a long cylinder. Finally, she wrapped the cylinder with the plastic wrap, set it aside, and followed the same process with the other lumps of colored dough.

"*Now* do we heat the oven?"

"Not for quite a while," Pamela replied, well aware that Bettina's patience was being put to the test. "The dough has to chill for an hour or so."

"It does?" Bettina's expression would have suited an actress of melodramatic bent reacting to a particularly heartbreaking plot twist. "What will we do in the meantime?"

"We could talk," Pamela suggested. Bettina stole a glance toward Richard Larkin's kitchen window and Pamela hastily added, "But not about . . . him. First, though, we can prepare the cookie sheets."

A few other topics presented themselves, failed to gain traction, and faded away, as each worked on her own cookie sheet, coating the surface with a thin layer of vegetable shortening. That task accomplished, Bettina fetched her phone to share with Pamela a video of Betty playing with Wilfred Jr.'s family's cat, Midnight. She was, in fact, so delighted to be revisiting the video that she was surprised when Pamela checked the clock and announced that the next step in the cookie making could commence.

Pamela explained her plan to Bettina while carrying out the steps that would create the cookies she envisioned. First she unwrapped the four cylinders of colored dough and cut each lengthwise into halves and then into quarters. She took one quarter of each color and reassembled the four different-colored quarters into a new four-color cylinder, repeating the process three more times.

"Impressive," Bettina commented, surveying Pamela's handiwork. "Now what?"

"We slice them," Pamela said, "just like that cookie dough that comes in tubes at the supermarket."

She followed the explanation with action, and soon each cookie sheet held rows of colorful cookies, each a neat round divided into quadrants of purple, yellow, pink, and green. The light that signaled the oven was heating clicked off, and Pamela bent over and opened the door. Leaning into the waft of hot air, she slid each cookie sheet onto its own rack and closed the door.

"They hardly take any time at all," she said, "and we don't want them to get even the tiniest bit brown."

The aroma of baking cookies—warm and sugary and buttery—began as a faint hint but soon filled the kitchen, all the more so when Pamela opened the oven door to rotate the cookie sheets.

"Five minutes," she announced, and indeed five minutes later the cookie sheets sat side by side on the stove top. The cookies were now much larger and their baked texture promised a light and tender crumb.

Bettina sampled one cookie, still warm, and pronounced it "divine" as Pamela used a spatula to loosen all the cookies. Then Bettina divested herself of Wilfred's apron and set off for home with it draped over her arm. Pamela busied herself with further preparations for the Knit and Nibble meeting.

She set out wedding-china cups, saucers, and small plates on the dining room table, with her favorite vintage lace tablecloth spread beneath. Six white linen napkins with lace trim were added, fetched from the linen closet, and spoons for the tea drinkers, as well as Bettina, the only coffee drinker who didn't take her coffee black.

Back in the kitchen, Pamela selected a teapot from her collection, this one striped in a way that suggested an Easter egg, and measured in loose tea. She slipped a paper filter into her carafe's plastic filter cone, ground coffee, and tipped the grounds into the filter. Finally, she arranged the cookies on a wedding-china platter and stretched plastic wrap over it.

There was time for a quick dinner of a grilled cheese sandwich and a tomato salad, and a trip upstairs. In her office, Pamela checked her inbox and found nothing pressing. Across the hall, she studied herself in her bedroom mirror and decided the charcoal-gray sweater she'd put on that morning didn't fit the mood of a mid-April day, or the anticipated reunion with Richard Larkin.

Her gaze was drawn to a sweater midway down a stack of sweaters on her closet shelf. Its pale amber color stood out against the other, more somber shades, and she reached up to slip it gently from among its companions. She'd made it some years back, she recalled, from a cotton and linen blend yarn she'd treated herself to at the fancy yarn shop in Timberley.

The doorbell's chime summoned Pamela just as she finished exchanging the charcoal-gray sweater for the pale amber one. From the landing she could see two figures on her porch, not Richard Larkin, and even before she reached the bottom of the stairs a third figure had joined them. She opened the door to greet Holly and Karen, with Bettina hovering behind.

She glanced next door before greeting them. Richard Larkin's olive-green Jeep Cherokee was in his driveway, but he had left it there while he was gone and it had been there all day and all the previous days. No lights were on in his house, so he mustn't be back yet.

"Karen and I came early," Holly said with an eager smile. "We're longing to hear the story behind the story before Nell gets here, because you know how she is about people minding their own business."

Holly stepped over the threshold and Karen followed. "But first"—Holly tilted her head to scrutinize Pamela's face—"are you okay?"

"Fine," Pamela said. "Really."

"That's a relief! Anyway, Marcy Brewer's report in the *Register* was very vague. So, quick, what caused the 'altercation' at your house, and what did that have to do with Corinne confessing to the murder?"

"Nell is walking," Karen chimed in, "and she hadn't left yet when we started out in the car."

"Maybe we can at least sit down then." Pamela led the way to the living room and perched on the hearth as Holly, Karen, and Bettina lined up across from her on the sofa. The three were a study in contrasts, Holly in black—an oversize sweater over slim leather pants, Karen in pale blue, and Bettina in vivid fuchsia.

"I'm thinking," Holly said, "that you had somehow figured out Corinne was the person who killed Ellen . . ." She paused, and her eager look turned the statement into a question.

Pamela described coming upon the cookbook by Camille Chartreuse in the discards from Ellen's apartment.

"The photo of Camille Chartreuse on the cover was very glamorous, but Corinne still looks enough like her younger self that I asked her if she was the cookbook's author. People change their names for all kinds of reasons. She acted so strange that I did an internet search, and discovered that she'd changed her name because she'd been a key figure in a murder case a few decades ago."

"So she's a murderer twice over?" Holly's eagerness was replaced by surprise.

"Not quite." Bettina spoke up. "She baked an almond cake at the request of an employer who was in love with her and wanted to murder his wife, but the murder was his idea and he was the one who added the cyanide to the cake and served it to his victim."

"Corinne was trying for a comeback with a new cookbook," Pamela said, "and the last thing she needed was for that detail from her past to be brought to light."

"Which was exactly what Ellen Weatherby proposed to do." Bettina took over again.

"Ellen needed money. Being an egg influencer doesn't pay all that well, and before her divorce, I suppose she'd had her husband's income as a cushion. She was hoping that the *Eggotist's Cookbook* would repair her fortunes, but the chance of a big payout from Corinne in exchange for keeping mum about her secret was too good to pass up."

Footsteps on the porch interrupted then. Pamela felt her heart thump. She rose from the hearth and started toward the entry without waiting for the doorbell, and its chime rang out just as she opened the door. Nell and Roland stood on the porch in midconversation, Roland's words "my own supply" audible before he turned his attention from Nell to Pamela. Richard Larkin's house was still dark.

"A convert to the animal cause," Nell explained as the new arrivals entered.

"I plan to make an elephant," Roland said, pausing en route to his usual perch on the hassock at the far end of the hearth.

"Sit closer to me tonight." Nell beckoned as she lowered herself into the comfortable armchair that was her customary seat when the group met at Pamela's. "I'll get you started."

Pamela yielded the rummage-sale chair with the carved wooden back and the needlepoint seat to Roland, and took his place on the hassock. Once settled onto the chair, which had been pulled up next to Nell's armchair, Roland opened his elegant briefcase to reveal a skein of lavender yarn shot through with silver lurex.

"Did you finish the argyle sock?" Holly inquired in her most sociable tones. Her knitting bag sat on her lap, unopened as yet.

"Socks, plural," Roland replied, "and yes, obviously. I wouldn't be starting a new project otherwise."

"That yarn looks familiar." Bettina's knitting bag, likewise unopened, reposed on the carpet at her feet. Only Karen, among the early arrivals, had managed to combine knitting with the discussion of Corinne's confession and arrest. She was already busy with the pale yellow yarn she had claimed at the last Knit and Nibble meeting.

"It looks familiar because it *is* familiar. It's left over from another project."

Pamela remembered the project. It had been a most un-Roland-like creation, a tiny sparkly sweater for his cat.

Roland went on, uncharacteristically chatty. "Seeing that bag of leftover yarn last week made me realize that I also have a lot of leftover yarn. And with the argyle socks finished, I'm ready for a new challenge."

Holly beamed at Roland and cooed, "Lavender with silver sparkles will make an awesome elephant. You picked the absolute best possible yarn, and some little child is going to be very happy!"

"I didn't pick it because it was the absolute best," Roland responded. "It's the yarn I had the most of. I certainly wouldn't want to run out midway through." He extracted a pair of knitting needles from the briefcase and tugged a strand of yarn loose from the skein.

"Nell has made lots of multicolored animals," Bettina observed. "If she runs out of one color, she just splices in another."

"A multicolored elephant wouldn't be realistic." Roland looped the loose strand into a slipknot and slid it onto one of his needles.

"But lavender with silver sparkles is?" Bettina's comment elicited a giggle from Holly, but Roland ignored it. Turning to Nell, he inquired, "How many stitches do I cast on for an elephant?"

Pamela settled into her own knitting then, the sleeve

that had been half-finished the previous week and was still not much further along. She was happy that she was well past the deep ribbing at the cuff, which would have required keeping track of knit stitches and purl stitches as thoughts of Richard Larkin intruded. Instead, guided by her fingers, her needles advanced and retreated automatically, looping the yarn back on itself as row was added to row.

Conversational possibilities at any rate were limited, given her seat on the hassock at the far end of the hearth. Roland, happy to focus on his work in silence, separated from his chatty fellows, was the hassock's usual occupant. The sofa was all the way across the room and the fireplace was between the hassock and the armchair. Voices reached her only as quiet murmurs, Holly, Bettina, and Karen discussing an upcoming event at the library, and Roland conferring with Nell about the progress of his elephant.

After a time, though, Bettina's voice cut through the murmur with a whispered "Pamela" loud enough to catch Pamela's attention. When Pamela looked up, it was to see Bettina mouthing the word *coffee* and pointing at her watch. Indeed, it was ten minutes to eight, Pamela discovered when she twisted sideways to consult the clock on the mantel. Bettina started to rise as Pamela rose, but Pamela waved her back into her seat. All that needed to be done was to boil water for coffee and tea. Besides, Pamela had the sneaking suspicion that given the chance—and the view of Richard Larkin's kitchen window—Bettina would once again bring up her favorite topic.

As Pamela stood at the kitchen sink running water into the kettle, it was impossible not to notice that lights were now on in Richard Larkin's kitchen. That meant he was back. But how long had he been back? It had been an hour since she checked his house while welcoming Nell and Roland.

She stared at the window. He could walk into his kitchen at any moment, his tall form approaching the sink, bending toward it, his eyes under his strong brow intent on . . .

A gurgling sound drew Pamela's attention to her own sink. The kettle was overflowing and water was running down the drain. She turned off the faucet and tipped the kettle to drain out all but enough water to make coffee for four, but the thoughts that had distracted her from her task remained. If he'd been home an hour, and he'd really been eager to see her, why hadn't he come right over—if only just to say, "Hello. I'm back."

She set the kettle to boil and filled a small saucepan with water for the teapot. Maybe Bettina was right. There were plenty of fish in the sea. He'd pursued her at first, in a gentlemanly way, and he'd stepped back when it became clear that, despite the years she'd been a widow, she wasn't ready for a new relationship. Lately, though, she'd made her interest plain, more than plain—at least she thought she had. Iceland was full of attractive women, though, and he'd have been a glamorous prospect, lecturing at the university. She'd waited too long, and now it was too late. He'd been emailing frequently, like a person who wanted to keep a relationship alive. But now he was over there in his own house, not nearly as eager to see her in person as she had imagined he might be—or as she was to see him.

Chapter Ten

"What are you doing in here?" came Bettina's voice from the doorway. "I could hear the kettle whistling all the way out in the living room."

Bettina crossed to the stove, clicked the burner off, and seized the kettle, which she tilted over the filter cone balanced atop the carafe.

"And what about water for tea?" she inquired. "Is that what's in that saucepan?"

Pamela nodded listlessly.

Within a few moments, the spicy aroma of brewing coffee collided with the herbal aroma of brewing tea as Bettina stepped away from the counter and approached the platter of cookies waiting on the kitchen table.

"Dining room," Pamela murmured. "Everything else is out there."

"Not cream and sugar." Bettina veered toward Pamela and peered up into her face. "What on earth is wrong with you?" she demanded.

"Nothing," Pamela said. "Nothing at all. Just"—she waved toward the carafe—"take the coffee out, or get the cream, or something . . . and tell them to help themselves . . ."

"You're sure?" Concern had erased any hint of cheer

from Bettina's mobile features. "Are you having some delayed reaction to being attacked by Corinne?"

Bettina's I-told-you-so reminder about fish in the sea would be too hard to bear, so Pamela replied, "I'm fine." Then she added, "Please, just . . . make sure there's enough sugar in the sugar bowl."

Holly appeared in the doorway, but before she could advance, Bettina whisked the plastic wrap off the cookies and picked the platter up. Circling around Pamela, she presented it to Holly with instructions to put it on the dining room table and tell everyone coffee and tea were coming. Bettina herself removed the filter cone from the carafe and followed Holly to the dining room, with the carafe in one hand and the teapot in the other. A minute later, she returned in quest of cream and sugar.

Pamela lowered herself into one of the chairs that flanked the kitchen table, closed her eyes, and took a deep breath. Her future stretched before her, alone, except for cats and the view of Richard Larkin's kitchen window, with him, inside, enjoying his life with someone else—another fish in the sea that he had chosen because she had waited too long. It occurred to her that perhaps she should move away from Orchard Street.

She sighed and stirred in her chair. The longer she stayed in the kitchen, the more explaining she would have to do when she finally emerged, so she took another deep breath, let it out slowly, and stood up. As she stepped toward the doorway to the dining room, she could hear voices, even laughter coming from the living room. Seemingly no one but Bettina had interpreted the temporary absence of their hostess as evidence of something gone amiss.

A solitary wedding-china cup lingered on the lace tablecloth, with its saucer beneath it. She tilted the carafe over it and watched the dark liquid swirl into its pale porcelain depths. The cookies had been popular, she judged—fewer than half the original number remained on the platter. She set one on a wedding-china plate, picked up a napkin, and slipped around the corner onto the hassock. Only Bettina noticed, greeting her with a relieved nod and smile.

The wooden chair with the needlepoint seat had migrated back to its usual spot at the end of the sofa and was now occupied by Holly. Nell had joined Karen and Bettina on the sofa, and the four were deep in conversation. Occasional words like *compost*, *seedlings*, and *perennials* suggested that the topic was gardening. Roland was on the hearth, nibbling meditatively on a cookie and looking at nothing in particular until Pamela's gaze met his.

His lean face brightened and he swallowed. Raising his hand with fingers clutching the remains of the cookie, a mostly-yellow quadrant, he said, "Excellent!"

The four people sitting across the room all looked up, first at Roland and then at Pamela. "Yes!" Holly exclaimed. "Your cookies are *amazing*! Perfectly delicious, and the colors are so much fun! How ever did you do that?"

"*I* know how," Bettina said, but paused while Karen spoke, her compliments echoing Holly's.

Pamela was happy to let Bettina describe the process by which each cookie had ended up divided into four precise quadrants, each a different color. She sipped her coffee, barely tasting it, and the cookie she had taken remained untouched on her plate.

As the description proceeded, Roland set his coffee cup on the hearth and made a discreet check of his watch. He then shifted his attention to Bettina and her audience, apparently trying to gauge how much longer the description of cookie making would last. Bettina noticed him, and interrupted herself to say, "There's no need to wait for someone to collect your dishes if you're ready to start knitting again, Roland. You know where the kitchen is."

Roland checked his watch again, stacked his cup and saucer atop his plate, and headed for the kitchen. When he returned, he took up his knitting, which had already begun to resemble an elephant, though minus the head and trunk.

The others slowly resumed knitting as well, after taking Bettina's hint and returning their own dishes to the kitchen without prompting. Back in the armchair, Nell bent toward Roland for a brief conference, the wisps of her white hair nearly touching his carefully barbered head. Pamela left her own dishes right where they were on the hearth and took up her knitting again. The action was more automatic than willful, and she was even more happy that she'd chosen the out of the way hassock for her seat. The image of Richard Larkin's kitchen window, bright with evidence of his return, remained in her mind.

As the evening wound down, Bettina assumed the role of hostess, rising when Roland snapped the latch that sealed his briefcase and climbed to his feet. Holly and Karen began tucking their yarn, needles, and projects away. Nell did likewise, and accepted the ride they offered. The group moved off into the entry, chatting with each other and murmuring thank-yous in Pamela's direction. Bettina closed the door behind them with a last good night and crossed the entry floor to stand in the arch that led to the living room. Pamela was still sitting on the hassock.

"They're all worried about you," she said. "Couldn't you tell?"

"Not really. They acted like they always do. Besides, there's nothing to worry about." Pamela mustered a smile that even she knew was unconvincing. "I'm just a little tired, and I think I'll go right to bed."

"It's not like you to leave dishes unwashed."

"I'll wash them first." Pamela stood up. "And then I'll go to bed."

"You're sure . . . ?" Bettina didn't move.

"Definitely. I'll wash them, and then I'll go to bed."

"You know what I mean." Bettina's expression blended irritation with concern. "Are you *really* sure you're okay?"

Bettina took a few steps in Pamela's direction, but then she suddenly whirled around to face the front door. "You have a visitor," she whispered. "It's awfully late."

The doorbell's chime confirmed the report.

Bettina edged warily toward the door. A bright patch on the entry carpet showed that the porch light was still on, and Bettina's sudden shift of manner indicated that she recognized the visitor through the lace that curtained the window in the front door. A moment later, she swung the door open to greet Richard Larkin.

He dipped his head to clear the doorframe as he stepped over the threshold, the lifetime habit of a tall person. Then he stopped, just inside the entry.

Pamela heard him say "Bettina!" in a surprised tone. "I thought you were gone."

"Do you want me to be?" Bettina replied, adding a good-natured laugh.

"Is . . . Pamela . . . ?" Feet sounded on the entry floor.

Pamela remained where she was. Richard Larkin had advanced beyond the arch between the entry and the living room, radiating an energy that stilled her breath and left her unable to move. His expression was stern as he appeared to struggle for words, a struggle that resolved itself in silence as he stared at the carpet.

When he looked up, it was to say, "I didn't want to interrupt your meeting."

"You could have . . ." The words squeaked out.

"I didn't know if you'd expect me to come right over . . ."

Out of the corner of her eye, Pamela noticed Bettina creeping toward the sofa, where she seized her knitting bag and then retreated.

The searching look in Richard's eyes made his expression almost desperate.

"I didn't *expect* . . ." Pamela paused. Now it was her turn to study the carpet. "Or I mean," she began, as she raised her head to meet his gaze, "I expected you to do what you wanted to do."

Stop tiptoeing! said a voice in her mind that might as well have been Bettina's.

"No!" she amended. "I did expect you to come right over. I *wanted* you to come right over. I really, really wanted to see you. I—" For some reason, she was weeping, and she covered her face with her hands, feeling her cheeks hot and sleek with tears. "I missed you," she murmured into her cupped hands. "I thought about you. I've been thinking about you for a long, long time."

"Come here." He reached out and pulled her against his jacket, cool and smelling of the spring evening.

The front door creaked and then closed with a delicate thud as Bettina made her exit.

Epilogue

"Welcome back, neighbor!" Bettina exclaimed as Pamela's front door swung open to reveal Richard Larkin.

Bettina was the first to arrive, dressed for this mild June evening in a pink linen sheath and matching sandals, but voices drifting from the sidewalk heralded the approach of Holly, Karen, and Nell.

"We all came on foot," Holly called as they drew closer. "Why drive on a lovely night like this?"

Bettina lingered on the porch as they headed up the walk and climbed the steps.

"Did you have a wonderful, wonderful time?" Holly inquired, tilting her head to make eye contact with Richard. Her dimply enthusiasm, mirrored—though without dimples—by Karen and Nell, made clear what response she expected.

Richard complied with a smile, rearranging features that had always seemed stern in repose. He studied the threshold uncertainly for a moment, as if newly interested in its design, and then stepped back, saying, "Come in, come in, everyone."

"Here's Roland." Bettina had edged aside as the more recent arrivals proceeded toward the door. She was keeping an eye on the street, where Roland's white Porsche was coming to a stop along the curb.

Roland climbed out, glanced at the group on the porch, and lifted his wrist to check his watch.

"You're not late, and your car is fine on this side," Bettina assured him as he hurried up the walk.

The group surged into the entry with Roland in the rear. As he approached Richard, he shifted his briefcase to his left hand to free his right hand for a handshake.

"Congratulations," he said. "Very good news." So formal were his tone and manner that he might have been congratulating a colleague on an impressive legal outcome.

"And where is the bride?" Holly peered toward the kitchen doorway.

"Here she is, here she is!" Nell sang out.

Pamela had just emerged from the dining room. She paused halfway across the living room carpet and surveyed the group, her friends.

"Marriage agrees with you!" Nell advanced, holding out her arms, and Pamela stepped forward to meet her.

Nell's face was glowing, despite the wrinkles, and her faded eyes were bright. "We are all so, so happy for you," she murmured as she hugged Pamela. Over Pamela's shoulder, Nell's gaze strayed to Richard, who had slipped around the group to station himself at Pamela's side. "And you too, Richard. I meant 'you,' plural."

Pamela in fact was looking very well. Still not a shopper, even when a significant life change was involved, she was wearing a gift that Penny had given her a few years back. It was a silky blouse with a rounded collar and wide cuffs, green, but dyed in an ombre effect with the color shading in waves from intense to pale and back again. Her straight, dark hair hung to her shoulders, enhancing the effect of well-modeled cheekbones, expressive eyes, and shapely lips. Lately though, smiles and even giggles had disturbed the elegance of her features on the most unexpected occasions.

"Sit down, please, everyone." Pamela waved at random toward sofa and armchair, flustered by being the focus of so much attention. "Nell, the armchair is reserved for you."

Nell was very soon settled at one end of the hearth and extracting her current project from her knitting bag. A few inches of vibrant orange knitting dangled from a needle, and an empty needle and a ball of the same orange yarn soon appeared. Roland, too, was seated, on his usual hassock at the other end of the hearth. His briefcase snapped open and he lifted the lid and peered inside.

"How was Cape May?" Holly was still on her feet, and she addressed the question to Richard, who was on the point of escaping toward the stairs now that the serious business of knitting seemed about to commence.

"Warm." He nodded. "But not too warm because of the ocean. Relaxing . . ."

"Romantic?" Holly prompted.

A giggle escaped from Pamela, and she glanced across the room at Richard.

"The architecture is very romantic," Richard said, trying to disguise a smile. "All those Victorian houses, and gardens . . . like the setting for a novel."

"Yes!" Pamela interjected. "It was very, very romantic, and not just the architecture." Skin that seldom blushed made an exception. "And, sweetie"—she addressed Richard—"you can retreat to your book now, but be sure to come back for the nibble."

"At eight p.m. sharp." Roland, already at work, looked up even as his busy fingers kept his needles in motion.

A slight bustle ensued as Bettina, Holly, and Karen arranged themselves along the length of the sofa and Pamela moved the wooden chair with the needlepoint seat to a spot more conducive to chatting.

"Luckily no murders occurred while you were gone," Karen observed once Pamela was settled.

"Whatever will we talk about, then?" Nell's twinkly expression made it clear that, as the group member least in favor of what she considered unbecoming gossip, she was teasing.

"Where will you live now?" Holly leaned forward. She was farthest from Pamela, at the very end of the sofa.

"Here." Pamela nodded. "Richard likes my house, despite the yellow kitchen."

On Pamela's first encounter with Richard Larkin, long ago when he was her new neighbor, he'd voiced his disapproval of yellow kitchens. She still remembered, and she remembered the attraction she'd felt to this tall, serious-appearing man, even then.

"I was determined to keep them on Orchard Street," Bettina said, "or at least in Arborville."

"You didn't have to do much persuading." Pamela had been rummaging in her knitting bag, but she paused to lay an affectionate hand on Bettina's shoulder. "About Arborville, anyway."

She went back to rummaging. Bettina opened a knitting magazine she had brought and pondered a photograph of a cowl-neck pullover fashioned from indigo mohair yarn. Holly tipped her head toward Bettina and leaned closer to the page, dislodging a wave of raven hair that strayed over her cheek.

"Awesome," she murmured, "and if you start it now you'll be finished in time for cool weather."

"I didn't buy the yarn yet." Bettina closed the magazine. "I'm still trying to decide . . ."

"There are elephants to be made," Nell called from the armchair, "and donkeys. The children at the women's shelter like a choice."

She reached down into her knitting bag and came up with a large ball of green yarn, which she tossed across the room. It fell short of its target and rolled under the coffee table. Suddenly, a streak of black fur darted in from the entry and dove after the ball of yarn.

Holly laughed. "Catrina can still move awfully fast when she wants to."

The yarn emerged from under the table, followed by the cat in hot pursuit. It leapt forward to seize the ball of yarn with both front paws, then rolled onto its back and hoisted the ball of yarn aloft. Back paws joined the front paws to enclose the yarn in an embrace, and the cat flopped onto its side, spinning the ball of yarn in its paws while biting it.

"It's not Catrina." Pamela and Bettina spoke at once. Pamela elaborated, adding, "It's Richard's cat, Frank Lloyd Wright."

"Four cats in one household now?" came a voice from the hassock at the far end of the hearth. The voice belonged to Roland.

"They're all getting along fine," Pamela said. "In fact—"

"Pamela!" Holly exclaimed.

She had leaned toward Pamela as Pamela began to speak, but instead of focusing on Pamela's face, her glance had strayed to Pamela's lap, where the knitting project she had extracted from her knitting bag awaited resumption. At present, it consisted of a few lacy inches of work wrought from the finest yarn in the most delicate of pink shades.

Staring intensely at the needles and the bit of pink knitting dangling from them, Holly whispered. "Pink. Baby.

Clothes." She raised her eyes to Pamela's face now. "Does this mean what I think . . . ? Could you possibly be . . . ?"

Even Roland was riveted.

Pamela let the suspense linger until even the cat, responding to the breathless silence, took notice.

"It's for Penny," Pamela said, "or rather for—"

Again Holly interrupted, this time with a squeal. "Penny's going to have a baby!"

"Not so much of a surprise," Pamela said.

"I knew she and Aaron were married," Holly said.

"That wasn't so much of a surprise, either," Bettina observed. "There was a spark, that's for sure, even way back then."

"The surprise is, though, that they're planning to settle out here." Pamela had begun knitting, but she lowered her work to her lap as she continued to talk. "After her graduate school in Illinois and his work in Guatemala, they could have ended up far far away."

"But they didn't." Bettina finished up the thought. It was obvious that she was as pleased (and relieved) as Pamela to know that Penny would once again be close, and there would be a new granddaughter to spoil—not quite her own granddaughter but as good as.

Pamela took up her knitting again. As if responding to the example of their hostess, the other knitters bent toward their own work, Bettina casting on from a second ball of yarn provided by Nell, who declared that the ball of green yarn could be consigned to Frank Lloyd Wright.

A murmured conversation between Holly and Karen provided a soothing background for Pamela's thoughts. She still felt Michael Paterson's presence here in the house they had labored over together. A fixer-upper was to become a forever home, for both of them, until Michael, an architect, was killed in a tragic accident on a construction site. She'd resisted moving on for so long until, just as a shift in perspective can make sense from random details, she'd realized that loving Richard didn't negate the love she'd had for Michael, and that being loved by two men was a double gift.

Holly and Karen continued murmuring and time passed. The bit of pink knitting on her needles grew row by row and began to resemble the sleeve it was destined to become. Then a motion across the room, at the far end of the hearth, distracted her momentarily. She glanced over to see that Roland had set his project down and pushed his immaculate shirt cuff aside to reveal his watch. His lips seemed to be moving as he counted off the seconds.

Before he could announce that eight o'clock had arrived, however, the doorbell chimed. As if she had been expecting a caller, Bettina sprang up and hurried toward the entry. She opened the front door to admit Wilfred. Pamela started to rise, but Bettina waved her back into her chair.

"Wilfred and I are taking care of the nibble tonight," she said. "Remember?"

A mysterious bakery box had arrived that afternoon, and Pamela had resisted the urge to peek inside. She returned to her knitting, though the other Knit and Nibblers were stirring, tucking projects into knitting bags, straightening backs and stretching necks that had been hunched over busy hands.

A faint glow from the direction of the arch leading to the dining room suggested that the chandelier hanging over the table was alight. Clinking sounds from that direction indicated that the table was being staged for refreshments, and the seductive aroma of brewing coffee was in the air.

Bettina appeared in the dining room arch. "You can all come in now," she sang out, beckoning with a coy smile.

Richard was suddenly at Pamela's elbow, and they were farthest from the destination, but everyone stood aside to let them go first. Wedding-china plates, cups, and saucers awaited, and napkins and silverware, with a row of champagne flutes as an unexpected addition. But the focal point of the arrangement was a cake, three graduated layers covered in smooth white icing and accented with cascades of pink buttercream roses. Figures of a bride and groom decorated the top.

"Congratulations!" the voices rang out, all but Wilfred's.

A subdued pop from the direction of the kitchen heralded his arrival. He bore a dewy champagne bottle partly wrapped in a linen napkin, the wisp of vapor escaping from its neck evidence of its recent opening.

"Eloping is romantic," Bettina observed, addressing both Pamela and Richard, "but you can't deny the Knit and Nibblers a chance to celebrate."

Another bottle of champagne was fetched, and the two bottles provided enough champagne for eight glasses to be raised in a toast. It was led by Wilfred, his ruddy face the very picture of cheer. Bettina insisted that Pamela and Richard cut the first slice of cake, then she took charge of portioning it out.

Soon everyone was back in the living room, crowded around the coffee table with dining room chairs pressed into service, cake plates on laps and steaming cups of coffee or tea on the table before them. As if not to be left out of the festivities, four cats were lined up in the arch leading to the entry—Catrina, Ginger, Precious, and Frank Lloyd Wright.

Pamela surveyed the group, so many dear people (and cats). Dearest of all, and right next to her so she had to crane her neck to study his face, those stern features softened now by a smile that showed no sign of fading, was Richard Larkin.

KNIT

Easter Bunny Hand Puppet

Nell Bascomb hasn't yet made knitted hand puppets for the children at the Haversack women's shelter, but this project is certainly one that she would approve of. It comes together in just a few hours and makes a fun Easter gift for a child or grandchild. To see photos of the completed puppet, visit the Knit & Nibble Mysteries page at Peggy Ehrhart.com. Click on the cover for *Easter Egg Murder* and scroll down on the page that opens. References to photos on my website in the text below are to this page.

Use yarn identified on the label as "Medium" and/or #4, and use size 7 or 8 needles. The puppet requires about 85 yards of yarn and a small piece of felt, about 4 × 4 inches. You will also need two buttons for eyes, and black embroidery floss if you want to add whiskers. I used white yarn and pink felt but you can use whatever colors you like.

If you're not already a knitter, watching a video is a great way to master the basics of knitting. Just search the internet for "How to knit," and you'll have your choice of tutorials that show the process clearly. The puppet is worked in the stockinette stitch. To create the stockinette stitch, you knit one row, then purl going back the other direction, then knit, then purl, knit, purl, back and forth. It's easier to understand "purl" by viewing a video, but essentially, when you purl, you're creating the backside of "knit." To knit, you insert the right-hand needle front to back through the loop of yarn on the left-hand needle. To purl, you insert the needle back to front.

Casting on and casting off are often included in internet "How to knit" tutorials, or you can search specifically for "Casting on" and "Casting off." The puppet uses the simple slipknot casting on technique.

Body—make two.

The puppet's torso, arms, and head are knit as one piece, and the front and back are the same. Cast on 22 stitches. Work 22 rows. On the next row (knit row), cast on 5 more stitches when you reach the end of the row. Purl the next row and cast on 5 more stitches when you reach the end of the row. Now you will have 32 stitches.

Work 7 rows. On row 8 (purl row) cast off 11 stitches at the beginning of the row. On row 9 cast off 11 stitches at the beginning of the row. Now you will have 10 stitches.

To shape the head, add a stitch at each end of each row for the next 3 rows. To make a nice edge, add the stitches after the first stitch and before the last. In each row, work a stitch, add a loop of yarn, go on until there's 1 stitch left in the row, add another loop of yarn, and work the final stitch. Now you will have 16 stitches.

Work 5 rows, starting with a knit row. Then decrease 1 stitch at each end of the next row by purling 2 stitches together. Knit the next row. Decrease as above on the purl row. Knit the next row. Decrease as above on the purl row. Knit the next row. Decrease as above on the purl row. Now you will have 8 stitches.

Knit 2 together, cast off 4, knit the last 2 together, and cast off the last stitch.

Ears—make two.

Cast on 6 stitches. Knit 1 row. On the next row (purl row), increase 1 stitch at each end, using the technique described above. Then work 10 rows. Decrease 1 stitch at each end of row 11 by knitting 2 stitches together. Purl the next row. Decrease 1 stitch at each end of row 13 by knitting 2 stitches together. Now you will have 4 stitches. Purl 1 row. Knit the first 2 stitches and the last 2 stitches together. Purl the last 2 stitches together, clip your yarn, slip the loop off the needles, thread the yarn tail through, and pull tight. Trim the yarn tail to about ½ inch.

Trace around the edge of an ear to make a pattern for the felt lining. Draw a second line about ⅛ inch inside the outline of the ear and cut that shape out. (You want the lining to be slightly smaller than the knitted ear.) Using the paper pattern, cut two ear shapes from the felt.

Smooth out one of your knitted ears, wrong side facing up. Lay one felt ear on the knitted ear with a bit of knitting showing around the side edges. Pin the felt ear in place. Hide the tail left at the top of the ear between the felt and the knitted ear, and use a sewing needle and regular thread to sew around the edges of the felt ear, fastening it to the knitted ear. Repeat the process for the other ear.

Create the puppet's face.

It's easier to create the face if you do it before sewing the puppet's front and back together. Use either of your body pieces for the puppet's front. For the puppet's nose, cut a felt triangle, about the size of a fingernail, with rounded corners. Sew it and the eyes in place with a regular needle and sewing thread. Consult the photo of the completed puppet on my website for positioning of the nose and eyes. Embroider whiskers with black embroidery floss if you wish.

Assemble the puppet.

Stitch the body front to the body back, up the sides, around the arms, and up the sides of the head. Leave the bottom open and leave a space at the top of the head wide enough for the ears. If the tails left from casting on are long enough, you can use them, or thread a yarn needle with more of the yarn you used for the puppet. When you complete your seams, hide the remaining tails by working the needle in and out of the seam for half an inch or so. Pull tight and clip the small tail that remains.

To attach the ears, anchor them first to the back of the head with the base of each ear about 1/8 inch below the upper edge of the head. Use a sewing needle and regular thread that matches the yarn you used for the body. Smooth the front of the head into place overlapping the base of the ears, and use a regular needle and more sewing thread to anchor the front of the head to the ears. A photo on my website shows the ears in place and anchored securely.

NIBBLE

Festive Easter Cookies

An Eggy Way to Die, Pamela bakes a batch of cookies when it's her turn to host the Knit and Nibble group. Inspired by Easter egg colors, she turns an ordinary sugar cookie recipe into a festive treat appropriate to the season. For a picture of the completed cookies, as well as some in-progress photos, visit the Knit & Nibble Mysteries page at PeggyEhrhart.com. Click on the cover for *Easter Egg Murder* and scroll down on the page that opens. References to photos on my website in the text below are to this page.

The recipe makes about 72 cookies, each about 2 inches across.

Ingredients

1 cup butter (two sticks)
¾ cup sugar
1 teaspoon vanilla
1 egg
2 cups flour
1 teaspoon baking soda
½ teaspoon baking powder
Not quite ½ teaspoon salt
Food coloring

Cut the butter into little pieces, place the pieces in a large bowl, and allow them to soften. When you are ready to start the recipe, cream the butter, adding the sugar slowly and then the vanilla. Continue to beat for a few minutes, until the mixture is pale and fluffy. Beat in the egg.

In a separate bowl, whisk the flour, baking soda, baking powder, and salt until thoroughly mixed. Add it to the butter-sugar-egg mixture a little at a time, stirring thoroughly with a wooden spoon. It takes a bit of patience to blend everything together, and you can use your hands if you don't mind getting them sticky.

Divide the dough equally into four small bowls. A rubber spatula is helpful. Use the food coloring to tint the dough in each bowl a different color. (I used deep pink, orange, green, and purple for the website cookies.) There are photos of these steps on my website.

Scrape the contents of each bowl, one at a time, onto squares of plastic wrap. As I said, the dough is very sticky, so use the plastic wrap to maneuver each batch into a long roll about 1 inch in diameter, and then wrap the plastic snugly around the roll. There are photos of this process on my website.

Refrigerate the rolls of dough for about an hour. You can refrigerate them longer if you want to postpone baking the cookies.

When you are ready to bake the cookies, unwrap the rolls of dough. If the dough is too chilled to work with, let the rolls sit for 10 minutes or so. Push on the ends to make the ends of the rolls about the same diameter as the rest of the roll. Cut each roll in half lengthwise and then cut the halves into quarters lengthwise. A paring knife works well for this step. Arrange two quarters of different colors lengthwise side by side and then place one each of the two remaining colors on top of those. Press them all together to make a smooth roll composed of all four colors. Repeat the process until you have four rolls, each composed of four colors. There are photos of these steps on my website.

Prepare one or more cookie sheets by greasing them or lining them with parchment paper. The cookies spread a lot while they bake, so a cookie sheet measuring 10 × 15 inches will accommodate only 18 at a time, or about one roll's worth. You can save two or more of your prepared rolls to bake the rest of your cookies later. If you don't plan to bake them for a while, the dough freezes fine. Just thaw it a bit before you cut your slices.

Preheat the oven to 350°F. Cut each roll into slices about ½ inch thick. Arrange the slices on your cookie sheet (or sheets) a few inches apart. Bake the cookies for 12 to 14 minutes, rotating the cookie sheet (or sheets) half-way through. The cookies will not be brown when they are done. Gently remove them from the cookie sheet with a spatula while they are still warm.

Note: The cookies are all the same flavor, vanilla sugar cookies. The colors are just for fun. If you're squeamish about including food coloring, you can skip that part of the recipe. Just scoop spoonfuls of the dough from the bowl and place them a few inches apart on your prepared cookie sheets. Dampen your fingers with water, flatten the scoops of dough slightly, and sprinkle them with sugar if you wish. They will spread out as they bake. Follow the baking directions above.